# WITHIN *the* SANCTUARY *of* WINGS

## A MEMOIR BY LADY TRENT

# MARIE BRENNAN

TITAN BOOKS

Within the Sanctuary of Wings
Print edition ISBN: 9781783297788
E-book edition ISBN: 9781783297795

Published by Titan Books
A division of Titan Publishing Group Ltd
144 Southwark Street, London SE1 0UP

First edition: April 2017
1 2 3 4 5 6 7 8 9 10

Bryn Neuenschwander asserts the moral right to
be identified as the author of this work.

© 2017 by Bryn Neuenschwander
Interior illustrations by Todd Lockwood
Map by Rhys Davies

A CIP catalogue record for this title is available from the British Library.

Printed and bound in the UK by CPI Group Ltd.

What did you think of this book? We love to hear from our readers. Please email us
at: readerfeedback@titanemail.com, or write to us at the above address.

To receive advance information, news, competitions, and exclusive offers online,
please sign up for the Titan newsletter on our website.

WWW.TITANBOOKS.COM

# WITHIN *the*
# SANCTUARY *of*
# WINGS

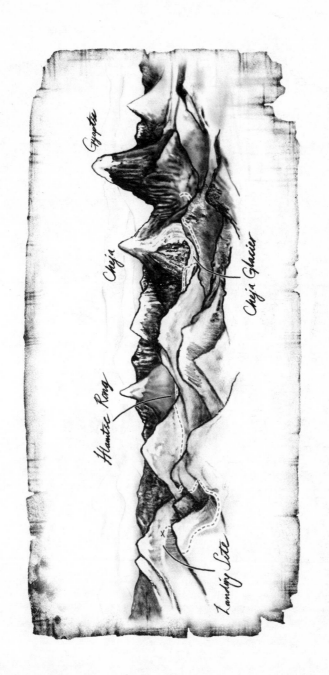

Gyyptu

Chyja

Chyja Glacier

Hlamtse Rong

Landing Site

X

# PREFACE

Writing the final volume of one's memoirs is a very peculiar experience. This book does not chronicle the end of my life, as I am not yet dead; indeed, I am still hale enough that I hope to enjoy many years to come. It does not even chronicle the end of my career: I have done a great many things since the events described herein, and am rather proud of some of them.

I suspect, however, that any *sequelae* would inevitably be a disappointment for the reader. Compared with what preceded it, my life in recent decades has been quite sedate. Harrowing experiences have been thin on the ground, the gossip about my personal life has long since grown stale, and although I am very proud of what I have learned about the digestive habits of the so-called "meteor dragon" of northern Otholé, that is not something I expect anyone but a dedicated dragon naturalist to find interesting. (And such individuals, of course, may read my scholarly publications to sate their thirst.) This book is not the conclusion of my tale, but it is the conclusion of *a* tale: the story of how my interest in dragons led me to the series of discoveries which have made me famous around the world.

For you, my readers, who are already so familiar with the tale's conclusion, the version of myself I have presented throughout these memoirs must seem terribly dense and slow of thought. Consider me akin to our ancestors who believed the sun revolved around the earth: I could only reason from the evidence before me, and that evidence was for many years incomplete. It was not until I had the final pieces that I could see the whole; and acquiring those final pieces required a good deal of effort (not to mention peril to life and limb). I have endeavoured here to re-create the world as it seemed to me at the time, without allowing it to be coloured overmuch by current knowledge. For the inevitable inaccuracies and omissions that has entailed, I apologize.

But we must not rush ahead. Before we reach the end of my journey, there is more to be told: the scientific advances of the time; the various conflicts which came to be termed the Aerial War; and the fateful encounter which sent me into the dizzying heights of the Mrtyahaima Mountains. I hope my words may convey to you even a quarter of the sheer astonishment and wonder I experienced—and, perhaps, a fraction of the terror as well. After all, without both sides of that coin, you cannot truly know its worth.

Isabella, Lady Trent
Casselthwaite, Linshire
10 Ventis, 5662

# PART ONE

*In which the memoirist acquires
a most unexpected ally*

# ONE

*Life as a lady—A lecture at Caffrey Hall—My husband's student—*
*The state of our knowledge—Suhail's theory—*
*A foreign visitor*

Members of the peerage, I need hardly tell you, are not always well behaved. Upon my ascension to their ranks, I might have become dissolute, gambling away my wealth in ways ranging from the respectable to quite otherwise. I might have ensconced myself in the social world of the aristocracy, filling my days with visits to the parlours of other ladies and the gossip of fashion and scandal. I might, were I a man, have involved myself in politics, attempting to carve out a place in the entourage of some more influential fellow.

I imagine that by now very few of my readers will be surprised to hear that I eschewed all these things. I have never been inclined to gamble (at least not with my money); I find both fashion and scandal to be tedious in the extreme; and my engagement with politics I have always limited as much as possible.

Of course this does not mean I divorced myself entirely from such matters. It would be more accurate to say I deceived myself:

surely, I reasoned, it was not at all political to pursue certain goals. True, I lent my name and support to Lucy Devere, who for years had campaigned tirelessly on behalf of women's suffrage, and I could not pretend anything other than a political motive there. My name carried a certain aura by then, and my support had become a meaningful asset. After all, was I not the renowned Lady Trent, the woman who had won the Battle of Keonga? Had I not marched on Point Miriam with an army of my own when the Ikwunde invaded Bayembe? Had I not unlocked the secrets of the Draconean language, undeciphered since that empire's fall?

The answer to all these things, of course, was *no*. The popular narrative of my life has always outshone the reality by rather a lot. But I was aware of that radiance, and felt obliged to use it when and where I could.

But surely the other uses to which I put it were only scholarly. For example, I helped to found the Trent Academy for Girls in Falchester, educating its students not only in the usual female accomplishments of music and literature, but also in mathematics and various branches of science. When Merritford University began awarding the first degrees in Draconic Studies, I was pleased to endow the Trent Chair for that field. I contributed both monetary and social support to the International Fraternity for Draconic Research, an outgrowth of the work Sir Thomas Wilker and I had begun at Dar al-Tannaneen in Qurrat. Less formally, I encouraged the growth of the Flying University until it formed a network of friendships and lending libraries all across Scirland, catching in its net a great many people who would otherwise not have had access to such educational opportunities.

Such things accumulate, bit by bit, and one does not notice

until it is too late that they have eaten one's life whole.

On the day that I went to attend a certain lecture at Caffrey Hall, I was running behind schedule, which had become the common state of my life. Indeed, the only reason I did not miss it entirely was because I had purchased a clock of phenomenal ugliness, whose sole virtue—most would call it a flaw—was its intolerably loud chiming. This was the only force capable of rousing me from my haze of letter-writing, for our butler had recently joined the army, our housekeeper had left us to care for her elderly mother, and I was not yet on good enough terms with their replacements to rely on them to evict me from my study by force.

But they had the carriage waiting when I came flying down the stairs, and in short order I was on my way to Caffrey Hall. At the time I was grateful because I would have been sorely disappointed to miss the lecture. In hindsight, I would have missed out on a great deal more.

The crowd on the street outside was large enough that I directed my driver around the corner, where I disembarked and entered the hall by a side entrance. This deposited me much closer to my first port of call, which was a room near the lecture hall proper. I pressed my ear to the door and heard a voice murmuring inside, which warned me not to disturb him by knocking. Instead I eased the door open and slipped quietly through.

Suhail was pacing a narrow circuit across the floor, sheaf of papers in one hand, the other fiddling with the edge of his untied cravat as if it were a headscarf, muttering in a low, quick voice. It was his habit before any lecture to make one final pass through his points. When he saw me, though, he stopped and took out his pocket watch. "Is it time?"

"Not yet," I said. One could not have guessed it by the hubbub, which was audible even through the door. "I am dreadfully late, though. There was a new report from Dar al-Tannaneen."

This was the home of the International Fraternity for Draconic Research, and the report concerned the honeyseeker breeding effort, which was establishing the boundaries of developmental lability. Tom Wilker and I had discovered that principle quite by accident during our time there, while trying to determine how much environmental variation a draconic egg could endure without aborting or producing a defective organism; further research had confirmed that the issue was not so much defectiveness as mutation, which (when successful) adapted the resulting creature to its expected environment.

Of course the theory was not yet widely accepted. No such theory ever is: it has taken an astonishingly long time for the concept of germs to catch on, even though it has the benefit of saving lives. I cannot claim any such grand result for my own theory. But slowly, one generation of honeyseekers at a time, the Fraternity's work was laying a foundation even the most skeptical of critics could not assail.

Suhail's expression lightened into a smile. "I would say I am surprised . . ."

". . . but it would be a lie. They have a new idea for how to encourage the growth of larger honeyseekers. I had to read it, and see if I could offer any suggestions. Speaking of which: is there anything you need, before you throw yourself to the wolves?"

He turned to lay the papers he held in a leather folder, lest his hand render them sweaty and crumpled. "I think it is beyond even your tremendous capabilities to produce a second Cataract

Stone for me, which is what I most truly need."

A second such artifact might exist; but we had been lucky even to find the first, and could not count upon a repeat of that good fortune. The Cataract Stone, which I had stumbled across in the jungles of Mouleen, was that most precious gift to linguists, a bilingual text: its upper half was written in the indecipherable Draconean script, and its lower half in the much more decipherable Ngaru. Proceeding from the assumption that the two halves contained the same text, we had, for the first time, been able to discover what a Draconean inscription said.

Being not a linguist myself, I had, in my naivete, assumed that would be enough—that with the door thus opened, the Draconean language would promptly unfold its secrets like a flower. But of course it was not so simple; we could not truly *read* the Cataract Stone. We only knew what it said, which did not assist us in deciphering any other text. It gave us a foothold, nothing more.

And while a foothold was a good deal more than we'd had in the past, it provided only a narrow place to stand while searching for the next step. Suhail lifted one hand to run it through his hair, then realized he would disarrange it, and put his hand back down again. "Without a more certain framework for the entire syllabary," he said, "much of what I have to say today is guesswork."

"Highly educated guesswork," I reminded him, and reached out to tie his cravat. He did not need me to do so for him; when he began to adopt Scirling dress, he swore he would not be the sort of aristocrat who could not even tie his own cravat. Nor, of course, did he favour the elaborate knots and folds so beloved of my nation's dandies in those days. Still, there was a simple pleasure in undertaking that task, feeling the rise and fall of his breath as I folded the cloth and pinned it into place.

"But guesswork nonetheless," he said as I worked.

"If you are wrong, then we will know it in time; the hypothesis will not hold up. But you are not wrong."

"God willing." He laid a kiss on my forehead and stepped back. In a Scirling frock coat or an Akhian caftan, my husband cut a fine figure—especially at moments like these, when his thoughts were bent to matters academic. Some ladies' hearts are captured by skill at dancing, others by poetry or extravagant gifts. It will surprise no one that I was taken in by his keen mind.

"You have a substantial crowd waiting for you," I said, as the noise from outside continued to rise. "If it is all the same to you, I will take a seat at the back, so that others will have a better view." I'd already enjoyed a private box for the development of his ideas, of which this was only the public revelation. Given the size of the waiting audience, I suspected more than a few people would be standing for the duration of his lecture, and I would gladly have ceded my chair to another; but being a peer, and a lady besides, I knew I would never succeed. The best I could hope for was to displace some fit young fellow, rather than an older gentleman who needed the seat far more than I.

Suhail nodded, distracted. He was always like this before a lecture, and I took no offense. "Then I will see if Miss Pantel needs anything," I said, and slipped back out of the room.

I could hear chanting outside, with a distinctly unfriendly tone. The rise of interest in Draconean matters had sparked a concomitant rise in Segulist zealotry, which decried our newfound obsession with the pagan past. Suhail's lecture was likely to inflame them more. Fortunately, the manager of Caffrey Hall had taken the precaution of hiring men to stand guard at the doors, and the worst of the rabble-rousers were kept outside.

That still left a great many people inside the building. The decipherment of the Cataract Stone and the discovery of the Watchers' Heart in the depths of the Akhian desert had sparked a fad for that ancient civilization, with a great many cheap books of dubious accuracy or academic worth being published on the subject, and Draconean motifs becoming popular in everything from fashion to interior decoration. Earlier that same week, the poet Peter Flinders had sent me a copy of his epic poem *Draconis,* in the hope that I might endorse it.

But even in the depths of such a craze, historical linguistics is a sufficiently abstruse topic that it attracts a more limited audience, of (dare I say) a more elevated class. I do not necessarily mean birth or wealth: I saw men there who would never have been permitted into the august halls of the Society of Linguists. They had a serious look about them, though, as if they knew at least a little concerning the topic, and were eager to learn more.

It was a mark of how much Scirling society had changed since my girlhood that I was not the only woman there. Even in sedate afternoon dresses, the members of my sex stood out as bright spots amid the dull colours of the men's suits, and there were more such spots than I had anticipated. There have been lady scholars for centuries, of course; the change was that they were finally out in public, rather than reading the articles and books alone in their parlours, or in the company of a few like-minded friends.

One such lady was on the stage, adjusting the placement of the large easel that would hold the placards illustrating Suhail's argument. A goodly portion of the scandal that once attached to myself and Tom Wilker had moved on to Erica Pantel and my husband; there were far too many people who could not believe a man might take a young woman as his student, and mean the word as something other than a euphemism. I had lost count of the number of times someone implied within my hearing that I must be terribly jealous of her—especially as I was getting on in years, being nearly forty myself.

This troubled me very little, at least for my own sake, as I knew how false those rumours were. Not only did Suhail have little interest in straying, but Miss Pantel's heart was already spoken for, by a young sailor in the Merchant Navy. They were madly in love and had every intention of marrying when he returned from his current voyage. In the meanwhile, she occupied herself with her other passion, which was dead languages. Her attachment to Suhail sprang from his familiarity with the Draconean tongue, and nothing else. Our fields of study might differ, but I considered her a fellow-traveller on the roads of scholarship; she reminded me a little of myself in my youth.

"Is everything in order?" I asked her.

"For now," she said, with a meaningful glance toward the audience.

The manager of Caffrey Hall might be keeping the obvious rabble-rousers outside, but I had no doubt a few would slip into the building. And even those who came for scholarly reasons might find themselves incited to anger, once they heard what Suhail had to say.

I said, "I meant with the placards and such."

"I know," she said, flashing me a brief smile. "Is Lord Trent ready?"

"Very nearly. Here, let me help you with that." The placards had to be large, in order to be at all visible from the back of the hall; the carrying-case Miss Pantel had sewn to hold them was almost as large as she, for my husband's student was a diminutive woman. Together we wrestled the case into position and unbuckled its straps. She had cleverly stacked the placards so they faced toward the wall, with the first card outermost, which meant we need not fear anyone catching an advance peek at Suhail's ideas.

Unless, of course, someone were to come up and rifle through them. Miss Pantel nodded before I could say anything. "I will guard them with my life."

"I doubt that shall be necessary, but I thank you all the same," I said with a laugh. No dragon could be a fiercer guardian. "If you don't need anything further from me, I shall go play hostess."

I meant the phrase as a euphemism. Necessity had taught me to be a hostess in the usual sense, though I still vastly preferred a meeting of the Flying University to a formal dinner. A baroness does have certain obligations, however, and although in my youth I would have thrown them off as useless constraints, in my maturity I had come to see the value they held. All the same, my true purpose in circulating about the hall and the lobby was to take a census of men I expected to cause trouble. I made particular note of a certain magister, whose name I shall not disclose here. If his past behaviour was any guide, he would find something to argue about even if Suhail's lecture concerned nothing more substantive than the weather—and my husband would be giving him a good deal more fodder than that.

When it was time for the lecture to begin, I dawdled in the lobby for as long as I could. By the time I entered the main hall, every seat was filled, and people lined the walls besides. Despite my best efforts, however, my attempt to discreetly join the gentlemen at the back wall failed as expected. The best I could do was to accept the seat offered to me by a fellow only a little older than myself, rather than the venerable gentleman who was eighty if he was a day.

Following a short introduction by the president of the grandly named Association for the Advancement of Understanding of the Draconean Language, Suhail took the stage, to a generous measure of applause. Our discovery of the Watchers' Heart (not to mention our romanticized wedding) had made him famous; his scholarly work since then had made him respected. It was not interest in Draconeans alone that brought such a large audience to Caffrey Hall that afternoon.

Suhail opened his speech with a brief summary of what we knew for certain, and what we guessed with moderate confidence, regarding the Draconean language. Had he been speaking to the Society of Linguists, such an explanation would not have been necessary; they were all well familiar with the topic, as even those who previously showed no interest in it had taken it up as a hobby after the publication of the Cataract Stone texts. But the Society, being one of the older scholarly institutions in Scirland, showed a dismaying tendency to sit upon information, disseminating it only by circulars to their members. Suhail wished the general public to know more. After all, it was still very much the age of the amateur scholar, where a newcomer to a field might happen upon some tremendous insight without the benefit of formal schooling. Suhail therefore delivered his lecture to the world at large, some of whom did not know declensions from décolletage.

It began with the portion of the Stone's Ngaru text that gave a lineage of ancient Erigan kings. This was of some interest to scholars of Erigan history, and of a great deal more interest to linguists, for proper names are much more likely than ordinary words to be preserved in more or less the same form from one language to the next. The names of the kings gave us a foundation, an array of sounds we knew were likely to be in the Draconean text, with a good guess as to where in the text those sounds fell. Although incomplete, this partial syllabary gave us a tremendous advantage over our past knowledge.

Having a sense of Draconean pronunciation, however, does not get us much further. What use is it to have confidence that a given symbol is pronounced "ka" when I do not know what any of the words containing "ka" mean? In order to progress further, linguists must try a different tactic.

The word "king" occurs eight times in that recitation of lineage. Suhail and his compatriots had analyzed the frequency with which different series of symbols occurred in the Draconean text, seeking out any grouping that occurred eight (and only eight) times. They found a great many, of course, the vast majority of which were coincidental: the fact that the combination "th" occurs eight times in this paragraph before the word "coincidental" is not a significant matter. (Anyone reading this memoir in translation will, I suppose, have to take me at my word that eight is the proper count.) But the linguists became confident that they had, through their statistical efforts, identified the Draconean word for "king."

This is only the tip of the dragon's nose, when it comes to the methods of linguistic decipherment, but I will not attempt to explain further; I would soon outpace my limited expertise, and the means by which they identified the inflection for plural nouns or other such arcana is not necessary to understand what follows. Suffice it to say that on that afternoon, we knew two things with moderate certainty: the proper pronunciation for roughly two-fifths of the Draconean syllabary, and a scattered handful of words we had tentatively reconstructed, not all of which we were capable of pronouncing. It was a good deal more than we once had; but it was a good deal less than the entirety of what we hoped for.

My husband was an excellent lecturer; he laid all these matters out with both speed and clarity (the latter a quality so often lacking among scholars), before embarking upon the main portion of his speech. "Ideally," Suhail said, "we should only use direct evidence in carrying our work forward. Hypotheses are of limited use; with so little data available to us, it is easy to build an entire castle in the air, positing one speculation after another whose validity—or lack thereof—can be neither proved nor disproved. But in the absence of another Cataract Stone or other breakthrough, we have no choice but to hypothesize, and see what results."

Miss Pantel, knowing her cue, moved to the next placard in the series. This showed the entire Draconean syllabary, laid out in something like a chart, with the characters whose pronunciations we knew coloured red. Scholars had made charts of the symbols many times before, in many different configurations; as Suhail had just noted, what facts we possessed could easily be poured into any number of speculative molds. This one, however, had more than mere guesswork to back it.

My husband's resonant voice carried easily throughout the hall. "This is a modified version of the chart assembled by Shakur ibn Jibran, based on what we currently know regarding the pronunciation of established Draconean glyphs. He noted an underlying similarity between the symbols for 'ka' and 'ki,' and another similarity between 'mi' and 'mu,' and so forth. His hypothesis is that each initial consonant possesses its own template, which is modified in relatively predictable ways by a vowel marker. By grouping the symbols according to these templates and markers, we may theorize as to the pronunciation of glyphs not included in the proper names of the Cataract Stone."

The process was not, of course, as straightforward as his description made it sound. Languages are rarely tidy; with the exception of the Kaegang script, designed a century ago for use in writing Jeosan, they show a distressing tendency to break their own rules. Although many linguists had accepted Shakur ibn Jibran's general principle in arranging the glyphs, they argued over the specifics, and easily half a dozen variant charts had their own partisan supporters. Already there were murmurs in the hall, as gentlemen grumbled at not seeing their preferred arrangement on display.

Those murmurs would grow louder soon enough. For now, the chart gave us a place to begin—and Suhail's own speculation depended upon his fellow countryman's as his foundation. Miss Pantel revealed another placard, this one with lines of Draconean text printed upon it, interleaved with an alphabetic transcription.

My husband said, "If we take that speculation as provisionally true, then this selection—taken from later in the Cataract Stone text—would be pronounced as glossed here. But we have no way to test this theory: here there are no proper names to guide us. We will never know whether this is accurate . . . unless we speculate again."

Taking up a long pointer, Suhail underlined a word in the first line. "Presuming for the moment that our chart is correct, these characters would be pronounced *aris*. One of the fundamental principles of historical linguistics is that languages change over time; tongues that are spoken today may have their roots in older forms, now extinct. The Thiessois word *terre* and the Murñe word *tierra* both derive from the Spureni *terra*, meaning 'earth.' So, too, may we hypothesize that *aris* gave rise to the Lashon '*eretz* and the Akhian '*ard*—also meaning 'earth.'"

Had I been inclined to place a bet with myself, I would have won it in that moment, as the lecture hall burst into uproar.

Linguists had spun theories of this kind before, imagining the Draconean language to be ancestral to a wild variety of modern tongues, Lashon and Akhian not excepted. After all, the deserts of southern Anthiope were the most likely homeland of that civilization. But the common wisdom held that the Draconean lineage was linguistically extinct: the Draconeans had been a separate ethnic group, ruling over their subjects much as Scirland currently ruled over parts of Vidwatha, and with the downfall of their empire their language had vanished forever. It was almost literally an article of faith, as everyone from Scirling magisters to Bayitist priests and Amaneen prayer-leaders agreed that our modern peoples owed nothing to those ancient tyrants.

I had advised Suhail to stop after that statement, lest the clamour drown out his next words. He took my advice, but the pause lasted longer than either of us had anticipated. Finally he gave up on waiting for silence and went on, pitching his voice to be heard above the din of audience commentary. His point did not rest upon that single example: he believed he had found cognates for a number of words, methodically connecting them to examples in Akhian, Lashon, Seghar, and historically attested languages no longer spoken today. It was, as he had said to me, guesswork; all he could do was tentatively identify specific glosses from the Ngaru text, and then extrapolate into speculation on other Draconean inscriptions. One tablet from a site in Isnats, for example, seemed to be a kind of tax record, as he found probable words for "sheep," "cow," "grain," and more.

Any one example could easily be shot down. Assembled together, however, they constituted a very reasonable theory—or so I thought. But I was not a linguist, and there were gentlemen in the audience that day who laid claim to that title. They were more than prepared to disagree with Suhail.

When I heard voices rising at the back of the hall, I assumed it was an argument over the substance of the lecture. The magister I mentioned before, ten rows ahead of me, had risen to his feet so as better to shout his disagreement at my husband; presumably the noise behind me was more of the same. When I turned to look, however, I saw a small knot of men at the door, facing one another rather than the stage.

Surely they would not begin an altercation over a matter of historical linguistics? But I have spent enough of my life among scholars to know that academic conflicts and fisticuffs are not always so far apart as one might expect. Rising from my seat, I went to see if I could defuse the situation before it reached that point.

But the argument at the door had nothing to do with Suhail's lecture. From my seat, I had been unable to see the man at the center of the knot; now that I drew near, I caught a glimpse between the shoulders of the other men. He dressed in the manner of a northern Anthiopean and had his hair trimmed short, but a suit did nothing to change his features. The man was Yelangese.

Now, on the surface of it there was nothing so terribly strange about a Yelangese man attending a public lecture in Falchester. Ever since long-range maritime trade became a common feature of life, there have been sailors and other immigrants in Scirling ports, Yelangese not excepted. At the time of Suhail's lecture, though, we were firmly in the grip of what the papers had dubbed our "aerial war" against Yelang, wherein our caeligers and theirs jockeyed for position all around the globe, and our respective military forces clashed in a series of minor skirmishes that kept threatening to break out into full-scale war. Men of that nation were not exactly welcome in Falchester, regardless of how long it had been since they called the empire home.

Furthermore, readers of my memoirs know that I had quarreled with the Yelangese on multiple occasions: when I was deported from Va Hing, when I stole one of their caeligers in the Keongan Islands, and when they made organized efforts to sabotage our work at Dar al-Tannaneen. This was public knowledge at the time, too—which meant that the gentlemen near the door, seeing a Yelangese man show up at my husband's lecture, had leapt to some very hostile conclusions.

I kept my voice low, not wishing to draw any more attention than this incident already had. Fortunately, the magister who had stood up was still on his feet, along with another man who was attempting to shout over him. "Gentlemen," I said, "I suggest we take this matter out into the lobby. We do not wish to disturb the lecture."

There are benefits to having a famous reputation. The men recognized me, and were more inclined than they might otherwise have been to heed my suggestion—which was, of course, a thinly disguised order. One of them shouldered the door open, and we escaped into the relative quiet and privacy of the lobby.

"Now," I said, once the door had swung shut behind us. "What appears to be the problem?"

"*He's* the problem," the tallest of the Scirlings said, jerking his chin at the foreigner. He topped the Yelangese man by more than a head, and was using his height to loom menacingly. "I don't know what he thinks he's about, coming here—"

"Have you tried asking him?"

A brief pause followed. "Well, yeah," another man admitted. "He said he was here for the lecture."

"Anybody can *say* that," the tall man scoffed. "That doesn't mean it's true."

"Nor does it mean it's false," I said. In truth, though, I suspected there was indeed more to the story. The Yelangese stranger, though doing his best to keep a bland expression, had clearly recognized me. Which was all well and good—as I have said, I was very recognizable—but something in his manner made me suspect I was his reason for coming to Caffrey Hall that day.

My tone was therefore sharp as I addressed the stranger. "What is your name?"

"Thu Phim-lat," he said, in a heavily accented voice. "Lady Trent."

So he would not attempt to pretend that he did not know me.

Under the circumstances, none of us would have believed him anyway. "How long have you been in Scirland?"

"Three weeks."

My heart stuttered in its beat. Perhaps you think it was a foolish reaction; I will not argue with you. But I had been on the receiving end of Yelangese trying to kill me, and could not forget that so easily. Had Thu Phim-lat been a longtime resident of Falchester, I might have persuaded myself that he was no threat. But if he had just arrived . . .

I decided to press the matter. "You may be here for the lecture, Mr. Thu, but I doubt that is your only purpose. Tell me what you hope to accomplish."

His eyes darted from side to side, taking in the men watching us. They had arrayed themselves quite close, clearly ready to interpose their bodies if Mr. Thu made a single move toward me. "Oh, come now," I said impatiently—as much to myself as to them. I did not like feeling afraid in my home city, and I liked even less feeling afraid when I had so little cause. "If he wished me any harm, there are far easier ways for him to achieve it than by walking into a public lecture hall." He could have accosted me on the street, appearing out of the crowd before I even knew he was there. A cosh to the back of the head, a knife between the ribs . . . but that was foolishness. Yelang had only troubled me when I troubled them, by investigating dragons in their country or attempting to breed my own for the Royal Army. There was no reason for them to assassinate me at home, unless I had made a much more personal enemy than I knew. And doing so would only make them look dreadful in the court of public opinion.

The Scirling men looked unconvinced, but I had persuaded

*Thu Phim-lat*

myself, and reassured Mr. Thu enough that he answered me. "I wished to meet you," he said, speaking very slowly. I realized later that this was because his grasp of the Scirling language was far from perfect, and he wanted to make certain he committed no errors of grammar or word choice that might cause his point to be taken awry. "I have news of a thing I think you would like to hear."

"News may be sent by letter," I said. "Or you could present yourself at my townhouse—its location is hardly a secret. Why come to a public lecture?"

"If I came to your home, would I be let in the door?" he asked. "Would my letter be read?"

"Yes, or else my servants would have a great deal to answer for. I do not pay them to make such decisions on my behalf."

"Ah," Mr. Thu said once he had taken in these words. "But how would you know?"

I dismissed this with a wave of my hand. "Clearly you have not been rebuffed in such fashion, or you would have said as much already. Let us not waste time with hypotheticals. What tidings are you so eager to convey?"

At many points in my life I have been on Mr. Thu's end of such a conversation, stumbling along in a language of which I have only a rudimentary command. My rapid speech and elevated diction had lost him. "Your news," I said, when I saw he did not understand. "You have found me; say what you came to say."

He glanced again at the men so energetically looming at him. "A dragon," he said at last. "The body of a dragon. Not like any kind I know. I think not like any kind alive."

My heart stuttered again, this time with excitement instead of irrational fear. *Not like any kind alive.* An extinct breed . . . I had scoured the world, corresponding with scholars from a dozen countries and more, trying to find evidence of the dragons created by the Draconeans so many thousands of years ago. Could it be this man had found what I sought?

It was unlikely. Even if he had only discovered evidence of some other extinct strain, though, he had my keen interest. "Where?"

"In the mountains," Mr. Thu said. "You will see."

# TWO

*At my house—The Mrtyahaima—Bog bodies and woolly mammoths—
The Khiam Siu—My support*

**F**urther discussion of extinct dragons had to wait. The
lobby of Caffrey Hall was no place for such matters,
especially with a phalanx of overeager bodyguards ready
to pitch Mr. Thu out on his ear. And it was clear that the barrier
of language would hamper any attempt on his part to explain; we
would proceed much more rapidly with Suhail's assistance.

I arranged for Mr. Thu to come by my house that evening,
assuring him that my footman would certainly let him in. I also
gathered the names of the gentlemen who had accosted him—
ostensibly so I could thank them properly for their assistance, but
also as insurance. When Mr. Thu was gone, I said to them all, "If
he does not arrive safely, I will be most vexed." Whether they
would have caused trouble for him or not, I have no idea, but I
felt it was best to issue a warning just in case.

By the time I made it back into the main room, Suhail's lecture
had, as expected, devolved into a public debate. This went on
until the organizer ejected us from the premises; then it continued

for a time in the street outside, with several opinionated fellows cornering my husband to argue some more. "Thank you," Suhail said fervently, after I rescued him by worming my way to the center of the crowd and asserting my superior claim to my husband's person. "I'm fairly certain they would not of their own accord have stopped before dawn tomorrow."

"I hope you are not too tired," I said. "I suspect that we have an interesting evening ahead of us."

He listened with growing surprise as I told him about Thu Phim-lat. When I was done, Suhail said, "He is not the first man to claim he has evidence of some undiscovered breed, Draconean or otherwise."

"Oh, I am skeptical," I assured him. "But also curious. If this *is* some Yelangese plot against me, then whoever crafted it has done their work well. I cannot let Mr. Thu go without at least inquiring further."

The delay also gave me time to contact Tom Wilker, so that there were three of us waiting when my visitor came calling a few hours later. Tom spent the time between his own arrival and Mr. Thu's pestering me with questions. "What did he mean by 'the body of a dragon'? A skeleton, or a recent carcass? Which mountains? What makes it so different from current breeds?"

"I spent all of five minutes speaking with the man, and half of that dealing with excessively zealous protectors," I said with some asperity. "Wait until he gets here; then you may question him to your heart's content."

Judging by Mr. Thu's wary posture when he arrived, he expected precisely the kind of interrogation he was going to get. I did my best to put him at ease with introductions and an offer of refreshment; he turned down both tea and brandy, and perched on the edge of his chair as if afraid it would sprout manacles around his wrists if he relaxed. I said, "My husband speaks some Yelangese, though not fluently. My hope is that between that and your own knowledge of Scirling, we will be able to piece together a proper explanation. Now. Tell us what you know."

It has been my habit in these memoirs to smooth over my own awkard conversations in other tongues, for the sake of not taxing my readers' patience; I will do the same for Mr. Thu here, bypassing the many halting exchanges in Yelangese which punctuated his Scirling comments, and his sporadic failures of grammar or vocabulary. (Among other things, there are multiple Yelangese languages, and the one Suhail spoke was not Mr. Thu's mother tongue. But they were both fluent enough in it that we got by, albeit with difficulty.)

"I found the body of a dragon," he said. "Or rather, part of one. It was incomplete, but there was enough for me to be certain that I did not recognize its breed."

"Are you a natural historian, that you are very familiar with different kinds of dragons?"

Mr. Thu shook his head. "No, Lady Trent. But I have been in the mountains before; I know the dragons that are found there. This was not of any kind I know."

Tom frowned. When questioning someone, it is often effective to have one interrogator behave in a skeptical fashion, while the other is more credulous; but I fear both Tom and I took on the role of skeptic at the start of that evening. He said, "It might not be a mountain breed."

"Perhaps. But then what was it doing there?"

"Where is 'there'?" I asked. "Which mountains?"

"The Mrtyahaima."

His answer startled me into silence. The Mrtyahaima Mountains are, of course, one of the great geological features of the Dajin continent. Comprising a number of interlocking ranges, they dwarf what we call "mountains" in many other parts of the world. If the measurements of surveyors are accurate, the fifteen tallest peaks in existence are all found in that region, each one more than eight thousand meters high.

Long famous to the inhabitants of Dajin, they had become more well known in Anthiope since the advent of mountaineering as an athletic activity. Our early climbers were content to test themselves against the lesser peaks of the Vystrani Mountains or the Netsjas in Bulskevo, but as more and more of those were conquered, the ambitious turned their attentions to Dajin and the Mrtyahaima. No one even knew whether it was possible to climb an eight-thousand-meter peak: could human beings survive at such altitude? Nowadays we believe they can, but no one has yet succeeded in reaching a summit that high.

The Mrtyahaima were of interest to us for other reasons as well. The various ranges grouped under that name, running as they do from near the northern coast well into the interior, almost bisect the continent. To the east lies Vidwatha; to the west, Yelang. And Scirland, of course, had various colonial possessions in Vidwatha—which meant the two nations had spent years glaring at one another across the nearly impassable barrier of the mountains.

I racked my memory for what I knew of Mrtyahaiman draconic breeds. It was disappointingly little: the region was so remote, what reports we had largely came from non-scholarly sources.

They described everything from small, cat-like dragons supposedly kept as pets by the peoples of the high valleys to demonic beasts composed entirely of ice. "Describe to me what you found. It was a fresh kill?"

Mr. Thu shook his head. "No. I don't know how long it had been dead, but it must have been at least a year. Or longer."

Could bones preserve naturally under the geologic conditions of that range? I had no idea. "With only a skeleton to study, how can you be sure it was a strange breed?"

"It was not a skeleton," Mr. Thu said. "No bones at all. Meat and hide."

We ground to a halt for a terribly long time on this point, for Tom and I were sure that something must be going awry in the translation. But Suhail, questioning Mr. Thu in Yelangese, suddenly uttered an oath. In Scirling, he said, "Like a bog body!"

"What?" I asked, even more confused than before.

He hastened to explain. In Uaine and some parts of Heuvaar, ancient societies made a practice of sacrificing people by strangling them and sinking their bodies into peat bogs. The chemical composition of the water naturally pickles the flesh, preserving the soft tissues that would ordinarily decay—but it dissolves the bones, leaching away the calcium until what remains is, in Suhail's words, "a slimy, boneless sack."

A similar thing had happened to the specimen Thu Phim-lat found, but for entirely different reasons. The bones of the dead creature had long since disintegrated, as is common among draconic species. But the carcass, high in the Mrtyahaima peaks, had frozen after death, which kept the flesh from rotting as it ordinarily would. "They've found mammoths in the permafrost of northern Siaure," Tom pointed out. "This sounds much the same."

"Half mammoth, half bog body," I murmured. The prospect was enchanting. Paleontologists, scientists who study extinct organisms, are accustomed to working from nothing more than skeletons. In my field of research, where we are rarely so lucky as to have skeletons to study, the evolution of draconic species is a near-total mystery. We had some theories, but most of them had fallen to pieces with the discovery of developmental lability. Facts were very thin on the ground, and preserved tissue was nothing short of a miracle.

But when I asked Mr. Thu where the specimen was now, he shook his head sadly. "I do not have it any longer. I think it froze above the snow line, and was carried by an avalanche down to a warmer elevation. By the time I found it, much of it had decayed, or been eaten by scavengers."

"*Much* of it," I said. "Surely there must still have been *something,* though, or you would not be here, assuring me it hailed from an unknown species."

"Yes. The head, the neck; a little material below that, badly torn and malformed. Scraps detached from the remainder of the body." He spread his hands helplessly. "I brought what there was with me to our camp, but we had nothing with which to preserve it. I made sketches, though."

"Your camp," Tom said, before I could spring on that word "sketches." He was frowning and tapping one fingertip against his knee. "How many of you were there? Where precisely were you? And what, pray tell, were you doing there?"

His tone was colder than mine, and with good reason. While thoughts of dragons had carried me away, Tom had remained with his feet firmly grounded in current reality. Yelang's easternmost territory was Khavtlai, the high plain to the west of the Mrtyahaima. They did not lay claim to any land in the mountains themselves—not yet. So what was a Yelangese party doing there?

Mr. Thu hesitated. I exchanged a glance with Suhail, and saw that he, too, was troubled. Then Mr. Thu nodded, as if concluding an internal argument. He said, "We were a party of mountaineers, exploring the high ranges."

"Looking for a way through," Tom said.

My blood chilled. A way through the Mrtyahaima . . . such things existed already, of course. The mountains are not wholly impassable; only mostly so. The nations of the high ranges, Tser-nga and Khavtlai and Lepthang and Drenj, had conducted trade with one another for centuries. But the major passes are not well known to outsiders, and are closely guarded besides; any attempt to bring an army through them would meet with stiff resistance. Yelang was looking for other routes, ways to slip a force across and gain a foothold on the eastern side, from which to control the whole region.

It was almost precisely the same tactic the Ikwunde had attempted in Eriga, approaching Bayembe from its theoretically unassailable southern border with Mouleen.

Controlling my voice took effort. "The only thing that persuades me not to throw you out right now is my perplexity. Why on earth should you admit that you are a scout for the Yelangese army?"

"Because sooner or later someone would discover it, and then I would look dishonest for not admitting the truth." Mr. Thu sighed. "And also because I am not a scout for the army. I *was* one. But no longer."

"Why not?"

"They discovered I was Khiam Siu," he said.

My interest might lie primarily with matters scientific, but even I could not escape recognition of that name. Some fifteen years previously, Yelang had begun to suffer internal difficulties, in the form of a revolutionary movement that wished to overthrow the current Taisên Dynasty (which had ruled for nearly three hundred years) and replace the emperor with a new claimant. This movement called itself Khiam, or Renewal, and the Siu were its adherents.

As Mr. Thu explained to us, he had not been a member of the army per se. He was a mountaineer, hired to work with surveyors so that Yelang might have more accurate maps of the mountains to their east. But it seemed he had made copies of those maps and passed them along to his Khiam Siu brethren, whose leaders had been driven out of Yelang after a tremendous defeat at Diéziò. Someone above him in the imperial hierarchy had discovered this fact, and Mr. Thu barely escaped with his life.

He delivered this tale in the simple, matter-of-fact tone one might use to relate events read from a news-sheet. To many people this might have seemed like evidence of falsity, but for me, it made the entire affair ring true. I knew that tone well, for I have used it myself when I am deeply upset by a thing, and must detach myself from it so as not to surrender my dignity before strangers. When he finished by saying, "So you see, I am an exile," I felt a pang of sympathy.

"I am very sorry to hear that," I told him, and was quite sincere.

An awkward silence fell, until Tom took it upon himself to break it. "But why come here?"

"Because of Lady Trent," Mr. Thu said, with a little bow toward me. "I wish her help. In exchange, I offer what I know."

"What manner of help?" I asked warily.

He straightened his back, hands placed precisely atop his knees. Now we had come to the heart of it, for which all the rest had been prelude. "Your support. We—the Khiam Siu—have approached your government, seeking an alliance against the Taisên. But many look at us and see only Yelangese, and say we can never be allies. You can speak against them. You can help us gain our alliance."

I would have a great deal of difficulty speaking if I did not first retrieve my jaw from the floor. The proposed alliance with the Khiam Siu was a matter of hot debate. The magazines and newspapers generally fell into two camps: those who, as Mr. Thu said, saw only Yelangese, and trusted them no further than the door; and those who understood the Khiam Siu to be the enemies of the Taisên, but saw no reason we should not stand back and let the two chew on one another to their hearts' content. In less public corners the issue was acknowledged as more complex— but relatively few with the power to do anything were inclined to show favour to the Khiam Siu. Mr. Thu was quite right in thinking they needed support.

Where I parted company with his reasoning was the point at which he thought *my* support would get him anywhere. I might have engaged with politics more often than I intended—for we cannot pretend the education of girls and the forging of international bonds for the well-being of dragons are apolitical acts—but that did not make me anything like a force to be reckoned with on the diplomatic front.

Tom had resumed the role of skeptic, while I attempted to find my tongue. "What assurance do we have that this information of yours is any good? You could feed us a load of rubbish, and we would never know until after Lady Trent staked her reputation on you and your allies."

"It is not . . . rubbish," Mr. Thu said, employing the new word with quiet dignity. "And I have faith that you and Lady Trent would see through it if it were."

I had my own question for Mr. Thu, which was as much a test as it was a genuine query. Looking him directly in the eye, I asked, "What makes you think I will trust you? My history with your countrymen has not been good."

He nodded, unsurprised. "You do not like Yelangese. I understand this. But they say you care more about dragons than things such as that. I am hoping this is true."

And, of course, it was.

# THREE

*Political suspicions—The deeds of Justin Broadmay—Tea with Lady Astonby—Mr. Thu's evidence—A second specimen*

W e met with predictable disbelief when we presented our situation to members of the Synedrion.

My brother Paul laughed in my face. I approached him first, for while we were not close, we were at least on cordial terms (my elevation to the peerage having done a good deal to mend my contentious relations with the bulk of my family.) As he still held a seat in the Open House of the Synedrion, I thought I stood a better chance with him than with someone I knew only from public functions. "It's a trap, Isabella," he said over dinner at my house. "I thought you clever enough to see that on your own."

"A trap to what end?" I asked. My impatience, I fear, was not as well concealed as I might have wished. "To lure me off into the Mrtyahaima Mountains so I may be killed? Dear heaven—if someone wants me dead, there are far less convoluted ways to arrange it."

"And what if they want to capture you instead?"

"Yes," I said dryly. "It is *so* much easier to do that by hunting me down in the icy wilderness of the world's highest peaks than by, say, knocking me over the head on my way to visit a friend. Besides, he is Khiam Siu, not a follower of the Taisên. They want our assistance; foul play would hardly aid them in that goal." (I forbore to mention that certain members of the Synedrion might applaud them for doing me in.)

Paul put his fork down with an impatient clack. "What other reason could these Yelangese have for approaching *you*? If they believe this information is so valuable—a point which I am not at all prepared to concede—then why not have their envoy formally present that offer to the Synedrion?"

Suhail laughed, as much to defuse the tension as from amusement. "Because they know our dear Lady Trent well enough to understand what good bait this is." When I gave him an exasperated look, he said, "My heart, you know it is true."

"That it is good bait, yes." I could hardly pretend otherwise, when it had already produced such a marked effect. "But what benefit do they gain from spearing *me* on their hook?"

"Your vote, for one."

We were then in that odd period between the passage of the Female Peers Act and the General Representation Act. The former gave me the right to vote in the Closed House of the Synedrion, as befitted my rank as a baroness who held the title in her own right; prior to the passage of that bill, I would have required a male family member to occupy my seat and vote in my stead. (Ordinarily this would have been my husband, but since another law prohibits foreign-born individuals from holding seats in either house of the Synedrion, I would have had to look farther afield.) The latter, of course, extended the right of suffrage to all women—but at the moment, I had the odd privilege of voting on Synedrion bills, but not in the elections which filled the Open House of that body.

Still my vote did not count for much. "If it comes down to so close a division that a single vote makes the difference, they are depending on a very slender reed."

"It would be one vote more than they had before," Suhail said. "And I would not undervalue yourself. If you speak in favour of this, it will have an effect."

I gave him a dry look. "An effect, yes. But a positive one? That remains to be seen."

My undertaking thus did not begin well, nor did it improve much in the following days. It seemed that everyone had a theory for what this supposed conspiracy might hope to accomplish. "He'll feed us false intelligence," Lord Rossmere said when I met with him a few days later. My readers may recall him as the brigadier who sent Tom and myself to Akhia—and as such, a man who knew how well the prospect of dragons would motivate me to action. "He'll say things about the mountains to lead our own men astray, so that we won't find a way through to the western side."

"We're in the mountains, too?" I said, startled.

"Of course we are. We've had surveyors there for the past two years. Ostensibly just to measure the peaks more accurately, but Yelang knows perfectly well what we're doing. Just as we know what they're up to."

I frowned, one finger tapping my lip. "Have any of them reported finding unusual remains? Carcasses, bones—"

Lord Rossmere gave me a look fit to freeze a specimen solid.

"They are not there to study the wildlife, Lady Trent. Their attention is on other things."

Thu Phim-lat had spared a fragment of his attention for this matter. Assuming, of course, that he was telling the truth.

He was maddeningly close-mouthed about his find. I knew why; it was his one bargaining chip, apart from what he knew about the terrain of the Mrtyahaima, which the Khiam Siu were not going to surrender without gaining a good deal more in return. Mr. Thu did let slip at one point, however, that the location was not of any particular use for invading Yelang, as the mountains there were much too difficult to traverse.

That narrowed down the list of places he might have been . . . to only half of an impossibly large area. It was still too much. I tried again with Paul, this time accosting him at a garden party. "Mr. Thu believes more specimens may be found in the region, if we search. But if we wait, someone else will discover them first, and then we shall lose this scholarly coup. Possibly even to Yelang!"

Paul only snorted. "No one in the government cares about that, Isabella. Dragon specimens, however interesting, have no military value."

I swallowed the impulse to point out that the bone specimens we discovered in Vystrana had turned out to have tremendous value, both military and otherwise. Bringing up that matter would only do me more harm than good.

Despite my restraint, one Synedrion member (who shall remain nameless here) was blunt enough to say it to my face, in the lobby of the chamber where the Closed House met. "Why in God's name do you expect anyone here to do you favours, Lady Trent? It's your fault we're facing caeligers from half a dozen nations in this aerial war, instead of just Yelang."

"I had nothing to do with Mr. Broadmay's actions," I snapped. The words came out by reflex; it was not the first time I had uttered them.

The gentleman grunted, as if the response he wanted to make was a good deal more vulgar. "Do you deny that you encouraged him?"

"I most certainly do. That I spoke out against the slaughter of dragons for their bones, I confess; but I never spoke directly to Mr. Broadmay, and had he introduced himself and explained his plan, I would have dissuaded him."

I would have tried, at least. Even now, I am not certain how sincere I would have been in my hypothetical attempt to stop him. Justin Broadmay, having heard my lectures and read my essays, had sought out a position at one of the factories producing synthetic dragonbone. His express intent, as confessed before a judge, was to learn both the chemical makeup of the substance and the process used to give it the proper structure, and then disseminate his collected information around the world.

I cannot even say that I think he was wrong. Once upon a time, I feared that the discovery of a method for preserving natural dragonbone would have disastrous consequences for the beasts, as humans slaughtered them for material. I had poured all I could afford and more into pursuing a replacement, especially once the preservation method became known in other countries. When Scirling scientists finally developed that replacement, however, I realized that it had created a new problem.

The availability of a form of dragonbone we could produce at will, in the shapes desired, spurred a great many subsequent developments, not least of all in the field of war. And if other countries wished to keep up, they would have no choice but to harvest as much as they could . . . from natural sources.

The only solution was to make the replacement formula as widely available as the one for preservation. It did not entirely remove the competition, of course: now everyone was racing to acquire the necessary raw materials, and flogging their own engineers to build newer and better devices from this miracle substance. But there was no putting that jinni back in the bottle; once preservation had been achieved—and it was inevitable that someday it should be—we could only move forward.

For better or for worse, Justin Broadmay had the courage of his convictions—a courage I myself lacked. As a consequence, a judge had sentenced him to prison two years previously, and ultimately he spent the greater part of a decade there. It was only through the efforts of my legal-minded and charitable friends that he was freed so soon.

But the whole Broadmay incident left me on less than advantageous footing with Her Majesty's government. In the end, I only achieved my goal by trading shamelessly on a connection I was not even supposed to have: my past encounter with Queen Miriam herself.

I did not meet with Her Majesty in person. A baroness I might be, but a title alone does not grant sufficient clout to be able to call upon the sovereign at will—especially when the circumstances in which we met were, at the time, still considered a state secret. Instead I had tea with Lady Astonby, whom my readers may recall as "Hannah," the woman whom, along with then-Princess Miriam, I met on the island of Lahana in the Broken Sea.

A conversation over tea is not as irrelevant as you might think.

Lady Astonby was not a peeress in her own right; she had her title by virtue of marrying her husband, and as such she had no vote in the Synedrion. But she belonged to that cadre of noblewomen surrounding the queen who participated in politics by other means. Through their social duties as hostesses, they gathered information; through their patronage and networks of friends, they dispensed influence. It was indirect, but not ineffective, and it permitted the queen to exercise more control over the Synedrion than she might otherwise have had.

"You believe this man's offer to be of value," Lady Astonby said, once I had explained the situation to her.

"Yes. I know that most would consider such information to be insignificant at best; but I believe it may be a discovery of great import to my field. And while draconic studies are not so impressive as the movement of armies, achievements in that area do raise our credit with other nations."

Lady Astonby studied me with a gaze that took in everything and gave nothing back. "But gaining that information requires you to support the Khiam revolutionaries. I would not have expected you to extend such charity to the Yelangese."

She had observed the Battle of Keonga, and I had to assume she knew of my other unpleasant encounters. I said, "I have been kidnapped, threatened, and otherwise mistreated by Eiversch, Bulskoi, Chiavorans, Yembe, Ikwunde, Keongans, Akhians, and my own countrymen. If I allowed that to discourage me, I should soon become a hermit, trusting no one at all."

It was a pert answer more than an honest one, but Lady Astonby allowed it to stand for the time being. "You have said in your publications and letters that you believe the Draconeans bred a unique species for their use. Do you think this specimen might be an example of that creature?"

I knew perfectly well that if I said "yes," my odds of success would go up dramatically. In theory any extinct variety should be of scientific interest; but that one, of course, was the Lost Ark of paleontological draconic research. Unfortunately, that would have been untrue, and I am not a very good liar. "As much as I might hope so, Lady Astonby, I doubt it. There were Draconean settlements in the lower reaches of the Mrtyahaima, but not up at the elevations where soft tissue might be preserved. And although we have evidence of breeding in various parts of the world, developmental lability makes it quite unlikely that the same species could have been bred in such a cold climate. Not without a great deal of effort, at least."

No doubt to Lady Astonby it looked like artifice when I hesitated. Upon my honour, though, it was genuine inspiration that made me go on to say, "Unless they bred more than one sort. Which is possible, I suppose."

The countess's eyebrows rose. "I see. But that is nothing more than speculation."

"I'm afraid so. Nonetheless . . ." I bit my lip, casting my gaze toward the ceiling. "I do not recall whether any breeding grounds have been discovered in the local ruins. My husband would know. Though of course a great deal depends on what we mean by 'local'—as we do not know where in the Mrtyahaima the specimen was found."

My intellectual enthusiasm had begun to run away with me once more. Lady Astonby brought me back to earth with a pointed question. "Other than greater scientific knowledge, what gain is there for Scirland in extending the hand of friendship to these revolutionaries?"

It was clear that my plea had made no impression, and was unlikely to do so. Still, I could not give up yet. "They oppose the Taisên," I said lamely.

"And if their rebellion were going well, that might be of use to us. Of course, if it were going well, they would not need our aid. So we are asked to gamble upon the possibility that they might succeed in overthrowing the Taisên."

Such a result would be beneficial to us in the long run, as it would remove an unfriendly dynasty and replace it with one that had reason to view us as friends. In the short term, however, it would require us to lay out resources and manpower, with no certainty of return. The mathematics of it made my head ache: this was why I stayed away from politics whenever I could. I was comfortable with risking my own life, but not those of our nation's soldiers.

Lady Astonby's gaze became curious. "Let us lay aside for the moment the question of the revolutionaries' chances, and the logistics of their rebellion. And let us also lay aside this dragon specimen of which you are so enamoured. Speaking only of the personal level—or the moral, if you will—do you truly support this alliance?"

When people asked my political opinion, their true question was usually whether I would support their pet cause or not. If Lady Astonby had any such purpose in mind, though, I could not discern it; and so I gave her question due thought, sitting silently for a long minute.

Finally I said, "There is a degree of hypocrisy in our opposition to the Taisên. Our two nations detest one another because we are too much alike: both of us are grabbing for territory and resources. We condemn them for their rapacity, and I would not be surprised to learn they condemn us for the same reason. But I do not believe we will ever find peace with the Taisên, and a continuation of the Aerial War will not be good for anyone—least of all the people whose lands we fight over. If the Khiam Siu take power, we might at least end that conflict. So yes, I support it." Then I permitted myself a small, deprecating smile. "But if you ask me to swear that my own self-interest plays no role in that statement, I'm afraid I shall have to decline."

Lady Astonby nodded, as if she had reached a decision. "So Lady Trent supports the Khiam Siu. We can use that."

I had cause to regret my words in the weeks that followed. Use me they did, in ways I should have predicted, were I not so determinedly naive in the realm of politics. Lady Trent extending the hand of friendship to the Yelangese made a noteworthy symbol, given my history of hostility with that people: they arranged for me to do so not just metaphorically but literally, during a diplomatic meeting with representatives from both the Khiam rebellion (including their would-be emperor, Giat Jip-hau) and members of the Synedrion. And that, of course, was only the beginning. I sat through endless state dinners, smiled and made small talk with Yelangese men and women who were as single-minded in pursuit of their cause as I was in pursuit of dragons. We had very little in common, and I found myself recalling, almost with longing, my perilous experiences in other parts of the world. At least there, I felt I was equal to the challenge.

In the end, however, I cannot complain too much. Thu Phim-lat obtained his alliance, and I obtained access to his notes.

"Is this all?" I said, gesturing at the small notebook on the table in my study.

Mr. Thu shrugged apologetically. "There was only the one specimen, Lady Trent, and only a few scraps of it at that. How much could I record?"

He had a point, but I had irrationally hoped for more. With Suhail leaning in at my left shoulder and Tom at my right, I opened the notebook and found myself looking at a pencil sketch of a decomposing dragon.

Pieces of one, at least. Mr. Thu had not been exaggerating the scantiness of his material. We were fortunate that he found most of the head; his theory was that it had been the last part to emerge from the snow and ice, and therefore the least damaged by the warmer temperatures and passing scavengers. Apart from this, there were a few scraps of flesh, one of which might have been part of a leg, and a piece of wing, so thoroughly separated from the rest of the body that it must have been torn off by an animal. "Or by the avalanche," Mr. Thu added. "Either before or after it died."

I shuddered to think of such annihilating force. I had taken up mountain climbing in recent years, partly as a hobby, but more to toughen myself for future expeditions. I had only rarely climbed above the snow line—almost every instance taking place the previous summer, when my son Jake persuaded me to take him on a holiday with the mountain pioneers Mr. and Mrs. Winstow to the southern Netsja Mountains—and had narrowly escaped what our Bulskoi guides assured me was a very small avalanche. A collapse strong enough to separate wing from body was harrowing even to think of.

"This can't possibly be the normal shape of its muzzle," Tom said. "Even allowing for the collapse of the bone within."

"The flesh is very—" Mr. Thu paused, searching for the word. "Dry, and thin."

"Desiccated," I said.

He nodded. "By the ice. And I think the weight of the snow crushed it over time, pushed it out of shape."

"That often happens with frozen bodies," Suhail agreed. "Like the pair found in the Netsjas thirty years ago. Without bone to provide support, I imagine the effect would be even stronger."

With Suhail's assistance, Thu translated the notes scribbled below and around the images. The head was approximately forty centimeters from back to front, and thirty centimeters from base to crown. Many of the teeth had fallen out, making dentition uncertain. There were sketches of the remaining teeth on the following page: a few incisors, one surprisingly small cuspid or "canine tooth," which Mr. Thu had tentatively identified as mandibular. A broken piece of what might have been a carnassial. We were lucky to have even that many, without bone to anchor them in place. The neck was set low on the skull, suggesting a head carried more high than forward. Mr. Thu could only guess at its intact length, but thought it was possibly quite short.

"Not surprising," Tom said. "In a cold climate like that, a long neck is only a way to lose vital heat."

Indeed, the neck of a rock-wyrm is much shorter and stouter than that of a desert drake—and the Vystrani Mountains are mere foothills in comparison with the Mrtyahaima. "What of the hide?" I asked.

In reply, Mr. Thu delved within his pocket and brought out a small silk bag. With great care, he opened its drawstrings and slid the contents onto the table.

It was a pair of . . . scales, I thought, but they were unlike any I'd seen before. One was long and thin: sized, I thought, to a beast much larger than that head would suggest. The other was a good deal smaller, and irregularly shaped. They were exceedingly pale and bluish in tone, but not the same colour; the larger one was mottled with darker grey spots. When I picked it up and tapped my fingernail against it, the sound was dull and heavy, though the scale itself was light.

"I had more," Mr. Thu said, "but they were confiscated by my commanding officer. I kept these only by hiding them in the lining of my clothing."

Tom and I grilled him on the shape, size, and thickness of the ones he had lost, and the details of where on the carcass the remaining pair had been found. At one point during this conversation, Suhail pounded his fist against the table in a rare display of frustration. "Oh, to have been there myself! I know you did not have much time to search," he hastened to assure Mr. Thu. "But there may have been other scales or teeth scattered along the ground, not obvious to the eye. And even looking at where they fell . . . we might have guessed at the path your carcass took on the way down, how the scavengers tore at it, and used that to tentatively reconstruct where the loose scales had been."

I understood Suhail's vexation, feeling much the same myself. It was maddening to have such disconnected fragments. I was no archaeologist, accustomed to making do with what little evidence the depredations of time and decay saw fit to leave behind; my subjects were usually alive or recently dead, and in either case they were whole. If only we had been there when this specimen was discovered, to see it with our own eyes!

My brain had not yet carried that thought through to its logical conclusion when I rose and pulled down the world map from its roller on one wall. I was thinking only of elevation, temperature, possible food sources. "Can you show me where you found this?"

Mr. Thu came to join me. "You do not have a more detailed map?"

"Not of that region. Though I can certainly obtain one."

He bent to peer at the area shaded to represent the heights of the Mrtyahaima. After a moment's consideration, he stabbed one finger onto the sheet. "Here. Roughly."

I looked, and my shoulders drooped. "Of course it was."

He had pointed at a spot in the hinterlands of Tser-nga, an area very poorly known to outsiders. Sheluhim and various emissaries had visited in past ages, but the kingdom periodically closed its borders, and at present they were shut. It was no surprise that Mr. Thu and his compatriots would have been exploring there: to their east lay the high plateau of Khavtlai, which had been a Yelangese possession for more than a century. Given the remoteness and seclusion of Tser-nga, if the Yelangese came through the mountains there, they could be well established on the eastern side before we heard anything of it.

It also made going there myself more than a little difficult.

Only then did I realize what plan had been taking shape below conscious thought. I said nothing of it yet, though. Instead I asked Mr. Thu, "And what was the terrain like where you found the specimen? You said it was above the snow line?"

"Not when I found it," he said, returning to his seat and opening the notebook to another page. It was not, I later learned, the same book in which he had originally recorded his observations, for that held too much in the way of other information he did not wish to share. Once the notes on the specimen were safely copied over, drawings and all, he gave the original to his Khiam Siu allies. But the copy included a terrain sketch of some truly forbidding mountains and the valleys beneath.

He indicated a specific location with the tip of his finger. "Here. But I believe it fell from higher up."

"Six thousand meters," Suhail said, translating the unfamiliar numerals written above. "More or less. Assuming I'm converting the units properly."

That elevation marked a high col or saddle between two peaks. If Mr. Thu was correct, the specimen had fallen several hundred meters down a nearly sheer face to the spot where he found it. "What makes you think it was up there originally?" Tom asked.

"It would not have remained frozen otherwise," Mr. Thu said with certainty. "Down in the valley, it is very sheltered from wind, and can become quite hot. And besides . . ."

His hesitation could not have been more effective at piquing my interest had he deliberately calculated it for that purpose. "Besides?" I prompted him.

"I think," he said, uncertainty dragging at his words, "there may have been another up above."

# FOUR

*Routes to Tser-nga—Why I must go—Jake's suggestion—Major-General Humboldt—Planning—Another for the mountains—Farewell to Jake*

From the moment Mr. Thu said "another," I believe my fate was set.

That Tser-nga was closed to outsiders was not enough to deter me; I had to go and see. "That site is barely within their territory at all," I said every time someone protested. "I can skirt their borders almost entirely, if I travel up the Lerg-pa River—"

But everyone who knew the first thing about the region assured me I could not possibly do that. The river, though it may look appealing on paper, is apparently the next best thing to impassable in person. "Very well," I said, "then I will come at it from the west—" But of course that meant Khavtlai, which meant Yelang. And no one was prepared to let me sneak into a country I had been formally deported from, with whom we were currently at war. Nor could I go through Tser-nga itself.

We were at an impasse.

"Just wait," people said to me, over and over again. "In a few years, when the Aerial War is over and Tser-nga has opened its borders—"

They presumed, of course, that the Aerial War would conclude in favour of Scirland, instead of with the Yelangese occupying Tser-nga and barring my entry even more thoroughly than the locals had. They also presumed that the specimen Mr. Thu had seen (if indeed there was more than one) would still be there in a few years, unharmed by the intervening time, rather than tumbling to the valley below and rotting away as the first one had.

"However old that first one may have been," Tom said, trying to reassure me, "it survived all this time. There's no reason to assume the others will perish in a few short years."

He was endeavouring to be optimistic, and so he did not say the rest of what we were both thinking: *it has already been more than a year since Mr. Thu found the first one.* It would be longer still before I got there, even if I went immediately. My chance might already be gone.

But I could not allow myself to believe that. I had to hold tight to possibility and move as rapidly as I could. At least then, if my hopes were dashed, I could tell myself I had done everything in my power.

How, though, to reach my destination?

My difficulties could have been worse. Had Mr. Thu found the specimen on the western side of the mountains, I would have needed to dodge Yelangese forces at every turn. But his expedition was unable to scout the Khavtlai edge of the Mrtyahaima satisfactorily; sickness in the district had turned them away, forcing them to seek an approach from the far side. And the area he indicated was so far removed from the Tser-zhag heartland that which nation controlled it depended on which map you consulted: some said Tser-nga, some Khavtlai and Yelang. Either way it was a mere fiction, for the mountains in between were uninhabited.

But never had such tempting bait been dangled in front of me, with so many obstacles between.

Suhail watched me chew on this problem for days. Then, one evening as we sat in my study, he said, "Please do not take this the wrong way. But . . . why are you so determined to go?"

Another man might have failed to understand the magnitude of my obsession with dragons, but not Suhail. He had come with me into the depths of the Jefi in summer; he knew that risking life and limb for knowledge was nothing new to me. His question carried a different implication. "You mean, why am I pursuing this so passionately, when there are other, easier goals I might more plausibly attain. Goals which would have a much better chance of furthering our knowledge of dragonkind."

"Even Mr. Thu is not certain there was another specimen in the col. He saw it through field glasses, not in person."

Meaning that I might go all that way, moving heaven and earth to do so, only to have nothing to show for it at the end. I rose and paced my study, as I so often did—to the point that my carpet had a distinctly worn track in it. "My scholarly contributions of late . . ." I sighed. "I feel like I haven't done anything."

This took Suhail aback. "But the Fraternity's work in Qurrat—your correspondence with the dragon-breeders in Bayembe—"

"Is all letters, letters, letters. Sitting on my posterior in this room, applying my brain to things, but not applying my *spirit*. And how much of my time is eaten up by other affairs? Patronage, public speaking, advice to others. It's all very useful, I'm sure." I meant the words to be sincere, but they came out scathing. My shoulders sagged. "I haven't been out in the field since we discovered the Watchers' Heart. I could go somewhere—Otholé, perhaps—but what would I do there? What question would I be answering, beyond some basic study of dragons not yet examined?"

Suhail rose and stopped me mid-stride, his hands on my arms. "Isabella. Why this doubt? It has never disappointed you to do basic study before." He smiled, trying to coax a similar lightness from me. "Sometimes I think there is nothing in the world you love better than to describe some characteristic or behaviour never before set down in print."

I had no answer for that. I could not explain the restlessness within me, the feeling that I must do something tremendous or my time would be wasted. Was it simply that I had grown so accustomed to making spectacular discoveries that the thought of doing the work of an ordinary scientist was tiresome to me? Dear heaven: if so, then I would have to go ice my head until the swelling went down. I had already been more fortunate than most scientists are in their entire lives.

Then the truth became clear to me. Without even thinking, I pulled free of Suhail's hands, turning away to resume my pacing.

"Isabella." His voice was very quiet, but no less fervent for that. "Tell me."

I could not face him while I said this—but it must be said. I fixed my gaze upon the wall map, pocked with symbols and notes marking dragon breeds and Draconean ruins. Addressing the map, I said, "I think I am jealous."

Silence fell. Then he said, "Of *me*?"

His tone was disbelieving, as well it might be. "I do not begrudge you your work," I said hastily, my hands twisting themselves into knots. "Never think I am jealous of *that*—indeed, it is one of the things I love best about you. But . . ."

I could not go on. Suhail finished the sentence for me. "But I have been making great advances in my field, while you sit here and answer letters."

"You have been *honoured* for your advances," I said. The sudden bitterness that coloured my words was not for him; it was for myself, and the realization that I had at last found the true core of what troubled me so. "Your lecture at Caffrey Hall was conducted outside the chambers of the Society of Linguists not because they would not have you, but because you *chose* to share your work with a broader audience. But the Philosophers' Colloquium will not have me. And they never will."

Unless I went on making discoveries so great, even that pack of hide-bound, close-minded sticks in the mud had to acknowledge them. At the time I would never have phrased it that way in public, but that was how I had come to think of them. And yet, despite my scorn . . . yes, I still wished to join their number.

This time I did not pull away. Suhail wrapped his arms around me and laid his cheek upon my hair. He asked no further questions; he only murmured, "Then God willing, we will find a way."

After that night, not a day went by that we did not pursue our goal of reaching the Mrtyahaima. I obtained a better map, tacked it to my wall, and began studying the topography of the region as obsessively as any mountaineer. Could we make our way along the range itself, from some starting point farther north? Not if I wished to arrive at my destination any time in the next ten years, Mr. Thu assured me. Perhaps I might approach from the west after all; I could dodge those Yelangese troops and come at the col from the far side. Nevermind that Mr. Thu had not the slightest notion what the terrain on the Khavtlek side looked like, and undertaking such an expedition would likely be suicidal. I was not so desperate as to gamble myself upon so slender a chance; but I was determined that I should not dismiss any possibility out of hand, however unlikely it might seem at first glance.

Which is, I suppose, why the answer came at the dinner table one night, when my son Jake was home from Merritford for a visit.

I had of course explained the entire situation to him, and introduced him to Mr. Thu. Jake's first impulse, naturally, was to insist that I must take him along. "There is no sea for thousands of kilometers," I reminded him as we sat down to dinner. Though he had scarcely begun at university, Jake had already made clear his intention to study the oceans as his life's work: our voyage aboard the *Basilisk* had left a stronger mark on him than I ever could have predicted.

"I'll find a way to rub along," he said, with a melodramatic sigh. "But the Mrtyahaima! How many people ever have an opportunity to go there?"

"One fewer than you are hoping."

Jake grinned. "You know that only encourages me to find a way."

"You are too large to fit into her baggage," Suhail pointed out. "I don't think you can sneak aboard without her noticing."

"Besides," I said, "we still haven't the slightest idea how we will get there." My own sigh was more full of discouragement than melodrama. "At the rate this is going, by the time I have a plan, you will have attained your majority. And then I will not be able to stop you."

Although Jake might not go so far as to sneak after us, he was quite serious about finding a way—for us, if not for himself. He said, "Have you asked Uncle Andrew?"

Much to the surprise of my family, the youngest of my brothers was still in the army. It was not his passion in life, but it gave him purpose and direction—and, dare I say, discipline—which was more than he had ever found on his own. "I have written to him, but he is only a captain. He cannot order the army into Tser-nga to clear a path for us."

Jake brooded over this as the footman brought out the soup course. Suhail and I began eating, but Jake only fiddled with his spoon. Since he ordinarily devoured his food almost before his dish touched the table, I found this worrisome. Before I could ask, though, he burst out with a sudden, uproarious laugh. "A path *through* Tser-nga, no. So you should go over!"

My spoon slid gently from my fingers and vanished up to the tip of its handle in my soup bowl. I did not attempt to retrieve it, staring blindly into the liquid.

*Go over.*

"Pardon me," I said. Abandoning my soup, with my son and my husband grinning after me, I went to write a letter.

My relationship with the military authorities of Scirland has always been a contentious one. I unwittingly undermined them in Bayembe, but aided them in Keonga; with Tom's assistance I strong-armed my way into a job posting they did not want to give me, but then redeemed myself with the discoveries in the Labyrinth of Drakes and the principle of developmental lability. I was instrumental in Scirland gaining knowledge of dragonbone preservation; lost that secret to foreign powers; funded the early research into synthesis; then inspired a man to spill the results as widely as he could. To say they detested me would be an overstatment . . . but to say they liked me would be false.

I would have gained no traction at all were it not for my brother Andrew. As I had told Jake, a mere captain had relatively little influence within the army—but he had once saved the life of another man in Coyahuac. Samuel Humboldt was a colonel at the time; now he was a major-general, and closely involved in the nascent enterprise that a few years later would detach itself from the army, becoming the Royal Scirling Aerial Corps. Thanks to his fondness for my brother, I was able to gain an audience and explain myself.

"Show me where you mean," Humboldt said when I was done.

I was quite incapable of reading the man's expression and voice for any hint of his thoughts. He had not laughed at me, though, and I chose to take that as an encouraging sign. I spread the map I had brought onto a large table already occupied by many other papers. The drawing was far from as detailed as any of us would like (maps of Tser-nga in those days being more imaginative than accurate), but it was the best we had, and supplemented by Mr. Thu's own observations. "There is a village up here," I said, indicating a spot at the foot of the massif which demarcated the edge of the inhabited zone. "We were hoping that it might be possible for a caeliger to fly us there—or if it cannot go that high, then as close as possible—so that we could explore around the col between these two peaks."

I expected the major-general to ask me what benefit this could possibly bring. The monetary costs, I was prepared to defray; the days when I had to scrape for patronage to fund my expeditions had ended for good the day we announced the discovery of the Watchers' Heart. Money alone, however, could not buy me the army's goodwill.

But Humboldt ignored that issue. He studied the map, one blunt finger tracing the edge of the massif, then venturing across the blank space between that and the eastern edge of Khavtlai.

How high, I wondered, could a caeliger fly?

The answer to that was a classified military secret. I had not gone terribly high on either of my flights—but those, of course, were carried out in some of the earliest dragonbone caeligers, before the art developed to its present state. Furthermore, none of us on board had more than the vaguest sense of what we were doing in flying the thing. A modern caeliger, with a skilled pilot on board . . . I had not the faintest clue what it might achieve.

But I might find out.

"It would be exceedingly dangerous," Humboldt mused, still looking at the map. "The winds are fierce at high altitudes, and while a caeliger is safe enough high in the air, any landing or takeoff risks the craft being flung into a mountainside."

He did not speak in the subjunctive or the conditional, as if speculating about what *would* happen if a caeliger *were* to test the heights. Someone, somewhere, had already flown one of those craft through similarly hazardous terrain—perhaps even in the Mrtyahaima itself. But not, apparently, at the western border of Tser-nga, where uninhabited mountains offered the chance to sneak a caeliger and its occupants across where they were not expected.

I curled my fingers around one another, uncertain of what to say. Back when Tom and I were hired to breed dragons, I had harboured reservations about the wisdom of allowing my research to be turned to a military purpose. Now I had planted a tactical notion in Humboldt's head, without at all meaning to.

It helped only a little to tell myself that someone would have thought of it eventually: if not the major-general, then someone else in the military or the government. If we had scouts in the Mrtyahaima, as the Yelangese did, then sooner or later someone might have looked at that blank stretch of map and contemplated its potential. After all, was that not the exact reason Mr. Thu himself had been sent there? And if feet would not avail us in that terrain, caeligers might.

I knew all that was true . . . but it did not erase my apprehension over being the one who first called the possibility to mind.

On the other hand, I had a strong suspicion that even if I abandoned my ambition on the spot, a caeliger might well be sent up into the peaks regardless. Much like the formula for bone preservation, that notion was a dragon that could not easily be stuffed back into its shell.

I drew a deep breath and thought of Suhail's common assertion, that I was both the most practical woman he had ever met, and the most deranged.

"If the army is willing to consider such a venture," I said, "then I should look into what an expedition would entail. Such things do not plan themselves overnight."

Not overnight; nor even in a month. It took far longer than I would have liked to make the arrangements, and I fretted at every day that passed.

For more than a month we hung in limbo, without even a

tentative assurance that a caeliger would attempt to bear us up into the mountains. Despite that lack, we spent most of our time on preparations, knowing that if this scheme gained approval, we did not want to delay our departure by so much as an hour. (It would only give those in charge time to reconsider the wisdom of their decision.)

Tom had turned green when he heard the plan, and was slow to recover his colour. He had ridden in a caeliger precisely once, when Natalie and her engineering friends debuted an experimental model (not composed of dragonbone) at an exhibition. Mountaintops and cliff edges did not trouble him—but as soon as the "floor" beneath his feet became an ephemeral thing of fabric and rods, his equanimity vanished. Jake elbowed him, grinning with all the irrepressible perversity of an eighteen-year-old boy. "Think you'll be able to do it, old chap?"

"I'm trying *not* to think about it," Tom muttered, but with a good nature.

Suhail had been in hot-air balloons before, as well as caeligers. They troubled him not at all; the frowning line between his brows was there for a different reason. He said, "It's all well and good to have ourselves flown in—but how will we get back out again?"

"If push comes to shove, we walk out. The Tser-zhag are in the habit of evicting outsiders found within their borders, not imprisoning or executing them." I laughed. My mood had improved tremendously since Jake put this notion into my mind. It mattered little to me that the possibility was so far-fetched; merely the dream of it was enough to give my spirit wings. "It might even make our lives easier if they capture us, so long as they do not do so before we complete our work. Then at least we would have experienced guides showing us the way out."

Tom drew in a deep breath and straightened in his chair. "Speaking of guides. Thu said they found the specimen a good four days' hike from the village—what's it called, again? Hlamtse Rong. That's a long way to go with nothing more than a small notebook sketch to lead us."

"He said they hired porters in the village. Presumably those men would know where the Yelangese party went."

Tom grimaced. "Assuming those men are still there, and haven't died or gone elsewhere for work. Assuming they're willing to hire out with more foreigners. Assuming they haven't decided that it's better to keep people away from where those remains were found."

He had a point—several of them, really—and after this many years together, I knew where his thoughts were headed. "You think we should bring Mr. Thu with us."

Jake had been leaning back in his chair so that it balanced on two legs only, a habit of which I had failed to break him. Now he almost overbalanced, and came down with a heavy thump. "That Yelangese fellow! The major-general will love that."

I thought it through out loud, speaking slowly as each part came to me. "He will say it is out of the question, of course, because they are still not certain of him—or of the Khiam Siu . . . but there will be three of us and only one of Thu Phim-lat. Not counting any soldiers they send along, of course. Even if we hypothesize his intentions to be false, no one can possibly suggest with a straight face that he has left an ambush waiting there for us. Not when our arrival is so improbable in the first place. If the Yelangese were doing anything there they did not want us to see, they would not send him to draw our attention; and if they have begun doing something since his exile, we are just as likely to wander upon it without him as with. The greatest danger is that he will, for some obscure reason of his own, lead us into the wildnerness to die."

"And that," Suhail said dryly, "is again just as likely to happen without his help as with. If not more so."

He did not exaggerate. Although we had done a bit of mountaineering in recent years, this was like someone who has dog-paddled across a quiet lake proposing to swim the channel between Scirland and Eiverheim. Of the lot of us, Mr. Thu was by far the most experienced. "We could take other mountaineers with us; Mr. Brucker has been to the Mrtyahaima before. But none of them will know the place we seek."

I looked at Suhail, and at Tom. It was not only my own life I would be placing in a stranger's hands.

My husband nodded. "We need someone. Let it be the man who found the specimen to begin with."

I got up and went to my desk, where I slid a fresh sheet of paper onto the blotter. "Then first let us see if he agrees."


Thu Phim-lat stared at me as if I were mad. "One day, I cannot be allowed to listen to a lecture without being thrown out. Now you trust me with this?"

"I see no reason not to."

His mouth opened and closed once, as if he had too many possible rejoinders, and none could make it through the scrum. I would not have heeded them regardless. He drew in a breath, then said, "And what if I do not wish to go?"

"Then I would ask *your* reason."

Mr. Thu spread his hands. "Here I am safe—as safe as I may be, at least. You ask me to go into danger again."

"We will be travelling for the most part through Scirling-controlled territory in Vidwatha, and Yelang does not have an eastern foothold yet. Would they have any cause to expect your return to Tser-nga?" He shook his head, and I gave him a bright smile. "Then one could argue that you will be even safer there than here, for the simple reason that no one will be looking for you there. Though I must allow that the risk of avalanches and rocks falling on your head is greater in the Mrtyahaima."

"Rocks and avalanches I fear only as much as they deserve." This statement reassured me more than if he had declared no fear at all. A man who has no fear in the mountains is soon rendered a dark smear upon the valley floor. Mr. Thu held his breath, considering, then asked his final question. "If I refuse, will this harm the Khiam cause?"

"No," I said. The major-general did not even yet know we wanted Mr. Thu to come, for we judged it best to get the man's cooperation before that of the authorities. In that moment, though, I wished we had done it the other way around, for I was certain my truthful admission would cause him to refuse.

He said, "But it would aid my people if I came."

"Among those who would take your participation as an encouraging sign of cooperation, yes. Among those who suspect treachery every time you sneeze, no. I cannot begin to tell you which might win out in the balance. But if this carries any weight with you, I should like to see you come. And not only," I hastened

WITHIN THE SANCTUARY OF WINGS        75

to add, "because your expertise would be useful."

"Why, then?" he asked curiously.

The last time I brought a man along on an expedition of this kind, it was because I loved him. In the case of Thu Phim-lat, my answer was much less scandalous. "Because you found the first specimen. You deserve to be there when—if—we find the second, and document it for the world."

I spoke with pure honesty, not out of calculation. My acquaintance with Mr. Thu was so short, I had no way of anticipating whether my words would move him or not.

Despite my ignorance, I chose the perfect reply.

Thu said, "Then I will come."


On the very day we received our permission to go, I sat down in my study for one final conversation—this one with my son.

"If you tell me not to go," I said, "then I will not."

Jake gaped at me. "Why would I say that?"

"Because the Mrtyahaima peaks are possibly the most lethal region in the world. I cannot promise I will come back alive." No more than I could have promised my survival in the Green Hell . . . but back then I had been grieving for my first husband, fighting to establish myself as a scholar, and fleeing a responsibility I had never particularly desired. Moreover, I was young and naive enough not to realize just how much risk I was facing. Now I knew, and a portion of my heart would have been content to remain at home, secure in what I had already achieved.

But not all of it—and Jake knew that. "If I wanted you to stay here," he said, "I would have already told you so. This is who you are, Mother. If you don't go, you'll always wonder what might have happened. What you might have learned. Besides, you need something new to shove in the faces of those—" (He used a phrase to describe the gentlemen of the Philosophers' Colloquium that I will not repeat here.)

My eyes pricked hot, and hotter still when he added, "But don't get yourself killed. Or arrested by some foreign government. Getting arrested at home is quite enough."

"I have only done that the once," I said. Our tones were light, but the sentiment behind them was not. Sniffling a little, I embraced my son; and not long after, I left Scirland for the heights of the Mrtyahaima.

# PART TWO

*In which the memoirist
signally fails
to get herself killed*

# FIVE

*Summing up—The caeliger base—Flight into the
Mrtyahaima—A less than perfect landing—The third
caeliger—We are alone*

Under any other circumstances, our journey from Falchester to Hlamtse Rong would be enough to fill half a book all on its own. Our party consisted of myself, Suhail, Tom, Thu Phim-lat, and one Lieutenant Chendley, on loan to us from the Royal Scirling Army for mountaineering assistance (largely because they did not trust Thu). We travelled in separate groups, the better to deflect notice; three Scirlings (one of those a woman), an Akhian, and a Yelangese man form a sufficiently motley assortment as to sound like the beginnings of a banal joke.

From Falchester we travelled in stages across the Destanic Ocean and along the eastern coast of Dajin to Alhidra, where we boarded river boats travelling up the Mahajanya into the interior. This is of course the "Father of Vidwatha," one of the two great rivers between which ancient Vidwathi civilization sprang up, and I could have remained there for months, quite happily. Like much of Dajin, Vidwatha boasts a number of river-dwelling dragons, who are often venerated and propitiated by the local farmers in the hopes of preventing destructive floods and drought. I was particularly curious to know whether there was any truth to the folklore which said all the dragons in the Mahajanya were male and all those in the Mahajani, female, the two coming together during the River Marriage Festival to mate. If so, it would have been a fascinating echo of the swamp-wyrms in the Green Hell, where the Moulish bring select males up to the Great Cataract to mate with the queen dragons in the lake there. (As it transpires, the folklore is not true; the physical differences between dragons of the two rivers are a matter of species differentiation rather than sex.)

But our aeronautical carriage awaited, and so I fixed my attention on the west and went onward. Unfortunately for us, the Mahajanya was in those days only partially in Scirling control: the people of that land did not much like seeing one of their spiritual parents in foreign hands (which is why Scirland controls none of it now). We returned to land once more and skirted the disputed stretch—a task which ultimately involved disguises and a good deal of lying, when my party discovered we had not skirted quite far enough—and then, after a brisk gallop away from bandits who attacked both sides indiscriminately, finally convened in the village of Parshe. But this portion of the journey, however lively a tale it makes in its own right, is a mere prelude to the true story, which is our flight into the Mrtyahaima peaks.

Here Lieutenant Chendley took the lead, as he was the only one among us who knew precisely where the Scirling caeliger base was located. Indeed, I never did find out its location, for the lieutenant went off alone and came back with soldiers, who blindfolded us and led our horses the remaining distance. All I know is that it lay approximately two days from Parshe and as close to the Tser-zhag border as they dared, so as to shorten our flight across the closed territory.

Even at that distance, we could see the Mrtyahaima.

Not in any great detail—though I'm told that when the air is truly clear, the vista becomes crisp enough for the knowledgeable to identify individual peaks. For the short time we were in Parshe, though, the air was sufficiently humid that the mountains were simply a dark haze, a hulking mass on the horizon. I thought at the time that we were seeing where we must go, and I marveled at the sight. I did not realize that this was only the edge of the great range, the chain geographers identify more precisely as the Dashavat Mountains. The Mrtyahaima proper lay behind, beyond my vision, rising even higher than I could imagine. Had I seen what I faced while still in Parshe ... I believe I would have continued, for my life has been a recurrent tale of my failure to truly understand my peril until it is too late for me to turn back. But I cannot be certain.

The base had a rather slapped-together look quite at odds with the usual Scirling military standards. I suspected it was a temporary arrangement, which did not surprise me; we were some distance from the nearest garrison, and of course they would not want their caeligers to spend much time out where others could seize them. It positively swarmed with activity, though, and the first person I saw when I dragged my gaze away from the mountains was my brother, Andrew.

I dismounted in a trice and threw my arms about him. "I

suspected I would see you here! But no one would tell me for certain."

Andrew pounded my back as if I were a brother rather than a sister. "It's all very hush-hush, isn't it? Fear of spies and all that. But of course I'm here; I couldn't send my favourite sister off into the Mrtyahaima without so much as a farewell."

His touching concern might have been a little more touching had he not called me his favourite sister. Since I was his *only* sister, the phrase was invariably a sign that he wanted something from me. "Andrew," I said, "you aren't hoping we'll bring you with us, are you?"

"Well, I certainly wouldn't mind—You there! Be careful with that!" He darted off to chide a private who was handling our belongings with insufficient care. That clinched it: my brother was never so diligent in showing his use unless he had some ulterior motive in mind.

Unfortunately for Andrew, I had no authority to bring him along. It is easy enough to add a person to a journey made by boat, horse, or foot, at least if rations are not too limited; but caeligers are another matter. The great limiter there is not space but weight, and all of the crew for long-range missions were at least twenty centimeters shorter than my brother. (Indeed, the army had made an exception to its usual regulations, actively recruiting into their nascent aerial corps men who would ordinarily have been deemed too slight.)

Even with our small party of five, we needed three caeligers for the journey; a single one, or even two, could not carry all of us, our gear, the pilots, and equipment for the caeligers, such as fuel for their engines and canisters of the lifting gas which made it possible for them to fly. "Will they go straight on after they leave us in Tser-nga?" Tom murmured, eyeing the vessels in their row, and the quantity of fuel in a depot some distance away. None of us knew the answer, and would not get one if we asked.

The caeligers themselves made for a striking sight. It is a very great pity that peacetime never spurs development as quickly as war: these craft bore as little resemblance to the caeligers of the Broken Sea eight years ago as an ancient longship does to a modern frigate. Those early vessels had been wired together out of natural dragonbone: shaped with saws where possible and fitted together most cunningly, but still peculiar and not quite suited to the purpose. The frameworks of these caeligers, being made from synthetic dragonbone, consisted of tidy rods and slats, with propellers far larger than any dragon species could provide (which I learned was a necessity for flying in the thinner air of high altitude). All of it looked quite ordinary, with nothing but its pale colour to hint at its origin.

That colour was a happy accident, for the purposes of a military caeliger. Seen from below, everything about these craft was pale, from the gondolas in which the crew rode to the undersides of the balloons, and every piece of structure that could be made light with bleach or paint. Being a natural historian, I needed no explanation as to why. Anyone standing on the ground would have a difficult time picking out the caeliger against the backdrop of the sky. The upper part of the balloon, of course, was painted with a camouflaging pattern, so that should another caeliger happen to overfly it (or the vessel come to ground in a low-lying area), an observer might not distinguish it from the terrain below.

The crew was minimal, so as to ensure we could bring

everything we needed. Our baggage formed a tremendous mountain, easily as large as the equipment for all my other expeditions put together (save Vystrana, where Lord Hilford had brought along a great many things for his own comfort that were not, strictly speaking, necessary). We had our scientific equipment, of course, including tools for the excavation of any specimens from the ice, and the means of preserving same. We had cold-weather clothing, which takes up far more room than it ought, along with tents, ropes, alpenstocks, snowshoes, and other tools of mountain travel—including a gift from our mountaineering friends Mr. and Mrs. Winstow that we would be very glad of in the coming days.

But the greatest bulk of it was food, for we could not be certain of buying or even hunting what we needed. Colonel Dorson, the commander of that base, had done what he could to gather up Tser-zhag coin, but it was not much; and we did not wish to draw attention to ourselves by paying in foreign currency. Besides, Thu warned us, the locals did not have much to sell. They scraped a marginal existence in a marginal land, and money would do them no good if they could not travel down to places where they might spend it and still return home in good time. As for hunting, although bears were not unknown in the region, the main large animals were the wild cousins of the yaks herded by the villagers. But these had been pushed out of their grazing meadows by those domesticated kin, leaving them few in number. And certainly no one would thank us if we shot their livestock.

We hoped it would be enough to sustain us. We had to plan our expedition carefully, for there are two seasons in which it is difficult to do much in Tser-nga: the winter, which was behind

*Military caeligers*

us, and the period of the monsoon, which lay ahead. In the lowlands that means rain, but at the elevation of Thu's valley, it would be snow instead. Foul weather during the sea crossing and our adventures making our way up the Mahajanya had put us behind schedule; we had hoped to depart for Tser-nga by the first of Nebulis, but it was already nearly Gelis. The monsoon would begin in a month, possibly sooner. But even if we did not make it back down to the lowlands before the snows came, we ought to have enough.

Unfortunately for our plans, everything seemed to go awry. Dorson had underestimated the weight of our gear, and after we had loaded the caeligers we found the distribution was entirely unsuitable, so it was all to do over again. Then the weather turned against us, with a hot and dusty wind that threatened to clog the caeligers' engines if we attempted to fly in it. The soldiers took precautions to guard the machines against the infiltrating grit, but when at last we set out for Tser-nga, we discovered the hard way that those precautions were insufficient.

I can only thank heaven that we discovered it before we were even so much as a hundred feet off the ground. Had the engine of our caeliger failed later than that, we would have been in dire straits, with no choice but to land in Vidwathi or Tser-zhag territory and attempt to repair it ourselves. Even with that good fortune, we had more than a few heart-pounding moments as our pilot guided the craft to earth once more. And as easy as our landing ultimately was, Tom staggered out of the gondola with his face white as parchment and collapsed to earth, shaking.

I knelt beside him. "Tom. If it is this hard for you—"

His jaw tensed and his fingers dug into the dirt. "I am not

turning back, Isabella. I will be fine."

To that I made no response. We both knew it was a lie.

Finally Tom shook his head. "I'd hoped to avoid this, but—well. Is there any task for which I might be needed during flight?"

"I don't imagine so. If the pilots need aid, the rest of us can provide it." If the hands of four others were insufficient, I doubted a fifth would make any difference.

"Then I'll just dose myself with laudanum." Tom climbed to his feet, brushing his hands and knees clean. "Better to be useless in flight than to not be there at all."

Two days later he suited word to deed, after we had repaired the engine and loaded the caeligers one last time, in yet another distribution of weight—one which left rather more of our gear aboard a single craft than I would have liked. Andrew helped Tom into the gondola, then came back out to bid me farewell.

"Are you *certain* I cannot come with you?" he asked. His tone was both anxious and wistful, as if he feared for my safety, and also regretted missing the grand adventure he imagined lay ahead.

I forbore to remind him that he was even less of a mountaineer than I, or that we had no cold-weather clothing in his size, or any of the other practical objections. Instead I said, "You would be absent without leave, and I'm given to understand the army frowns upon such things. Besides, in a few months we may need you to ransom us back from the Tser-zhag government."

It made him laugh, as I had hoped it would. "You're depending on me to rescue you from a diplomatic situation? Good God, you're doomed."

That was not what my nerves needed to hear. Despite everything, though, I held to my course. The next morning Suhail looked at me and asked, "Any second thoughts?"

"None I care to listen to," I said. Having given him one final kiss, I straightened my shoulders and marched across the camp to the waiting caeliger.

Although I had been in the air before, there was a part of me that wanted to curl up on the floor of the gondola with Tom, for I had never been on a flight like this one.

Suhail and I had never attained any tremendous altitude in our stolen caeliger, and much of our time had been spent over open water, where there are no features to threaten disaster or show you how far up you are. This time, we knew precisely where we were—especially as the lead craft carried a device called an altimeter which measured our vertical position, and the senior pilot, one Captain Adler, continually signaled to the others with flags when he decided to climb or descend. He did not test the upward limits of the caeligers, not yet; but we flew quite high in the air, the better to hide our presence from people below.

Any such people were mere specks from that height, difficult to see unless heralded by a dark stream of yaks making their way across a high meadow. We saw settlements, but steered clear of them when we could. Below us, the ground rose and fell, rose and fell . . . but rose more than fell, and we climbed yet again to keep our distance.

And ahead lay the mountains.

Even though I knew better, I had thought of them in terms of the mountains I had seen before, during my first expedition to Vystrana. I thought of dark trees, and those were there; I thought of alpine meadows, and those were there, too, fringed with snow in areas too sheltered for it to melt.

But in Vystrana, the peaks were little white hats atop the green beauty below. In the uplands of Tser-nga, life threaded through the valleys like branching fingers, clinging to the base of the mountains as if they might lose their grip at any moment. Above towered pinnacles of ice and snow and stark, unforgiving stone. There were fields of scree where nothing grew, passes which rose to sterile heights before descending once more to a level where humans might grudgingly be allowed to persist. I would never have guessed that so frigid a place might remind me of Akhia ... but only in the Jefi have I encountered a landscape so indifferent to my presence. Men and women might easily die here—indeed, they have done so—and the Mrtyahaima would take no notice.

The higher we went, the more likely that fate seemed. In order for the propellers to gain much purchase in the thin air, we could not fly too high; but flying lower meant subjecting ourselves to the fickle winds, sculpted into diabolical knots by the terrain. In the early stages of our flight Captain Adler had chatted casually with Suhail: now that gave way to silence and the occasional barked command for a new signal, which Suhail rushed to post. Watching the pilot's hands (for I could not long keep my eyes on the nearby peaks and slopes), I saw his knuckles whiten from the force of his grip. Tom's own knuckles were even whiter, gripping the nearest hand-holds, for the caeliger frequently jerked one way or another, slammed to and fro by the changing winds.

I crouched next to him. "I can fetch more laudanum—"

Tom shook his head in a tight gesture. "No. I may be needed after all, and quite soon."

In his shoes, I would not want to be drugged into a stupor either. It was obvious that matters were not going according to plan. Thu was nearby, clinging to the flapping edges of our map; he frowned and called out to Suhail in Yelangese.

My husband shouted something back. I could not understand his words, but his tone was clear: whatever Thu had said, Suhail had short patience with it. He bent to speak to Captain Adler, and I made my way to his side. "What is it?"

"We're too far south," Suhail said. "At least, Thu believes we are—who can be sure, with so little to go by. But there isn't a damn thing we can do about it. Heading north would require us to fly directly into the wind, and the engines don't have the strength for that, not at this altitude."

Ahead of us, the greenery ended in a forbidding wall of black and white: a range of peaks that might delight a dedicated mountaineer, but spelled death for us if we met them in flight. Below us lay the western fringes of Tser-nga, the scattered villages and herdsmen who fell under the authority of the Tser-zhag king only because there was no one else around to claim them. "What do we do?"

"Look for a place to land," Suhail said. "If we can."

My first two caeliger flights had ended in crashes. I drew in a deep breath, reminded myself of the later flights that concluded in perfect safety, and tried to believe they would be my model today. My heart, already racing from the altitude and thin air, kept up its pace.

The caeliger lurched. Adler swore. I wanted to ask Suhail how far we might be from our destination, but kept silent. The answer was irrelevant. We would land where we could; only after we were safely on the ground did anything else matter.

"There," Suhail said, pointing.

"I see it," Adler said through his teeth.

Up ahead lay one of those fields of scree. It was not exactly level—but given a choice between sliding on loose stone and risking our balloon's integrity on a treetop, our pilot clearly chose the former. The only problem lay in the preposition: the field lay *up* ahead. To reach it, our caeliger would have to climb once more.

Were it not for the cold, thin air, I might have thought myself back in the Keongan Islands. With the same blind faith as before, I followed the instructions of Suhail and our pilot, doing what little I could to assist. Our craft banked and rose, but not as quickly as the slope ahead drew near—and we were too far to starboard, I could tell. "If we keep on this way," I called out, "we shall miss it entirely!"

"Wait—" Adler shouted back, intent on the terrain ahead. He could not spare the attention for more.

Just as we drew abreast of our target, a gust of wind caught us and slammed us sideways. The caeliger's frame crunched with bruising force into the scree, knocking us all off our feet. For one irrational instant, I was certain our landing had broken the gondola—but of course dragonbone is not so easily cracked.

"Kill the lift!" Adler gasped, scrambling back to his feet. We were sliding on the scree, partly forward, partly down, and would soon come loose if we did not settle.

Suhail made it to the valve before I did, and the caeliger's movement lessened. I drew in a steadying breath. One of the other caeligers soon came to a halt above us on the slope; but the other overshot. Adler spat a curse, watching it go. We all stood, not breathing, until the third caeliger dropped out of sight behind a ridge.

It was, of course, the one carrying the majority of our gear.

But if only one caeliger were to suffer misfortune, I had rather it be the one with fewer people on board. In the meanwhile, as the lightest member of our brigade, I leapt from the gondola with a sack in hand and began to fill it with scree. The craft shifted ominously and slid several meters away as I turned to hand my bounty to Suhail, and I had to fill a great many more sacks before its position was secure.

Finally both caeligers were settled into position. I was by then tired enough to lie down on the rocks and declare my day over, but of course we could not do so. Lieutenant Chendley immediately tightened his boots and declared his intent to hike in the direction of the third caeliger. "I'll go with you," Tom said, lurching to his feet.

He clearly wished to be of use. I had no idea of how much laudanum remained in his body, however, and I was not at all certain he should be undertaking anything strenuous until his head had cleared. When I protested, though, he waved me off. "I am steady enough now that my feet are on the ground. And besides, they may need medical aid."

I could not argue that latter point, and he proved his fitness by scaling a nearby boulder. The sight alone was enough to exhaust me, for even a small exertion is utterly draining at such heights, and our flight meant we had not been given the usual chance to acclimate. It must have set Tom's heart to pounding, for bright spots stood out in his cheeks against the general pallor of his skin; but the laudanum at least seemed to have loosened its grip, and so we sent him off with Chendley.

The rest of us—myself, Suhail, Thu, and the four pilots allocated to the two remaining vessels—set about examining our craft for damage. I was relieved to see that while the canvas sides of the gondolas had torn in a few places, there was no harm that could not be mended.

While I helped cut a few pieces of spare canvas into patches, I heard Suhail address Adler. "What are your orders now?"

Silence followed this—apart from the wind, of course, which did not cease for even one minute during my time in Tser-nga. Then Suhail spoke again. "You cannot tell me, of course." He sighed in frustration. Or perhaps he was only catching his breath; none of us could speak in more than brief bursts, as our lungs clamoured for more air. "Then let me rephrase. Should we empty the balloons? There will be much less risk of attention if we do so."

"No, we'll keep them filled."

They had more than enough spare lifting gas to refill all three balloons and fly back eastward. If the pilot wanted them to stay as they were, it could only mean that they intended to fly onward, west across the Mrtyahaima—or at least as far as they could get. Could they return from their scouting mission the same way? I doubted it. In which case, how did they intend to get home? It was one thing for us to jest about the Tser-zhag taking us into custody and marching us back to the Vidwathi border. We were not in friendly territory, but neither were we at war with the locals. Every place the caeligers might plausibly reach, though, was either sufficiently inhospitable to life as to be uninhabited, or in Yelangese control. Unless the pilots managed to find and loot some caeliger supply depot over there, they could not hope to fly back. They would have to abandon the caeligers—likely destroying them first—and somehow sneak back to friendlier territory.

It says something about my own temperament, I suppose, that such a plan seemed astonishing to me. To creep into a hostile environment for the sake of scientific study, I understand; to do the same for military advantage is too daunting to contemplate—even though most would call the latter purpose far more comprehensible.

Had we landed without difficulty, I think the caeligers would have flown on as soon as they could repair the torn gondolas and unload our gear. But our pilots were military men, and would not so easily abandon their companions. Although they were clearly not happy with the delay (and concomitant risk of discovery), they settled in to wait for Tom and Chendley's return.

Our companions did not appear before dusk, which came shockingly early in that region, the sun vanishing behind the snowy rampart to our west. What warmth the air held—not remotely enough for my taste—vanished as if it had never been, and after some conference, we moved down to a more sheltered spot.

I sat looking at the western sky, still brilliant with light, but cut by the dark knife of the mountains. Suhail sat next to me and said, "Even if the caeliger crashed, most of our gear will have survived. Though it may be scattered halfway to Akhia, and the gathering may be difficult."

It sounds heartless, when I recount such words and thoughts. Yes, our gear had been on that caeliger—but so had Marbury and Lowe, two corporals in the Royal Scirling Army. What of them? But it was easier for us to talk of inanimate objects, while the fate of two people was in doubt. Both Tom and Chendley were experienced in field medicine; if anyone were injured, they would do everything they could to help. Until we heard from them, we could do nothing to assist. Forming contingencies for our own expedition at least gave us something else to think about.

Without our tents, the best we could do was to construct a makeshift shelter from stones and fallen branches, enough to cut the wind and hide our fire from eyes down below. Even in Gelis, which for that hemisphere is summer, the air was unpleasantly cold. I huddled next to the little flame, trying not to ask myself why I had volunteered for this lunacy, until Thu said, "I see light."

He had been keeping vigil since the shelter was done, watching in the direction the third caeliger had gone. We all scrambled to see. Sure enough, a fire twinkled in the distance. Then it vanished—and came back. And again.

"They're signaling," one of the junior pilots said with relief. "Army code. One of them has got a broken arm, but they're alive."

It is truly a wonder, how thoroughly circumstances can alter one's perception of a situation. I will not claim I slept warm and happy that night, but knowing the others were relatively unharmed did much to improve my outlook. In the morning, when there was sufficient light to travel safely across the intervening ground, the four of them trekked back to our camp.

According to Tom's report, our equipment had taken a bit of a tumble, but nothing we could not redress. "Then we stay?" I said, looking from him to Suhail, to Lieutenant Chendley, to Thu. I knew my own inclination—but this was our last chance to change our minds. After this, we were on our own.

They nodded. Adler said, "We can't fly the third caeliger out of here, not when one man has a broken arm."

I must confess my heart leapt a little, before logic caught up and hauled it back to earth. There was no way they would leave the vessel with us, and the gas and fuel to fly it: the risk of it being captured was far too great, and we had no real piloting experience among us. "I expect you will want to destroy it," I said.

Suhail made a muffled sound. The caeliger represented a tremendous outlay of resources and effort on the part of Scirland; now I proposed to simply throw that away. But he understood my reasoning—and, more to the point, that my reasoning was merely a guess at the army's.

"We'll cannibalize some of it for parts," Adler said. "But yes. And we have to move quickly, before others find us here."

He meant what he said. Crossing back to the broken vessel took us what remained of the morning, but by mid-afternoon they had stripped it of whatever equipment and spare components they thought they could use. "Now what?" Tom said. "Try to start a rockslide to cover it?"

"Too risky," Adler said. "And we have something better."

I had taken no particular note of the small canisters among the caeliger supplies, assuming them to be oil or fuel or some such. Now, however, the pilots uncapped them and began to scatter the liquid within across key portions of the caeliger. It hissed when it struck dragonbone, and to my astonishment, the bone began to crumble and break.

Standing beside me, Tom hummed low in his throat. "Of course they'd bring something like that," he murmured to me. "They can't let these vessels fall into enemy hands. I wonder—are they replicating the process that decays natural dragonbone, or is this something new?" But he pitched the question so it carried no further than myself and Suhail. Military men do not take kindly to civilians prying into military secrets.

When this task was done, pieces of dragonbone yet remained; the pilots had not troubled to douse the entire thing, likely because they could not spare enough of the dissolving reagent. Nothing of any possible use was left intact, though. And bits were still disintegrating when the pilots gathered up the salvage and prepared to head out. "We'll fly onward tomorrow morning," Adler said to my group. "If something goes wrong—if you change your minds—light a signal fire before dawn, and we'll wait."

I wondered how sincere the offer was. With one caeliger lost already, they would not be eager to spare another to fly us back east. Still, it was a kind thought. "Thank you, Captain," I said, and the others echoed me.

We did not light a signal fire. The next morning, at the very crack of dawn, we heard the buzzing of engines and saw the remaining caeligers lift into the air. Their pale undersides worked as intended, making them difficult to track across the sky, but I followed their course northeast until they came parallel to a gap in the peaks, whereupon they tacked hard to the west and out of sight. They had vanished into the empty heart of the mountains, and were gone.

That quickly, we were alone in the Mrtyahaima.

# SIX

A s soon as the caeligers were gone, Thu laid out a sheet of paper on which he had sketched his best guess at our location and the surrounding terrain. He said, "We are here." His finger tapped one spot along the ramparts at the western edge of Tser-nga. "The village of Hlamtse Rong is here." He tapped another, northward of us.

In between lay a forbidding stripe, roughly where I had seen the caeligers turn west the night before. "What is that?" I asked.

"A river gorge," Thu said. "I think it may be a tributary of the Lerg-pa."

Which we could not fly across. Before I could select from among the curses that rose to my lips, Suhail asked, "And the scale of this map?"

"If we could go directly there, two days? But we must go east, then north, then west again. If we are lucky . . . five days, perhaps. If we are not lucky . . ." Thu shrugged.

There was no use railing against the contrary winds that had kept us from landing closer to our destination. With the caeligers all gone or destroyed, we could only tackle the challenge thus presented, or give up—and none of us, of course, were willing to give up.

Unfortunately, there was simply no way we could carry all of our equipment the necessary distance. We would have needed the relative strength of ants to each toil along beneath a fifth of the pile, and that was without accounting for the harsh terrain. "We'll have to leave some of it here," Tom said reluctantly, "and send people back for it once we're established in Hlamtse Rong."

Chendley looked grim. "Even if we leave all of your scientific equipment, it's still too much. We'll need rations, shelter, clothing, equipment for crossing the river. Either we take twice the time making a supply depot at the edge of the gorge, or . . ."

"Or we need help," I said, finishing the thought he was too reluctant to voice.

Help might be available—but we would have to ask for it. And of the five of us, only Thu spoke Tser-zhag to any real extent (though Suhail had been practicing assiduously, and was making good progress). He would also attract less attention, I suspected; after all, the Yelangese had been through here before, and his features and coloration were not so wildly different from the local norm that he could be identified as foreign at a distance. Tom, on the other hand, would stand out like a daisy in grass, and the rest of us would not fare much better.

Chendley objected with great force when we proposed to send Thu to find the nearest village by himself. "You can't be serious," he said. "Handing him a pile of barter and letting him go off on his own—"

"Why, Lieutenant," I said with insincere mildness. "Whatever do you imagine will happen? Your concern for his safety is touching, but I think it unlikely that he will fall victim to a footpad out here, in the middle of nowhere."

His concern, of course, was for something quite other than Thu's safety. Although ostensibly the lieutenant had been assigned to us as an aid in mountaineering, we all knew perfectly well that he was also there to be Thu's watchdog—for, our newfound alliance with the Khiam rebels notwithstanding, the army was composed of suspicious types who did not trust anyone with a Yelangese name. Unfortunately for Lieutenant Chendley, his military associations did not give him any sort of command authority over the expedition, and so Thu went to the village alone.

He returned before sunset on the second day with two ponies. Chendley, scowling like a thunderhead, declared them utterly inadequate to our needs, but no amount of complaining would improve our options: those two were all the village could spare, whatever enticements Thu offered in return. (Indeed, we were lucky to have two.) I think Chendley had visions of all five of us riding, with a string of pack ponies to carry everything for us, such as recreational mountaineers often enjoy. Perhaps it is just as well that we could not. I have seen people riding Mrtyahaiman ponies, perched on saddles and piles of blankets so high there can be no possibility of communicating with one's mount by means of legs or seat. I might as soon have tried to communicate with the mountain through a meter of snow. The rider can only perch and offer prayers to whatever deity they honour that the pony will do as intended. Lacking enough to use as mounts, we loaded those two as high as we could with food and other necessities, thanked our lucky stars that Tser-zhag ponies are as hardy as mules, and carried what we could of the remainder upon our backs. Then, groaning beneath our loads, we began walking toward Hlamtse Rong.

The verb "walk" is wholly inadequate to what followed. No single word will suffice: we walked, crept, climbed, slid, dragged, laboured, and occasionally fell our way across the intervening terrain. And all this effort was made worse by the awareness that, if we descended just a little way, we would find ourselves on much more hospitable ground, below the worst of the ridges which made a washboard of the area we traversed. But the farther down we went, the more attention we would attract. None of us had any illusions that our presence had not been noticed, of course; Thu had gone into the village, and we had undoubtedly been spotted a dozen times by distant herdsmen and traders. Habitation here might be sparse, but that did not mean it was absent. But the more inconspicuous we remained, the easier it was for the Tser-zhag to shrug and let us pass.

Before we ever embarked upon this journey, Tom, Suhail, and I had discussed what to do if our most experienced climbers, Chendley and Thu, disagreed on routes or techniques. Ultimately we chose to trust in Thu's experience of that region, even if it meant frustrating our lieutenant. Which it most certainly did— but in one respect that journey to the village of Hlamtse Rong was beneficial to us all, for it gave Thu ample time to prove his competence in the face of Chendley's distrust. When we roped ourselves together, we did so in two groups: myself following Chendley, and Tom and Suhail behind Thu, because Chendley considered it his sacred duty to keep me alive, and would not let me dangle from a rope tethered to our Yelangese companion. But by the time we reached Hlamtse Rong, he had seen enough of Thu's skill and courage to accord the man his grudging respect. After all, it is difficult to question someone's integrity when you have seen him fling his full weight upon his alpenstock to arrest the headlong plunge of his companions into the river below, then hold them both while another man unropes from a horrified baroness and joins him to set up a rescuing belay.

(When Suhail and Tom were upon solid ground once more, I discarded our usual public reserve and clung quite tightly to my husband for some time. "Please tell me," I said, my nerves expressing themselves via unsteady humour, "that you did not engineer that incident merely to prove to Chendley that Thu is a good sort." Suhail's answering laugh was so shaky as to barely qualify, but it became a joke afterward among the five of us, that any setback or difficulty was a cunning ploy to create trust.)

I fretted at the slowness of our pace. How could I not? Every day we spent trying to reach Hlamtse Rong brought us one day closer to the onset of the monsoon. We moved at a crawl, for we could not carry every piece of our gear on our backs, and had to spend half our time raising it or lowering it over the same obstacles our bodies had to surmount—and raising and lowering our ponies, too. We were exhausted, gasping for breath, our hearts pounding at the smallest exertion. Our journey up to Parshe in the highlands had given us some time to acclimate to the increasing altitude, but from there to here we had leapt over a rise of more than a thousand meters, and every one of us felt the difference in our bones. Suhail suffered particularly, his hands and feet swelling, fatigue and dizziness threatening his balance as he moved. I fretted at not being roped to him, even though I knew he was safer with Tom and Thu, and examined him for fever or fluid in the lungs every time we paused to rest. It was a great relief when, after a few days, his symptoms began to subside.

But if I claimed I had no energy with which to conduct research during that time, you would know I had been replaced by an imposter.

I mentioned before the cat-like dragons supposedly kept as pets by the local people. One night, as I climbed out of the tent I shared with Suhail to deal with a certain necessity, I startled several creatures who were investigating our food stores. They froze—I took a step toward them—and they shot skyward in a burst of wings.

"Dragons!" I exclaimed, instantly awake with delight. I fear my voice was too loud; it disturbed Suhail, who (having not heard me properly) thought I was in some kind of distress, and his half-awake attempt to leap out of the tent ended badly enough that it roused Tom and Chendley both. With the two of them up and moving, of course, Thu could not long stay asleep.

"Oh," Thu said when he heard my tale. He did not sound impressed. "Yes. We should be more careful in storing our food, or they will eat it all. They adore fat."

At that altitude, it was not surprising. We had packed a large amount of pemmican (a mixture of powdered meat, fat, and berries), knowing that the cold and thin air would cause us to crave the fattiest, most filling food we could put down our gullets. I was fascinated to see it act as bait for dragons, though. "Are these the beasts you told us about? The mews?"

"Mew," of course, is not any kind of official name. The locals have a variety of terms for them: *drukshi, udrakor* ("noisy trickster"), and others less polite. But Thu and his companions had dubbed them the Yelangese equivalent of "mews," because of their call, which resembled that of a cat.

The Tser-zhag did not, as travellers' rumours had it, keep them as pets. Quite the contrary, in fact, as mews are scavengers who will paw through garbage, steal shiny objects, and even (in large enough groups) dive at yaks. The locals say this is an attempt to burrow through their dense wool and chew at the fat beneath, but I never saw one succeed; I think a yak would have to be very far gone indeed to let that pass without retort. But their failures notwithstanding, they are far from popular with the human inhabitants of the region. Suhail and Chendley soon came to detest them as passionately as Thu did, after they perpetually broke into our stores and played havoc with our gear.

But for Tom and myself, they were very nearly as interesting as the frozen specimen we hoped to find. They could not be counted as true dragons, for they had nothing resembling extraordinary breath, but we relished the chance to dispel a misconception among our peers—not to mention answer new questions. I was especially eager to know how the mews avoided losing too much heat through the thin membrane of their wings.

Our curiosity was not sufficient to make us delay our forward progress, of course. A bird in the hand might be worth two in the bush, but a dragon in the ice was worth half a dozen of its diminutive cousins digging through our supplies. The latter would still be there next year; the former might not be. Nonetheless, we made what observations we could as we trudged to Hlamtse Rong, leaving out bait at night, studying their tracks, and keeping watch for them during our hikes.

Of the mews I will say more later—but first, the village.

Hlamtse Rong is named for the valley it sits in, which points toward the nearby peak of Hlamtse as if laid out by a landscape architect. In those days it was a flyspeck too small to even appear on Tser-zhag maps, let alone those made by foreigners, and it is not much larger now. Were it not for Thu, we should never have found the place, nor had any reason to go looking for it to begin with. Its population numbered less than one hundred, eking out their living through a combination of yak-herding and growing crops on what narrow terraces they could carve out of the slopes. The only reason anyone had built a house there at all was because it was unclaimed land: the people of the village belong to the tiny Nying minority, whose members had been evicted from more favourable regions by the dominant Tser-zhag.

Living where they do, on the extreme edge of a country in which they do not enjoy power, the people of Hlamtse Rong take a very cautious approach to strangers. When we entered the village, we might have thought the entire place deserted: there was no one at all in the narrow dirt track that served as a main street, no one in front of the houses or visible through windows. But here and there we saw eyes peering over a low wall, or caught the movement as a shutter swung hastily closed, and we knew we were being watched.

This, as much as the mountaineering, was why we had brought Thu. He called out in Tser-zhag, which is not the native tongue of the Nying, but they speak it quite well. Under his breath, Chendley muttered, "How do we know what he's saying is friendly?"—but his heart was not in the suspicion; he said it more out of habit.

I could not deny that we were as much in Thu's hands right now as Tom and Suhail had been when they went over that cliff above the river. Whatever he said caused a man to emerge from one of the houses: a small fellow, with the broad face typical of his people. This man peered at Thu, who spoke to him in what even I could recognize as very halting sentences. I alternated between watching the two of them and watching Suhail, who had the abstracted look that meant he was bending all his concentration to the task of parsing their conversation. I envied him his facility with such things.

Finally the local man nodded, and Thu sighed in relief. "He remembers me," he said to us. "And no one has given them difficulty because we were here before."

Apart from the weather and the mountains themselves, this was the biggest danger we faced. The Nying of Hlamtse Rong were so separated from their Tser-zhag countrymen in the "lowlands" (by which they meant those living a mere three thousand meters above sea level) that they hardly cared that the government in Thokha had closed the borders. But they might have gossiped about the Yelangese explorers to someone in another village, and so on down the chain until it reached the ears of some official who did care. If such a man had taken action against this village, our welcome might have been even colder than the environment itself.

With that hurdle cleared, we laid out our gifts, like foreign diplomats at the feet of a very ragged potentate. We had brought things useful to the Nying: copper pots, good steel knives, waterproofed silk. The sight of these items lured the other villagers out of their wary hiding, and soon we had everyone from old grannies to toddlers barely old enough to walk poking at our gifts—and at the five of us, too. Thu they had seen before, and his features and coloration were not too dissimilar to their own, but Suhail's Akhian nose and cheekbones drew comment, and my pale skin and lighter hair even more. But they were the most fascinated by Tom, who was, as usual for him, already red and peeling from the sun, which is even more intense at high elevations than it is in the desert or at sea.

In exchange for these things (and the entertainment we brought), we were given leave to use the village as our base of operations while we attempted to search for another frozen specimen. "Have you asked them whether they've seen any other carcasses themselves?" I asked Thu, as we lugged our equipment to the house where we would be staying.

He shook his head. "Do not say anything of it to them yet."

"I hardly could," I said wryly, dropping my pack inside the courtyard wall. "Remember, I have not mastered above a dozen words of their tongue."

Thu apologized for his error, then went on. "They consider Gyaptse, the nearby mountain, very ill-omened—its name means it is cursed. They did not like us going up there the first time, but it is the lowest col in the vicinity—the only one we had any hope of using as a pass."

I thought of the Draconean site outside Drustanev, and the island of Rahuahane. "You did not see any ruins near there, did you?"

His answering look suggested I was mad. With justification, I suppose; no one builds structures of that kind at such an altitude.

Even the monasteries of Tser-nga are never above five thousand meters. Once I explained my reason for asking, he said, "No. It is cursed only because those who wander too much around the area have died."

And yet we proposed to go there ourselves. Well, it was not the first reckless thing I had done.

The houses in the village were all of a type common to the high regions: round and multi-storied, with livestock on the ground floor and the family above, and the attic space used for storage (which helps to insulate the people below). Shuwa, the woman to whom the house belonged, had been in the street for our arrival, and had raced ahead to make all ready for us—which, given that there was no guest room to prepare, largely consisted of brewing tea. When we climbed up the steep ladder into the living quarters, a tray was already set out, with five steaming cups on it.

It is natural that when we read a word like "tea," our minds supply the most obvious interpretation, as shaped by our own experiences. For a Scirling, this means black tea, sweetened with sugar and milk. For a Yelangese, it might be green tea. But we were in Tser-nga, and that meant those five cups contained butter tea.

I understand why the people of the region drink such a thing. When your body is desperate to stay warm and fed in an environment that wishes you to be neither, butter is an excellent way to sustain yourself. Naturally, then, it appears in any food where it might profitably be added, and on this front I have no complaint. But I feel that adding it to beverages is a bridge too far; however much I reminded myself of its beneficial qualities (and however much my body, on occasion, craved the sustenance),

I never reconciled myself to drinking the stuff.

My travels, however, have inured me to consuming many things I would not even consider at home, and despite its cheese-like odour, butter tea was less objectionable than some of the comestibles on offer in the jungle of Mouleen. The five of us arrayed ourselves on the floor of Shuwa's house, and I smiled and thanked her, thus deploying two of my dozen words of Tser-zhag.

She ducked her head and spoke with the intonation of a question, casting a puzzled glance around at our group.

"What is it?" I asked Thu. "Did I give offense somehow?"

The months that had elapsed since Thu's arrival at Caffrey Hall had given me some sense of the man's character. Now I recognized, by the way his hand rubbed at the nape of his neck where his queue had been, that he was embarrassed and uncomfortable. (The Taisên had imposed the queue on all males; therefore its severing was a common gesture among those Khiam Siu who wished to publicly declare their allegiance.) "No. She— she only wants to know, ah, how this group fits together."

Shuwa made a circling gesture that encompassed the four men in the party, then pointed at me, repeating her question.

"Ah," I said. "She is wondering what I am doing here, female as I am?"

"No." Thu sat very upright, then said in a rush, "She wants to know if all four of us are your husbands."

Some unknown span of time later, I realized I was sitting with my mouth open, and closed it very carefully. "*All* my husbands?"

"I did not think to tell you—it did not seem relevant. Here, women can marry more than one man. Brothers, to be precise. She is confused because we do not look like brothers."

"I should think not," I said faintly.

The custom is not a common one; polygyny, the marriage of one man to multiple women, is far more widespread. But polyandry—one woman and multiple men—serves an important function in the property laws of Tser-nga and some neighbouring regions. Farming and herding there are marginal propositions already; if land were to be divided up among a man's sons via partible inheritance, then within a few generations the harvest from each parcel would be insufficient to keep a mew alive, much less a human family. And simply practicing primogeniture would leave quite a lot of young men wandering about at loose ends, which tends to result in raiding, warfare, and murder. In other parts of the Mrtyahaima, excess sons are all shunted off to monasteries, with only the eldest inheriting anything at all. But in the highlands of Tser-nga, all brothers marry the same woman, and hold the property in common.

Suhail looked at me, bemused. I think I stared back. I have been married more than once in my life—three times, if one counts my temporary arrangement with Liluakame in Keonga—but never simultaneously. I tried to imagine being wed to both Jacob and Suhail at once, and felt as if I had sprained something in my head. The loss of Jacob still saddened me . . . but had he not perished in Vystrana, I could not imagine myself having met Suhail, or having considered him in anything more than a friendly light if we *had* met. How could I weigh that loss against what I had gained after? Even in Tser-nga, I do not think I could have had both: my Scirling husband and my Akhian one, the marriage arranged for me by my father and the one I impulsively made for myself. And so many joys have come to me as a result of that latter match, it is impossible not to think my life would have been impoverished without it.

There are no simple answers to such things. We can never know who we might have been had things gone differently. I only know that without Suhail, I would not have become the woman I am today.

Tom coughed, breaking the awkward silence. "You can tell her no—Isabella only lays claim to the one."

"Yes, of course," Thu murmured, and relayed this in Tser-zhag. Naturally he had known the answer, but I think the woman's question so discomfited him that for a moment he could not think of the necessary words in her tongue.

Our hostess had three husbands of her own, all brothers. Two of them were away at the moment, on a journey down to Phen Rong, where they could trade for some much-needed supplies. This was why she could accomodate us in her house, although with all five of our party added it was a tight fit. I did not consider this entirely a bad thing: privacy was impossible to come by, but the close quarters meant I could at least be assured of sleeping warm. The yaks penned below us might be fragrant, but their body heat rose up through the floorboards, and with Suhail to one side of me and Shuwa to the other, I never had cause for complaint.

Not while in the house, at least. Outside, it was another matter.

We woke the morning after our arrival to the sound of gentle rain. This did not deter Thu from making arrangements with some of the local men to retrieve the remainder of our belongings—a process that left us in some difficulty, for we had only the one companion who was anything like conversant in Tser-zhag, and he could not be in two places at once. Ultimately we dispatched Chendley with the retrieval group, while Thu stayed in the village, where our topics were less easily explored in mime.

I was glad not to be going with Chendley myself. Although my body had more or less settled in to the elevation, I was still quite tired, and knew I would need a rest before tackling the hike to the col. But the next day it rained again . . . and then, after a respite of one day, a third time . . . and long before Chendley arrived back in Hlamtse Rong, we knew the truth.

The monsoon had begun.

# SEVEN

*Seasonal considerations—Trapping mews—Diving behaviour—*
*Lessons in falconry—Breeding and bones*

Had we been able to land closer to the village . . . had our first attempt to fly west been successful . . . had we not been forced to evade bandits on our way to Parshe . . . had we only left Scirland sooner. I could list a dozen points at which we lost precious time, but it was no use wishing to have those moments back. The simple fact was that we had arrived in Hlamtse Rong too late, and now had no hope of journeying to the col before the snows made it impossible.

In my less bitter moments, I knew the delays were a disguised blessing. The monsoon that year began early, but we had no way of predicting that. Had we come to the village a week earlier, we would have set out in the cheerful confidence that we had plenty of time to conduct our research. The snows would have caught us at high elevation, far from shelter and support; we might all have died. But it was hard to weigh that hypothetical peril against my very present frustation, as I sat in the doorway of Shuwa's house and watched the rain pour down.

Suhail sat next to me, a warm and comforting presence. Tom had gone out with Thu to speak with the village headman, but we all knew what answer they would return with: we could not set out today, nor tomorrow, nor any time in the near future. Not unless our destination lay below us, eastward, back in the direction of Vidwatha. The heights of the mountains were far too dangerous now.

"Ventis," I said at last. I had not spoken in nearly an hour, but Suhail could follow my thoughts well enough. "Three months; that is how long they say the monsoon lasts." Assuming it did not overstay its welcome, as it had shown up too soon.

"You want to wait," Suhail said. "Attempt the search between the monsoon and the onset of winter."

Somewhere out there, Chendley and the villagers were toiling back toward us with a pile of equipment. "If we do not, this entire journey has been wasted. It would be one thing if I could be sure of trying again later—then it would only be resources and time we have thrown away. But do you really think anyone will loan us another caeliger? That the Tser-zhag government will not have tightened its watch, or the Yelangese overrun this place?" I did not speak of the thing we had come here for, the way our odds of success decreased with every passing day. If uncovered, it might rot; if entombed in fresh snow, we might never find it. I had gambled on the chance of discovery, and like a bettor desperate to make good his losses, I refused to walk away from the table.

Three months rotting in Hlamtse Rong, waiting. Hoping.

A chorus of mewing came from a nearby house. A Nying woman, cursing, used a broom to drive out several draconic figures that had evidently taken up residence among her livestock.

Suhail turned to me, grinning. "Whatever will you do to keep yourself occupied?"

Shuwa and her fellow villagers looked at us as if we were mad when we expressed our intention to study the mews.

I have of course encountered this reaction many a time—but never more so than in Hlamtse Rong, where the dragons in question were nothing more than vermin. Rock-wyrms and desert drakes may prey upon livestock, earning the enmity of the local humans, but their grandeur also commands respect. Mews enjoyed no such reputation. They were simply pests, no more admired in Tser-nga than stoats are in Scirland. (Indeed, less so, for they provide no fur.)

Chendley looked at us in much the same way after he returned. In democratic fashion, we held a vote: only the lieutenant was in favour of abandoning this whole matter as a bad job, and his strenuous arguments did nothing to sway the rest of us—though in fairness I should note that his arguments were good ones. It is not his fault they lacked the power to penetrate our thick skulls and effect any change within. We would stay in Hlamtse Rong until the monsoon ended, and make our attempt then.

In the meanwhile, we would study the dragons we had on hand. Inquiries around the village revealed that the hunting of mews, if the enterprise can be given so grand a name, is the domain of unmarried spinsters—of which there are more than a few, what with husbands being distributed in sibling batches. A wife who finds mews plaguing her household calls for assistance, and the spinster in question builds and lays traps for the creatures in areas which attract their attention, such as kitchen stores and refuse pits.

"You are not a spinster," Shuwa said to me (as translated by Thu). "Why on earth would you be interested in this?"

I searched for a diplomatic phrasing, then gave up; anything I said would be put through the grinder of linguistic differences regardless. "Please tell her," I said to Thu, "as politely as you can, that perhaps I may learn something that will help the Nying keep the mews at bay? Without suggesting that I think their own efforts have been deficient—after all, they've lived with the creatures for generations. But I *have* studied many kinds of dragons in other parts of the world, and it might be that the comparison will shed some useful light on the matter."

What Thu said to Shuwa, I have no idea. I only know that after a few minutes of back-and-forth she gave up on understanding his meaning, or my intentions, at all. Shaking her head, she merely said that if we wished to do something with the mews, it was our own lookout.

Tom and I began with their thieving behaviour, which did not require us to go any farther afield than a few houses in the village—though it did cost us some sleep. We sat up through the night on multiple occasions, observing how the mews raided storehouses, larders, and livestock pens. They proved to be cunning beasts, often sending one of their number ahead as a scout before descending to scavenge. Or perhaps that one might better be called a canary: if the advance mew is captured by a trap, it squawks a warning, and the others flee. "It might be more effective if the trap could be sprung upon them en masse," I said to Tom.

*A Mrtyahaiman mew*

"Yes, but how? It would require someone to sit up at night, in every place the mews might scavenge, and spring the trap by hand."

Given the number of possible locations, such a requirement was utterly impractical. But under the current approach, I suspected that each incident only taught the mews how better to avoid traps in the future. One of the spinsters we talked to, an old woman named Kyewa, agreed with this theory. A congenital deformity that twisted her legs from birth had ended her marriage prospects before they began, but she made very fine traps, and was careful to use different kinds in a rotating sequence. According to Thu, she did this so the mews might have time to forget past traps and become vulnerable to them again.

"Now that would be a fascinating thing to test," I murmured, as much to myself as to Tom. "Perhaps we could try laying out only two different kinds of trap in alternating sequence, then three, then four, to establish whether mews truly do learn from their errors, and if so, how long it takes them to forget those lessons."

Alas for my curiosity, the Nying would not hear of any experimentation that might cause them to lose more of their stores to the little dragons. I understood their reluctance, for they often walked too close to the edge of starvation to gamble with their future in such fashion; and we certainly could not squander any of our own food, for we were saving as much of that as possible for our autumnal expedition. In the meanwhile, Chendley, Suhail, and Thu (when we could spare him) lent their aid to the herdsmen, and hunted as much as they could. Our continued residence in Hlamtse Rong depended heavily on our not becoming a burden to them.

Tom and I spent some time with the herdsmen as well,

watching the diving behaviour of the mews. Suhail had devoted long hours to improving his own command of Tser-zhag, and put his growing skill to use in questioning the men about the little dragons. He said, "They all agree that mews eat the fat out of the yaks' humps, but I've taken a look at the beasts, and I haven't found a single one with scars or any other sign of chewing."

"It might be an old wives' tale," Tom said. "On Niddey, the grannies all agree that cats have to be kept away from infants, because they'll suck their breath away. I've seen a cat sniff a baby's face, but no more—and certainly we've seen mews dive at yaks, which could be exaggerated in the same way."

"But why on earth do they do that in the first place?" I tapped my fingers against my elbows, musing. The day was a bright one, and the alpine meadow around me dotted with flowers; at moments like this, it was hard to believe that bad weather was keeping us from our goal. The typical Anthiopean concept of the monsoon is a period in which it rains twenty-four hours a day, but even in the wettest regions, this is not the case. We had sunshine on an intermittent basis—along with enough rain to transform the hard-packed trail through the center of the village into a river of mud. I had only to look up at the wall of the high peaks, though, to be reminded of why we were passing the time with mews.

Tom was still pondering my question, rather than the weather. "Scavenging?" he said doubtfully. "Do they ever drive yaks into stampeding over a cliff edge? They might be hoping to feast on carrion."

Suhail asked on our behalf, but turned up no reports of such a thing. "Which could be due to the vigilance of the herdsmen," he said. "They do seem to be concerned that the mews will frighten a beast into injuring itself, if not falling to its death."

After another week spent in observations, we had no better answers. "Perhaps it is a kind of play behaviour," I said. "Like a cat toying with a mouse. The mews may simply find it entertaining to make a yak run."

We had greater luck in our other endeavour, which was the trapping of a mew—not to kill it, as the locals do, but for study. Even this was not so easily done; as I have said, mews are quite clever about learning to avoid traps. We caught one the second night we tried, but made the error of going to sleep rather than sitting up in watch, fearing that our presence might frighten the mews away. We realized our mistake when we awoke the next morning to find the thin wooden bars of the cage chewed clean through. Tom swore colourfully in the several languages we had acquired in our journeys and built a new cage. With the mews forewarned, it took us several more nights before we met with success again, but at last we had a mew—and, having seen the fate of the first cage, we made certain to incarcerate our new captive in a much sturdier prison.

Honeyseekers and desert drakes were the only dragons I had kept in captivity before then. In size the mew more closely resembled the former breed, but whereas a honeyseeker is relatively mild unless provoked (whereupon it will spit toxic saliva at the source of its annoyance), a mew is much less cooperative. Watching it pace the boundaries of its new cage, gnawing speculatively at the joins, I said to Tom, "It does remind me just a little of a cat, beyond the coincidence of its call. Andrew once caged a stray he found in the village, and it behaved much the same way."

"It's a pity the Nying can't set them after rats and shrews. It would do wonders for the grain situation here."

Much to the bemusement of not only the Nying but also our companions, Tom and I did make some efforts to see whether the mew could be trained. Suhail was a great deal of help in this, although he found the entire enterprise hilarious. During his fosterage among the Aritat nomads, his "desert father" Abu Azali had taught him the noble art of falconry, which Suhail had continued to practice after we purchased the estate of Casselthwaite in Linshire. He was able to show us how to fashion jesses and a hood, and then teach our captive mew to fly to a glove. He did this by placing tidbits of food on the glove and whistling in a particular manner, so that the dragon would come to associate him, the glove, and the sound with reward. This stage of the process went well enough, but Suhail was less than convinced. Watching the mew, he said, "I think it's cleverer than most falcons—too clever, even. You can almost certainly teach it to fly to a lure . . . but the first time you set it loose in the open air, it will be gone." He pondered for a time, then said, "I wonder if they would imprint, as an eyass does. Raising a bird from the shell requires a great deal of effort, and I cannot imagine that a mew would be any easier; but it does offer the best results."

We did not want to risk losing our mew by setting it after a lure, as capturing a replacement would be more trouble than it was worth. It therefore reigned alone in the shed we built for it— "the mews," as Suhail insisted on calling the structure, grinning every time he did so. (This is of course the proper name for the place where trained falcons are kept . . . but the pun entertained him far too much.)

Tom did contemplate a second capture, though not for the purpose of training. "It would be interesting to see if they exhibit developmental lability, too. We've got evidence of that in a few breeds now, but we'll need more before we can say for certain that it's a broad characteristic."

His phrasing was conservative. In truth, he and I had begun to formulate a theory which did away with the six criteria Sir Richard Edgeworth had used to distinguish "true dragons" from mere "draconic cousins," and put in their place only one: developmental lability. We did not yet have a good understanding of how the different breeds related to one another—indeed, this is a question that continues to vex dragon naturalists to this day—but we had long since begun to suspect that whatever the anwer was, lability played a large role in the diversity we see today. As it is not a characteristic anyone has documented outside the draconic family, it might serve as an admirably simple means of differentiating that family from unrelated creatures.

I would dearly have liked to try breeding mews, or at least conduct experiments with their eggs. After my conversation with Suhail in Falchester, a part of my mind was constantly examining my research, asking at every turn, *And what else?* It was a peculiar feeling. On the one hand, I lamented the loss of my girlish glee, the sense that it was enough simply to see a new thing and record it for other people to learn. On the other hand, it was also exhilarating, for I was challenging myself to look further, to think harder, to fit what I saw into a larger picture and then tease out its implications.

Unfortunately for our mew-related aspirations, we were again there in the wrong season. Unlike honeyseekers, who will mate at any time of year, mews did so only toward the tail end of winter, with their eggs hatching in mid-spring—"And if we are still here then, something will have gone *terribly* wrong," Tom said.

"Can't you trap a pair and try to carry them out?" Chendley said, when he heard this.

It was a mark of how restless our lieutenant had become that he showed any enthusiasm for the prospect. Even granting that we would carry a smaller quantity of supplies out of the mountains than we had carried in, adding a pair of caged mews to the pile would not make things any easier. But it was a moot point regardless. "If they're anything like yaks," Tom said with a wry grin, "they'll go toes-up from heat exhaustion at the searing temperature of fifteen degrees. But who knows. If all else fails, I'll have a shot at it."

One thing Tom and I did not attempt: bone preservation. We had not brought any of the necessary chemicals with us, as Thu's report had made it clear that we should not expect any bones to survive in one of his mystery specimens. Besides, the process had gone from a matter of great industrial import to a minor curiosity, of interest as a footnote in the history of dragonbone synthesis, but otherwise of use only to individuals like ourselves, who wished to study the skeletons of dragons at leisure. We did dissect several mews, working from carcasses provided by the spinsters who hunted them, and confirmed that their bones disintegrated according to the common habit of their kind; but for records we were dependent upon my drawings.

One other activity kept us occupied during the monsoon, and that was mountain climbing. Once Suhail had enough fluency in Tser-zhag to handle minor daily matters, Chendley went out on a regular basis with either him or Thu to hone their skills on the nearby ridges and peaks. Tom and I went less frequently, but the weeks we spent with the herdsmen involved a great deal of clambering around by routes that made the Nying laugh at us. It was preparation for what was to come: the snows would have made our route much more treacherous, and the five of us could not afford the suspicion and lack of coordination that had weakened us on the journey to Hlamtse Rong. By the time the monsoon ended, we were in the best fighting trim of our lives, and ready—we thought—for anything.

# EIGHT

*Leaving Hlamtse Rong—Across the glacier—*
*Gyaptse and Cheja—Speculations—Clear weather—Climbing—*
*Buried in the snow*

Although the Nying had been willing to accept us as guests, the strain upon their resources meant they were pleased to see us go—though not in the direction we chose.

I mentioned before that the nearby peak, Gyaptse, is named for its supposedly cursed nature. There are meadows below it which might be profitable for the grazing of yaks, but the locals never used them; they were certain that anyone who went there would die. They held to this certainty even though, upon questioning, none of them could name a single person who had done so within living memory—for this is how folklore works.

What caused this belief? Elsewhere in the world (that is to say, in Vystrana and Keonga), it had been the presence of Draconean ruins which inspired such dread; but as I have mentioned, it was deeply unlikely that any such things should be at so high an elevation, and Thu had seen nothing of the kind during his own exploration there. No, the fear had a more fleshly source . . . or so I suspected.

Elsewhere in the Mrtyahaima, there are stories of monstrous snow-apes, variously called *yeti, mi-go,* and an assortment of other names. But in Tser-nga, the stories tell instead of ice demons. Could these, I wondered, be derived from the creature Thu had found?

We had seen no sign of any such creature during our time in Hlamtse Rong, despite locals who swore up and down that they had seen them with their own eyes. Again, this is customary with folklore; Scirling farmers will swear equally blind that they have seen giants and fairy hounds on the country roads at night. But this did not mean that, once upon a time, *something* had not existed and roamed the mountains. Even if they were all gone now, their memory might survive.

Thu and Suhail managed, through weeks of effort, to persuade three youths from the village to help ferry our supplies to a spot at the foot of Gyaptse's neighbour Cheja, which we could then use as a depot while we explored the area. In addition to this we had our two ponies—which was still not enough to carry everything, but one of the virtues of our long delay was that we had learned which items we could, upon reflection, do without. Eight humans and two equines sufficed to convey the remainder, though we could not have hoped to do so were the ponies and Nying youths a whit less sturdy and tireless.

In theory it should have taken us four or five days to reach the valley below the col, where Thu had found his specimen. But he had been travelling in the spring; now it was autumn, and the snow lay deep on the higher slopes over which we must toil.

And toil we did. In the first day we climbed at least five hundred meters, counting ourselves fortunate that our monsoon-imposed delay had put us into so fit a state. That night it snowed, for while the season arrives quite abruptly, it does not depart in the same fashion; and by then we were at a high enough elevation for precipitation to come in solid form. But the snow was not so bad as the wind. This howled about our tents and proved to us that we had not pitched one of them securely enough; I think the only thing that prevented it from blowing away was its burden. (We were sleeping four to a tent in structures designed to hold three, so that our porters would not be left exposed. I was glad my nose had become entirely stuffed up, as it protected me from the aroma of so many unwashed bodies in such proximity—my own not excluded.)

But all of that was nothing compared to the obstacle that lay ahead, which was the Cheja Glacier.

This is named for its associated peak, the lesser companion to the towering Gyaptse. It descends off Cheja in a long, curving arc that wraps around the southeastern side of its base like a tongue. Until I took that holiday in southern Bulskevo, my image of a glacier was of a towering block of ice, intensely blue in its center, bordering a frozen northern sea. But glaciers, of course, can form on inland mountains provided they are high enough, and they are *far* from the uniform mass I imagined. Glacier ice flows: more slowly than water, to be sure, but it moves all the same. Where it moves quickly enough, it forms an icefall—the solid-state equivalent of a waterfall. Such areas are shattered with crevasses (into which one may fall) and seracs (tall pillars of ice that may collapse without warning on the unwary traveller). Even a short traverse of a glacier is exhausting at best, injurious or fatal at worst.

Upon reaching its edge, we sent one porter back with the ponies, those being our parting gift to the people of Hlamtse Rong. It meant we would have to move our supplies in stages, but that was unavoidable: no pony, however surefooted, could hope to manage what lay ahead.

Crossing that glacier was not a very technical challenge, compared with some of what we did in the following days. For the most part it involved exceedingly careful walking, with Thu or Chendley in the lead testing the ground with their alpenstocks, those iron-tipped, pick-headed staves which have proven so useful to the serious mountaineer. Where a crevasse divided the ground we sometimes crossed via a snow bridge, if our leaders judged it stable enough, but more often went around—assuming we saw the crevasse at all, as many of them are covered with a layer of snow thick enough to conceal, but not to support human weight.

We did not see the one into which I fell.

I do not blame Chendley for missing it. I was the careless one; rather than following strictly in his foosteps as I should have, I strayed leftward in my course. I had just enough time to think that the snow beneath my foot had settled rather more than usual before it gave way entirely, plunging me into the hidden blue abyss.

My shriek echoed off the walls around me, then cut short as the rope tied about my waist did its job and stopped my fall. My alpenstock slipped from my hand and scouted the depths for me. I did not hear it strike bottom, though I must admit I was not exactly listening.

When I could draw breath, I caught the rope with one flailing hand, steadied myself, and looked upward. To my horror, I saw Chendley's legs dangling over the edge of the crevasse. The collapse of the hidden snow bridge had taken him completely by surprise, and my fall yanked him straight off his feet. He had attempted to arrest his slide as a mountaineer should, by digging his alpenstock into the snow, but this only found purchase when he was almost in the crevasse with me.

What saved us was the gift I mentioned before, from the mountaineers who had trained Tom, Suhail, and myself. Before we left Scirland, the inestimable Mrs. Winstow had given us a brilliant innovation of her own devising, which has since become so vital to those who climb on ice: a framework one straps to one's boot, whose downward-pointing teeth provide far superior purchase compared to hobnails, without transmitting as much chill to the foot. This is called a crampon, and the sets Mrs. Winstow had gifted to us were made of synthetic dragonbone.

Suhail was behind me on the rope. When I fell and Chendley made as if to follow me into the abyss, my husband would also have been pulled down were it not for his crampons. They gave him sufficient traction that he was able to keep his feet and slam the point of his alpenstock into the snow, further stabilizing him. Had Chendley gone over the edge, committing his weight to the rope along with my own, this might not have been enough; but Chendley caught himself at the last instant, and Suhail held.

I did not know any of this until after I was safely on the surface once more, of course. At the time I could only dangle, for no part of the crevasse wall was quite within my reach, and I dared not swing for the nearest. Soon Chendley was up, though, and Tom joined Suhail; he belayed Thu as our Yelangese companion approached the edge and lowered the ropes he and the porters then used to raise me up.

When I reached the top, I could not immediately speak. Suhail enveloped me in a fierce embrace. I returned this as best as I could, notwithstanding the painful bruising I had received about the middle. (I recall thinking, rather inanely, that I had come a long way since my first experiment with abseiling in Vystrana, but that I did not recall my ribs hurting quite so badly back then. At the time I chalked this up to the difference in my age, but later I realized I had likely cracked one of the aforementioned ribs. Which I ought to have mentioned to those around me . . . but it seems I have never quite outgrown my youthful stupidity.)

Suhail might not have released me had Chendley not called out, reminding us that he stood on the opposite side of the crevasse. I tugged my clothing straight, managed a smile for the others, and said, "While I was down there, I looked about for any other frozen dragon specimens. Alas, I did not see any."

Thu stared at me, clearly wondering if he had suffered a failure of translation. Tom swore, laughing as he did so. Chendley, shouting across the crevasse, demanded to know what we were going to do next.

Roped as we were, we could not conveniently go around the gap; and after that scare, none of us were quite willing to unrope. But fortunately the crevasse had a nearby bit where the walls sloped more agreeably inward, and we were able to improvise a crossing. Our supplies we later brought by a much safer route, around the end of the chasm.

Such were the incidents that delayed us. I will not recount them all; our report on the journey was published years ago in the circular of the Peak Club. Any mountaineering enthusiast interested in the details may look up that account and marvel at the primitive state of the sport in those days, and our sheer dumb luck in not getting ourselves killed. For me, the next point of relevance comes after we reached the far side of the glacier, dismissed our remaining porters, and entered the little valley where Thu had found his specimen.

I must take a moment to lay the scene, for not all of my readers are familiar with the topography of mountains in general (much less that particular location), and the specifics are vitally important to the progress of this tale.

Gyaptse is the highest peak in the wall that marks the western boundary of inhabited Tser-nga, and a more forbidding mountain one would be hard-pressed to find. There are taller—it does not even come close to claiming the title in that regard—but few with so unfriendly an aspect. Its southern facet, the one visible from our approach, falls in an array of nearly sheer faces, of so dark a stone as to appear almost black in anything other than direct sunlight. Snow and ice can only cling to scattered footholds, and I could not help but mentally arrange their harsh, slanting lines into a face, as if the mountain were frowning at me. The peak itself is peculiar in shape, almost like a tower; and a more unassailable tower I have never seen. In recent years three expeditions have tried to assail it: none have succeeded, and one perished almost to the last man.

Fortunately for us, we had no need to climb the peak. Our initial interest lay in a valley below, the cirque between two aretes or ridges descending off Cheja and Gyaptse. The latter, which is the route by which those later mountaineers have attempted the peak, has come to be known as the Dumond Ridge, after the leader of the first of those expeditions. The other I attempted to name Thu Ridge, in honour of our companion (without whom none of us would have been there); and it is called so in Yelangese. But in my homeland this attempt resoundingly failed, and mountaineers there speak of it as the Trent Ridge instead.

Thu and his compatriots had come here in search of a route through the mountains. Staring up at the col between the two peaks, I spoke to Thu. My breathlessness owed something to the altitude and exertion—but not all. "You thought *that* could be your path?"

The saddle where the slopes of Cheja and Gyaptse meet is far lower than either summit, but still towers over the valley below. Like the southern face of Gyaptse, the descent from the col to the valley floor is the next best thing to sheer: more cliff than slope. There was no direct route from where we stood to the top, and the Dumond Ridge does not connect to it; one would have to traverse the face of Gyaptse to reach it from that side. The reasonable approach—I am tempted to scar the adjective with quotation marks—is up Cheja's ridge, along the mountain's shoulder, and then up again to reach the col. It was feasible, I thought, for any moderately skilled mountaineer; but not for people in quantity.

"We did not think it for long," Thu said wryly. "But we were trying to find *some* kind of pass, and this is the most approachable one for two hundred kilometers in either direction—if you can believe it."

Unlike his previous expedition, we were not searching for a way across; our attention, at least to begin with, lay in the valley below. By a stroke of good luck, this was not as deeply blanketed in snow as we had feared. The arrangement of the surrounding terrain shelters it a little from the prevailing monsoon wind, while its southern exposure means it receives a great deal of sun. A brisk little stream of snowmelt poured down the lower slopes; we pitched our tents next to this, too exhausted to attempt any reconnaissance that day.

What we intended as a brief pause stretched two days longer than planned, on account of the winds. We were fortunately spared additional snowfall, which would have made our task even harder than it already was, but neither Chendley nor Thu would allow any of us to venture toward the head of the cirque. Though the winds were not bad where we camped, they would be much worse up at the col, and they feared the risk of avalanche. Such an event, Thu believed, had brought down the specimen he found, for the valley was far too low for flesh to be preserved year-round by the cold. Indeed, there were times there when even I felt quite warm—a very incongruous sensation, when one is at high elevation and surrounded by snow.

This delay did not prevent Suhail from surveying the area with an eye toward planning our search. He looked at the deeper snow piled where previous avalanches had landed and shook his head. "If there is anything under that, I don't know how we'll find it. With a settlement, you can make educated guesses about where to dig based on buildings, streets, and so forth. But here? You could be half a meter from what you're looking for, and never know. And digging it all out would take all year."

"While the mountain drops more on your head," Tom muttered.

But Thu hastened to reassure us. "It was not where the snow is so deep. More to the right, I would say—though it is difficult to be sure." He looked embarrassed.

"Quite some time has passed since you were last here," I said. "Anyone would have difficulty remembering."

In the area Thu had indicated, the snow was thin enough that Suhail thought we might be able to at least attempt an organized search. He prepared a series of thin cords, and when the wind dropped to a more reasonable level he ventured out and staked them down, delineating a grid of squares. "We'll take these one at a time," he said, "one person per square. The snow there is only about half a meter thick. Stop if you find anything out of the ordinary: bones, teeth, claws, flesh, whatever you may turn up. I'll come take a look at it."

It was arduous, back-breaking, hand-numbing work. However warm the air might be, we were still digging in snow, half a meter down to the thin grass which was all that would grow here. And we had to paw through what we removed, just to be certain there were no small remains that might herald the presence of something larger nearby.

We could not work for very long each day. The surrounding terrain cut off our light with shocking speed even when the sky was clear, and it was often quite grey. Clouds wreathed Gyaptse more days than not, sometimes descending low enough to bury the col itself. Only four of us dug at any one time; the fifth rested and watched Gyaptse, in case an avalanche should begin.

Chendley was the one who raised an objection, after careful study of the area. "I don't think that thing was brought down by an avalanche," he said.

We stopped and looked at him, most of us grinding our knuckles into our backs during this respite.

He gestured at where we searched. "Either you're searching in

*The col*

the wrong place, and really ought to be digging into these big piles—or that thing wasn't where most avalanches land. Oh, I won't rule out the chance that some avalanches fall differently. Maybe that slide was one of the exceptions. But the odds say, probably not."

"Then how did it get down here?" Tom asked.

"Could have been blown by the wind. Happened with a fellow on the Feillon—do you know that story? He died ten or fifteen years ago, trying to prove it could be climbed by a new route, and though people could see where his body was, nobody wanted to risk dying themselves just to retrieve it. But one day it vanished, and then a hiking party stumbled across it, some ladies out for an energetic stroll. People later worked out that it must have fallen in a gale."

I was obscurely pleased that Chendley told this story without a single apology to me for speaking of such grim matters in front of a lady. "Where would our specimen have begun, do you think, if it fell on account of wind?"

He might not apologize for indelicacy, but his manners stayed with him well enough that he did not roll his eyes at me. A gesture upward sufficed to remind me why the question was foolish. We could barely even make out the col today, so shrouded was it in fog.

But none of us had forgotten what Thu said about seeing what *might* have been another specimen up there. If we could work out the path the first one had taken . . . .

I knew the truth. Every last one of us was hoping for a break in the weather that might allow us to attempt a climb up there. We searched below less because we expected to find anything of use, and more because we could not yet risk ascending higher. I am not often a religious woman, but I prayed for clear skies and calm winds.

In the meanwhile, we turned up nothing more than a few scraps of badly decayed flesh which might not even have come from a dragon. The night our search ended, I sat up with Tom and Suhail around the fire, discussing the entire situation.

"I do not think there can ever have been dragons living at the elevation of the col," I said. I was sitting with my knees up in front of me, arms crossed over them. Even this close to the campfire, bundled in nearly every stitch I'd brought, I was cold. The day's warmth fled promptly with the day's light. "Developmental lability can achieve a great deal—but not, I think, a dragon that derives its sustenance entirely from rock and ice."

Tom nodded. "Humans and yaks can adapt to living at altitude, and dragons might take it further. Insulation against the cold, more efficient respiration, that kind of thing. But they still have to eat. And nothing grows that high." Even where we camped, the pickings were slim indeed.

"So what was a dragon doing there to begin with," Suhail said. His intonation did not make it a question; he was instead stating the problem.

"Migration," I said. "Wild yaks have been known to climb barren passes. A dragon could do it, too."

Tom leaned back on his elbows and tipped his head toward the sky, thinking it through. "Then we have a few possibilities. One is that Thu was mistaken; there was only the one preserved carcass, and whatever he thought he saw in the col was only a rock or a strange formation of ice. The second is that more than one dragon tried at various points to cross that pass, and died in the attempt."

"Humans have died in this region," I said. "Remember the

stories the Nying told. There is no reason the same could not have happened to animals."

"And the third possibility," Tom said, "is that the breed was social. Which would be quite unusual for a dragon of that size."

Unusual, but not unheard of. "They could have been like savannah snakes, with unattached males hunting in sibling groups." I paused, tapping my fingers against my elbows. It had become more of a habit lately, as I often kept my arms tight around my body to retain heat. "But migrating in such a group would be quite useless. Sibling males cannot breed."

Suhail's snort quickly tipped over into immoderate laughter. Tom sat up, and we both stared at my husband, who seemed to have lost his reason entirely. "My apologies," Suhail said, once he'd regained a modicum of composure. He wiped his eyes. "It is the exhaustion at work, I suspect. But you made me think of those frogs you mentioned once, the kind that change their sex when needed. And then I imagined frog-dragons hopping their way through the mountains." He illustrated with one hand, springing over imaginary peaks.

I giggled, but Tom looked thoughtful. "It isn't impossible. Not the hopping, of course, but the other part. We already know that swamp-wyrm eggs can develop into either sex. The ability to change in maturity would be quite valuable to dragons living in a place like this, where populations can be very isolated."

"We aren't likely to be able to tell that from a carcass," I said. "Assuming we can find one at all. But yes—it's an interesting thought." I wondered if mews were capable of such a change. If nesting in tamarisk leaves and incubating the eggs at high heat could produce an orange honeyseeker with salty saliva, who knew what kinds of variation could occur in the wild?

None of that was the kind of question I could answer while camped in the shadow of Gyaptse. But until the weather cleared, speculation was all I had.

And then some benevolent deity smiled upon us, for the next morning we woke to find the skies a brilliant, frozen blue.

The only cloud to be seen was a wisp trailing off the peak of Gyaptse, which is a frequent phenomenon at that altitude. No sooner did we discover our good fortune than we scrambled to bring out the field glasses and examine the col above.

Looking at it directly was painful; we could only do so for brief periods of time. The same clear weather that blessed us with a view also reflected off the snow with blinding radiance—quite literally blinding, if we did not take care. We had goggles with darkened lenses, but these could not be combined with the field glasses without losing so much clarity as to make the whole exercise pointless. So we looked with unprotected eyes, and took it in turns to risk the light.

"If you see that horizontal band of bare stone," Thu said, "it was below that somewhere—I think." He did not sound as certain as a man who hauled us halfway around the world should have been.

We searched. After a time, we realized that the band of stone Tom, Suhail, and I had been looking at was not the one Thu meant. We found a dozen suspicious-looking lumps, spent far too much time trying to direct the eyes of others to those lumps, and then realized they were only stones or piles of snow. Or were they? We scrutinized them, arguing size, shape, piling speculation atop guesswork, optimism conquering pessimism and then being conquered in turn.

It was Tom who finally put his field glasses down and said, "We can't tell from here. Whatever you saw, Thu ... if it's still there, it's been too deeply buried by the snow for us to have any hope of finding it again. Not at this distance."

My shoulders sagged in disappointment. All this effort, and we had nothing. In the ordinary way of things my work with the mews should have pleased me—but not when I had hoped for so much more.

Then I realized what Tom meant.

I looked up to find him gazing steadily at me. I, in turn, sought my husband's eyes. Suhail's frustrated expression faded to quiet stillness; then a silent laugh shook his shoulders. I did not even have to explain. "God willing," he said with a half smile.

Chendley was staring at the three of us. He tumbled to it an instant later, for he had been in our company long enough to understand our habits. "You can't be serious. You don't even know that there's anything up there to find!"

"The only way to find out," I said, "is to go up there and look."

It was madness, of course. The decision to leave Scirland at all had been a gamble; this was a much larger one. The weather was clear now, but how long would that hold? "When we were here before," Thu said, with the cautious air of a man offering up a slender thread of hope, "we planned out what I think is a route to the col. We did not attempt it because there was no point—it had no military use—but I believe our group could manage it."

Assuming our skills were adequate to the task. Assuming the

weather did not take a turn for the worse. Assuming that Gyaptse did not live down to its reputation, and crush this group of foolhardy humans who thumbed their noses at its power.

I had not travelled halfway around the world only to give up at the end.

Tom shook his head, not in disagreement, but in a gesture so familiar to me from years of partnership: disbelief at what he was about to say. "Well. If we're going to get ourselves killed, we might as well get started."

By the standards of modern mountaineering, Thu's route up to the col is accounted a moderate challenge, but not a tremendous one. It is more than enough to deter the casual passerby, but within the reach of those equipped with ropes, alpenstocks, crampons, and the techniques of belaying. For this I am eternally grateful, because were it any more difficult, we should not have made it at all—and then not only my life but the field of dragon naturalism and, indeed, the world as a whole would have been quite different.

The first part was simply hiking, out of the valley and toward the ramparts of the neighbouring peak of Cheja. There we climbed the ridge I mentioned before and traversed the mountain's lower slopes, heading for the dark tower of Gyaptse once more. But two technical hurdles stood in our path, and these tested my own meager climbing abilities to the utmost.

To attain the higher elevation of that traverse, the shoulder which would permit us to approach the col, we had to ascend a narrow chimney: a gap in the rocks where one climbs not by clinging to the outside of the stones, but by bracing against their inward faces and using this pressure for support. This is most difficult, and most hazardous, for the one who goes first, as that individual climbs without the safety of a rope from above. If he falls, there is nothing to catch him. This chimney was only about four or five meters high, so our leader might hope to escape serious injury at the first impact—but the terrain at the bottom was such that he stood a great risk of tumbling out and over the nearest edge, whereupon those behind him would have to arrest his fall. And our own footing there was none too secure, as by then the friendly ridge which had borne us to that point was deteriorating into crumbling, rotten rock.

Thu insisted on leading the way up the chimney. Chendley granted this only when we pointed out that Thu was smaller than anyone save myself, and thus we had the best chance of holding on if the worst should happen. Our Yelangese friend made short work of the chimney, but I do not think I took a single breath until he was safely at the top. And then I had to hold it again while Thu belayed Tom up. This done, Tom edged past him to a better spot, anchoring both Thu and himself while I made the climb.

In the mountains of Anthiope, in those places where the climbs are considered suitable for the frailty of ladies, it is not uncommon to see women in skirts being hauled up such obstacles by the main force of the men above them. Indeed, experienced women mountaineers such as Miss Collier and Mrs. Winstow have often had to argue strenuously to prevent themselves from being subjected to the same assistance. Had I been in need of that kind of aid, I would have found myself in dire straits that day: the footing above was no better than at the bottom, and while Tom could loop the rope around a nearby stone for support, he and Thu could not have lifted me without endangering themselves. Although I had their belay for safety, I had no option but to do the work of climbing on my own. My shoulders and knees ached by the time I reached the top, and I did suffer a stabbing pain or three from my cracked rib . . . but I must confess I felt pride in the achievement, and grinned broadly at both men while I took my place in the line.

The second obstacle was the location we dubbed, by universal agreement, the Cursed Crack. This is without a doubt the most absurd bit of terrain I have ever set myself against, and I hope never to see a worse. This too is a chimney, but one far too narrow for a climber to fit inside. The only way to ascend it is to wedge one hand and foot into the crack, and with the other pair to grip whatever discolorations in the stone might pass for holds. One's instinct is to huddle as close to the crack as possible, but this will not do: safety lies in spreading oneself broadly, as if hugging the mountain. This is far from a reassuring position to be in, and Suhail exercised his creativity on the way up, formulating oaths in an astonishing medley of languages.

I felt no pride when I finally reached the top of the crack, for I was too exhausted. We had ascended at least a thousand meters since leaving Hlamtse Rong, likely more, and the change was palpable. The smallest exertion had me gasping for breath, much to the detriment of my ribs, and my heart never ceased its frantic pounding. Even the knowledge that our only remaining obstacle was a relatively easy trek across the icy expanse of the col to the area of our search could not put much life into my limbs, for each of them felt as if it weighed at least three times as much as usual.

No force in the world could have turned me back, though. It was difficult enough to accept that we must pitch our tents at the top of the crack, as the day was much too far gone for us to reach any other shelter before night fell, and the winds through the center of the col were vicious. (A fact for which we must be grateful: were it not for those winds, the snow there would have buried any specimens much too deep to ever be recovered.) But I do not think I slept more than two winks that night.

Dawn comes early in such a place: at that high an elevation, there are few peaks to block the sun. I was awake even before then, and although the air was most bitterly cold, I must confess that dawn ranks among the most glorious of my life. The light came first to the peaks of Cheja and Gyaptse, igniting them with brilliant fire, while below the shadowed slopes remained grim and dark. There is no contrast more stark in all the world, not even in the deserts of Akhia. It felt as if the descending line of the dawn was bringing life toward me one meter at a time, and when it arrived, the world transformed. Gut-curdling doubts about my decision to come to Tser-nga gave way to a bone-deep certainty that our quest would be successful. I had no scientific basis for this change of heart; but I was sure.

I was glad of that surety when we ventured out into the exposed space of the col. No sooner did we leave the shelter of Cheja's flank than the winds struck us with titanic force, carrying razor crystals of ice. We staggered one careful step at a time, mindful of the risk that a fall could be the trigger that began an avalanche. But the true risk lay above us, where the steep upper slopes of Gyaptse held a heavy load of snow, which might come loose at any moment.

My attention should have been on that, and on the ground

ahead. But although we had conquered no mighty peak, we shared with such pioneers a rare and precious experience: the knowledge that we were quite possibly the first human beings to stand upon that ground. And depending on the success of the caeligers, we might even be the first to look past the col into the uninhabited terrain beyond.

The ground on the western side sloped away in a much gentler fashion. To my right and to my left, the mountains circled in a formidable wall, as if to guard the peak in the center: a beautifully formed pyramid I thought taller than Gyaptse, reigning like a queen amid her subjects. It glowed like a diamond torch in the early light. In the shadows below lay deep valleys, low enough to support trees and meadows, some of them yet free of snow. Altogether, it had the appearance of an alpine paradise.

I came to realize Tom was standing at my right shoulder. We could not converse in low tones, for the wind flung our voices away; he had to shout as he said, "We can't do it, Isabella."

"I know we can't," I shouted back. In order to make this ascent, we had left a substantial portion of our gear at the base of Cheja; we carried only enough food for a few days, and no guns for hunting. Descending into those valleys would be suicide by starvation.

But Tom and I were of one mind. Looking down into that region, we both thought: *Perhaps they are not extinct. Perhaps that unknown breed lives in this place, isolated from all human observation, and if we go there we will see them alive.*

The season was too far gone; we could not plan any expedition there until next year at the earliest, and probably much later than that. And it would be exceedingly difficult to bring enough men and materiel up to this col, however much easier the descent might be on the other side. But with that possibility before my eyes, I would not be deterred: whatever it took, however much money I had to pour into the task and political maneuvering I had to engage in, I *would* come back and explore that lost world.

The cosmos has a fine sense of humour.


The col is not a perfect ridge; at its crest it flattens out, and even dips down slightly to create a shallow bowl. In the month of Seminis in the southern hemisphere, at six thousand meters of elevation, you would not think it is possible for one such as I to become overheated, but I did; the deep snow of this bowl reflected the sun like a mirror, and the slight shelter it provided gave enough respite from the wind that I found myself sweating heavily in my layers of wool and silk and fur. But I did not want to stop long enough to remove my pack and shed layers; and so I slogged onward, through the deep, wet snow.

Even with our goggles on, the light was blinding, and we could not effectively search while floundering through the snow. At regular intervals one member of the party or another stopped to catch their breath and look around, scanning for any hint of something other than snow, rock, and ourselves, praying all the while that we had not climbed up here for naught. However glorious the view, however tempting the vista beyond, we had come here with a specific purpose in mind. And it was Tom, the most eagle-eyed among us, who spotted it at last.

"There!"

It was a tiny thing, an aberration in the smooth expanse of snow. Near to a small shoulder of Gyaptse on the north end of the col, it protruded only about fifteen or twenty centimeters; had the snow been any deeper or the winds here less fierce, we would have missed it entirely, for the monsoon had gone a long way toward burying it. But that tiny thing was enough, and we set off for it with new life in our limbs.

Suhail dragged us to a halt a few meters away, quite literally grabbing our sleeves to stop us. "Wait. Wait!"

There was nothing in the world I wanted less to do. Sun-dazzled though my eyes were, I could see enough to make my breath race even more than it already did. A pale, pebbled surface very similar to the scales Thu had shown us. A flattened lump I thought might have been a brow ridge, before the bone beneath gave way and collapsed the flesh. We had at least part of a specimen, and the rest . . . the rest might lie just a little distance under the snow.

But if Tom and I were here for our expertise with dragons, and Thu and Chendley for their expertise with mountains, Suhail was here as our archaeologist, to make certain we did not damage what we had come so far to find.

As he had done when we discovered the Watchers' Heart, he made us proceed with care. While we hovered and twitched, he circled the visible remains at a safe distance, considering their disposition. Finally he said, "If the rest of the body is still attached, it most likely lies here." One hand indicated an area of snow. "But without the skeleton, we can't really be sure. It might have twisted in any direction."

The only way to know for sure was to dig.

We began at the head—or rather I should say Suhail began, for he did not want more than a single person's weight atop the snow there, in case it crushed something delicate. He brushed away the looser snow with his gloved fingers, exposing enough to reveal that we were indeed looking at the flattened head of some draconic creature. Then, with careful taps of a small pick, he began to chip away the older encrustation.

While he did this, the rest of us brushed the ground in a circle around the head, scooping away the snow. Ordinarily I would have stood back and drawn the scene, but not on this occasion, for two reasons: first, that my heavily gloved hand could not wield a pencil with any accuracy, and second, that I could not have stood back for any sum of money. I took the southern quadrant, where Suhail thought the rest of the carcass was most likely to lie; Thu was to my left and Tom to my right.

I did not have to dig far at all before it began. "I found something!" I exclaimed. Only a sharp order from Suhail kept Tom and Thu from hovering over me. But they turned their efforts toward mine, and we went on digging.

One centimeter at a time, it emerged. At Suhail's end, the collapsed head; at mine, a misshapen lump it took me a long time to be certain was a foot. Rather than chipping too far downward, I went horizontally, following the line of the leg. Hindleg, or fore? I kept changing my mind; we had not uncovered enough to be certain. Fore, I thought, based on the distance from the head, and the relative sizes—but then I reached something that did not look like a shoulder. And Tom, lying full-length to distribute his weight and digging between myself and Suhail, stopped without warning.

"Isabella," he said. "Look."

In science it is often possible to examine the bark so closely, one forgets the subject at hand is a tree, much less that it exists as part of a forest. I sat up, my back aching, and I looked.

At Suhail's knees, the head. At mine, the leg, twisted and flat, leading to a structure that was not a shoulder. And where Tom dug, another limb—smaller than the one I had uncovered, equally twisted and flat, but leading to a structure that most definitely *was* a shoulder.

From foot to head, the entire thing was not more than two and a half meters. And it was bipedal.

We stared at it in frozen silence, while the wind howled around us. Imagine it alive, with a skeleton inside; imagine it standing, with one foot outstretched and the shoulders thrown back proud. We had seen that image a thousand times, in statues, carved into walls.

It was a Draconean god.

# NINE

*A race against time—Gyaptse's wrath—Out of my grave*

What does one do, when one finds a mythical creature buried in the snow of the Mrtyahaima?

One keeps digging, of course.

We could not spare the time to discuss its implications. We were too exhausted, and there was no good place to set our tents on the Gyaptse side of the col; if we were to return to our previous campsite, we could not stay where we were for long. But all of us shared the fear that if we left the specimen where it was, exposed by our efforts, it would be destroyed or lost to the valley below, as the previous one had been. We must free it from the ice now, and carry it with us. That this would likely damage it, we must accept as preferable to the alternatives.

Further excavation only confirmed that we were not hallucinating on account of altitude. The carcass was that of a bipedal, dragon-headed creature, with a head large in proportion to its body, as a human's is. The first wing we uncovered was too poorly preserved for us to make any judgments; could it bear the body's weight? How would a creature such as this fly, when it was built to walk upright? With the muscles so withered by cold and desiccation, we could only guess at its living mass, its sex, whether it was a juvenile or an adult.

It was a race against time. We had barely set our hands to the task once more when Chendley, keeping a worried eye on the sky, said, "The weather's changing."

In the Mrtyahaima, storms can blow in with shocking speed and very little warning. I soon took off my darkened goggles, for the sunlight had vanished behind a fresh layer of clouds. The wind picked up as we located the second wing, renewing the stinging onslaught of ice. And, worst of all, more snow began to fall.

I cursed steadily under my breath as I worked. It was too unfair—finding something so astonishing, only to have the sky itself turn against us. This was no mere fouling of the weather, but a genuine storm, and every minute we stayed there endangered us further. One entire side of the carcass was still buried in ice when Suhail left off and hauled me to my feet. "No!" I shouted, struggling against him. "We can't leave it—we can't go back—no one will believe us if we don't have proof!" My scientific reputation was not powerful enough to support such a claim. They would think I was clawing for more attention, making up stories to inflate my notoriety. No one would believe that we had found a dragon-headed biped, not unless we could silence the doubters with a carcass.

But Tom was at my other side, helping Suhail drag me away. I knew they were right; I knew staying there would be suicide. And yet I fought them, even as we stumbled back across the col toward safety.

Then Gyaptse itself turned against me. "*Avalanche!*" Chendley bellowed, and the thunder began.

* * *

Had we still been roped together, as we had been during the climb, all five of us would have died. The rope itself would have broken our bones, yanked us this way and that, dragged us down into the torrent when we needed to swim for the surface.

Surviving an avalanche is a good deal like swimming—in violent, solid water. The snow overtook us before we got very far at all, but in the interim, we all charged to our right, desperate to get away from the cliff that dropped into the valley where Thu found the first carcass. If we went over that edge, we were dead. I ran with Suhail's hand gripped in my own, both of us stumbling in the deep snow and alternately helping one another to our feet—and then the hammer of God struck us from behind.

Suhail was ripped from me in an instant. I lost sight of him, of Tom, of my entire party, and could spare no attention for anything other than trying to survive. The racing snow bore me along at terrifying speed. I floundered at what I hoped was an angle, trying to escape its current and keep myself near the surface. But which way was which? I had lost all track; I was only flailing, desperate, certain I would be buried and never found again.

Then my leg struck something, and pain flared white-hot at the impact. My fingers hit a solid surface, but it was gone before I could grab it. On and on I slid, so disoriented I wanted to retch, and then, at last, it stopped.


I woke buried in snow.

By purest chance, I had come to a halt with my hand in front of my face. Because of this, when I began to flail in panic, I did the most useful thing I could have done, under the circumstances: I compressed the snow, creating a pocket in front of my face.

I could not have been unconscious for long at all, or I would have suffocated. And although I did not realize it until later, I could not have been buried very deeply, or the snow would have been too firmly packed for me to create that pocket. Spittle trailed down my face; it ran sideways across my cheek, and I retained sufficient presence of mind to realize that the surface must lie in the other direction.

Clawing my way free of the snow felt like climbing out of my own grave—as it could easily have been. I was less than half a meter deep, I think, but even that weight was exceedingly difficult to move. Only the sheer animal panic of being trapped gave me the strength to drag myself out.

The wind was still howling, the snow still falling. I lurched upright and nearly bit through my tongue when I put weight on my left leg; the only reason it held was because I was too cold to feel the pain clearly. But I was alive, and that was more than I might have had.

Where were the others?

For once it was not a stubborn refusal to contemplate the worst that kept me from thinking about how they might be dead. I was concussed; I was hypothermic; I was not thinking at all clearly, though I had the delusion that I was entirely rational. Since I was not dead, I must not have gone over the eastern edge of the col; since I had not gone over the edge, I must have been swept down the western slope, which was the direction I had been trying to go to escape the avalanche. Therefore—by the logic of my addled

*The frozen Draconean*

brain—I must go uphill to find the others.

I set off, staggering in the snow.

The pain faded from my leg as I went. I was no longer shivering. I went on, up a small slope and down the other side; I stumbled onward, looking for the correct slope. The ground went down and down and down, not obliging me. I lost my footing and slid a good distance, and when I rose I didn't know which way I was facing. The sky was much too dim for me to see anything clearly. I saw a spark of light ahead; that must be them. But then it went away, and I lurched in a circle, trying to find it again. This dizzied me, and I collapsed once more into the snow, which felt almost warm.

Just as my thoughts were fading, I saw them coming, and giggled in relief. I was all right. Suhail had found me. He and Tom and Jacob lifted me up and carried me to safety.

# PART THREE

*In which the memoirist*
*passes a most unusual season*

# TEN

*Fever dreams—My saviours—Theory as distraction—*
*The beneficial effects of gloating—Many observations—*
*Experiments in language—Names*

I was delirious for a long time after that, wracked with fever and the aftermath of what I later realized was a concussion.

I dreamt again and again of the avalanche, the rushing snow sweeping me away with titanic force, only this time it carried me over the eastern edge of the col. Sometimes I fell to my death, and sometimes I flew away on dragon wings.

I dug out the desiccated, boneless flesh of the Draconean god, and it woke up and spoke to me in a language I could not understand.

I was at home in Scirland, lecturing on what I had seen—but no one would believe me, even though my audience was made up of dragon-headed figures.

I was buried again, suffocating, certain I was about to die, even though the snow pressing me down was so warm and soft.

The whole time, I kept calling for those dearest to me . . . but they did not come.

\* \* \*

Then one day I woke with something like a clear head.

I was not in camp. Whether I was in Shuwa's house or someone else's, I could not tell: my only illumination was one small yak-butter lamp, and someone had hung curtains of thick wool all around me, which had the odd effect of making me feel as if I were in the tent of an Akhian nomad. I lay on a heavy fleece, with another one over me. Smiling weakly, I recognized this as the "snow" that had buried me during my illness.

Was I well enough to cast it off? I lifted it experimentally, and was not surprised to find myself no longer in my mountaineering clothes. I wore only a shift, the sort of thing that can easily be removed when caring for a sick individual. This was not quite warm enough for the air, but I was determined to stand and reassert myself as a living person, rather than the near-corpse I must have resembled since my rescue.

My left leg ached when I put weight on it. Searching with my fingers along my calf, I found a tender spot, and surmised that I had fractured my fibula during the avalanche. No doubt I had done this very little good in my stumbling through the snow; but if my illness had one benefit, it was that I had given the bone some time to heal. Nonetheless, I made sure to bear the greater part of my weight on my right leg when I stood. The floor beneath me was not composed of the wooden panels I expected, but quilted hessian, stuffed with something small and hard.

Once I was sure of my balance, I parted the curtains and stepped out into colder air. Only a single step: after that, it was not the temperature that made me freeze.

Three figures stared at me from the other side of a fire. Not Suhail. Not Tom. Not Thu or Lieutenant Chendley, nor any of the Nying.

Three *dragon-headed figures.*

I clutched at the curtain for balance. It tore free from its moorings and we went to the ground together, the curtain and I. One of the figures stood, and I wanted to blame all of this on continued fever and delirium, but I knew better. I was awake, and alert, and the living cousin of the creature I had dug out of the snow was coming toward me with its claws outstretched.

I did not react with wonder, nor delight, nor scientific curiosity. Quite frankly, I shrieked. And then I tried to scrabble away like an upside-down crab—but the heavy curtain tangled me and my injured leg failed me, so I did not get very far.

The creature coming toward me went instantly still. On the other side of the fire, one of them jerked upright and popped its ruff as wide as it would go. The other lunged to the side of the second and clamped one clawed hand around its muzzle.

Body language varies from place to place around the world, and a good deal more between species. These draconic figures did not behave quite like humans, nor quite like dragons, but owed a bit to both. The expansion of the ruff was either hostility or a fear response, making the creature appear larger and more intimidating. These thoughts stabilized me, breaking me out of my own fear response . . . though the fear itself did not entirely dissipate.

I tried to behave like a rational being, rather than a bundle of instincts held together by a very tenuous thread. It was more easily intended than done, however, as was putting together a coherent sentence. I licked my lips, drew in a deep breath, and managed the following triumph of eloquence: "Where am I?"

As soon as the words were out of my mouth, I knew they were futile. Sure enough, the creatures looked at one another with no sign of comprehension. Of course: why should they understand Scirling? Though my command of Tser-zhag was very nearly nonexistent, I could manage that simple of a question; but it elicited no better response. Perhaps they could not speak at all?

A foolish thought. The creature that had approached drew breath and spoke, but I did not understand a word it said.

Fear threatened to choke me again. For all the strange and dangerous situations I have been in before, none came close to this. All of my previous captors had been human, and with most of them I had shared at least a modicum of language. Here I had nothing. I knew I must be in the mountain basin that lay beyond Gyaptse and Cheja; my speculation on the col, that the species might not be extinct after all, was proved correct. But that meant I was cut off from human habitation. I could not even ask whether the others were here, Chendley and Thu and Tom and, most of all, Suhail.

I tried regardless. Even though I knew they could not understand me, I asked; when my question got no response, I clung to names alone, repeating them in a louder and louder voice as if volume alone would accomplish what words could not. On the far side of the fire, the creature spread its ruff again, and the one at its side cast a glance toward—

A door.

I could not bolt for it, not with my legs so tremulous and one yet weak from the fracture. Still, I did my best, which was a rapid and unsteady hobble. I did not get more than three paces before the creature that had approached me interposed itself, half spreading its wings to block the way.

My voice shook nearly as badly as my legs, but I made it as

strong as I could. "I have to look for the others. I do not *care* that you cannot understand me, I *must*—"

Before I could work myself up to a proper shout, the creature in front of me reached up and held its own muzzle shut, just as one of its compatriots had done to the ruff-spreading one. It is a thing I have seen people do to dogs who bark too much, and I realized it must be the equivalent of holding a finger to one's lips. The creature was trying to hush me.

I almost screamed. Not out of fear, but out of defiance: if they wished me to be quiet, then perhaps the best thing I could do was to be as loud as possible. I had been a prisoner before, and had not liked it on any occasion.

But these creatures had taken care of me. I was not hungry, nor stained with my own filth; more to the point, I was *alive*. Whoever had rescued me from the snow, it had apparently not been my companions. Was it these three? Or others like them? Either way, it did not matter. They had looked out for my well-being, likely at a great deal of inconvenience to themselves. I owed my life to three winged, dragon-headed creatures out of Draconean myth.

No—not myth. I stared up at the tall figure in front of me, standing with its feet apart and its wings slightly spread, in a pose I had seen so many times before. The epiphany came upon me like a lightning strike, so astonishing it momentarily drove all fear and despair from my mind. All those statues and reliefs and painted murals, showing humanoid figures with wings and dragon heads, with humans making offerings to them . . . we had assumed those figures were gods. And perhaps, indeed, ancient humans had worshipped them as such.

But they were not gods.

They were, quite simply, the Draconeans.

That ancient civilization had not been a human edifice. It was the creation of beings like the one in front of me, who ruled over their human subjects until their downfall. The evidence had been before us for thousands of years ... but when the Draconeans were overthrown, their existence faded into legend, easily disbelieved without the proof of it in front of us.

The one that had approached me gestured toward my bed, with words I still could not understand. It did not seem hostile. Numbly obedient, I limped back to my rest. Two of them worked together to hang again the curtain I had torn down, closing me into my little shelter, shutting away the sight of their hybrid, impossible bodies.

I lay under the yak fleece and shivered, but not from cold. The truth had crept into my mind while I was occupied with other things, but now, alone in my nest, I could avoid it no longer.

I was alone. Though the avalanche remained a terrifying maelstrom in my recollection, it was not so chaotic as to erase one simple fact: I had been torn away from my companions, from my husband. I went one way and they went another, and then in my disorientation I compounded that separation by staggering west. They were on the other side of the mountains, or—

Though I tried to tell myself not to think it, such discipline was beyond me. *Or dead.*

What the Draconeans made of my sobs, I do not know, but they left me in peace.

\* \* \*

One of them brought me food some time later: porridge not much different from what the Nying ate. Accepting it, I tried to study the Draconean's dentition, but it kept its mouth shut. Not wholly carnivorous, it seemed, although I had seen before, on the living and the frozen, that they had quite prominent cuspids. They could not give me porridge unless they farmed grain, and would not bother to farm grain unless they ate it. Which made sense, given the terrain; this region could not possibly support a large population of obligate carnivores. Perhaps their diet was like that of bears, omnivorous.

Such thoughts were the lifeline that kept me afloat while I ate my Draconean porridge.

They lived. They were *real*. How could I make space in my mind to accommodate that fact?

I found myself thinking of the egg from Rahuahane, and the cast I had made of the vacuoles in its petrified albumen. Lumpy and imprecise as it was, the cast had not given me a good picture of the lost embryo; but it had shown enough to be perplexing. The unexpected proportions, the odd configuration of the legs. All quite wrong for a quadripedal creature . . . but in hindsight, quite natural for a bipedal one.

How was it even *possible*?

I will not trouble my readers by recounting every occasion on which I lost the thread of my reasoning and sank once more into tears. I could not think of Rahuahane without thinking of Suhail, who had been there with me; I could not think of the egg without thinking of Tom, who had puzzled over its mysteries with me. Moreover I was still quite weak from my trials, and weeping exhausted what little reserves I had, so that I spent far more time

asleep than I would have liked. I knew that I must try to get out of
that place and back to human civilization; I told myself the others
were waiting for me there, as a spur to my determination. But I
also knew that if I tried to flee now, then regardless of what the
Draconeans did, I would be a dead woman in short order. I was in
no state to face the mountains.

How long had I been in that house? My hands and toes showed
clear signs of healing frostbite. I did not think it had been
dreadfully severe, as I still had full sensation in all the affected
areas, and my skin was not sloughing off. But it had been bad
enough to blister, so I had been more than merely nipped by the
cold. Judging by my current condition, and the state of my leg . . .
I feared I had been there at least a fortnight, if not longer.

Even if the others were alive, they would be certain I was dead.
I lost a great deal of time to that realization, and could barely eat
the food laid at my side.

What pulled me up again was the conundrum before me, the
inarguable existence of living, breathing, dragon-headed
creatures. If I could not escape them, I would study them. And
perhaps my study would lead me to some useful understanding.

But first, I had to reach some equilibrium on the matter of my
companions. I forced myself through the possibilities with
ruthless logic.

If I assumed them to be dead, and they proved to be alive, then
my mourning would be to no purpose. If I assumed them to be
dead and was correct, I did not think my mourning would be
lessened at all; I would only feel a new wave of grief upon
confirmation of their loss. Contrariwise, if I assumed them to be
alive and was wrong, my grief would be dreadful; but in the

*My Three Saviors*

meanwhile I would enjoy a greater use of my faculties, which would undoubtedly be of use in returning me to the human world. And finally, if I hoped for the best and proved to be right . . . that would be the best of all possible outcomes. I therefore resolved to behave in all ways as if they were alive, until I had proof to the contrary.

Did it work? Of course not; no mere resolution could hold back all fear and uncertainty. But it did help. With that vow to support me, I could address myself properly to the question at hand: how could the Draconeans be possible?

Developmental lability had to be the answer; there was no other explanation. Very well, then: under what conditions could a draconic egg develop into something half human?

It must be exposed to some kind of human factor in its environment. Not a house or the sound of literature read aloud or anything of that sort; no, the factor must be biological. And then I thought of the murals in the Watchers' Heart: the inscriptions, their glyphs painted red, descending on an egg below. The "precious rain" referenced in the Cataract Stone—and the clause that followed after, which might be read as an elaboration of the previous, telling of the "sacred utterances of our hearts."

Blood. Bathe a draconic egg in human blood, and perhaps a Draconean would result.

How often could that possibly occur? The more extreme the mutation, the less likely the embryo is to be viable; the experimentation carried out at the House of Dragons in Qurrat, both mine and that of my successors, had established that quite clearly. Something like this would not succeed one time in a thousand, I suspected. Or perhaps it was somehow done in more gradual steps—I had no way of knowing. My only certainty was that it *had* been done, for the proof of it kept bringing me porridge to eat.

Lying in my nest, slowly regaining my strength, I imagined sharing my speculations with Tom and Suhail. This was comforting, and soon I imagined myself standing in a place like Caffrey Hall, lecturing to the public on the Draconeans I had met. Unexpectedly, I found myself giggling. (The sound may have been a little hysterical; I muffled it in my blankets.) It had come to me that one way or another, I had my victory. Either this discovery would at last force the Philosophers' Colloquium to accept me as a member, and I would have the satisfaction of having broken through that door . . . or they would continue to refuse me, and I could wash my hands of them entirely. I had dreamt for years of achieving status as a Fellow, to the point where I could not surrender it easily—but if this did not suffice, then they would prove themselves a pack of hidebound reactionaries not worth a moment further of my time.

Of course, that would only be true if I had a chance to tell them.

Therefore, I must survive and return to the outside world. I would not give them the satisfaction of tut-tutting and shaking their heads over the sad demise of a woman whose aspirations exceeded her worth.

I will not pretend this washed me clean of all distress. Every minute I stayed in that place was another minute my husband believed me to be dead. I remembered all too well my grief when Jacob died; the thought of Suhail enduring such a loss was wrenching. However joyous our reunion would be, I could not envision it without first thinking of his suffering, which quite countered the effect. But rubbing the Colloquium's collective noses in my achievement? That was quite a powerful motivator, and every time my will to carry on faltered, I thought of the satisfaction that awaited me.

My trio of Draconeans permitted me to rise from my bed and hobble about so long as I neither shouted nor broke for the door. I did wonder what would happen if I made too much noise: would I provoke an avalanche? Attract a predator? Disturb the local peace and bring wrath down upon my captors? No one came into the house but those three; I could not even be certain there were others out there. I suspected there were, though. Had I been able to stay longer at the top of the col and survey the land on the other side, what might I have seen?

I shook aside such thoughts in favour of more immediate matters. In order to hobble about, I had to fashion a splint for my leg, to avoid doing it any further mischief. The Draconeans, when they realized what I was after, attempted to bind the splint about my knee; my insistence on placing it around my shin provoked much conversation among them. Of course: they would have little experience with broken bones, when their own were so close to indestructible. Crutches, on the other hand, they understood quite well, for they could damage their tendons and ligaments just like any other creature.

With my health thus addressed, I turned myself to the task of observation. I began with the Draconeans themselves. They were somewhat over two meters tall: enough to loom over many humans, but I had seen men as large, especially in the Keongan

Islands. In the chest and shoulder they were quite broad, presumably to support the musculature of their wings—could they fly? I suspected they would have difficulty, compared with their quadrupedal cousins; their bodies were not shaped for horizontal balance. They might be able to glide, though. They also appeared stockier than their ancient cousins, perhaps as an adaptation to the cold. Their scales were darker than those of the frozen Draconean we had found in the col; whether that was a seasonal difference, a sex-based one, or merely the equivalent of the colour variation seen in horses, I could not yet tell.

I had ample opportunity to study them, however, as they wore very little clothing while indoors. Although I found the air outside my blanketed shelter quite chill, they seemed perfectly comfortable in loose, plain trousers that did not fall below their knees. I knew that was not all they wore, though. They came and went, and although I kept my distance from the door, I could see through it to some kind of room beyond—an antechamber, I thought, where they donned and doffed heavier clothing, jackets and boots and the like. It would have been wildly insufficient to keep me warm, but it was clear their tolerance for the cold far exceeded my own.

(Why had the Draconean in the col not been clothed? I will never know for certain, but I do know they can suffer the effects of hypothermia. This sometimes causes people to succumb to a kind of madness wherein they strip off their clothing, feeling themselves to be far too warm. The lost one may have done just that.)

So much for the Draconeans, at least for the moment: next I turned my attention to their environment. The outside world was presently beyond my reach, but I could and did observe their house. It was not the kind of monumental structure I associated with the Draconeans; but of course I knew from Suhail that the ruins which awe us today are only the great edifices of their civilization, comparable to the Temple in Haggad or the Hall of the Synedrion in Falchester. Ordinary people had lived in more modest buildings.

(Were all of those ordinary people human? Or had Draconeans been numerous enough that there were Draconean peasants as well as rulers? My list of unanswered questions only grew longer with each passing day.)

The architecture differed in many ways from that of the Nying. Although the house in which I dwelt was round, it was clearly not built atop a livestock pen as is done in Tser-nga. Instead the floor was covered with that quilted hessian I had noted before, which was remarkably effective at insulating us from the cold—I did not learn why until later. The furnishings were sparse, just a few chests and shelves which held practical items such as pots and blankets. The fire sat in a broad, shallow bowl of bare stone; it was here that my caretakers slept, on thin mattresses they put away during the day. The smoke rose through a hole in the low ceiling (it barely cleared the heads of the inhabitants); the hole must have been shielded in some fashion, for I could not see the sky when I peered into it.

Our only light came from that fire and a handful of lamps whose odour I recognized: it was yak butter. Unless they traded with the Nying, and the entire region had conspired not to breathe a whisper of it to my party, they must herd their own yaks. They did indeed eat a mixed diet, grains and meat and dried fruit, along with the same staggering quantities of butter and fat I had seen among the Nying. And that, too, inclined me to believe these three were not alone, for it was unlikely in the extreme that they could supply themselves with such variety—especially when no more than two of them were ever gone from the house at one time.

I could not ask questions about any of it, though, until we could speak with one another. And that led me to my next task.

We began almost immediately. After my leg was splinted, I came to sit with them by the firepit, swaddled in a blanket, with my three hosts watching me warily. Looking at them, I said, "Anevrai?"

This was how Suhail had pronounced one of the words from the Cataract Stone. We had not known then whether it referred to the Draconeans or to their gods; now that I had conflated those two categories, I thought it would be a good guess. But they only cocked their heads and said nothing.

I was not half the linguist my husband was . . . but Suhail was not there, and so I must make do. I remembered him saying the words that changed the least were usually the most basic, and cast about for something that was both in the room and a word he had reconstructed. Pointing at the fire, I said, "*Irr?*"

This only seemed to deepen their confusion, but I kept trying. Leaning forward, I tapped one of the stones that ringed the fire and said, "*Abun.*" Then I pointed at the fire again. "*Irr.*"

The three Draconeans looked at one another and talked in low, rapid tones. One seemed to be asking a question, and the other two encouraging it—but perhaps that was only me laying meaning atop behaviour I could not understand. Finally the one turned back to me and pointed at the fire. "*Rrt.*" Then it tapped a stone. "*Vun.*"

My heart leapt. *Fire. Stone.* Two tiny footholds on the slope of an unimaginably large mountain; it was a long way from those two to conversation. But it sounded, to my linguistically amateur ear, as if Suhail was right. The Draconean language was ancestral to those of southern Anthiope—which meant it was *not* wholly alien to me. By looking for the points of commonality, I could leverage my way up to comprehension.

You must not imagine that this epiphany unlocked everything, any more than the Cataract Stone instantly unveiled the secrets of all Draconean inscriptions. It did nothing of the sort. Being raised in the Magisterial religion, I had never studied Lashon (and now cursed that lack), but my Akhian was passable, and gave me a much better starting point than the few fragments of vocabulary Suhail had tentatively reconstructed. But of course things had changed a great deal since those ancient days; the language my host spoke was not that of its ancestors from thousands of years before. Sounds evolved into completely different sounds, following rules my husband might know, but I did not. Words hived off to mean only a single concept related to the original, while something else came in to fill the void: the Akhian word for "to weave" seemed to be a distant cousin to the modern Draconean word for "cloth," while their "weave" was unlike anything I had heard before. Progress was excruciatingly slow.

But what else did I have with which to fill my time? Until they allowed me to leave the house, the most useful thing I could do was learn to communicate. Perhaps (I thought with another stifled giggle) I might find a place among the Society of Linguists, if the Colloquium would not have me. And although I am not talented at languages, it is amazing what one can accomplish when one has nothing else to focus on.

It is not true, though, to say I had *nothing* else to occupy me. One day—I assumed it was day; in truth I had no way of telling time other than by the wakefulness of the Draconeans and my own hunger—my three caretakers held a quiet and tense-looking conference, huddled in a fashion that made it clear I was not welcome, even though I could not have understood them yet. Then, stiff with obvious tension, two departed, leaving one behind.

The remaining Draconean took down my curtains and urged me to the back of the rounded room, as far from the entrance as possible. There it made a nest of the curtains for me and enacted a pantomime. I was to sit in that nest and, if someone came through the door, pull one of the curtains over myself and hide.

This was my first evidence that I was not supposed to be there at all.

I watched this Draconean closely. I had begun to tell them apart: the one who spoke to me in our halting language lessons was the tallest, with pale streaks running down the sides of its neck, and so I called it Streak. Another, with narrower shoulders, most commonly took the task of cooking, and so I dubbed it Cook. This was the smallest and stockiest of the three, and I referred to it as Wary—for of the three, it was the most obviously afraid of me.

Afraid of *me*! I was half a meter shorter and half its weight, with no claws or teeth to speak of, and yet it feared me. Much of their conference, I thought, had been about persuading Wary to stay with me while the other two went away. How long would they be gone?

Watching the Draconean from my nest, I realized something else. All this time, I had been observing them with a naturalist's eye, noting conformation, coloration, behaviour. We had begun to communicate . . . but not yet to treat one another as people.

I caught the Draconean's attention and pointed at myself. "Isabella."

It stared mutely. Confused? Or too wary to speak?

To clarify, I went through the words we had established so far, naming the fire, the stones, my blanket, and more. Then I pointed at myself again. "Isabella." This I repeated, several more times, with slow and careful enunciation. Then it was time to point at the Draconean and make an inquisitive noise.

It understood me, I was sure. But it only turned away and bent itself to the task of cleaning the porridge-pot.

Either they did not use names, or this one was unwilling to share its own. I made a private wager on the latter.

The other two were gone for a long time, the remainder of which Wary and I spent in silence. Finally we heard sounds outside, and Wary gestured fiercely for me to hide myself; I complied without hesitation. But I peeked through a tiny gap in the blankets, and when the door was safely closed behind the familiar pair, I emerged once more.

I hoped their return meant I might be permitted to go outside. They had never before taken the precaution of hiding me, which meant today was unusual; it might have heralded that welcome change. Unfortunately, I had no such luck. But I repeated the process of naming myself, and this time, it bore fruit.

Streak understood my meaning immediately. After a glance at the others—I could see Wary silently willing its companion not to speak—the Draconean turned back to me, pointed one claw at its muzzle, and said, "Ruzt."

The one I had dubbed Cook followed suit. "Kahhe."

Then they glared at Wary until it muttered, "Zam."

Now all of us had names. They were no longer creatures to me; they were people. And that marked the beginning of many changes among us.

# ELEVEN

*Out of the house—Yaks and mews—A winter of learning—New arrivals—Kahhe's wing—Hibernation—*
*The utility of art*

"Zabel." This was how they tended to pronounce my name. They were not incapable of providing it with its initial and final vowels, but in their speech such things tended to fall away, and I answered readily enough to the truncated form. Ruzt had gone out for a time; now it was back, and it held in its claws my mountaineering clothes, carefully mended.

A thousand possibilities collided in my mind. I was to be escorted home; I was being tossed out on my ear; I was to meet other Draconeans at last; I was being taken to my execution. Would they bother to mend my clothes before killing me? I chided myself for foolishness and dressed with alacrity. Only one thing could I be sure of: I was going outside at last. After so long cooped up in that house, nothing sounded more wonderful.

Despite my still-splinted leg, my step was light as I followed Ruzt through the door it had blocked me from before. The antechamber was stuffed with all manner of sacks and crates;

clearly it served as a storeroom for those things which would not suffer from the cold. The wall it shared with the inner room was covered in more of that quilted hessian. Ruzt took garments from a nearby rack, snow-caked enough that I understood why it did not bring them inside, where they would leave meltwater all over the floor. The sight should have warned me of what I would face outside, but I was so caught up in the thought of freedom that I did not follow my observation to its logical conclusion.

Ruzt led me to the exterior door, set a little distance to the side of the first (so the wind would not blow straight through to the interior), and opened it.

I stepped out into a world of diamonds. The sky overhead was a brilliant, unforgiving blue, and the sun reflected off a thousand surfaces around me. From the col I had seen greenery in the valley below; unless Ruzt and the others had taken me someplace entirely different, that green was all buried now. Icicles decorated the eaves of the buildings, hung in dense strings from the trees. Directly ahead of me, dominating the mountain basin, was the peak I had seen from the col, dressed entirely in white. My first step sank me almost knee-deep into the snow, and the air was the coldest I had ever felt.

While I lay ill and then healing inside that house, winter had begun.

Oh, by the calendar perhaps it was not yet there. But in the Mrtyahaima, winter does not wait upon the solstice to come calling; it arrives early and stays late. Though much of the precipitation falls during the monsoon, as rain in the valleys and snow in the heights, winter is not without its storms; and during that season, travel is all but impossible.

I stood as if turned to ice myself. All thoughts of departure withered on the vine. It did not matter how much I had recovered; it did not matter whether the Draconeans helped or hindered me in going. Any attempt to leave this place before spring would be a death sentence—and spring would not show her face before Fructis at the earliest. At a conservative estimate, I would be trapped here for at least four months.

Four months, during which everyone I loved would believe me dead.

Ruzt said something I could not understand. When I did not respond, it bent to peer at me. I shook myself to something like life and nodded, numbly. I could not encompass that thought yet; I would come to terms with it by degrees, for to take in the whole at once would break me. For now, I distracted myself with my surroundings, which I was at last free to explore.

The house stood on the edge of a village. It should, I thought, have looked more exotic; after all, this was a Draconean settlement. But the truth is that sensible architecture stays much the same regardless of species. The steeply pitched roofs were not far different from those of the Nying—or, indeed, those one might find in Siaure or northern Bulskevo. Where there is a large amount of snow, there is a need to shed it, lest it crush the roof with its weight.

I turned the other direction and saw that I had not come so terribly far. The familiar tower of Gyaptse stood proud in the sky, with Cheja alongside. From here, the path up to the col was comparatively easy. But I had no illusions that I could chance it: even if I made it across, I would die attempting to descend the other side alone; and even if I survived the descent, I would still be in the Mrtyahaiman wilderness, with a glacier between me and the nearest human settlement.

When I turned back, all three of my Draconean hosts were watching me. I suspect they guessed my thoughts, but I do not know for certain.

All three of my hosts. Where were the remainder?

Just as when we had come into Hlamtse Rong, I saw no one on the paths between the houses; unlike in Hlamtse Rong, there was no one peering out at me from cover. I could not even see many tracks in the snow. What few I saw, I suspected came from Ruzt, Kahhe, and Zam.

This was why they had permitted me to leave the house. Because no one else was here to see me.

So where had the inhabitants gone? To winter quarters, perhaps? Leaving behind my three, who made no objection as I tentatively began to explore. They let me walk up to one of the other houses; when I knocked on the door, they only looked puzzled. Clearly it was not the Draconean custom to announce themselves in such fashion. Did they clap, as people do in other parts of the world? I had no idea. But the door opened when I tried it, and although Kahhe followed me closely, they permitted me to go inside. The layout of the house was much like the one I had left, but clearly packed up for the season, its inhabitants not expecting to return any time soon. Here, though, part of the quilted hessian had split, exposing the stuffing. Poking at this, I found it was filled with scales like the ones that adorned my companions, but paler.

"Insulation," I murmured, stepping back to study it. The same material that helped protect their bodies could easily serve the same purpose on their houses. Did the Draconeans shed their scales each year? The quantity suggested they did, and the colour suggested the scales bleached over time, likely as a seasonal adaptation. (In wintertime a pale hide would camouflage them more effectively against the snow, while a darker hide would be much less conspicuous among the trees and bare stones of summer.) They must save their scales with care, stitching them into new fabric casings when the old ones failed.

Zam was hissing something to Ruzt when I came out of the house. It still did not trust me; that much was palpable. I wished I could ask why.

Since I could not, I continued exploring. There seemed no point in going into any of the other houses, but below me on the slope was a building unlike any of the others. It was low and square, but enormous in area, at least compared to everything else in the village. To give the roof a steep pitch would have required it to soar into the sky; instead its gentler slope was oddly lumpy, which I soon realized came from the pine boughs that carpeted it. These could be pried off as needed, taking the encrustation of snow and ice with them, and replaced with a clean covering from a storehouse built for the purpose.

Of course my first thought was "temple." We humans have a long history of attaching that name to any monumental Draconean structure whose use we do not understand; this one might be constructed of wood and rough field stone rather than the carefully shaped blocks of the ancients, but what other purpose could motivate them to build so large a place?

I should have guessed the answer, for the parts of the village I had seen thus far had one exceedingly obvious lack. But it was not until I drew close and smelled the odour arising from it that I realized the truth.

Ruzt unbarred the door and ushered me inside the yak barn.

It contained what I presumed was every single yak belonging to the village, penned in a series of smaller enclosures. In each enclosure, the beasts shared a common style of nose-ring, which I understood to be owners' marks. Wherever the rest of the Draconeans had gone, they had left behind their livestock—and, I soon realized, it was the duty of these three to care for them until spring.

I spent a good deal of time in that yak barn during my stay in the village. I knew from past experience in other parts of the world that assistance with daily tasks goes some way toward establishing friendly relations, and it was no different here (though my aid did little to thaw Zam's heart). But my motives were not entirely altruistic: owing to the number of beasts inside the barn, it was also the warmest place in the village, unless I wished to spend the months huddled right next to the Draconeans' fire. Furthermore, there was something of great interest to me inside that barn.

From above us I heard a familiar cry.

"Mews!" I said in startlement, looking at the Draconeans. Naturally this meant nothing to them, and none of the Tser-zhag words I tried had any better effect. But Ruzt led me up a ladder to an attic space—a mews, I thought, remembering Suhail's laughter at the word—filled with familiar draconic shapes. These, too, were marked, though in their case it was with paint on their hides rather than rings through the nose.

In the days that followed I discovered that the mews were an integral part of how three Draconeans could care for such a large quantity of livestock all by themselves. In Hlamtse Rong we had wondered whether mews could be trained; in the Draconean village, which was called Imsali, I learned that they could. It works far better, however, when the trainer is not human, though the reasons for this are still a mystery. But I received my answer on the matter of the mews' diving behaviour, for this is clearly a degenerate echo of the action they use to herd yaks.

Yes, my Draconean hosts used mews as their aerial sheepdogs. The little dragons helped them drive groups of livestock out to areas where grazing could still be found—for yaks can nibble up shreds and patches of grass from beneath the snow. If they have fed well enough in summer, they can survive all winter on such fare. We supplemented this with dried fodder in the barn, but to keep them there the entire season would be detrimental to their health. My hosts therefore took them out in a steady rotation, one Draconean and cluster of mews per herd, with at least one caretaker remaining behind in the village.

Even my fascination with dragon behaviour could not persuade me to volunteer myself for such excursions, not in a Mrtyahaiman winter. It was therefore in some ways fortunate that the Draconeans clearly did not want me to leave the village. Instead I engaged in chores there: mucking out the yak barn, caring for the mews not currently on duty, and working diligently to establish some command of the local language, with the help of Ruzt.

It is difficult to tell the story of that winter among the Draconeans. I kept no journal during my time there (lacking a notebook to keep it in, or a pen with which to write). Even if I had, I could not tell you when and how I learned everything; too much of it seeped into my head by some osmotic process, assembled from a hundred little clues until one day I knew a thing, without ever quite having been told it. Even when my education was more overt, it is difficult to recall the sequence and cause. Certain details are vital enough to this tale that I will keep them in their proper places; but for the rest, I shall let them fall where they may, without undue concern for chronology.

My progress often felt painfully slow—in part because it was, and in part because it came not in grand leaps, but by small degrees. There was no moment at which I began having conversations with Ruzt. We started with the vocabulary of my immediate environment, progressed to basic verbs, muddled through the fundamentals of grammar by a great deal of trial and even more error, and by the end could tackle some abstract concepts through extensive circumlocution—all of which was great progress over where I began, but it happened so slowly that at times I doubted it was happening at all.

That I achieved so much success I largely attribute to my husband's brilliant deduction, connecting Draconean to the languages of southern Anthiope. Familiar though I was with the concept of evolution, I was not in the habit of applying it to languages; and on my own, I do not know if I would have looked for the patterns that would allow me to extrapolate from the tongue I knew to the tongue I did not. (There is, of course, a hazard in leaning too heavily upon such analogies: I spoke very Akhian-flavored Draconean, as I instinctively defaulted to the grammar of the more familiar language whenever my attention wandered.) But with that theory in hand, I could apply my naturalist's mind to the problem, and after a while I was able to make educated guesses as to Draconean words I had not yet learned. These were rarely correct, but they often led me toward the proper word by a faster road.

The remainder of my success is due to Ruzt. If we, analogizing to biological evolution, think of Lashon and Akhian as the domestic housecat and the lion—differing in a variety of respects, but obviously near relations—then the modern Draconean tongue is like a dog: still derived from a common ancestor, from whom all three languages have inherited some important characteristics, but much more widely separated by millennia of change. Fortunately for me, Ruzt spoke what I eventually recognized as an older, religious form of the language, comparable to Scriptural Lashon; this lay much closer to the ancient roots than their modern tongue. The language she spoke with Kahhe and Zam contained a vast number of words that I suspect derived from another tongue entirely—perhaps a human language, though it did not, to my amateur ear, appear to be Nying or Tser-zhag.

Despite this, I learned a few things, beginning with the shift my alert readers may have noticed already: my hosts were in fact hostesses. Ruzt, Kahhe, and Zam were three sisters, which is the typical household arrangement among the Draconeans. Males are fewer in number, but rather than following the polygamous structure a human society might assume, the Draconeans practice no real marriage at all. Their males live together, in several larger buildings where they are sorted according to their age group, while sister-groups maintain independent houses. They consider the sibling bond to be much more significant than the parental one, and the sororal more significant than the fraternal.

Imsali was not the only village in the region. On a clear day I

could see smoke arising in other places around the Sanctuary—
for that was how I came to think of the basin that encircled the
great central peak, known to the Draconeans as Anshakkar. The
ring of mountains surrounding it (of which Gyaptse and Cheja
are but two) is nearly impassible; the col by which I entered is one
of the lowest points in that ring, and as you have seen, it is not
easy to traverse. Mountaineers may scale it, of course—but it is
only in recent history that mountaineers have begun to frequent
the region, people well equipped for the climbing of ridges and
peaks, and motivated less by the search for new pastures or arable
land or even trading routes than by the desire to conquer
untrammeled terrain. For the inhabitants on all sides, the way is
too forbidding to be worthwhile. What good would it do to enter
such a place? Departure is too difficult; anyone who lived within
would be isolated from the world without.

But the land inside is hospitable—at least by Mrtyahaiman
standards of hospitality. The valleys are quite deep, and at most
times of year the surrounding mountains block enough of the
wind to make the interior relatively pleasant. Farming is possible,
and the herding of yaks; and while humans would find it quite
hard going, the Draconeans, with the advantage of their adaptable
biology, made do quite well.

How had they come to be there? Speculation alone could not tell
me, but my command of the language did not yet suffice to address
such abstract, complex topics. I had a strong suspicion that, as I had
theorized before, folk memory in Tser-nga preserved knowledge of
the Draconeans—for surely these were the "ice demons" feared by
the people of Hlamtse Rong. Had they dwelt here since ancient
times? Nothing in their architecture reminded me of the ruins I

had seen in other parts of the world . . . but of course it would be absurdly difficult to build such things in a place like this. For one mad moment, I wondered if the inhabitants of the Sanctuary even knew that the larger Draconean civilization had fallen thousands of years before, far outside their isolated home.

Had I been able to explore, I might have learned more, and more rapidly. Three things, however, militated against my departing from Imsali. First, of course, was my own weakness and injury, though in time I overcame that issue. The second was that although it does not snow as heavily in the winter as during the monsoon, it does still snow; and winter is the primary season for the wind to come howling through.

The third is that we were not alone in that place.

In our village, yes. (If I may be permitted to term it "our village," when I was only a temporary guest there.) But as it transpired, each of the villages within the Sanctuary had its own set of yak caretakers. This I discovered one day when Kahhe swooped down and bundled me straight back into the barn, without so much as a by-your-leave.

I do mean *swooped*. On that day I discovered that, while Draconean wings cannot support full flight, they are sufficient for a degree of gliding. Kahhe landed before me in the snow, clapped one scaled hand over my mouth, and hauled me bodily through the doorway. It is a mark of how much I had come to trust the sisters that after my first, muffled yelp of surprise, I made no protest at all. If she felt I needed to be removed from sight, I assumed it was for my own protection—and so it was.

Voices came from outside. By then I had heard enough of the three sisters that I could recognize their tones, and knew the new speakers were neither Zam nor Ruzt. Kahhe pointed with one claw. I stared. She pointed again, wings fluttering. I knew what she meant; it was only reluctance that held me back. But I had no better option, and so, obedient to her instructions, I climbed over the railing into one of the yak enclosures and wormed my way between the beasts until I was far enough back to be thoroughly concealed. Then she went outside.

Common sense told me to stay where I was. But I am, as Suhail is fond of saying, deranged as well as practical. I could learn a great deal by watching my three Draconeans interact with others . . . and I did not relish the thought of staying among the yaks, made fragrant by their enclosed quarters.

I crept back between them and went to the barn door, where I peered out through the crack. In the street outside I saw two new Draconeans speaking to Kahhe. Before long her sisters joined them, and then the conversation devolved into an argument.

The wind was too fierce that day for me to hear much of what they said, and I doubt I would have understood more than one word in ten even if I could hear. Though by then I had some facility with the language, at least within the narrow scope of my daily affairs, I still required my interlocutors to speak slowly and clearly— which is not a thing people generally do in natural conversation.

Watching their body language, however, kept me fascinated enough to forget the intense chill coming through the crack of the door. Their gestures were not those of humans: Ruzt kept holding up one hand, fingers spread and palm out, which among us would have been a sign of placation or a request for quiet while she spoke. Here it seemed to be a way of indicating refusal, like a shake of the head. At one point a newcomer half spread her wings; Kahhe responded by spreading her own to their fullest extent. The other followed suit, and the two commenced what I could only think of as a staring contest, except with wings instead of eyes. When Zam had lifted her ruff my first day awake, I had interpreted it as a fear response; here I thought the increase in apparent size signaled some kind of dominance challenge instead.

Kahhe won the contest, but in the end Ruzt curled her fingers inward and turned her palm toward her body, which signaled assent. All five Draconeans turned and came toward me.

I scrambled for cover once more. Whether any of the Draconeans took particular note of the restless and protesting yaks in one of the enclosures, I cannot say; by then I was crouched as low as I could be in the far corner, praying that the nearest beast would not decide to saunter away and leave me exposed. I only know that no one commented on my presence, which meant none of the strangers had noticed it.

They climbed up the ladders and were gone for some time. I heard a creaking from the upper attic, where fodder was kept, above the mews. I considered trying to shift to better cover, but did not quite dare; the risk of being caught in the open was too high. Finally they came back down, bearing sacks of the richer feed we gave to yaks that seemed to be languishing in their winter quarters. So: the argument had been about feed, and whether our village would give any to the visitors. Were their yaks wasting away, or had something gone wrong with their feed, or were the newcomers simply bullies extorting surplus from their neighbours? I never did find out.

Kahhe retrieved me once they were gone. Leaving the barn, I saw something that stopped me—in my tracks, I should say, but it would be more accurate to say in front of them. The ground by the barn door was thoroughly trampled, but I had been roaming about earlier, and the snow away from the usual path showed my footprints clearly.

Human footprints. Would anyone here recognize them as such? They certainly did not look Draconean, by size or by stride length.

When Kahhe saw what had alarmed me, she immediately went to consult with her sisters. After that I was issued a broom with which to blur my tracks, and the trio frowned more on me going anywhere they had not already trampled a path. (After a day or two of carrying the broom, I instead improvised a kind of straw skirt, which would drag behind me as I walked without need for special effort. As this also had the effect of insulating me further against the cold, I did not mind the additional burden.)

"What would have happened if they saw me?" I asked, staring in the direction the strangers had gone. I spoke in Akhian, as had become my habit; I was more focused on learning Ruzt's language than teaching her any of my own, but the odds of her understanding a stray word or two were higher if I spoke that tongue.

She made no reply, and I doubt my meaning came through. In a sense, I am glad I did not get an answer then, for I would not have been prepared for the consequences.


That night I approached Kahhe and asked, by means of mime, whether I could examine her wings.

Ever since I woke up and discovered that Draconeans were not only real but alive (or at least since I had collected my wits in the aftermath of that discovery), I had wondered about their wings.

Their ancient kin might have inhabited places like Akhia and Keonga, but these three dwelt in an exceedingly cold climate. A thin structure like a wing loses heat rapidly, because the blood vessels are unavoidably close to the surface. How did they deal with this problem?

I had noted that my rescuers had a habit of crouching close to the fire with their wings partially spread, as if cupping the heat to themselves. They most often did this immediately after returning from the outside, in the manner of a human warming their hands at the flame, and that made sense to me; but they also did it before departing, and I wanted to know why.

So I pointed to Kahhe's wings and said in her language, "What?" By now this was well established as my way of asking for vocabulary, and so she answered me, "*Kappu.*" I repeated this process with my eyes and received the word *ika* in return. Then, employing my new acquisitions and some accompanying mime, along with their word for "please," I inquired whether I could examine her wings. Kahhe seemed puzzled by my interest, but let me approach, and did not flinch away when I touched her.

In the course of my career I have handled any number of dragon wings. Many of them, however, have been on carcasses, and most of the remaining number belonged to very small breeds of dragon, such as the honeyseeker. My only experience with a larger wing on a living creature was when I had to assist Tom in doctoring a drake in Akhia, and in that instance she was drugged to her ruff.

Kahhe's wing was entirely different, not for any reason of anatomy, but simply because it belonged to a living, wakeful, self-aware creature. The muscles that controlled it shifted under my hands, Kahhe not quite willing to relax entirely into my grip. I felt the warmth of it—we had been inside for some time—and her pulse when I used my fingertips to locate the main alar artery.

A pulse which vanished a moment later. I think Kahhe believed I wanted to pinch off the blood flow, and was trying to assist me; and so she did, but not in the way she intended.

Her action told me what I would not otherwise have known: that Draconeans can voluntarily control the blood flow to their wings. When in strong sunlight or near a fire, they open those vessels and draw in as much heat as they can, but when they go into the cold, they reduce the flow to their wings, the better to preserve that heat.

They cannot do this forever, of course, as it greatly restricts the mobility of that limb; and the longer the wings remain dormant, the longer it takes them to return to full function. (It is for this reason that spreading the wings is a dominance challenge, at least in winter; to leave them exposed is a test of endurance.) Judging by the way she moved in the aftermath of the strangers' visit, Kahhe had strained a muscle swooping in to hide me, likely on account of the cold and lack of blood flow. But it is a very clever adaptation—a kind of localized anatomical hibernation.

The notion of hibernation should have occured to me much sooner. (No doubt the more scientifically inclined of my readers have thought of it already, and wondered that I have not addressed it before now.) In my defense I can only say that I had spent my entire tenure in that village either unconscious, in hysterics, or reeling from the flood of new information; and as a consequence, I had the attention span of a gnat: no sooner did I begin pondering one aspect of the puzzle than some equally interesting angle distracted me.

But as soon as I thought of it, I was certain that the rest of the village's inhabitants had not gone to winter quarters—or rather, that "winter quarters" for them consisted of hibernation. It is a common biological response to cold weather, for it allows the organism to survive on a much reduced diet when food is scarce; I had seen its more unusual summer cousin, aestivation, among the desert drakes of Akhia.

The Draconeans could not all go into hibernation, for they would wake to find their yak herds annihilated by the harsh winter. (Wild yaks may survive without undue trouble, but their domesticated kin have more difficulty.) My three fought their instincts, staying awake through the frozen months to ensure their kindred's livestock would be waiting when spring came. They ate tremendous quantities of food—a fact I had noted but, having nothing to compare it against, had assumed was their ordinary diet—and chewed a certain leaf in much the same fashion as human men chew tobacco. Initially I abstained from trying the leaf myself, knowing that what was edible to them might not be so to me; but Ruzt pressed some upon me when I had an abscessed tooth, and although the taste was unpleasantly astringent, it helped to numb my mouth while she drained the abscess. After that I chewed it somewhat regularly, for I found it improved my health and mitigated the effects of the high altitude.

Not long after I examined Kahhe's wing, I tried to ask about hibernation. Our communication was not anything like fluent enough yet to cover such a topic, and so once again I had to ask in mime, pointing at empty houses and then feigning sleep. At first I thought my meaning still too muddled, for Ruzt only cocked her head and then walked away. As this persisted, however, I became certain that she understood me perfectly well, and was using incomprehension as her shield against my questions. I did not press.

You must not think that I had suddenly mislaid my curiosity. My list of mysteries to solve was a kilometer long; but language was still a tremendous barrier, and moreover I was eternally cognizant of the fact that the line between "prisoner" and "guest" might be exceedingly thin. That my three hostesses were friendly to me, I was certain—well, certain in two cases; Zam still gave me a wide berth whenever she could, and watched me with a gimlet eye. But Kahhe's swift action to hide me when the neighbours came calling made it obvious that I could not expect so hospitable a reaction from their kin.

And whether I was correct about hibernation or not, I knew beyond a doubt that eventually the other inhabitants of Imsali would return. When that day arrived, I needed to be out of the Sanctuary and back to my own people, which I could only do with the help of my three caretakers . . . or I needed that trio to be my shield against whatever might come next.

My communications with Ruzt and the others improved dramatically when I realized that I was thinking too much like my husband.

This was ironic because I had been trying not to think about him at all. I was frequently unsuccessful; over the past five years I had grown accustomed to having Suhail at my side, and his absence felt like a missing limb. As I have said, though, I often lost myself to despair in those days, for it was easy to imagine that I would never escape the Sanctuary (how ironic that name would then be!), and therefore would never see him again. I could banish my demons with unyielding determination to prevail . . . but this only worked for a time, and drained me tremendously. It was better to lose myself in the challenges I faced, addressing what lay immediately before me, rather than allowing my thoughts to stray too far ahead.

But one cannot live in a marriage like mine without each spouse shaping the other—not when one of your primary joys lies in sharing your interests and fields of knowledge. It was only because of Suhail that I had made as many linguistic strides as I had, and I followed his principles and theories in establishing a common vocabulary with my rescuers.

My change of course came about because of a brilliant dawn. A nightmare had woken me, as it often did; rather than disturb the sisters with my restlessness, I slipped quietly through the door to the antechamber. I had to bring my outer clothing with me, naturally, for the air there was cold enough to give me frostbite if I did not take care—and there is nothing like the unforgiving slap of freezing air to wake a person. Since sleep was now beyond me, and I had gone to such effort in dressing myself in all the necessary layers, I thought I might as well go outside.

Dawn had come to the summit of Anshakkar, that central peak. Though most of the Sanctuary yet lay in shadow, the mountain burned like a flame with the light of the rising sun. Looking on it, I was reminded of the dawn when I stood atop the col with Tom, gazing into the west; and I understood why humans have been known to worship mountains. Anshakkar's beauty was of a divine sort, sharp and untouchable, as far distant from my own concerns as I was from the concerns of an ant. Pencil and paper, had I possessed either at that moment, could not possibly have captured the effect, and I have never had much skill with oils . . . but never in my life have I wished so strongly to render a moment on canvas, even if I knew my effort would fall short. It seemed to me in that frozen moment, caught between the remnants of sleep and the wakefulness of an icy dawn, that no one could hope to understand my time in the Sanctuary unless they saw that mountain, ablaze with morning's light.

The feeling passed—but the idea it had planted in my mind did not.

Prior to the discovery of the Cataract Stone and subsequent breakthrough regarding their language, we had two sources for our fragmentary, erroneous knowledge of Draconean civilization. The first was folklore: memories preserved in Scripture and humble tales, mutated by time until they were scarcely recognizable. The second was the material remains of their age, the buildings and artefacts and, above all, the images—the painted murals and carved reliefs that had once adorned their world. We had misinterpreted so much of that, but it was still the one means by which the ancients could speak to the modern human, transcending the barrier of language.

Could I not communicate in the same way?

I had no proper supplies for the purpose, just a few scraps of paper that had been tucked into the pocket of my coat; my pencil had gone astray during the avalanche or my wanderings afterward, never to be seen again. But humans made art long before we had paper or pencils, and I would not let that lack hinder me.

The interior wall of the yak barn, plastered with white lime, was my primary canvas. By the time the sisters roused to feed the beasts and muck out their enclosures, I had laid out my tale in charcoal, doing my best to mimic the style of ancient Draconean art: Thu, finding the remnants of a Draconean in the valley; Thu again, meeting with myself and Tom and Suhail; then five of us climbing up to the col, where we found the second carcass; then the avalanche. As a coda, myself on one side of the mountains, my companions on the other, in postures of sorrow.

(I was fortunate that the barn, inhabited as it was by so many yaks, was warm enough that my tears did not freeze. My nose ran dreadfully, though, and I had only one handkerchief with which to address that issue, which I had already worn to a rag. Yak-wool scraps make abysmal tools for the purpose.)

The sisters were already upset when they came in, I think because they woke to find me gone from the house, and had to follow my brushed-over tracks to locate me. The simple existence of my picture was enough to deepen their consternation, long before I had a chance to show them its details. Zam in particular was angry: although the charcoal would wash off quite easily, or could at least be smudged into illegibility if the need should arise, I had left a blatant sign of my presence in a relatively public building.

But in time they calmed, and then Ruzt and Kahhe studied my pictures. I exercised my vocabulary, pointing to each bit like a teacher: Draconean, Zabel, mountain. Then, once Ruzt understood, I drew a final image. This one depicted myself and the others together again, in the posture from ancient art that we believed to indicate rejoicing.

Ruzt understood me, I am sure, when I turned to her with a pleading, hopeful expression. But she stared at the wall, neither meeting my gaze nor responding.

Kahhe asked her a question, in a tone I recognized as dubious, and jerked her head in the direction of the mountain Anshakkar.

This set Zam off like a firecracker. Whatever Kahhe had just suggested, Zam was adamantly against it. Ruzt silenced them both with a snap of her wings. I lifted a bucket of water, and she nodded; I began to wash my images from the wall.

What was at the mountain? I had my suspicions, but could not be certain. And I was not ready to pursue them just yet, not when it might lose me some valuable goodwill—or simply kill me outright.

But in the meanwhile, we had a new mode of communication, which aided me in expanding my vocabulary. I essayed some experiments with Draconean writing as well, hoping to establish for certain the pronunciation of the different glyphs, but made scant progress; Kahhe and Zam were clearly illiterate, and while Ruzt understood a little, she was very reluctant to help. Suspecting some kind of religious control of writing, I desisted. For my purposes, writing was of little use anyway, as it could only set down the words I heard. Images were better for eliciting new words entirely.

Ruzt and Kahhe seemed very respectful of my newly revealed skill. Their wooden tools and their pots were decorated, but only with abstract designs; as with people in many cold climates, they passed much of their leisure time in carving. Nowhere, though, had I seen any figurative art. The part of me that, despite evidence to the contrary, persisted in thinking of them as particularly clever dragons had taken this as only natural—but of course they were more than that; they were people, albeit only partially human, and their ancestors had been quite capable of both drawing and sculpture. Modern Draconeans did still have representative art, only not in casual use. And it is fortunate they did, for had they possessed no concept of artistic representation, they would not so easily have understood my pictures.

In time I came to understand that figurative artists form a special class in Draconean society, one that is much admired. Without realizing it, I had, by demonstrating my skill, made myself a good deal safer among them.

# TWELVE

*A fire in the yak barn—Into the Sanctuary—Herding with mews—The*
*perennial question—In search of yaks—Up the path*

In the history of scientific discovery, it is my opinion that
insufficient credit has been given to the behaviour of the
humble yak.

Oh, I could say that what happened next was due to a fire in
the yak barn. This would be true as far as it goes; without the fire,
the beasts would not have panicked, and nothing of interest
would have occurred. But had it been a fire only, with no ensuing
complications from the yaks, I believe I would have remained in
that village for the whole winter, and what ensued thereafter
would have proceeded entirely according to the plans of my
hostesses. Instead I departed from Imsali, learned things the
sisters did not intend, and made a great deal of progress I had not
anticipated in the least.

The carelessness which began the fire was not my own. The
interior of the barn was exceedingly dim, even with the doors
thrown wide; we often set butter lamps in strategic locations, the
better to see what we were doing. Ordinarily we exercised some

caution in where we placed the lamps, but errors happened—and on that transformative day, Kahhe made a mistake.

One of the yaks, wandering about its enclosure, jostled the beam on which the lamp lay.

Had either of us been right there, we would have seen the lamp fall, and could likely have extinguished the fire before it grew too large. But I was outside the barn when the trouble began, and Kahhe had gone to fetch a new basket in which to carry away the yak manure; the first one she found was torn, and by the time she replaced it with a usable one, the fire had well and truly taken hold.

Ruzt and Zam were out with portions of the village herd for grazing, which left the two of us to fight the blaze on our own. We first attempted to suffocate the fire with the best material we had to immediate hand—which is to say, yak manure. (Dried, their droppings are often used for fuel. But these were not yet dry.) Had the yaks remained calm, we might have succeeded. Alas for Kahhe and myself, they did not.

The group nearest the fire stampeded first, with their neighbours hard on their heels. The enclosures were not meant to withstand a concerted attempt to break out; the railings splintered and fell. Kahhe bent her knees and sprang upward, snapping her wings out in a desperate attempt to gain altitude; it lifted her high enough to seize one of the overhanging rafters. For my own part, I could only run—sideways to begin with, out of the stream of yak flesh, as if they were an avalanche like the one that had brought me to Imsali; but then onward and out of the barn entirely, for the spreading fire and the stampede soon had the entire place in an uproar.

Kahhe, it must be said, kept her wits rather well. By the time I had steadied my nerves and could re-enter the building without fear of being pulped, she was back at the fire, beating it out with anything that came to hand. This was not only courage at work: without the barn, the sisters could not hope to care for all the herds of Imsali by themselves. And without the herds, their village would starve in the coming year. I had no way of guessing how community-minded the Draconeans were; I did not know whether other villages would contribute bulls and cows to keep their neighbours going. Now was not the time to ask. I tied a rag over my face, seized a bucket, and began dousing one edge of the flames from the nearest water trough.

We got the fire out in time, although it destroyed one corner of the barn. This the sisters could patch after a fashion, with yak hides and bracing beams; the greater damage, in the immediate term, was the near-complete scattering of the herds.

In this I was both a liability and an asset. Although I lacked the physiological adaptations that made the Draconeans of that region better suited to withstanding the cold, I could endure if I had to, and my presence meant the sisters had a fourth pair of hands to help restore order. Four, however, was not enough: multiple people would be necessary to track down the missing beasts and bring them back to the village, but the village itself needed looking after, especially as the yaks returned. The sisters would have to call on the neighbouring villages for help . . . and that, in turn, risked the revelation of my presence. The only solution was to send me out with two of the sisters on yak-retrieval duty, while a few neighbours from the nearest villages helped keep order at home.

I was not so loath to wander the Sanctuary as you might expect.

True, the conditions I would have to endure out there would be dreadful; I did not look forward to any part of that. But my situation, which confined me almost wholly to the sisters' house, the yak barn, and points between, was beginning to send me mad with claustrophobia. I thought I would be happy to endure some freezing cold, if it meant I could see new surroundings.

(Of course it is easy to think such things from the comfort of a relatively warm building. I did regret that impulse more than a few times in the days to come.)

Three of us therefore set out: myself, Ruzt, and Zam, with Kahhe remaining behind to repair the barn. I spent a miserable night alone in a small snow shelter when reinforcements arrived, lest they see me about the village; then the other two joined me with a pack of mews, and we sallied forth, into the depths of the Sanctuary.

Much of what followed does not make for good telling, unless one is keenly interested in the finer points of herding yaks in mountainous terrain. The yaks, having fled, were safe enough for the moment; they are bred for that kind of environment, and need very little grazing provided they are in good enough health and fatness. But of course they might slip and fall, or fail to find any grass beneath the snow, or simply wander so far afield their owners would never see them again. We therefore spent more than three weeks tramping through the nearby folds of the Sanctuary, following signs of the beasts' passage, and herding them back toward the village once found.

I was miserably cold, as you might imagine. By my best estimate, we were then in the depths of Messis, which in the southern hemisphere is the nadir of winter. The limited diet on offer in the Sanctuary was beginning to take its toll, with scurvy loosening my teeth and sapping all my energy. My warmest moments came when I was chasing yaks; my coldest came at night, when I had neither movement nor sun to counteract the bitter air. Ruzt and Zam had brought along a tent, into which we all packed—not only the three of us, but also the mews. The little dragons arrayed themselves around the tent's interior perimeter, and I slept tucked between my Draconean hostesses—an exceedingly odd sensation, I must own, but the only way I had of preserving myself against the weather. They were not nearly as warm to the touch as a human would have been, but they were preferable to the icy wall of the tent.

One of the things that kept me from giving myself wholly over to misery and self-pity was my awareness of how my companions also struggled. Until the fire drove us forth, I had not realized how vital the warmth of their house was to counteracting their hibernation instinct. Deprived of that regular haven, they chewed enormous quantities of their stimulant leaf to remain alert. To complain of my own difficulty seemed like whinging in comparison—especially when I realized they did not *have* to suffer so much.

We could not wander the Sanctuary in this manner without travelling near other villages. They are widely spaced, as the region will not support a denser population, but we ranged far enough afield that we passed several other settlements. In each instance, Ruzt would lead me in a wide arc around, while Zam went in to speak with the inhabitants. My years in the field had given me some facility for moving with stealth, but I have never been in sharper practice than during that journey; for even when we were not near a village, we often had to be cautious of other caretakers leading their herds out to graze.

The significance of this all sank in after Zam came back from the second village bearing both food and a sullen expression. Her mutter to Ruzt, though too quiet for me to make out, sounded resentful.

In a fit of sudden clarity, I said, "You would be sleeping in the village, if I were not here."

(What I actually said was "You sleep in the village, if I am not here." Although by then I could converse passably well on our most common topics, I had not yet figured out either the conditional or subjunctive conjugations of their verbs.)

Zam glared at me. "Yes."

For once I had no doubt as to why she disliked me. "I am sorry," I said. Then, floundering for more words: "I will sleep alone in the tent. It will be all right."

This was sheer bravado, courtesy of my wish to mend fences with Zam. Ruzt shot it down without hesitation. "No, Zabel. We must—" The words that followed were incomprehensible to me; I had never heard them before. But when I asked for clarification, she brushed off my question and returned to the task at hand.

If I could not free them to rest warm and snug in someone else's house, then at least I could lend every last scrap of energy I had to hunting down the missing yaks. I suspect neither Ruzt nor Zam expected much on that front, though; they had brought me along only to ensure that none of the Draconeans helping Kahhe stumbled upon me by accident. Although by then I had been assisting in the yak barn for two months, I was still a novice herdswoman at best.

My lack went further than that, however. As I have said, the Draconeans use mews in their work, much as a Scirling shepherd uses a sheepdog. Suhail, Tom, and I had experimented with training the beasts in Hlamtse Rong during the monsoon, but our model had been that of falconry; the Draconean method is quite different. They employ neither jesses nor hoods, and direct the creatures with a complex series of whistled commands. Each pack of mews is paired with a specific herd of yaks, and is not much use in shepherding unfamiliar beasts.

How any of this was achieved quite perplexed me. Ruzt tried to explain, but we spent enough time attempting to circumlocute our way to simple agreement on what a word meant that digging deeper, into the actual concepts represented by those words, was beyond me. (At home, in a comfortably warm house, I might have managed it. Not with my brain frozen into a block of ice.) Even now it is a mystery. The customary explanation is that the rapport between Draconeans and mews is based on some kind of "shared draconic instinct"—but of course that is no explanation at all, any more than one can explain the survival of fish in water by recourse to some kind of "inherent piscine ability." Fish survive by means of gills; what the Draconeans use to create understanding between themselves and mews, I do not know.

Whatever it may be, I lack it utterly, and so I could not make use of the mews. I was not quite so useless as Zam expected me to be, though. One cannot spend one's lifetime tramping through every kind of wilderness the world has to offer in search of beasts without acquiring a modicum of tracking ability; and I had more than a modicum. I doubt I could follow a human or Draconean who sought to hide their passing, but yaks have no such subtlety.

I suspect I could track one even now, when my vision is far from what it used to be.

I therefore spent much of my time ranging away from my companions, identifying whether a given set of prints belonged to an errant herd or one being overseen by a Draconean from another village. When we located our beasts, Ruzt and Zam used the relevant pack of mews to round them up, and then Zam escorted yaks and mews alike back to Imsali. These were my coldest nights, especially as the task wore on: without Zam, and with the number of mews inside the tent dwindling steadily, there were many fewer bodies to heat the air inside.

One night while Zam was gone it began to snow again, and Ruzt resorted to sheltering in a small cave on the flanks of Anshakkar itself, that central mountain. (I call it central: in truth it is somewhat off-center, being closer to the eastern edge of the Sanctuary than the western.) There she built a fire, and erected the tent so that it stood between the flames and the outside air, with a gap for the smoke to escape. Without such precautions, I suspect I would have died that night—and even Ruzt might have gone to sleep, not to wake again until spring.

After we had finished eating, I spent some time examining one of the mews. Those bred by the Draconeans are noticeably more docile than their Tser-zhag cousins: an unsurprising difference, but what was its cause? Had the Draconeans tamed and domesticated wild mews, or were those outside the Sanctuary the feral descendants of escapees?

It was one of many questions I lacked the linguistic facility to ask. I confined myself to physical examination instead, which I had not had much leisure for in the preceding days. My recollection

of the mews Tom and I had dissected in Hlamtse Rong told me
the main alar artery was located in a different position on them
than it was on the Draconeans—in fact, it ran through a channel
in the bone, where I could not feel it with my fingertips. Holding
up the mew I had been studying, I asked Ruzt, "Do they close it?
In the wing, as you do."

She understood me, and circled her head in the motion they
used to indicate that the answer was neither yes nor no. "Not as
we do. They close . . . part of it? In the spring—" Her own wings
were partly spread to capture heat from the fire; now she tapped
one claw-tip against the membrane and made a dropping motion
with her hand.

The membrane of the mew's own wing had not felt especially
warm to my touch, nor especially cool; upon reflection, it was
about the same temperature as the surrounding air. The only
warmth I felt was contained along the wing's leading edge—as if
that were the only place where blood yet flowed.

"They *moult*," I said in fascination, staring at the mew. When I
tried to tug at its wing, it yowled indignantly and squirmed away.
Which is probably just as well; I later saw a fight between rival
packs of mews, in which one tore the membrane of the other's
wing clean off. I might have done the same by accident. They do
indeed moult when spring comes, growing in new membrane to
replace the old. It is an inconvenient time for the Draconeans, as
the mews are of no use whatsoever during that time; and indeed
they are of decreasing use as the winter progresses, for they lose
maneuverability on account of both this adaptation and the
damage they may suffer without feeling it.

I made a halfhearted attempt to catch a second mew in my

hands, but they were having none of it, and I lacked the energy to pursue them further. Ruzt watched this entire process in silence; then, when I was settled once more, she said, "Why do you ask these questions?"

Never in my life have I been so ill equipped to answer that query. It is hard enough when I must explain myself in my native tongue; in Draconean, I could barely string together an entire sentence that was not about yaks. Floundering, I said, "It is . . . what I do. I—" At every turn, I ran up against the limits of my vocabulary. "Begin to know? As I begin to know these words."

"*Azkant,*" Ruzt said.

I hoped that was indeed the word for "to learn." It was recognizable as a verb, at least; but I had on previous occasions thought I was asking for one word, only to discover later that Ruzt, misunderstanding, had supplied me with a different one. "I learn about . . . mews. And other animals." I had not realized before now that I had no general word for "dragons." There were none in the Sanctuary save the mews and the Draconeans themselves. The next time I had an opportunity to draw, I would sketch a variety of other breeds—rock-wyrms, desert drakes, queztalcoatls—and see whether Ruzt had a word that encompassed them all. She might well not. Her ancient ancestors might have created enough breeds to need such a term, but here in the Sanctuary, such a thing would fall into disuse and be forgotten.

Ruzt was clearly still confused. "As you herd yaks," I said. "I learn about animals. It is what I do."

My sentences were clear; my calling was not. There were no universities in the Sanctuary, no intellectual societies of scientists who pursued knowledge regardless of practical use, any more than there were in Hlamtse Rong or Keonga or Mouleen. I might as well have said it was my profession to load myself into a cannon and shoot myself to the moon: that would have been equally beyond her ken. And I had neither the will nor the words to try and explain. We bedded down without carrying the thought further, and did our best to sleep.

When I woke the next morning, the only thing that persuaded me to leave my blanket was the knowledge that I would be warmer if I moved around. Ruzt was sluggish as well, and we, by unspoken agreement, left our belongings where they lay. If the next night was anything like the previous, we would need the cave's shelter again. If it were not . . . then we would be glad of a more comfortable night we did not have to walk very far to obtain.

Once outside, we separated and began to search. The terrain there was not so fierce as to pose a danger to either of us; if it were, the yaks would not have been as likely to venture into onto Anshakkar's flanks. Unfortunately for us, it was a sighting the previous day that had led us here, not tracks, and so all we could do was quarter the area in the hope of stumbling upon some further hint of their presence.

Had the night not been so bitter, I suspect Ruzt would have sent me in the opposite direction from the one she chose—but her brain was not working as swiftly as usual.

I headed up a small ridge, thinking it would give me a good vantage point from which to survey the area. It is a mark of what effect the Mrtyahaima has on a person that I thought of the ridge as "small"; at home it would have been a good stiff hike. I shambled up it like an automaton, hunched in on myself against the cold, until I neared the ridge's crest. There the morning sunlight found me, and I opened up like a timid flower, uncurling the tiniest bit to see if it was safe.

Earlier in this text I said that my awareness of how my Draconean companions suffered in the cold was one of the things that kept me from sinking entirely into my own misery and self-pity. The sight that greeted me atop that ridge was another.

Throughout the Mrtyahaima there are stories of a secluded mountain paradise. The nature of this paradise varies from place to place; in some regions it is the abode of the gods, in others it is the afterlife, and in some—though I did not know this until later—it is the bastion of some lost, idyllic civilization. I will not claim the Sanctuary was a paradise in the true sense of the word, and certainly it was neither divine nor idyllic . . . but its beauty I cannot deny. And from my vantage point I could take it in, from the encircling ring of mountains to the peak of Anshakkar towering above me, from the stony cliffs to the river that vanished into a steep-sided gorge, from the snow-coated trees to the flatter areas I suspected would be fields after the thaw. It was a wonderland of ice and snow, and so sublime was the vista that I forgot, for a few blessed moments, how cold I was.

What recalled me to myself was the realization that I was standing like some kind of brave explorer posing for her portrait—and that, in so doing, I had made myself quite visible atop that ridge. Even if there were no Draconeans nearby save Ruzt, this was not the wisest thing I could have done, and I hastily crouched to reduce my profile.

The shift in posture made me notice something else. The way

up to the ridge had been a real scramble in places, but that was because I had chosen to take the most direct route to its top, rather than circling around to come at it from a lower point. Had I done so, the way would have been remarkably easy: the crest of the ridge was broad enough for at least five people to walk abreast, and quite flat.

Suspiciously so. It was too heavily shrouded in snow for me to examine its surface, but the manner in which it rose from the valley floor looked a great deal like a road.

And a road, of course, must lead somewhere.

As if I were a puppet and Curiosity herself pulling my strings, I turned to look in the other direction, up the slopes of Anshakkar.

There could be no doubt. It *was* a road, rising along a ramp either natural or Draconean-made; and although I could not properly see its end, something about the shape of the mountainside up ahead struck me as less than entirely natural.

I cast a quick glance about. Ruzt was not in sight, having gone in the other direction around that particular flank of Anshakkar; in the distance I could see smoke from one of the villages we had passed, but no one moving about. Inconveniently, no yaks had made their way up the road, which might have given me an excuse—

—but there were some yaks grazing not far off, on the other side of the road.

Wrestling one of the cows away from her herd and up the road was not so easily done, but I persevered. I knew, of course, that I should likely not be climbing Anshakkar to see what was there. If Ruzt wanted me to know, she would have brought me there herself. But the joy of discovery was my sustenance, when everything else in my life had been taken from me; and I did not have it in me to turn around and walk away. This way, at least, if anyone asked why I had gone there, I could say truthfully (if incompletely) that I was following a yak.

The beast finally received my messages and trudged up the road. The path was steep, but not arduously so, curving through a series of lacets that snaked their way up the mountain's face. I could see my destination long before I reached it, but only in tantalizing glimpses of some monumental entrance, its lower parts blocked from view by the remainder of my route. Above that I thought I glimpsed something else, but it was even more difficult to see.

My wind had improved greatly since I first woke up in the sisters' house, as had my injured leg. When at last I reached the road's end, I was breathing hard, but not gasping. If my breath faltered, it was for the sight in front of me, and no physical weakness on my part.

The entrance carved into the mountainside looked like it belonged to the ancient world—and yet not quite. I could see the heritage of the Draconeans in the flaring, leaf-like capitals of the pillars which flanked the doors, but their bases were much wider than those I had seen elsewhere in the world, and no inscriptions marked their sides. The lintel above would have borne an intricate frieze if this place were in the Labyrinth of Drakes; here it showed only an abstract, geometric pattern, akin to those I had seen on pots and wooden implements in Imsali. And the doors—well, it is unfair to say how the doors compared, for the only surviving doors from ancient times I had ever seen were those in the Watchers' Heart. But these were heavy and bound with corroded bronze, as if to hold out winter's presence.

Had it been necessary to swing open one of those enormous portals, I would never have gone inside. The snow blanketing the flat, courtyard-like area in front of the doors was not terribly thick, on account of the continual wind, but it was still enough to hamper the swing of a door; and these were large enough that I would have had difficulty moving one even at the height of summer. But set into one of the doors was a smaller gate, such as one often sees in the main entrances of large Anthiopean tabernacles, through which an individual can pass without troubling to open the entire thing. And when I put my hand to this little door, it shifted.

Whatever this place was, I knew I should not be there. If anyone caught me, I might find myself in a great deal of well-deserved trouble.

But I had not forgotten the day I drew pictures on the wall of the yak barn. Kahhe, I thought, had suggested bringing me here, or at least telling me about this place; she had nodded her head in the direction of Anshakkar, and the mere suggestion had enraged Zam. I could only guess at what Kahhe thought to achieve—but knowledge was power, and right now I sadly lacked that resource. Sooner or later my life here would change, and if I went into that transition blind, I did not like my chances. However much I trusted Ruzt and her sisters, I did not want to leave myself wholly at their mercy.

I looked at the yak, who was ambling around nosing into the snow, as if wondering why I had brought her to a place with no grass. "No one will believe I chased you inside," I said to her. She flicked one disinterested ear. "But I am not willing to relinquish you, either. Therefore, you will have to stay out here."

There were five posts in the forecourt, whose purpose was no doubt ritual in some way or another. I tethered the yak to one of these. Then, before I could let myself think the better of it, I hauled the door open far enough to admit me and slipped inside.

# THIRTEEN

*The temple—A discovery upstairs—Exploration—*
*The trespasser found—Images of the past—Nowhere to run*

The interior was quite dim, but not wholly dark. Several unglazed openings above the entrance admitted both light and a small quantity of snow to the chamber beyond. These gave enough illumination for me to identify freestanding braziers around the edges of the room, with small objects set on shelves built between the legs of the braziers. When I bent to examine one of these, I found it was a lamp—much like those I had been using these past two months, but more finely made. The yak butter within was solidified, but kindling sat in the brazier above, bone dry. It was the work of a mere moment to light the brazier, and then I held one of the lamps above it to warm while I looked at my surroundings.

We humans have long been prone to identifying every impressive Draconean site as a temple, but I had no doubt that I stood in the antechamber of a holy place. Historically speaking, there are two types of buildings to which people will devote great amounts of labour: the religious and the kingly. It was possible the Draconeans of the Sanctuary had a king or equivalent ruler, but the remote location of this place did not lend itself to political use. This was, of course, assuming that Draconean motivations were like those of humans—but my experiences with Ruzt, Kahhe, and Zam gave me moderate confidence that their ways were not so alien as that.

The walls of this antechamber were richly decorated, in elaborate circular patterns reminiscent of the mandalas found in many Dajin countries, but different in style. Their meaning was opaque to me: I could recognize that it must be there, for nestled among the spirals and geometric figures were repeated symbols, but they could have signified anything. Each was painted in vivid colour, predominantly yellow, blue, and white, with rare touches of red. The artist in me wished to examine these more closely, because I was curious about the pigments they used; surely the Draconeans did not trade with the outside world to obtain the necessary materials. But the white and yellow might be derived from lead-based minerals, and the blue . . . copper? Cobalt? There might even be lapis deposits in the region; certainly they were known elsewhere in the Mrtyahaima.

I shook myself from my trance. The yak butter had warmed enough for me to light my lamp; with that in hand, I set forth to investigate.

Three different paths lay before me. Staircases ascended from the right and left corners of the entry hall; between them stood a pair of doors, almost as large as those through which I had come, but much more elaborately carved. I suspected they would be easier to move, for they were not a tenth so weathered as their exterior brethren, but for the time being I chose to leave them untouched. Instead I took the right-hand staircase upward.

Partway up this lengthy, spiral path, I realized why the climb was so fatiguing: the steps had not been cut for human legs. The Draconeans I knew were all a good thirty centimeters taller than me, and their legs were long to match; this meant that a comfortable step upward for them was a heave for someone my size. "I feel like a child again," I grumbled to myself—and then snapped my mouth shut as if I could somehow swallow my words.

For as I spoke, I came around the final curve and found myself at the periphery of a large, open room ... which was full of sleeping Draconeans.

Their tidy ranks stretched far beyond the reach of my puny lamp. But here, too, clerestory windows admitted dim light from without, disclosing lines of bodies that carpeted the floor from one wall to the other. Had I come up here without a lamp, I might have trod upon the nearest before I noticed they were there.

I stood as motionless as a mouse under the gaze of a hawk. Had my voice disturbed them? The unsteady light of my lamp (unsteady in part because of my trembling hand) made it seem as if those close to me were moving, but I steeled my nerves and did not bolt. Long moments passed. In time I realized that I was holding my breath, and made myself expel it quietly. No one had shifted or made any sound. I was, for the moment, safe.

And I had found the remainder of the Draconeans. Whether this was everyone who dwelt in the Sanctuary, I could not say; the room stretched back into the mountain, farther than either lamp or windows could show me, and I was not about to risk tiptoeing between them just to see. Certainly there were hundreds of them. For the first time, I found myself wondering about the size of the population here—were they in danger of inbreeding? But developmental lability might help to mitigate that issue; I had no idea one way or another, though it was an intriguing question to investigate later. It also helped to steady me. Very well, then: they hibernated, as I had surmised. Bars made a lattice of the clerestory openings, and below I could make out larger windows, shuttered and barred. Why both, the former open and the latter closed? Regulation of light, perhaps, while still admitting a quantity of cold air, which no doubt helped to keep them asleep.

I was very grateful for the cold air.

One careful movement at a time, I crept back downstairs. Brief investigation of the staircase on the other side of the entry showed me that, as I suspected, it led to the same place. For ritual reasons? Or practical ones? (Were I a Draconean, I would not have wanted to face the lengthy queues that would result from everyone there trying to ascend or descend by a single route.) Had Kahhe intended to bring me to that chamber? Wake someone inside? Or perhaps some other purpose altogether; I had not yet explored the entire place. I therefore turned my attention to the great carved doors.

I was glad to see that the hinges of these were well oiled—I was still thinking of the sleeping Draconeans, though it was doubtful that a squeaky hinge would be enough to rouse them from their seasonal slumber. The handles were two large brass rings, still bright gold, in contrast with the green patina on the fittings of the exterior doors. Telling myself that it was unlikely to budge, I gripped one and pulled.

Many thousands of years had passed since the construction of the Watchers' Heart, but the Draconeans either had not forgotten the techniques of hanging an exceedingly heavy door, or had rediscovered them. It swung open far more easily than I expected.

"Well," I murmured to myself in a near-soundless voice, "hanged for a fleece, hanged for a yak."

Once again, my tiny lamp did not throw its light very far, and the small windows of the entry hall were no help at all beyond this threshold. But reflective flickers answered my lamp from all around the room; the nearest, to my right, was another brazier. Holding my breath—a foolish impulse, but difficult to quash—I lit the oil inside.

Colour sprang to life all around me. This room too was painted, with more of those mandala-like designs, interspersed with elements I suspected were purely decorative. But the image that dominated the room was familiar to me from Draconean sites: a circular disc, from which extended two stylized wings. Where it is found painted upon walls, that disc is invariably yellow, but here, as in the hidden chamber of the Watchers' Heart, it was made of hammered gold.

Our best theories said the disc represented the sun, though why it should be winged, no one knew. Equipped with my knowledge that dragon-headed people were real, I found myself re-evaluating the basis of Draconean religion: was the sun itself perhaps what they worshipped? The winged disc often held a central place at any site, either hovering over Draconean figures, or on its own. Then again, real Draconeans did not rule out the possibility of mythical ones as well. After all, human religions have often depicted the gods as human in shape. Moreover, I had no certainty that the faith practiced here was the same as that which had prevailed when the Draconeans reigned over a worldwide civilization. Indeed, I should be surprised if it had *not* undergone changes.

With a wry smile, I added "religion" to the list of topics I must broach with the sisters when time and vocabulary permitted. The list was approximately a thousand items long, and grew with every passing day.

I turned my attention once more to my surroundings. The chamber was large, but not large enough to accommodate together all the Draconeans I had seen upstairs. Its furnishings were sparse. The reflections I had seen were from the winged disc and the gold tracery adorning the braziers, all of which had been polished to a mirror sheen. Finely carved benches occupied part of the floor, but not all. Beneath the sun disc stood what I presumed was an altar, with what appeared to be offerings. Approaching, I found branches of greenery and a bowl of seeds. The former were still springy to the touch; they could not have been cut more than a day or two before.

Which meant that someone visited this place during the winter. Did the temple, too, have a caretaker? Or did the wakeful herdswomen come to pay their respects?

Either way, it meant I should not linger. I had already been longer in the temple than I intended; I should collect my yak and go. But there were curtained openings off the central room, two flanking the altar, several along the side walls, and I could not depart without at least glancing inside. I pulled aside one of the curtains near the entrance and found a corridor behind, hewn, like the rest of the temple, from the living rock of the mountain.

(It did occur to me to wonder if this place, like the Watchers' Heart, had any hidden doors. But I could hardly spare the time to

*Hibernation*

hunt for such a thing, especially when I had no clues to guide me, such as we had enjoyed during our search in the Labyrinth.)

The corridor led me on a short way before debouching into a smaller room. A mandala adorned one wall, but this one was different; a Draconean figure dominated the center of the design. I could not help but evaluate it with an artist's eye, noting the similarities to ancient art as well as the changes. A great deal of time had passed since the height of their civilization, but religious artwork is often highly conservative, harkening back to the styles and motifs of one's forebears. Gone was the strange perspective which depicted figures in a combination of profile and facing stances, but the Draconean still adopted a familiar posture, striding forward with its hands at its sides.

I caught myself thinking of the figure as "it," and shook my head. "Truly," I murmured under my breath, "I *must* contrive a way to see some male Draconeans." Thus far I had no data on sexual dimorphism among their kind. Certainly the sisters had no breasts, which was only to be expected among organisms that laid eggs. (Monotremes notwithstanding—that is to say, the platypus and certain kinds of echidna—mammals are not generally oviparous.) There might well be some males upstairs, but I did not quite dare to go back up and search for them.

Indeed, I should have departed already. With one last glance about the room, I hurried back down the corridor, my little lamp flickering with my speed.

When I flung the curtain aside, two Draconeans spun to face me.

*    *    *

Ruzt leapt forward, clapping one hand over my mouth. She needn't have bothered: by then the instinct to remain quiet was deeply ingrained in me. I sagged in boneless relief, for it was only Ruzt and Zam, not strangers, who had come upon me.

My relief did not last long.

Zam wrenched me from Ruzt's grasp, snarling. I had seen the sisters confront their neighbours who came begging; I had never seen one in a true fury before. Her ruff stood up high, her wings spread, and her lips peeled back to expose her formidable teeth. The words she spat at her sister and myself were too gutteral for me to have any hope of making them out, but I could guess at their meaning: she was enraged that I had trespassed upon their holy place.

My reasoning in entering the temple was sound. But reasoning is of very little use when faced with a sight like that; guilt and fear came down upon me in equal quantities. I could only babble apologies in my broken Draconean: "I think no bad" was the closest I could come to "I meant no harm." But "I am sorry" came easily to my tongue, for it was a phrase I had used a thousand times before, albeit never with such heartfelt fervor.

Zam was not mollified. She divided her snarls between me and her sister. When Ruzt stepped forward, hands outstretched, Zam hurled me toward the altar. I had seen her lift heavy sacks of feed, but had never been on the receiving end of that strength before. I was briefly airborne; then I struck a bench and went sprawling. Instinct told me to stay down, to appear as contrite and unthreatening as possible. Zam disliked me; Zam had feared me from the start. Now she could kill me with one swipe of those claws.

When she seized me again, all the restraint in the world could not keep me from yelping. Zam dragged me to my feet and shoved me forward, in the manner of one marching a prisoner to execution. But a swift, terrified glance showed me that Ruzt was re-lighting my fallen lamp and following along behind. Surely I could trust her to protect me, if Zam had decided upon my death? I did not know. Perhaps she had concluded that this enterprise was a failure, that they never should have troubled themselves to rescue a human from the snow. Our legends and Scripture were filled with tales of murderous Draconean rituals, and a part of me expected to be the victim of one now.

Zam shoved me through the opening to the left of the altar. I did not expect stairs, and half fell down several of them, catching myself against the walls. When Ruzt passed through the curtain, providing a pittance of light, I saw the path led downward in a spiral much like the one I had followed upstairs. More hibernating Draconeans? The ruler of this place, who would decide my fate?

Neither. Reaching the bottom of the steps, I stumbled into another small room, this one painted with murals in a much older style.

Zam took me by the scruff of the neck and spat out the first intelligible word I'd heard from her that day. *"Look."*

I would have looked even if she had not forced me to. The murals were crude imitations of those I had seen in the Watchers' Heart, but I could follow their meaning clearly enough. On the right, which was the customary beginning for Draconean sequences, adoring humans knelt at the feet of a splendid dragon-headed figure, who dispensed livestock, baskets of grain, and other largess to its subjects. But this was soon followed by scenes of strife: layered bands in which humans turned their backs on pleading Draconeans and set fire to buildings or killed cattle in pointless slaughter. Warfare ensued.

"This is the past," I whispered, heedless of which language I was speaking. It might have been Akhian; it might have been Scirling. I cannot recall. "The past as you remember it." Their account differed from ours rather a lot: Segulist and Amaneen scriptures tell of tyrannical rulers who lived in decadence and oppressed their subjects until the Lord's prophets led the people to overthrow them. Stories in other parts of the world have their own variations on that theme.

The central image dominating the back wall also have parallels in our tales, though I had never thought to connect my own evidence to them. Human figures, now grown monstrously large, poured black liquid over a field of eggs. Inside the shells, tiny Draconean figures in postures of agony turned to grey stone.

My knees gave out from beneath me, and Zam let me fall.

The eggs on Rahuahane. I had wondered at the process that petrified them, turning the albumen to the gem we call firestone. We found that gem in so many places worldwide, often associated with Draconean sites . . . I had not thought it through, because my attention was on the disintegrated embryos, not the matrix that once held them. Why so much firestone? Why so many petrified eggs?

Because ancient humans had poisoned them. They had found some compound that, when poured over the eggs, induced a fatal change of state. It was the slaughter of the children from Scripture, the punishment the Lord levied upon those ancient tyrants for their sins. It was the Keongan hero Lo'alama'oiri, travelling to the cursed isle of Rahuahane and turning the *naka'i* to stone.

We had done that—we humans. Our ancestors had massacred unborn Draconeans in untold numbers.

Zam left me there on the floor. It was by my own will that I turned to see the end of the tale: weeping Draconeans, murdered by humans, or fleeing in terror. Retreating into mountains, hiding. The Sanctuary in which they now resided.

No wonder Zam feared me. No wonder the sisters were so determined to keep me out of sight. I was the monster of their myths: a human being, a vicious, merciless beast. Never mind that they towered thirty centimeters over me and had teeth and claws I could not hope to match. We fear poisonous snakes a hundredth our size, for they can kill us in an instant.

Were the Draconeans' eggs hidden somewhere in this temple? Did Zam think I had come here to turn them to stone?

I had to choose my words with exquisite care. I could not let my distress hamper my speech; Zam was clearly in no mood to wait while misunderstandings were sorted out. Three breaths were necessary to steady me: then, still kneeling upon the floor, I turned to face the two sisters.

"I am sorry for this," I said, indicating the story upon the walls. Now was not the time to quibble over historical interpretation, to debate whether the ancient Draconeans had been loving rulers or hideous tyrants. We had slaughtered their children; I was indeed sorry for that. "We now—humans—" I had to use the Akhian word; I did not know what the Draconeans called us. Likely nothing flattering. "We do not know about this—about *you*. We have forgotten. I do not want to hurt you. No one wants to hurt you."

That last was only true because no one knew about them, not

*The Downfall*

as anything other than vague ice demons defending the borders
of the Sanctuary. I could not blame them for hiding.

I looked at Ruzt. Zam could not be reasoned with right now; I
could barely speak with her, given the archaic cast of the words I
had learned. But Ruzt, I thought, was the mastermind of this
entire scheme, the decision to hide me away and teach me to
speak. "Why?" I asked. "If I am this—" I gestured at the walls
again. "Why did you take me into your house?"

It was the question I had been wanting to ask them since I
awoke. I had avoided it until now because I did not trust my
command of the language to carry me through so complex a
matter; but now I felt I had no choice.

Ruzt, I think, had delayed for the same reason. Now she
paused, clearly choosing her own words carefully, so that I would
understand. Finally she pointed at the leftmost panels and said,
"For a long time we have run. Humans come, and we hide.
Humans come again, and we hide again. Now we are here—
where else can we go? Are there others? Like us?"

Isolated in the Sanctuary for who knew how many years, decades, centuries . . . if there were other enclaves, they would long
since have lost contact with them. My answer came in a whisper.
"I do not think so."

Ruzt bowed her head. "As we thought. Then—we are the last.
When humans try to come here, we defend ourselves. One here,
two there. Not many. But we watch, because what if one day there
are more?"

It would happen, inevitably. The Sanctuary was too inaccessible
to be worth settlement by anyone who did not want to hide—but
sooner or later a human would escape their border guardians and

bring tales of dragon-headed beasts to the outside world. Most would laugh at the notion, but not all . . . and then more would come, and more, until someone showed up with an army. And then the Draconeans would have nowhere left to run.

The sisters had saved my life as an experiment. To see whether a human could be reasoned with.

I must, on peril of my life, be reasonable.

"Humans will find you," I said, employing the word I had heard her use. It was not related to its Akhian counterpart, and I wondered what root it derived from. "Murderer," perhaps. "You are right. I wish it were not so, but . . ." Explaining the Aerial War was beyond me. Ruzt did not need it, though; she nodded in resignation.

Slowly, keeping Zam in my peripheral vision, I stood. She still watched me with hostility, but made no move to strike. She had brought me here to confront me with my people's crimes, not to kill me.

Addressing both her and Ruzt, I said, "You have my help. What can I do?"

# PART FOUR

*In which matters
become exceedingly complicated*

# FOURTEEN

*Plans for the future—How I was found—A change of perspective—*
*Caring for Draconean eggs—*
*Origin stories—Politics*

Once the last of the scattered beasts had been collected and I returned with Ruzt and Zam to Imsali, I had cause to be glad that my yak-herding vocabulary was by that point quite well developed. We no longer devoted more than the bare minimum of our attention to such chores; all our efforts were bent to a different set of topics.

Ruzt's plan, as she explained it to me, was frighteningly simple—and I was certain it was *her* plan, though she always spoke of it in the plural, as something she, Kahhe, and Zam had developed together. They would keep me concealed until spring, when the hibernating Draconeans awoke . . . and then they would reveal my presence, using me as proof that humans were reasonable creatures with whom the Draconeans could attain peace. Between now and then, my chief task was to prepare for the discussions that would ensue.

"What if I am not ready by then?" I asked.

Zam glared at me. Kahhe laughed, though she did not sound amused, and said, "Be ready."

It would not do to keep me hidden longer, even if I were insufficiently prepared. The sisters had been able to manage it before because everyone else in the village was making arrangements for their winter sleep; the day they left me with Zam was the day they went out and persuaded the villagers who had drawn the short straw that year to let the three of them take over the task of caring for the herds. (I doubt it took much persuasion. Remaining awake was considered an unpleasant duty, and while Imsali settled this by the democratic means of drawing lots, I later heard that other villages fobbed it off on whomever was least popular among them. Fortunately there was a law that said no one could take on that burden two years running, as winter wakefulness was considered detrimental to their health.)

But once the Draconeans awoke, I could not long remain concealed in the sisters' house. I must sally forth, ready or not, and represent my entire species to those who dwelt within the Sanctuary of Wings.

For it was not only myself who called that place the Sanctuary. That was the Draconean name for it as well: in their tongue, *Sratar Vrey,* the Sanctuary of Wings. "Anevrai," I said to Ruzt when she taught me the phrase. "That is how we have been saying the name of your people—at least, we believe that word refers to your people. But you do not call yourselves that." The word I had learned for the Draconeans was *mranin,* which clearly came from a different root.

"It is a very old word," she said. "For those who ruled in ancient days. We have not gone by that name since the Downfall."

She paused, remembering. "You said that to me once before, didn't you? When you woke up. I was so nervous—I didn't even recognize it. You pronounced it so strangely."

I could not conceive of what that must have been like: rescuing a dying monster in the hope that she might prove a friend. "How did you come upon me? I have been meaning to ask for ages, only I did not know how."

This was something of a fib. I could have managed, if I were determined—as I was managing now, for you must not imagine that my conversations were as simple and straightforward as I am presenting them here. Circumlocution and mime were still my frequent tools, along with my charcoal drawings, whenever I could not come directly at my target. I had allowed the difficulty to turn aside my curiosity because thinking about that day would remind me of too many things I did not wish to dwell on: the avalanche, and the unknown fate of my companions.

But I had a better heart for it now, and so I asked. Ruzt said, "We are watchers, the three of us—we look for signs of humans at our borders."

"Do you cross the mountains?" I said, intrigued.

"We used to. We stopped years ago."

The Nying had pushed almost to the limits of possible habitation, short of entering the Sanctuary itself. Patrolling outside the ring of mountains risked beginning the confrontation the Draconeans had striven so long to avoid. "But you saw me?"

"We saw two humans," she said. "Up there." I followed her pointing claw to the col; the day was sunny and nearly cloudless, which made it look only a short stroll away. Tom and I had ventured a little distance to the west when we first stepped out, so as to look down into the valley beyond. Likely it was the two of us whom Ruzt saw.

But a great deal of time had passed between that moment and when I stumbled half dead down the western slope, not to mention a storm. "Were you watching us dig?" Even though the sisters were now my friends—two of them, at least; I was not certain I should count Zam as such—the thought of them spying on us from concealment was unsettling.

Ruzt denied it. "Zam insisted that we collect our weapons first. And we argued. As we were climbing, the mountain came down, and she said you must all be dead. But we agreed to search before we gave up."

"I was very lucky that you did," I murmured. "I should certainly have died otherwise." At no point had the sisters carried weapons in my sight. Where did they keep them? What did they arm themselves with? Not firearms, I suspected; I had observed nothing in the Sanctuary that led me to believe the Draconeans had the technology to manufacture anything so complex. Bows and arrows? Swords? I was surprised Zam had not insisted on arming herself around me, every waking and sleeping minute.

As it turned out, I was not the only one who had been sitting on her curiosity. "Zabel," Ruzt said, "why were you *there*? You do not live here."

She did not mean in the Sanctuary. My pictures and attempts at storytelling had made it clear to them that I hailed from a more distant land—and of course they had seen the Nying from a distance, and knew I was no kin of theirs. But I suspected that my rough charcoal attempts to sketch dead Draconeans in the snow had not made much of an impression when I scrawled them on the plastered wall of the yak barn.

To answer her, I made more drawings, these of a wide array of draconic creatures: everything from drakeflies to desert drakes, swamp-wyrms and *tê lêng* and fire lizards. "These are all dragons," I said, giving her the Akhian word, and resuming the conversation we had abandoned that night in the cave, when I was examining the wings of a mew. "As all birds are birds, but different kinds. Does that make sense?" Ruzt nodded. "My task is to understand dragons: that is what I do for my people. I have been doing it for most of my life. We believed . . ." I hesitated, searching for the correct words. "There are many . . . places in the world, like your temple, but old and fallen down."

"Ruined."

"Yes, ruined. From the days of the Anevrai. There are pictures of the Anevrai in those places, but we did not understand them; we thought they showed—" Here I floundered, for I lacked the word for "gods." Rather than fall down the pit of religion, I merely said, "We thought there were no such things, outside of the mind. We did not know *you* existed."

Ruzt pulled back in startlement. "You—did not know we were here?"

"Not at all. When I woke up and saw you, I was very surprised!" I could laugh about it now, with my delirium and terror so far behind me.

This was so astonishing to Ruzt that she insisted on sharing it with Kahhe and Zam before we went any further. Zam stared at me, frankly incredulous. "It is true!" I kept insisting. Then the sisters retired for a conference—not, I think, because they wished to keep their discussion secret from me, but because they did not want to slow themselves down for my sake. It was only then that I realized their plan had been predicated on the assumption that humans knew they were in the Sanctuary (or at the very least, that they existed), and had simply not bestirred themselves to wipe the remaining Draconeans out.

It did not change anything in the immediate term, of course. We were still waiting for spring, and I must still prepare. Ruzt and I returned to our interrupted conversation the next day. I told her, "I thought the Anevrai were human, and had bred some special kind of dragon for their own use. When a man named Thu Phim-lat told me he found a strange body out there, I wanted to see for myself what kind it was."

"A body of one of ours?" Ruzt said.

I described to her what we found in the col, how its bones had dissolved and its flesh frozen hard in the endless cold. "That was when we discovered that the Anevrai were not gods." I laughed, this time with a wry smile. "Just before the mountain fell down." We had not gotten around to establishing the word for "avalanche," I think because it amused us both to go on using that phrase. I did not even know how to say it in Akhian, as the word is not often needed in the desert.

Then my perspective changed, yet again. When we dug that Draconean out of the snow, I had seen it as a specimen: the carcass of a mysterious creature, hailing from a species unknown to us. But if Ruzt had become a person to me . . . then the carcass was the sad remains of another person, one who froze to death in the icy heights of the mountains.

In a quiet voice, I asked, "Do you know who they were? The two we found."

"I think so," Ruzt said. "Years ago—when I was only a hatchling—the rains came terribly late. The land was so dry, and there were fires . . . worse on the other side of the mountains, I think. We could see the smoke from here. The elders decided that we should keep a closer watch on our borders for some time after that. Two of the guards were lost in a storm, not long before the sleep."

"What were their names?"

My question clearly startled her, for her ruff twitched slightly. She said, "Seymel and Yaminet."

Thu had found one in the valley; the five of us had uncovered the other. I did not think we would ever know which was which. "What do you ordinarily do with your dead? Do you bury them, or burn them, or . . . ?"

Ruzt said, "They go to the sky."

At first I took this for a euphemism, much as we might say that a late relative has gone to a better place. But while the Draconean religion is indeed very oriented toward the sky, she meant it in a somewhat more literal sense. It is their custom to leave the bodies of the deceased out in the open, where scavenging birds may consume their flesh and carry it into the heavens—with the bones, of course, falling to dust.

It was some comfort, then, to think that the Draconean who fell from the col met with something like the treatment his people would have wanted. The other, I feared, had vanished beneath the snow; he might never be found again.

My mental phrasing snagged against another thought in passing. "These guards who were lost. Were they female, or male?"

"Female," Ruzt said, as if it were obvious. "None of our border watchers are male."

So I still had not seen a male Draconean, even one frozen and squashed flat. They had begun to acquire a mythical status in my mind, as if they were a fiction invented by female Draconeans to explain where hatchlings came from.

Male Draconeans were real enough, naturally, and I met some in due course. But such thoughts led me to inquire about reproduction—for one cannot be a naturalist without losing a great deal of the delicacy one is expected to have in speaking of such matters.

"I am not asking where your eggs are," I said hastily, thinking of Zam's hostility. She was not so wary of me as she had been; but she still did not entirely trust me, and I wished to avoid provoking her. "But I am curious—am I right in thinking you must be very careful of the conditions in which the eggs are kept?"

This was a thing that had perplexed me since I compared the hatching grounds on Rahuahane to those in the Labyrinth of Drakes. Given the sensitivity of draconic eggs, how could the Anevrai have bred their own species in such disparate environments?

Part of the answer went a long way toward explaining why we had long mistaken firestone for an ordinary mineral. Underground chambers enjoy far more stable temperatures than those above; though Ruzt did not say so, I felt certain the Draconeans of the Sanctuary incubated their offspring inside the mountains, insulated from the killing cold of the outside. Whether they had one hatching ground or several, and whether any of them were in that temple carved into the side of Anshakkar, I did not ask.

But however deeply one burrows into a mountain, the Mrtyahaima was not the Broken Sea. My error, I eventually realized, lay in thinking of the Draconeans as a uniform species, bereft of variation. This is not true of humans, who vary a great deal across the world; why should it be true of Ruzt's kind? Of course she had never seen her ancient kin, and had no proof of the ways in which island Draconeans had differed from those in the desert. But she agreed with me that such variation was quite likely, for she averred that too much warmth during incubation was "bad" for the resulting offspring. While cold in too great a degree killed them in the egg, heat might produce perfectly healthy hatchlings . . . who would then perish in their first hibernation.

My readers may also be wondering how they had maintained their hybrid nature, after countless generations cut off from all human contact. Many gruesome stories have circulated in answer to this question, all upon the theme of Dreadful Human Sacrifice: they kidnapped Tser-zhag and Nying and others from around their borders with which to feed their ravenous eggs; or they kept a stable of human slaves bred and slaughtered for that purpose. One especially unpleasant version of that latter said the last of their slaves died off not long before I arrived, and the entire scheme to use me as their ambassador came about because they needed to replenish their stock.

It is all nonsense, of course. The creation of the Draconeans before the dawn of their civilization may have required human blood—offered by ancient humans as part of their primitive rites—but once their population was established, they bred true. They had no need for special conditions to ensure a new generation of dragon-headed bipeds; they had only to protect their offspring against factors that might cause harmful mutation.

When I said something about this to Ruzt, though, I met with an odd reaction. It took me some time to find out why. Finally I asked her, "How do you believe your kind came to be?"

"How do you think *your* kind came to be?" she countered. I think she meant this partly as a challenge, for my questions had nettled her; but she also meant it as a way of ensuring she understood what I was asking.

It had the effect of making me realize the question was more complicated than I had thought. "We have many different stories to answer that," I said at last. "Religions around the world each tell their own—that the first humans were carved out of trees, that we were made from the body of a sacrificed god, that a bear became human after many long trials. The religion I was taught as a child says the first man was made from dirt, and the first woman from his rib. But people like me—scientists—" I used the Akhian word; it had no parallel in her tongue. "They have established that we descend from apes. Do you know apes? Or monkeys?"

She did not, as there were none in the Sanctuary or its surroundings. "They are very like humans," I said, for lack of any better description. "Much as mews are somewhat like you—though the differences there are much greater."

Ruzt accepted this, as if it were only natural. "Of course mews are like us. But your scientists are wrong. You do not descend from apes."

I could not restrain my eyebrows from shooting upward. "Oh? Where do we come from? And how do you know such things, when you have never spoken to a human before me?"

"Like mews, you descend from us," Ruzt said. "Draconeans were born of the sky: the sun's heat made wind, and the wind took solid form as four sisters, and the scales they shed became the mountains. The weight of the mountains dragged the sisters down, and they wept to lose their flight, which made the waters of the world. When they bathed for the first time, new creatures were made: the water of their mouths made the first brother, the water of their fronts made humans, and the water of their backs made dragons. We usually say mews, but I think it means the other kinds of dragons as well."

This tale astonished me enough that I was rendered temporarily mute. It had a certain poetic logic to it: the back, which featured both wings and larger, more prominent scales, was more obviously draconic, while the front, which had a more human configuration, bore a stronger resemblance to my own species. And her comment about the weight of the mountains dragging the sisters down almost sounded like a mythic explanation of gravity. As origin stories went, I quite liked it.

But not only was it scientifically inaccurate, it was not the tale I had seen depicted on the wall of an ancient Draconean temple.

"That is why you were the subjects of the Anevrai," Ruzt said, clearly reading my hesitation and disbelief. "Because you came from us."

One of the benefits of limited fluency is that one is forced to stop and consider one's words before speaking them. "The Anevrai told a different tale," I said at last. "I have been in an ancient hatching ground, one left untouched since the Downfall. It depicted a dragon egg being bathed in blood to create a Draconean. And my own research supports the notion: changes in the environment of an egg can provoke all manner of mutations, many of them detrimental, but some successful—such as a dragon-human hybrid."

(Rendering that argument into her tongue took approximately

eight times as long as it appears here.)

"But where did dragons come from, if not from us?" Ruzt was obviously skeptical.

"That is a very good question, and one I would like to answer. From some kind of reptilian relative, clearly—but when and how your unique mutability arose, I cannot say."

We argued a great deal over this in subsequent days. I was not surprised that Ruzt might have difficulty accepting the theory of evolution; she had never dreamt of such a thing before I spoke of it, and it was not well accepted when first introduced among humans, either. (Indeed, there are some who do not accept it today, despite an ever-growing body of evidence in support.) Challenging someone's deeply held beliefs is a difficult thing to do, for it threatens to tear away the foundations upon which they have always stood.

I think Ruzt would have dismissed my words out of hand were it not for the fact that I could cite Anevrai artwork to support my point. It was peculiar for me to realize that her forebears were almost as mythical to her as they were to me—though it should have been obvious that thousands of years, a cataclysm, and continual flight into ever more remote parts of the globe would not leave a culture unchanged. I had seen more of the remains left behind by her ancestors than she had. But however mistily they might be recalled, the Anevrai were a name to conjure with: if they had believed they came from the influence of human blood on dragon eggs, then perhaps it might be true.

(I had an unfortunate suspicion, as I debated this point with her, that my scientific query might wind up sparking a religious schism. Faiths have broken into warring camps over far less.)

You must not think, however, that we spent the remainder of the winter discussing ancient history and theology, or the finer scientific points of Draconean nature. By far the larger portion of our time was devoted to planning for what would happen when the others awoke.

Recalling with no little trepidation my past experiences in other lands, I made a point of inquiring as to the political arrangements of the Sanctuary. I discovered that each cluster of villages is led by a sister-group—by which I mean a set of female Draconeans, sometimes as few as two or as many as five, but usually three or four—hatched from the same clutch. (Daughters hatched from the same mother in other clutches are also considered sisters, but in a lesser degree; the Draconeans use a separate word for that relationship.) These leaders are joined by a single male, elected from among his brethren to advise them and govern certain aspects of society.

But when it comes to the Sanctuary as a whole, it is the opinion of the Draconeans that allowing a sister-group to rule together would be inadvisable, on account of the strength of the familial bond. They instead have a council of elder females, most of whom are advanced enough in years that their clutchmates have gone to the sky. This council likewise has a single male adviser; he is drawn from the ranks of the elected representatives, but wins his more elevated place through a strenuous competition against his peers.

This council was the governing body to which Ruzt intended to present me, for they were the only ones who could make decisions for the entire Sanctuary. When I heard this, I muttered to myself, "I hope I do not cause any of those venerable ladies to drop dead of an apoplexy."

As I have said, it was my habit there to speak Akhian when not attempting Draconean, because of the greater odds that Ruzt might comprehend a little of what I said. "Venerable" and "apoplexy" were much too arcane for that, but the word "dead" would certainly have come through; she gave me a sharp look. I waved it away. "Tell me how to behave so I will neither scare them nor give offense."

We had debates over that, too—or rather, Ruzt debated with Kahhe and Zam, for on that subject I was wholly uninformed. We shaped plans and discarded them, sometimes thrice a day. We more than once lamented the entire enterprise, and wished we had never embarked upon it—though in my case not seriously, as that would mean either that I had died in the snow, or that I had never come to the Mrtyahaima. I still did not know the full cost of that latter decision . . . but I could not, without proof of tragedy, bring myself to regret it.

But that did not mean the road ahead would be an easy one. As the days lengthened and grew imperceptibly warmer, my thoughts turned to the world outside the Sanctuary of Wings—a world that was not ready in the slightest to meet the surviving descendants of their ancient rulers.

Late at night, when the sisters were asleep, I lay in my nest of yak-wool blankets and stared at the embers of the fire, wrestling with an impossible question.

How could I keep them all from being killed?

# FIFTEEN

*The Draconeans awake—Meeting the elders—Back into the Sanctuary—
The opposition registers a protest*

The seasons would not slow their turning for my sake. Spring came at its own pace, heedless of my readiness or lack thereof; I counted down the days until the Draconeans awoke with far more trepidation than had attended my first wedding. After all, it was only my own future which would be secured by *that* day. What happened in the Sanctuary of Wings would affect a great many more people than myself.

My countdown was quite literal, for the day of waking was set. The temple had its own caretakers—I was fortunate in the extreme not to have encountered them—and at dawn on that day, they would go into the hibernation hall and throw open the shutters I had seen. The hall being aligned with the rising of the sun at that time of year, the great quantity of light thus admitted would act as a wake-up call, disturbing the sleep of the Draconeans enough that the ringing of an enormous gong at the back of the hall would rouse them. They would file downstairs, enjoy a great feast prepared by the other caretakers, and then return to their home villages.

"It takes *forever*," Kahhe said with feeling, when I inquired about the process. "The stairs are so narrow. And if you are at the back of the crowd, all the best food is gone by the time you get downstairs."

I appreciated her perspective, for it humanized the Draconeans for me—if that word is not inappropriate in this context. By then I was accustomed to thinking of my three hostesses in such terms, but I suspected I might lose hold of that thought when I was surrounded by a mob that was angry, frightened, or both.

At dawn on the day of waking, I went outside one last time, tipping my face up to the thin spring sun. We had agreed that it was best not to surprise a group of sleepy Draconeans with an unexpected human; rather we would allow them a few days to resume their normal lives before the sisters presented me. But that meant I would be confined to the house for the intervening time, and I was not looking forward to the wait.

In fact it was every bit as bad as I had feared. Although the weather had improved enough for the Draconeans to wake, it was still quite cold outside; one could reasonably expect that I would be glad of a reason to take refuge in the warmth of the sisters' house. After so much time spent out-of-doors, however, my enforced seclusion was positively suffocating. I missed the fresh air, and I missed the sunlight even more, weak though it still was.

My fretfulness grew with the onset of noise outside. Each village had a local ceremony to mark the return from hibernation; I did not dare peer out the exterior door to watch Imsali's, but the sound of drums, flutes, and singing came through regardless. Draconeans chattered as they went to and fro, asking what had happened to the yak barn, and the sounds produced both yearning and fear in me. Yearning because I had gone for such a long time with no company apart from the sisters—I was overwhelmed by a surge of loneliness and homesickness. My habit had been to keep such things at bay by focusing upon the challenges before me ... but waiting in the house, listening to the community outside, I missed my own with a longing so profound it was almost a physical pain. And thinking of the challenges that remained was no help, for that only brought on the fear.

I had more than enough fears to keep me occupied. Fear that someone would come inside, looking for one of the sisters, and I would not hide myself in time. Fear that Ruzt's optimism was misplaced, and her fellows would tear me limb from limb on sight: I have faced danger many a time, but it is always the most frightening to me when it comes from thinking, rational creatures.

Above all loomed the fear that I would fail the sisters who had saved my life. I would not win over their kin; or I would succeed there, and fail among my own kind.

I had agreed to three days' wait, but a part of me would gladly have run out the door and flung myself before the Draconeans with no warning whatsoever, simply to end the unbearable tension.

Instead I waited. For while I may not be a patient woman, I am quite good at pigheaded determination. I had agreed to three days. And so we passed the time, myself, Ruzt, Kahhe, and Zam, waiting for the world to change.

"Are you ready?" Ruzt inquired.

"That may be the most absurd question anyone has ever asked me," I said. In Akhian, which meant she understood very little of it; but my tone was clear enough.

I was dressed in clothing we had made during the winter—for you must not imagine my mountaineering garb would have survived a whole season's wear without suffering quite a bit, and I would need it when I left the Sanctuary. We had debated the merits of dressing me in my own clothing for this occasion, but ultimately Kahhe's argument had prevailed, that I would be less intimidating if clad in the familiar furs and yak wool of their own people. My body was sweltering inside the layers, for it was warm inside the house, but my hands and feet were cold with apprehension.

Zam had brought the word just a little while before: the council of elders was in Imsali. Ruzt had gone to speak with the temple caretakers more than a week ago, begging the council's presence today; the message was given to them when they woke, and it seemed they had complied. Nine elderly female Draconeans waited for me outside, all without knowing what they waited for.

Nine elderly female Draconeans—and the entire population of Imsali, who must be wondering what the sisters were up to.

I forced my thoughts into the Draconean tongue. "Waiting will not make me more ready."

Ruzt nodded. I found myself noting her posture and body language, filing it away under "nervousness, Draconean, signs of." Such things are soothing to me, at moments like that.

Ruzt opened the door and led me outside.

Sunlight and cold air came in from the exterior door. Through the gap I could see a crowd of Draconeans, tall and small, waiting. One of them—a juvenile, judging by size—spotted me as I passed through the darkness of the antechamber, and tapped at an adult's thigh in an unmistakable gesture. Though I could not hear the words through the roaring in my ears, I knew what they must be:

"Mama, what's that?" Or at least the Draconean equivalent.

I stepped into view, and the world went silent.

My imagination supplied a thousand Draconeans. In truth, there were less than a hundred. But when every last eye is upon you, the number seems far greater; and then, like a blow, I heard someone hiss a recognizable Draconean word: "*Human.*"

Silence broke, and pandemonium reigned.


The sisters bracketed me in a triangle. They had anticipated the rush of bodies that would occur, as the more energetic and warlike of their kin leapt to defend the council from my small, winter-starved self. Zam, who had once seized me and thrown me across the temple, bodily checked another Draconean who seemed bent on doing the same. Ruzt was shouting, her wings furled and her hands raised high. Kahhe stood ready to hurl me back through the doorway if necessary, where they could more easily guard me against attack.

But it was not necessary. One of the elders snapped her wings open, then another; the rest followed suit in short order. As if that were a gavel pounded upon a judge's bench, the crowd fell into a muttering hush, and then quiet. A crisp order from one of the elders sent the various Draconeans back to their places, restoring the empty space that had surrounded my entrance.

I judged this the right time to speak. I had no wings to wrap around my body, but I performed the human approximation, laying both my hands atop my breast in the Draconean gesture of respect. Raising my voice, I spoke the words I had painstakingly rehearsed with the sisters. Only a faint tremor marred them.

"May the sun bless you and keep you warm. My name is Isabella, and I mean you no harm. I owe my life to these three sisters, who rescued me from certain death in the mountains. If it meets with the approval of you nine, the revered elders of the Sanctuary, I would like to repay their generosity and kindness by assisting your people in any way I can."

My listeners could not have been more astonished had one of their yaks reared up on its hind legs and begun speaking. The only sounds were the constant rush of the wind and the dripping of icicles melting off the eaves. Then one of the elders said, stammering, "H-how does she know our language?"

I was in trickier waters now. My first speech was rehearsed to be fluid and well pronounced, but from here on out I must rely on my ability to comprehend and speak at speed. Since I was still more conversant with the older, religious form of the language than the one spoken in daily life, the potential for error was quite large. But just as my growing skill had caused me to see the sisters as people rather than creatures, so must I use conversation to prove to these elders that I, too, was a person.

My reply came more slowly than my initial greeting. "I have been studying all winter to learn it. There is a human language that is a little bit the same. My knowledge of that language helps."

"You taught that thing?" one of the elders snapped at the sisters.

"If I had not learned," I said before Ruzt could reply, "I would not be able to thank you now." It came out more heavily accented than I would have liked, and more than a little tinged with Akhian elements. I still defaulted to these when my attention slipped. But I made myself understood, and that was enough.

One of the elders strode forward. Ruzt let her pass, so I stood my ground. This, too, we had expected and prepared for: the elder took me by the chin and tilted my head upward, so she could study my face more closely. To maintain direct eye contact would have been a challenge; to drop my gaze entirely would have made me look weak and vulnerable. Instead I fixed my gaze upon her muzzle, making no attempt to resist.

She turned my head this way and that, pulling off my hat to finger my hair, which must have been very strange to her. I was abruptly conscious of its ragged, matted state, and the smell it must have carried. (I had washed it a handful of times during the winter, but under the circumstances, a wet head was less than wise.) When she attempted to peel back my lips, however, I pulled away. "If you want to see my teeth," I said, politely but firmly, "then ask."

I could see that my response amused her. This, however, did not prevent her from turning a gimlet eye on Ruzt and the other two. "You know you have broken a law."

All three sisters brought their wings forward, around their bodies. Ruzt said, "We know. We would not do so without good reason."

"And what is your reason?" This came from one of the other elders, the one I suspected to be the oldest of them all. Draconeans show few signs of aging compared with the grey hair and wrinkled skin of humans, but her eyes were sunken and her bone structure more pronounced, and her movements were slow and cautious.

My command of the language did not suffice to let me follow Ruzt's reply in its entirety, but its content was familiar to me. These Draconeans knew themselves to be confined to the Sanctuary, with no place more remote and protected to which they might flee; now she told them they were likely the last of their kind. Contact with humans, she warned them, was inevitable. They could wait for it to happen on our terms—by which I mean those of my species—or take the first steps themselves, in a fashion they might hope to control. And the first step was to acquire a single human, to see whether she could be reasoned with.

"But why did you hide her?" another elder asked. The one who had examined me was among her peers once more, watching this all with a thoughtful eye. "Why not inform us at once?"

"We thought she was going to die," Zam said. The bluntness of it shook me, even though the danger was by then long past— the danger of dying from my ordeal in the mountains, at least. My current peril was still an open question. Ruzt had promised to do her best to help me escape if the situation turned against me, but her best was likely to amount to a temporary stay of execution at most.

Kahhe intervened before anyone could think too much about the merits of following through on the notion of my death. "Also, it was almost time for hibernation. We could not ask the revered elders to stay awake, and so nothing could happen before spring at the earliest anyway. We thought we could use the winter as a test—to see whether we could learn to speak with her, and how she would react to us."

I thought of my screams and weeping. My first impression could not have been a good one. But no one here needed to hear of that, and so I offered up, "I helped with the yaks."

The elder who had examined me laughed at that. Her reaction pleased me, for laughter is a great reducer of tension. A number of Draconeans glared at her, elders and villagers alike, but I had one person here besides the sisters who did not view me as an imminent threat.

I would need to convince a great many more, though, before we could make anything like progress. "If you please," I said, "I would like to tell you about the places outside the Sanctuary. Whatever you decide to do, there are things you should know. But it will take me a long time to tell you, because my speech is not as good as I would like." With a nod toward Ruzt, I said, "This honoured sister's help would make it easier."

That last was my own addition, and it made Ruzt start with surprise. She was not the only one conversant with the religious form of the language; most of the elders spoke it quite well. With that as a bridge, I could manage with them almost as well as I did with her. But she was the one who had started this all, persuading Kahhe and Zam to take the risk of contacting the human world. If it ended in disaster, she was already condemned, and I could do nothing to save her. I wanted to make certain, though, that if it ended in success, she received the credit she deserved. And for that to happen, she must remain a part of what followed.

As it turned out, however, my comment was based on a foolish optimism. The eldest Draconean said, "All three of them will be coming with us. They must face—"

Her last word was one I did not know, but I could fill in its meaning for myself: *judgment*.

I do not know whether it failed to occur to the council of elders that they should take steps to ensure word of my presence in the Sanctuary did not spread, or whether they gave it up as a lost cause from the start. If it was the former, they were foolish; if the latter, quite pragmatically wise.

To say that the entire Sanctuary knew before the day was out would be an exaggeration, but not much of one. I had not realized that mews, in addition to acting as aerial yak-dogs, could also be trained in the manner of carrier pigeons; they are not used for this during the winter, on account of the cold and the limited need for communication. But now the weather had warmed, and news of a human in Imsali quite literally flew from one settlement to another. In my ignorance of Draconean ways, I had argued for Ruzt's continued presence without realizing the whole sister-group would be called to accompany us; but all three proved necessary, for my journey from Imsali to the place of the elders was anything but quiet.

The mountain basin was quite transformed from its appearance earlier that winter, when we chased the yaks of Imsali hither and yon and I trespassed in the temple. Although snow still lay deep in many places, particularly on northern slopes or where trees provided shade, the thaw had begun; the sound of snowmelt streams was as constant as the wind. Six months previously I would never have dreamt of calling the temperature balmy, but after what I had endured, I almost felt I could survive with only three layers on.

By far the greatest transformation, however, was one of movement. All winter long the Sanctuary had lain quiet, with only the occasional yak herd or accompanying caretaker with mews to disturb its stillness. Now there were Draconeans everywhere: chivvying their livestock along, travelling between villages, assessing the state of their fields and fences, chopping wood to make repairs. Their total numbers were not so large; even the most densely settled parts of the Sanctuary, west of Anshakkar, were still almost uninhabited compared to the Scirling countryside, which is much flatter and more arable. But after months of near-total solitude, I felt as if I were on the busiest street in Falchester—and all the more so because it seemed like every Draconean within five kilometers of our path diverted to see me with their own eyes.

Our party was not one that could pass in stealth. The nine elders made quite a crowd on their own; and of course they could not be expected to travel in rough fashion, given their advanced age and great status. Compared with an Anthiopean potentate, their entourages were not worth the name; but each had at least one attendant, in many cases two, whose duty was to ease their way. To this we added myself, Ruzt, Kahhe, Zam, and a sister-group of four from Imsali who had volunteered to come as supplemental guards. The dominant one among them, a tall Draconean named Esdarr, made no secret of the fact that they did not trust me in the slightest: along the way I learned that they were the ones who ought to have had winter duty that year, and their relief at being spared the task had soured greatly when they discovered the reason.

Altogether it made for a cavalcade of thirty—a draconicade, one might more accurately call it, except that is not a proper word. (The Draconeans made no use of ponies, and for good reason. The poor equines come near to dying of fright at the sight or scent of a Draconean.) I travelled in the center of it, insulated from the gawping locals by the ring of the elders and their attendants, and insulated from the elders by the Draconeans of Imsali.

None of this arrangement did any good when we passed through a narrow defile scarcely ten meters wide.

I had, on that journey, attempted to rein in my natural curiosity, lest it look like spying. Although I longed to see as much as I could of the Sanctuary—male Draconeans most particularly, as I had been too distracted during the revelation in Imsali to look for them—I kept my eyes fixed on the path ahead of me, gazing no farther than the limits of our group. But when a scrabbling sound came from overhead, I could not stop myself from looking up. I have too often been in wilderness where that sound might herald a predator or a dangerous rockfall to let it pass without suspicion.

Even as I looked up, wings blotted out the sun.

They descended upon us with bone-chilling battle cries, leaping from concealment down into our midst. I ducked—the instinctive reaction of a creature faced with an airborne threat—and claws swiped above, close enough to tear my hat from my head. For an instant I was nineteen again and on my way to Drustanev, having my first encounter with a wild dragon.

Then the present day reasserted itself. My attacker was no rock-wyrm; it was a Draconean, one of several who had launched themselves into our midst. The other sister-group from Imsali had come to protect people against *me,* and so they were slow to react to this new threat. But Ruzt, Kahhe, and Zam did not hesitate: they instantly formed up around me, correctly guessing that I was the target of this assault.

I could do no more than crouch in their midst, trying to watch in every direction at once lest an enemy slip through. The attackers wielded curved knives whose blades flashed viciously in the sun. Beyond the mêlée I could hear the elders calling for a halt, but no one was paying them any heed. A scream cut through the snarls: someone fell, and in the chaos I could not see whether it was a friend or a foe. Then the flow shifted, surging away from me, and a Draconean leapt into the air, rowing hard with her wings in an attempt to gain enough altitude to escape our crowd. But someone else leapt after—Zam—and dragged the fleeing one down to earth once more.

The final tally was three dead out of eight; two sister-groups had banded together for the ambush. Five of ours were wounded to one degree or another, including both Ruzt and Zam. But none on our side had perished, and the sheer relief of that turned my knees to water. I knew very well that if someone had died defending me, the loss would have poisoned minds against my cause, perhaps beyond repair. As it was, the death of three attackers was bad enough, for it was my presence that had provoked them to this extreme.

One of the elders confronted me after order had been restored. Her name was Tarshi, I thought; I was working hard to familiarize myself with them all. Without preamble, she said, "You did not fight."

"I do not know how," I said. It was more or less true: my brother Andrew had made good on his offer to teach me a few things I might use to defend myself, but they would have been of limited use against Draconeans, who had a tremendous advantage in both height and mass, and claws and knives besides. Honesty prompted me to add, "And if I fought, what would you think of me then?"

She made no reply to that, simply turning away and rejoining her peers. It was not my most glorious moment; but at that particular moment, glory would have served me ill. The dreadful human, heir to a legacy of murder and rebellion, cowered in the face of Draconean fury. Under the circumstances, it amounted to a diplomatic master stroke—albeit a wholly inadvertent one.

# SIXTEEN

*The place of the elders—A male Draconean—*
*Conversations with the elders—A decision at last*

The ambush shook everyone in the party, I think, for we travelled with a great deal more care after that. The elders were not accustomed to thinking of themselves as the targets of a threat—and they had not been even in this instance, as the attack was directed primarily at me and secondarily toward the three sisters who had brought me there. But their society is agrarian and scattered enough that they rarely if ever face the kinds of conflicts that are familiar to the rulers of more populous and concentrated states, and the realization that my presence might spark an actual rebellion was an unpleasant surprise.

For my own part, I did not like the feeling that every step I took shook the ground, that simply by existing within the Sanctuary I was spreading fear and discord. But how much worse, I reasoned, would it have been had this first contact happened under different circumstances? Everything that made me vulnerable—my lack of companions, my lack of martial capability—also made me less of a threat. In a sense, I traded my safety for theirs . . . albeit not by my own choice. This was the decision of Ruzt and Kahhe and Zam, who leapt on the opportunity presented by a lone human, bereft of support.

It was with a great deal of trepidation that I came to the place of the elders. This was the phrase used to describe it, and so generic were the words that I had no idea what to expect. Not the temple, that much I knew; we had rounded the base of Anshakkar, leaving those sacred chambers far behind. A palace, perhaps?

That term will do as well as any, though it implies a much grander structure than the reality. The place of the elders was the set of buildings where those nine Draconeans dwelt, along with their male counterpart. Although the greatest of these was smaller than the yak barn of Imsali, it was far larger than any ordinary house, and much more finely made, with carved decoration outside and painted inside. In the summer months the terrain around the compound was a kind of garden, consisting mostly of sculpted rocks, in which they would plant flowers and other beauteous greenery; when I arrived, however, it was of course still mired in winter's leavings.

The three sisters and I were given a chamber to sleep in, while the four who had come as our guards were dispatched back to Imsali. This was by decree, not the sister-group's voluntary choice; the elders had security enough there, and I suspect they did not want the disruption our self-appointed watchdogs might bring. I took the decision as an encouraging sign, for it also sent away several Draconeans who were hostile to me, leaving us greater peace and quiet in which to speak. Of course this did not last; nearly every village in the Sanctuary sent representatives to the place of the elders, to examine me or render their opinions on what ought to be done. But we had a little breathing space before those began arriving.

Our meetings I expected to take place in the central chamber of the largest building, which was an audience hall. We did indeed spend a great deal of time in there—enough so that the place became nearly as suffocating to me as the sisters' house, though that was due as much to my desire to leave the Sanctuary as to the amount of time I spent inside. But we were also outdoors a great deal, weather permitting, for the Draconean religion as it was practiced in the Sanctuary revolved around the contrast between two extremes: the secrecy and protection of a cave, and the vitality of the sun in the open sky.

This I learned from the first male Draconean of my acquaintance, a fellow named Habarz who was the counterpart of the ruling council of elders. I tried not to show my excitement upon being introduced to him, but I fear I did not succeed very well.

Physically Habarz was not much different from the females: sexual dimorphism among their species is much less apparent than in humans, consisting primarily of a larger and more interestingly patterned ruff, which is considered their most attractively masculine feature. His was far from the most impressive, though at the time I had no real basis for comparison. Unlike some males of his kind, who earn their keep through what I can only term stud service, Habarz was a scholar.

His work bore little resemblance to mine, of course: scholarship in the Sanctuary was far more theological in nature than scientific. Male Draconeans, as I have said, are in the minority of their species; they constitute no more than twenty percent of the population, with any given clutch ordinarily containing several sisters and a single brother. Although no one admitted it openly to me, by reading between the lines, I came to understand that their eggs were kept communally—likely somewhere in or near the temple; I was not about to ask—where a cadre of elder males watched over them. Once hatched and old enough to travel, the juveniles were sent back to their home villages, where again they were in the custody of the oldest male age group. They do pay attention to which eggs came from which female, and not only that Draconean but all of her immediate sisters are considered the mothers of that clutch; but the care and education of the young is the responsibility of the males en masse.

In light of this, it is unsurprising that those same males should predominantly occupy the intellectual roles of Draconean society. Much to my amusement, I had once again marked myself as peculiarly masculine—but not for quite the same reasons as usual. My tendency to wander about and put myself into danger is a quality associated with female Draconeans (who, being more numerous, are more easily risked); my drawing skills, on the other hand, acquired in childhood as part of my feminine accomplishments, are more commonly seen as masculine. The sisters frequently whittle geometric patterns, but it is their brothers who paint figurative art.

Figurative—and religious, for the two go hand in hand. Males form not only the majority of the artistic class I mentioned before, but the majority of the spiritual leadership; or rather I should say it in reverse sequence, for it is the latter which leads to the former. Their religious role also leads to the greater rate of literacy among males, as a modernized version of the ancient script is used primarily for religious texts and important historical documents.

After all, there is little need for reading or writing when one spends the majority of one's summer either farming or herding yaks, and the majority of the long and idle winter asleep.

(My readers now may be wondering about Ruzt. I had indeed found a kindred soul, in the sense of one who did not quite fit her society's usual mold: her knowledge of the archaic tongue and small skill at reading were both quite unusual for her gender.)

So: these were the male Draconeans, and Habarz was their chief representative. He and I spoke quite a lot during my time at the place of the elders, for reasons he presented quite frankly. "Regardless of what happens with you," he said, "we should have a record of it for future generations to consider."

I decided to risk a little levity. "Then I hope what you record is not, 'on such-and-such a day we cut off the human's head.'"

He laughed, and from then on I was more at ease with him. But he did not tell me that my fears were unfounded ... for we both knew they were not.

Establishing new diplomatic relations is a difficult enough task under any circumstances. Now imagine, if you will, that this difficulty is compounded both by a lack of fluent communication, and by the diplomatic ineptitude of the ambassador. The proceedings seemed as if they would drag on until the following century.

The question that so vexed us was, what to do next? It was all fine and well to make contact with a lone human, but that was only the first step along a very long and treacherous path. I laid the groundwork by explaining to them the situation of the world outside—a subject that could have filled a year on its own, even without the interference of linguistic obstacles, but I confined myself to the most basic elements only. All of it was in the service of making a fundamental point: that whatever they chose to do with me, further contact was inevitable. With armies sharpening their bayonets on both sides of the Mrtyahaima, sooner or later someone would come tramping through the Sanctuary, and that someone would probably be armed. When that happened . . .

I had long feared for the safety of dragons, once we knew the secret of preserving and using their bones. My new fear was to that one as the Great Cataract was to the melting icicles outside. So few in number were the Draconeans, it would take very little to exterminate them.

And as much as I wished to pretend otherwise, I knew that extermination was a distinct possibility. My extraordinary circumstances had induced me to see the sisters as people rather than as monstrous beasts, but how many others would pause long enough to look beyond their initial impressions?

Any plan that did not end in my imprisonment or death also required the elders to see *me* as a person, rather than as a monstrous beast. We spent long hours on historical debates over the Downfall, with me citing our own body of evidence, the picture it presented of merciless tyrants overthrown for their cruelty. The basic facts of the Downfall were not particularly in question, though my poor knowledge of Scripture hobbled me on more than one occasion; what we argued about was motivation, until my head ached. Finally I said, in utter weariness, "Oh, what does it *matter*? I have no doubt there were good Draconeans and bad humans. But they are all thousands of years dead and gone, and what anyone thought or did then is of less import than what they will think and do *now*."

"The human has a point," Tarshi said to her fellow elders. "And if we do not let go of that question for now, another thousand years may pass before we get anywhere." Habarz grumbled—his scholarly soul longed to establish the truth—but to my relief, the council accepted Tarshi's point, and we moved on.

One aspect of being at the place of the elders was an unmitigated benefit: I ate better there than I had since leaving Vidwatha. The elders received taxes in kind from villages all over the Sanctuary, and although it was all dried, smoked, or otherwise preserved (as fresh food was still quite some ways off), the variety was much greater. I confess that I ate them out of their entire stock of a certain dried berry, which I craved from the moment I tasted it; this berry has properties similar to those of citrus fruit, and made a dramatic change in my health. And I cannot help but think that also benefited my diplomatic efforts, as an ambassador weak from malnutrition makes a very unimpressive show.

I made a point of taking walks in the garden with each of the elders, starting with Sejeat, the one who had tried to examine my teeth in Imsali. (I was glad I had prevented her. Devouring those berries meant I ultimately lost only one tooth to scurvy, but at the time the interior of my mouth was not a pretty sight.) Sejeat was by far the most curious and accepting of me; Urrte the least so—and to my surprise, Urrte was also the youngest of the lot. But although it is often true that the elderly are the most set in their ways, the least receptive to new ideas and change, it is not by any means universally true. My suspicion was that Urrte, being not only the youngest but the newest to the council, felt the need to establish her devotion to Draconean tradition.

"Are your sisters all dead?" Sejeat asked me one day.

"I never had any," I said, and laughed a little. "I am more like the opposite of a Draconean; all my siblings are brothers. But my mother, sun be praised, birthed us all singly, rather than in a group." Having endured childbirth once, I shuddered to imagine even twins, let alone anything more.

Speaking of my brothers was safe enough, but she continued to question me about my family, which led inevitably to those closer to my heart: Suhail, my son, all those who had found a place in my life by routes either personal or professional. I struggled to maintain a stiff upper lip—and then, upon reflection, wondered if that was truly the best course of action. Would it not help for the Draconeans to see that a human was capable of feeling?

Enough time had passed since the avalanche that I was able to speak of my loved ones without collapsing into tears as I had before. Indeed, such conversations gave both me and my purpose strength: as the Sanctuary warmed, the day when I might attempt the col drew nearer. My passionate determination to be reunited with them interwove itself with my passionate determination to aid the Draconeans, and both blazed higher with every passing day.

I worked half the night with Ruzt to prepare my words to the council, so that I could present my vision for a path forward without confusion. The next morning, I requested permission for us to meet outside; this was, I said, a matter for sunlight, not a cave. The latter was the place for inaction, careful contemplation before any decision might be made. My aim that day was to spur them to action.

The servants at the place of the elders had tidied the garden for spring planting, though it was still winter-barren. I tipped my head back, turning my face to the sun—a gesture natural to me, but also one with significance to the Draconeans, having the effect of a silent prayer. Then, drawing in a deep breath, I began.

"My people," I said, "*must* become accustomed to the notion of your people as real creatures—*before* they see one in the living flesh. It is likely that this has already begun: unless my companions all perished in the avalanche, they will by now have spread the word of our discovery in the mountains. If you permit me to return to the outside world, I can fan the flames of enthusiasm for all things Draconean, which have been burning since we discovered the lost hatching ground." I had told them of this—not omitting the fact that I wept to see the tracks of those ancient Draconean hatchlings, who perished waiting for caretakers who would never come. The memory shook me even more now than it had then, when I thought the creatures only dumb beasts, but I went on.

"I can declare my intent to find a living population. Both my fame and my connections in the scholarly community will draw support to my cause; I can begin a movement for the preservation of the Sanctuary even before it is 'found.' When your existence is revealed to the world, there will be humans standing ready to support you, and together they will act as a defense for your well-being."

The elders did not like this plan, and I cannot blame them one bit. It would be a gamble on a scale so large, no word in any of our languages could encompass it—though they certainly made a thorough hunt for one, ranging through vocabulary far beyond my ken. Sejeat was on my side, and Tarshi seemed willing to consider it, but the remainder . . .

"Only a few should know of us," Kuvrey said. She was the eldest of the lot, and tended to assert her seniority. "If you carry a message from the council to some human government—"

"Then that government will take the situation out of both my hands and your own," I said, before this suggestion could garner much support. "They can slaughter you all in secret, and the general human public will never know the truth. I could tell them—but that would do you little good once you are dead. Or perhaps they will simply come in here and—" I did not know the Draconean word for "subjugate," having foolishly not thought to obtain it for this conversation. I made a gesture with my hand instead, clenching my fist tight. "They will keep you in pens, as you keep yaks. And it does not matter which government I tell; the risk will be the same." As much as I liked Queen Miriam and generally thought well of her, there was the Synedrion to consider. And my influence would be less than nothing at the court of the Vidwathi or Tser-zhag kings—much less that of the Yelangese emperor.

These hazards did not vanish under my plan, of course. But popular sentiment at least stood a chance of acting as a check on such actions—a better chance than any other possibility I saw.

"What if we sent our own representative out?" Sejeat asked. "Someone you can take in secret to negotiate."

"Where would I take that person?" It came out more curtly than I would have liked, but my body was stiff with tension. "I could not even get them to Thokha before someone saw us, much less to my own homeland. And they would be in even more danger than I am here, with less protection. Your—" I paused, looking at Ruzt, who supplied the word that had already slipped through the gaps in my increasingly leaky mind. "Your representative would be killed. I wish it were not so, but it would happen." I did not know the Draconean word for "suicide," and could not muster the will to ask for it, but I believe my meaning came through.

When all was said and done, only one thing carried us through that morass of difficulty: the fact that contact with the outside world was a matter that had troubled the council of elders for a generation or more. That it was inevitable and necessary, they agreed, but no further had they gotten; they had, in the manner of councils everywhere, dithered without reaching any conclusion. But much of their dithering had hinged on the lack of information to guide their actions, and now that lack was resolved. Furthermore, my presence forced their hands. As Tarshi said bluntly, "We cannot simply disregard the problem. We have three choices: keep her here, send her out again, or kill her."

It took all my will not to flinch when she said that last. By then I was fairly certain Tarshi was on my side; she only mentioned that possibility out of scrupulous fairness. Other elements on the council, however, were not nearly so sympathetic, Urrte chief among them. And every day messengers came from various parts of the Sanctuary—Draconean messengers; this was far too important for mews—urging them to that final course. Fortunately for me, the remainder knew that such action would solve nothing, and only squander an opportunity that might not come again. (How often does a dragon-friendly wanderer fall into one's lap, under conditions that dispose her to be grateful to one's people?)

Indeed, the hostility served my purpose in a peculiar fashion, for it also weighted the scale against keeping me in the Sanctuary. While in theory my continued presence would give the Draconeans a chance to acclimate themselves to humanity, in practice we all knew it would only inflame sentiment still further.

My murder, I told Sejeat quite bluntly, would bring all the ills of my execution and more, as it would only deepen the rift between the progressive, outward-looking faction and the reactionaries who wished to remain isolated. Furthermore, if it were ever to be discovered by humans, it would poison public opinion against the residents of the Sanctuary.

Even when there is no good choice, a choice must be made: lacking anything better, we chose what appeared to be the least of the available evils. By a narrow margin, and by means of a great deal of acrimonious wrangling, we finally arrived at a decision.

Kuvrey spoke for the council, in the sunlight, where decisions are made. "You will leave the Sanctuary," she said. "Go forth to your people, and tell them of us; then come find us again when they are ready."

I did not say to her, *they will never be ready.* I had not been ready to meet the elders, but had gone ahead regardless, for there was no other choice. We had already fallen from the cliff face: we must find a way to fly before we reached the ground.

# SEVENTEEN

*To the col once more—A sharp boundary—Miracles—Too many*
*conversations at once—Silence for a query—*
*A new plan—Above the col*

I was not alone as I travelled toward the edge of the Sanctuary, to the col between Gyaptse and Cheja. For the return to Imsali, I had not only my three hostesses but an honour guard from the place of the elders—the latter partly for my own protection, and partly for the protection of the dignitaries who travelled with me. Urrte had campaigned to be one of my escorts, making no secret of the fact that she looked forward to wishing me good riddance; fortunately for the pleasantness of my journey, she was voted down. Instead I had Sejeat and Kuvrey to represent the council, and Habarz to bless my departure. We went by less-trammeled paths, and arrived in Imsali without difficulty.

Even had I been the most beloved figure in the Sanctuary, I would not have tarried long in Imsali. Over the long months of winter I had mostly succeeded in turning my thoughts away from the circumstances under which I vanished: the avalanche, the unknown fate of my companions, and the certainty that the world believed me dead. But now that my departure was under way, the weight of those concerns returned in force, and I chafed at every delay.

I will not pretend that I felt no trepidation at all. So long as I remained where I was, everything outside the Sanctuary was like a hand of cards dealt but not yet examined. They might be good or they might be bad; once I lifted them from the table, all possibilities but one would vanish. I might lose the dread of tragedy . . . or I might lose the buoyancy of hope. Until I looked at my cards, I suffered the one, but also clung to the other.

But it is not in my nature to hide from such things when I have the option of moving forward. So far as I am concerned, uncertainty and inaction are among the worst forms of torture: it was much easier to head for the col than to hide in the Sanctuary, ignorant of what lay beyond.

And so I dressed myself once more in my mountaineering clothes—now rather baggier than before, owing to the weight I had lost over the winter. I was a far cry from the trim, fit woman who had approached the col from the east, though trekking to the place of the elders and back had done a small amount to put me back in condition. My hair was ragged, my skin weathered by sun and cold wind, my limbs pale as rawhide and every bit as stringy. Alone, I stood little chance of crossing the border of the Sanctuary; the western slope might be forgiving enough to spare a hypothermic, concussed woman staggering along on a cracked fibula, but the eastern side would put an end to me in short order. I doubted I could even make it down the Cursed Crack on my own, by any means other than falling.

Fortunately, I would have Draconean aid in the first part of my travels. The sisters did not dare help me much outside the Sanctuary, but their limited capacity for flight was sufficient to at least carry me over the worst parts of the descent along Cheja's slopes. After that . . . the impending mental and physical challenges of crossing the Cheja Glacier solo gave me something to think about besides more personal fears.

First the col; then the journey to Hlamtse Rong; then I intended to get myself deported by the Tser-zhag. (What I had once spoken as a jest had in truth become the most practical method of leaving the country.) Once in Vidwatha, my true undertaking would begin.

Even for a woman who has faced as many trials as I have, it was a daunting prospect.

Habarz's blessing was a simple one. He marked a yellow spot on my forehead with some kind of pollen—the symbol of the sun—and recited a prayer comparing my journey to that of the sun, which vanishes into an abyssal cave each night only to reappear the following day. There were butter lamps, whose flame and fuel are both reminiscent of the sun; there was a bell, to drive away any ill fortune that might follow me. I wished the ritual were known to me, for then I might have taken comfort in its familiar shape. As matters stood, it did nothing to calm my nerves, and I fear I was more brusque in my farewells to Kuvrey and Sejeat than I should have been.

But they did not take offense. "May we see you again soon," Kuvrey said. With an awkward curtsey, I departed.

Four of us set out from Imsali: myself, Ruzt, Kahhe, and Zam. The bright air and singing birds made it feel like a springtime ramble, but the sisters were irritable, for they were in the process of shedding their scales. These had indeed bleached pale during the winter, and I was pleased to see my theory confirmed, with the new layer much darker than the old. They also collected their shed scales, as I had surmised, and saved them for later use as insulation.

The moulting process likely did not explain all of their irritability; nerves also accounted for a great deal. But we were all happy to blame the situation on biology, rather than speak of our impending lunacy. Conversation fell away as we approached the col, until we marched in almost complete silence.

I was just as glad not to be speaking. Even a small gain in elevation can have a shocking effect on the body, and my reduced condition meant I was breathing hard long before we neared the top. I skidded often on the rocky slopes, making errors I would never have committed a year before, and could ill afford if I were to make it to Hlamtse Rong alive. Each slip motivated me to sharpen my focus, until we reached the snow line, above which the mountains never thawed.

Then I stood, gazing at the col. It is rare that profound changes in one's life are marked by so sharp a geographic boundary: the woman I had been on the eastern side of that ridge was not the woman who now stood on the west. Crossing over would not transform me back into my former self—and I would not accept such a reversion if it were offered. I only hoped that my return journey would not bring a second transformation, one into a life of disaster and sorrow.

It seemed that exhaustion and nerves had the power to turn me maudlin. I shook off those sentiments, turning to the sisters and saying, "Should we attempt our crossing today?"

After some conference, we agreed that we should camp below

the snow line and wait until the following day. Apart from strong winds, we had relatively little to fear from the weather in this season—this was the time of year my companions and I had originally aimed for in our own plans—and as much as I wished to move forward, I knew the respite would do me good.

That night I sat outside our tent, looking at the stars and thinking of the night before my human companions and I began our assault on the col, when I had sat around the fire with Suhail and Tom, discussing the biology of an unknown draconic species. The prospect that either of them could be dead—or both—gripped my heart so painfully, I honestly thought for a moment that I might be suffering a heart attack. Such things have been known to strike people who exert themselves too much at high elevations. But it was only fear; and the only cure was to rejoin the human world—where, I told myself firmly, I was certain to find them alive. I would accept no other prospect.

And to find them, I myself must survive what lay before me.

Dawn on this side of the range was a cold, grey affair, though Anshakkar burned like a torch to light our way. Despite fierce winds that would make crossing the col difficult, we set out early, not wanting to be caught cold and tired on the descent, where we would rapidly lose our light.

I am grateful to the sisters, who formed a team as effective as any *cordée* of mountaineers. Their irritability notwithstanding, they worked together in a harmony that was almost supernatural, anticipating each others' moves without a word being said. In skill they were not comparable to the humans who challenge themselves on the slopes and peaks of the world; but the structure of their society, which treats the sister-group as the highest bond, fosters an enviable degree of cooperation. (In its best form: I will not pretend all groups achieve or maintain such cordiality.) Although I was not included in that harmony or familiarity, I benefited from it all the same, and by the time we neared the crest of the col an upwelling of confidence buoyed my tired limbs. The sun had risen high enough to light our slope; to reduce the risk of another avalanche, we were making our way along a stony little rise at the margin of the snow slope I had wandered down months before.

Then Zam's powerful arm reached out and slammed me sideways, flattening me against the rock.

She did not mean me harm. It was the instinct of a Draconean who has long guarded the borders of her land: she saw movement, and acted swiftly to hide us.

I had blithely assumed we left the risk of ambush behind in Imsali. But if someone wished us to vanish quietly, without causing a fuss . . . what better place to do it than here, on the edge of the Sanctuary, where no one was present to see?

My smoked-glass goggles were long gone, having vanished along with my spare alpenstock during the avalanche, but I had contrived a slitted eye mask to protect my vision against the glare of snow. Now I pulled it off, the better to see what lay ahead.

The movement was at the top of the col, near the flank of Cheja. A figure—no, two of them, moving back and forth along the snow. I recall thinking, with the cold-blooded calculation of fear, that it was peculiar behaviour for ambushers, who surely must wish not to be observed before they struck.

Then I measured the figures against the surrounding terrain.

Zam was too slow to stop me. I charged forward, scrambling up the slope at a pace much faster than was wise, shouting as I went. The wind tore my words away. I kept losing sight of the pair, for I had to look where I put my hands and feet lest I fall to my death; and to go through the snow would be no faster, as then I would only flounder along as if through mud. But I glanced up as often as I could—and then my next glance showed me one of the figures sliding down toward me at a pace even more unsafe, dislodging stones that could easily have rewarded us with another avalanche.

But the mountains, ever my perverse ally, held their peace. And then the figure skidded to a halt and remained where it was, as if all strength had fled. The task of crossing the remaining ground fell to me. I staggered upward, a name already on my lips, even though the man in front of me was so heavily bundled in clothing that to claim recognition was sheer hubris. I knew him; I would know him anywhere. *"Suhail."*

His hands were shaking as he dragged his goggles loose. They disclosed a face as weathered as my own, and eyes spilling over with disbelieving tears. Though the wind tore the sound away, his lips shaped the words, "All praise to God."

Nothing in my life has ever felt more like a miracle. I collapsed to my knees at his side; and we were still locked in embrace when Thu, descending with a great deal more care, arrived to witness our reunion.


The story came out in pieces, for neither of us was coherent enough to make it through more than half a sentence at a time.

Although my career has been built on a foundation of careful observation, I doubted the evidence of my own eyes. How could those two men be there? It was far too early in the spring for them to have returned to Tser-nga; for me to chance the heights at this date was ambitious, and possible only because I began from so nearby. Had I let myself dream of my companions' return, I would have calculated it for a month hence.

The answer, of course, was that their departure point was equally close. Suhail and Thu had spent the winter in Hlamtse Rong—not because they were snowed in, as I had been, but because they refused to leave.

They had no expectation of my survival. But Suhail would not hear of leaving my body in the mountains; he was determined to wait until spring, and then comb the path of the avalanche until he found my remains and gave them a proper burial. To his mind, the only question was who would stay with him, and who would go to inform the Scirling army of my death and the results of our expedition.

All of my companions had survived. I went as limp as Suhail at that news; I could not have stood up for all the iron in the world. They had escaped the worst of the avalanche, faring much better than I did; but their attempts to find me in the aftermath had comprehensively failed, though they risked their lives in the search. Only the certainty that all four of them would die if they remained at the col had finally driven them down—and even at that, the other three had dragged Suhail away by main force. By the time the storm passed, there was no hope of finding me alive; and indeed, by then I would have been dead were it not for my Draconean rescuers. They returned to Hlamtse Rong in grief, and there agreed that Chendley and Tom would leave, while Suhail and Thu would stay.

Why that division? I did not ask immediately, though I did wonder. Chendley's duties called him east, of course; and Suhail, as I have said, insisted on waiting for spring. To send Chendley off on his own would have been much too hazardous, and so he needed a companion. But why was it Tom who had gone, and not Thu?

The answer to that came later. In the meanwhile, they had a question of their own, to wit: how in God's name had I survived?

I finally broke from my daze enough to look around. The sisters had not followed me in my uphill charge; that was hardly surprising. But what on earth could I possibly say to explain my presence here, if I could not point to a Draconean as the answer?

They must have conducted a rapid argument amongst themselves, while I was lost to the world in my own reunion. When I looked up, Ruzt was concealed among the rocks not far away, watching me with a steady eye. I met her gaze, and something passed between us. We were not sisters, to read one another's minds through long familiarity; but we had built a rapport over the winter months, in which we learned to communicate by means both verbal and otherwise, and I knew what she was saying now.

With my heart beating so strongly I could taste my pulse upon my tongue, I nodded my agreement.

She stepped out from behind the rocks, standing tall in the sun. "There," I said, my voice pleasingly steady. "There is the Draconean who saved my life."


The side of a mountain above the snow line is not the best place to conduct an extended conversation. At some point during

what followed, we agreed to retire to a more comfortable spot—
still on the western side of the col.

Suhail and Thu had known for months that such organisms
existed: humanoid bodies with draconic heads. And Suhail, of
course, had both his archaeological knowledge and his familiarity
with my draconic expertise to draw on in forming conclusions
based on that fact; moreover, he had the entirety of a long
Mrtyahaiman winter in which to contemplate the possibilities.
But as I myself had discovered, it is one thing to find a frozen
specimen, and quite another to meet the living cousin face to
face. (Or rather three of them, as Kahhe and Zam had, with
palpable reluctance, joined Ruzt in view.)

I could scarcely tear my gaze away from my husband. Winter
had left its marks upon him, as it had upon me. For many years
his family had pressured him to become a prayer-leader; the
colloquial phrase for this is "to grow one's beard," as Amaneen
prayer-leaders do not shave their faces. I assumed Suhail was no
more inclined to the religious life now than he had been, but he
had at least grown his beard: a useful addition to the face in a
Mrtyahaiman winter, though one I hoped he did not intend to
keep. This, I eventually realized, was a source of some hilarity to
Zam, who had found my own hair astonishing enough; she had
not realized that the males of my species could grow it upon their
chins as well.

But there was little hilarity in those initial moments, as we
were all too busy reeling from our various shocks. Suhail's own
gaze kept alternating between me and the Draconeans, pulled
this way and that by his dumbfounded relief on the one hand, and
his astonished curiosity on the other. When I explained the

situation to my caretakers, his expression took on the abstracted cast I knew so well; it was the look he bore when the greater part of his mind was devoted to efforts linguistic. "You were right," I said to him, breaking off my explanation. "Their language *is* related to Lashon and Akhian. No doubt you'll be more fluent than I am in a week."

The complex tangle of languages caused no little difficulty. My Draconean companions were accustomed to hearing me mutter to myself in Akhian, but Scirling was wholly unfamiliar to them, and it made them nervous: to them it had the sound of a code, used so they could not hope to guess at what I was saying. But it was the only language Thu and I had in common; and he and Suhail still resorted to Yelangese on occasion, which they had used a great deal during their own winter sojourn. Together with Draconean, there were four languages tumbling around in our conversation, and matters often ground to halt while a concept was carried through the necessary chain of translations.

My first task was to explain to the sisters who these two men were. This went with relative ease, for they recalled my story of how I came to be in the Sanctuary—and I think that Ruzt and Kahhe at least were very glad to see my fears laid to rest, though Zam may not have cared overmuch. After that, however, I was peppered with questions from both sides: Why had Suhail and Thu come back? How many Draconeans were there? Were other humans coming over the col? Where had I lived all winter? Could the men be trusted not to speak of what they had found? Could they be permitted to see a Draconean city?

"Enough!" I exclaimed at last. I honestly cannot recall which language the word emerged in, but the meaning was clear to everyone. I pressed my hands to my aching head and tried to marshal my thoughts into order. Then I turned to the Draconeans and said, "You are safe for now; there are only two of them, though we should discuss what will happen next. But will you let me explain matters to them first? I think they are much more confused than you."

Permission thus obtained, I began to direct the traffic of the conversation in a fashion that even I will admit was imperious and high-handed. It was the only way to retain my sanity, for individuals on both sides kept breaking in with new questions. By the time I had satisfied everyone's initial curiosity to an acceptable degree, it was almost midday, and my throat was so dry I felt I could have swallowed all the snow on Gyaptse.

Silence fell after I stopped talking. Suhail finally released my hand—he had not parted contact with me since we were re-united, save when the practicalities of moving to a more sheltered spot required it—and climbed to his feet. Kahhe was the nearest of the sisters; he approached her with his hands extended. "May I?" he said, doing her the courtesy of addressing her even though she could not understand the words.

I translated his query, expanding upon his meaning, and Kahhe nodded. Suhail walked a circuit around her, studying her with open fascination. As he came again to his starting point, he began a process familiar to me from my earliest days in their house: pointing to objects and suggesting words for them, based on his attempts to reconstruct the Draconean language. When I tried to answer him, he waved me off with a fond smile. "You have talked yourself hoarse already," he said. "And I cannot pass up the chance to learn from them."

He would learn from them regardless—assuming that we could form a plan for what should happen next. No one had yet broached that subject. I accepted a skin of water from Ruzt and went to sit next to Thu, who had been watching with quiet intensity for most of this time, turning a pebble over and over in his fingers.

"Thank you for coming to look for me," I said. "Even though you thought I was dead."

He bent his attention to the pebble. "My reasons were not noble."

I was uncertain how to answer that, and words came reluctantly from my throat after so much talking. But Thu took my silence for a query, and went on. "I am the reason you came here. If I left the mountains with the news that you were dead—conveniently lost in an avalanche . . ."

His use of the word "convenient" called to mind all the suspicion that had greeted his initial appearance in Falchester. How many people had cautioned me that surely the Yelangese meant to lure me to my death? And lo, I died—or so he thought. "Tom and Suhail would have vouched for you," I said. (Chendley as well, no doubt; I do not mean to slander him. But he was not at the forefront of my thoughts the way the others were.)

"Of course. But if Wilker had stayed, and I had gone with Chendley, neither of them would have been there to vouch." He lost his grip on the pebble; it rattled away, and he bent to pick up another. "I knew it would look more honest if I helped to retrieve your body. I am sorry."

"What do you have to apologize for?" I said in astonishment. "Had I been dead in truth, the last thing I would have wanted was for you to be blamed. It is only sensible that you should do everything you could to protect yourself; if I am upset, it is because such caution was necessary. And," I said as an afterthought, "because you were forced to endure such a winter."

This induced him to smile, as I had hoped. Then we sat in a more companionable silence, with me emptying the waterskin as fast as my stomach could accept it, while everyone girded themselves for the next peak to climb.

I do not mean Gyaptse or Cheja, of course. I mean the question of what we should do now.

With my voice somewhat restored, I explained to Suhail and Thu the plan I had agreed upon with the Draconeans, which had sent me toward the col that day. I did not go into a great deal of detail, such as explaining the council of elders; that was neither pertinent to the immediate question, nor a thing I felt I should share until we had decided whether the men would continue on into the Sanctuary or not. But they grasped the problem quite rapidly; and while they considered it, I turned once more to the Draconeans.

"What do you want me to do now?" I asked. "I can carry on more or less as we agreed; it will be easier now, with these two to help me out of the mountains. But they would be of much more help to me if they came to know your people, even if only briefly, before we departed."

Suhail and Thu were talking quietly; Zam watched them with an untrusting eye. "You, we know. These two, we do not know."

"They will not speak," I assured her. "That is—I believe they will help me do what I planned." Suhail certainly would. Thu might choose not to assist, but I was confident he would not work against me. "You trust me, and I trust them."

Zam and Kahhe both looked unconvinced. Even Ruzt was

dubious; she said, "You lived with us for months before you met the others. And then it was one human, not three."

And three humans in the Sanctuary would cause more than three times the disturbance. At least I could be reasonably confident they would not attempt to hold the men hostage for my own good behaviour while I proceeded with my mission: that would be the worst of both worlds, introducing all the chaos of a human presence while also letting word of the Draconeans go into the outside world.

"Then we can continue on as planned," I said. "Well—not immediately. It is far too late in the day to try and cross the col; we would be caught on the far side without sufficient light to descend safely. But we can camp for the night, and make our crossing tomorrow."

I expected this to please Zam, who surely must be eager to see the back of us all. To my surprise, however, her scowl did not abate. Ruzt noticed this as well, and questioned her as to the reason.

"You want us to lie again," she said.

Again? Understanding came, only a little tardy: as they had lied when they concealed me in their house. The elders had deferred judgment on the sisters' transgression—if my mission turned out well, they could hardly punish those who made it possible—but they might not be so lenient if the sisters failed to report the arrival and departure of two more humans.

I spread my hands. "I will do whatever you decide. Take the time you require; this need not be something we settle in—" How did the Draconeans measure the hours of the day? It was not a thing I had learned yet, so I could not say "five minutes" or its equivalent. I paused, trying to think of a way to convey the concept; then I gave it up as not worth the effort, given the exhausted state of my brain. They seemed to understand me regardless, for Ruzt nodded, and the sisters began to converse amongst themselves once more.

When I turned back to my human companions, I found that Suhail had very quietly lost his composure. The novelty of the Draconeans could only hold back the tide for so long; now the impact of it struck him with full force, that I was not dead as he had believed. I sat wordlessly at his side and we gripped one another's gloved hands hard, while Thu pretended he was very occupied in studying the springtime landscape of the Sanctuary.

There was no sound to warn me, for the wind was still blowing ferociously from the west—a profound blessing, as it turned out. I did not know what was happening until I saw Zam staring past me, up the slope toward the col, and I twisted to look.

A caeliger hovered in the air of the pass. Its position wavered from side to side, and I could not fathom what it was doing; why did it not advance? Was it searching for Suhail and Thu?

Then it suddenly veered off, almost into the upper slope of Cheja, and I understood.

Its pilot was trying to fly the craft through into the Sanctuary, but the winds were holding it back. The caeliger vanished behind Cheja, then reappeared; he was repeating his approach, once more pitting his engine against the headwind. I realized I was holding my breath. Then I realized I was holding it not because I hoped the pilot would make it safely through, but because I hoped he would *not*.

Everything came crashing down on me at once. The caeligers that had flown us into Tser-nga the previous year—they had not come this way, but the gorge they used as their passage through the walls of the Sanctuary must be the same river gorge I had glimpsed in my own treks. Assuming they had not crashed, their flight path would have taken them directly over this hidden basin.

Would they have been able to make out the houses and farmland below? Perhaps; perhaps not. Certainly they would not have known the inhabitants were Draconean—not without landing in the Sanctuary, and people surely would have said something if they had. The caeliger was not here to rescue me, for everyone believed me dead; nor was it here to investigate the mysteries of this place. It was here because its pilots had seen a relatively hospitable-looking region, beyond the edges of the Tser-zhag king's control. Of course they wanted to investigate further.

Behind me, Zam snarled. In a voice so guttural I could barely make out the words, she growled, "*What is that?*"

"It is a—" My sentence died on my tongue. Of course there was no word for "caeliger" in their language. And what explanation could I give that would not simply describe what Zam already saw with her own eyes? The Draconeans did not even use carts, on account of the ruggedness of the terrain. I could hardly call it a flying yak. "It is like a basket," I said, my voice faltering so much I am not even certain she heard me. "A basket carried by . . . the air."

Ruzt's reply was thick with tension. "Humans?"

"Yes."

The caeliger veered off again. We all waited, every one of us on our feet, watching the col with fists clenched. The seconds ticked by with agonizing slowness; the caeliger did not reappear.

"They've given up," Suhail said.

"For today," I replied. "But when the winds are more favourable, they will try again." Which could be as soon as tomorrow.

I pivoted to face the sisters. "When they bring that basket to earth, I must be there to greet it. If I am not . . ."

If I were not, then all the horrors I had envisioned might come to pass even sooner than expected.

# PART FIVE

*In which the fate
of the Sanctuary
is decided*

# EIGHTEEN

*An unexpectedly swift return—A prayer to the sun—No sleep—*
*Waiting for the caeliger—More reunions—*
*A foreign nation—The mystery revealed*

Catching a caeliger on foot is impossible even in the flattest terrain. In the Sanctuary of Wings, even to attempt such a thing would have been suicide, for I would have broken my neck thirty seconds into any sprint.

The only way to be certain I could greet the caeliger upon landing was to arrange for it to land in a place of my choosing. It was with this intent that I skidded back into Imsali, hard on the heels of Ruzt and Kahhe and Zam, and gasped out a desperate request for the brightest cloth or paint they could give me.

Suhail and Thu were not with us. I knew better than to charge into the village with two more humans at my back; that would only cause more alarm. And although I very much wanted the Draconeans to be suitably alarmed, the presence of my husband and our Yelangese friend was too likely to tip matters over from "suitable" to "excessive." Eventually I must admit their presence . . . but not until I had explained the caeliger and what it portended.

Kuvrey's last words to me had been that she hoped to see me again soon. Her next words were, "We did not expect you *this* soon. What is going on?"

I tried to let Ruzt explain, trusting her vocabulary far more than my own, but that did not work; Ruzt, of course, did not fully understand what the caeliger portended. Between the two of us, we got the point across, albeit in tangled and uneven fashion. The news that more humans were attempting to breach the Sanctuary did not go over well. The more warlike of their people—chief among them Esdarr's sister-group, who had escorted me to the place of the elders—were in favour of meeting this incursion with knives and the short spears they used for hunting.

"You will die," I said flatly, making no attempt to soften it. "They have objects that hurl spear points farther than any arm, so quickly that no one can hope to dodge them. If you threaten them, they will kill every last one of you, to protect themselves."

Not long before, I had been assuring them that humans were not the murderous monsters of legend; now all that good work was undone. But I was willing to accept temporary damage to the reputation of my species in exchange for not provoking a confrontation that would guarantee even more hostility going forward. "I can keep them from hurting you," I said, putting more confidence into the words than I felt. "But I need to be there when they arrive."

"This was your plan all along," Esdarr spat, wings spreading. "You led them to us!"

I cannot blame her for thinking so. In a sense, she was even correct: it was my decision to come to Tser-nga that had sent the first caeligers over the Sanctuary. The army would likely have tried that sooner or later, but they might have tried it elsewhere in the Mrtyahaima—not here. Not where it would threaten the Draconeans.

I turned to the elders. "Have you seen this before? Last spring, a little before the monsoon. Two baskets like that one. They would have come in over the river."

"Someone in Eberi said they had," Sejeat said. "But no one believed them."

With the caeligers painted to blend with the sky, it was not difficult to overlook them—especially when no one expected such a thing in the air. "Those two sent for others," I said. "Or they went astray, and this one has been sent to look for them. It hardly matters. This means more humans are coming; there can be no hope of a slow revelation now. And if I am not there to meet them, you will not be able to talk to one another, which will only make everyone more afraid, and therefore dangerous. *Please*—I beg you. Give me fabric or paint, something bright, so we can bring them down where we want them."

My words were even more garbled than usual, fracturing under the strain of distress and difficult subjects, but by then Ruzt was accustomed to piecing my utterances together. "How will those help?" she asked.

I closed my eyes, trying to calculate how large an image must be for someone to reliably spot it from the sky. "I need to make a target."

Sejeat was observant. In the short time I had been in the place of the elders, she had learned to read my moods well; now, in the kicked ant-hill that was Imsali, she took me aside and asked, "What are you not saying?"

I had known all along that I could not keep Suhail and Thu hidden forever. Had Sejeat not drawn me off, I would have done the same to her; the sisters and I had agreed that of all the people I could speak to first, she was by far the best choice. "You recall that I came to the mountains with companions," I said, not bothering to prevaricate. "Two of them stayed the winter outside the Sanctuary. We met them in the col today, where they were looking for my body. They were with us when we saw the caeliger."

Perhaps it was the consequence of piling shock upon shock; eventually one reaches a point where additions have little effect. Sejeat stared at me, as unblinking as a lizard. Then she turned and bellowed in a powerful voice for the scant handful of carrier mews that had not already been dispatched to the place of the elders.

These went out shortly thereafter with a postscript to the previous message. This done, Sejeat insisted that Kahhe go out and bring the two men down. I do not think she especially wanted to add them to the chaos of the village; but it would be worse if they were discovered by chance, or left to wander freely.

I will not trouble my readers with a detailed account of the furor that greeted them. You can imagine it for yourself; for the curious, it was a second menagerie come to town, and for the suspicious, it was proof positive that humans were coming to kill them all. I was grateful beyond words for two things: first, the presence of the two elders and Habarz, without whom I am sure the situation would have degenerated into violence; and second, for my husband's fine memory. At one early point, while everyone else was shouting, he whispered into my ear, "Is there a religious leader in this crowd?"

"Two," I whispered back. "Esmin is local, but Habarz is something like a head priest for the whole Sanctuary. Why?"

Suhail's answering smile was more than a little tinged with nerves. "I put my time waiting to what I hope will be good use."

Moving slowly, so as not to startle anyone, Suhail approached Habarz. The shouting abated, except in a few quarters; Esdarr very much wanted to step forward and protect the elders. But Suhail stopped a safe distance away and knelt. Then, in a voice strong and clear, he recited words I could only partially make out—words in an approximation of the Draconean language.

It was one of the texts he had been working on back in Scirland. His transliteration of the script was imperfect, his pronunciation flawed, and the language itself was even more archaic than the religious form used in the Sanctuary . . . but it was recognizable. The words were a prayer to the sun, that it guide the beneficiary down the right path.

If my own first speech had been akin to a yak standing up on its hind legs and saying hello, now the yak was leading a worship service. The reactions would have been comical, had the situation not been so tense; as it was, I still had to stifle a laugh. Habarz stared at Suhail with his wings drooping so their tips almost trailed in the mud. The shouting stopped utterly; the only voices I heard were villagers murmuring to one another, asking what on earth the human had just said.

Kuvrey was the first to recover her wits. "Quite remarkable," she said dryly. "But I think we need more than the sun to help us now."

"Then let my companions help," I said. "I will vouch for them. And call for all the aid you like, neighbouring villages with their knives and their spears; you may need them. But *please,* do not hurt these men."

The elders stepped aside to confer with the ruling sister-group of Imsali. Suhail rose and returned to my side, not even bending to brush the mud off his knees. Thu was watching all of this with an unreadable expression: wariness, perhaps, but also very rapid thought. I did not know him well enough to guess at those thoughts.

When the elders came back, I knew by Sejeat's posture that I was not going to like what they had decided. "You may make your picture," Kuvrey said, "and meet with the humans. But we will hold these two." She gestured at the men. "If the others coming here are as dangerous as you say, then we must have protection against them."

I swayed on my feet. *Hostages.* Suhail and Thu would be hostages after all. If I failed in my goal . . .

It took me an agonizingly long time to force my reply into Draconean. "I cannot—" The word "promise" had fled my mind. "The men who come in the basket, I do not control them. I will try. But my trying may not be good enough." My companions were looking on, uncomprehending; they could see only that a sudden wave of fear had come over me.

"With these two in our keeping," Kuvrey said, "you will try your very best."

I scarcely slept a wink that night. A good deal of time was taken up in creating the sign I needed; there was no proper paint in the village, but the white lime ordinarily used to plaster the yak barn served well enough. I also had to discuss with the villagers the best place to lay that sign out. We needed a suitably large and flat meadow, where the snow had melted enough that my sign would be visible to a caeliger entering through the col, and the craft would have a reasonable chance of landing. And of course we had to negotiate the specifics of who would be where when that happened—my human companions included.

After that, though, there were still some hours in which I might have slept. I passed them instead in Suhail's arms, trembling with nerves. "I am so sorry," I murmured, knowing the words were laughably inadequate. "I should not have brought you here."

His arms tightened around me. "To Imsali?"

"Or the Mrtyahaima."

"Don't be absurd," he said lightly. "I wanted to come—well, not *quite* as much as you did, because that would be difficult to equal. But I certainly would not have sent you off without me. And if you had not come, none of this would have happened, good *or* bad."

"But you are a hostage now, because of me. I should have sent you back across the col. Back to Vidwatha, where you could warn someone—"

This time the pressure of his arms was stronger. "Don't even think of it. No force in the world could have persuaded me to leave you. Not when I had just found you again."

His words silenced me for a time. It was bravado to say I would have sent him away; I could no more have parted from him than he from me.

But the choice, in the end, might not belong to either of us.

"What if I don't succeed?" I whispered. "What if—"

Suhail kissed the top of my head. "You'll do very well. There is no one in the world better suited to this than you."

A bitter, frightened laugh shook my body. "True. But only because there is no other human in the world who speaks their language."

"That is not all of it—though I'll grant that it's a necessary precondition. But Isabella . . . you have thrown yourself into the thick of things before. You are fearless. Not in the sense that you feel no fear; I know better than to think you that foolish. But you do not let it hold you back, and there is power in that. You will hurl yourself in front of that caeliger and refuse to accept anything less than cooperation, and you will bend whoever has come to your will. I believe this, with all my heart."

We lay in silence again, while I tried to ensure I could speak without my voice wavering too badly. When it was steady at last, I said, "All the same. I want you and Thu both to be prepared to do . . . whatever you have to." Defend yourselves, I thought. Run away. Whatever it took. I had lost one husband in the mountains; I would not lose another.

"We will," Suhail promised. "Now sleep."

Perhaps I did, a little. But my memory is of an all-too-short time at his side, before Suhail rose for his dawn prayer and Kahhe came to say it was time.


The worst part was the waiting.

I laid my sign out in the meadow we had chosen, just below the point at which the greenery of spring thinned out to the barren rock of the upper slopes. It was an enormous sheet made of yak-wool blankets hastily stitched together, a square of suspiciously regular brown, with a huge white star painted in its center—a shape snow was unlikely to melt into. Below that I had written "LAND HERE" in the largest letters the space allowed, but I could not be certain anyone would be able to read them from the air.

There were so many things I could not be certain of. What if they did not enter between Gyaptse and Cheja? There were other cols, or the river gorge through which the first caeligers had passed. I had no idea when the caeliger was coming; if its base was very far away, they might not return today, or even tomorrow. We might sit out here for a week without anything happening—and then I would wonder whether I should stay, or make my dash for the outside world in the hope of preventing more flights. (How I might do that, I could not even begin to guess.) They might overlook my sign, or crash in attempting to land, or see movement nearby and rake the ground with their rifles before touching down.

I had all the time in the world to think up one disaster scenario after another, for the caeliger did not come at dawn, nor at noon. The only mercy of this was that waiting dulled the edge of my fear, which cannot remain sharp for so long without something to hone it. The whetstone finally went to work in the early afternoon, when movement at the col drew my gaze. The caeliger had returned, and this time it looked like it would succeed in clearing the pass.

My lips formed soundless prayers. Though ordinarily I devote little attention to religion, in that moment I begged for the mercy of any deity that might care to listen, from the Lord of my childhood Assembly-House visits to the sun the Draconeans worshipped.

The caeliger almost scraped the snow of the col; I think a downdraft must have pushed it unexpectedly to earth. But then it shot forward at a slant, as if it were skiing down the western slope, and attained the free air of the Sanctuary.

A pole lay on the ground at my side. I seized it and, with all the strength in my arms, began to wave its banner back and forth: a piece of yak wool, the brightest blue the limited dye palette of Draconean fabrics could offer. Surely they would have scouts looking below; they must see this movement, a spot of unusual colour against the expected hues of spring, and shapes too regular for nature. I had not intended to speak, knowing my voice would be lost before it reached so high, but holding back proved impossible; I shouted at the top of my lungs, begging them to see me.

And the caeliger flew on. It soared past me and my increasingly desperate cries, dropping altitude as it went, until it was nearly on a level with me. Then it began to turn, and I realized it was simply preparing its approach. I ran for the edge of the meadow, flagpole in hand, to get out of their way.

I did not choose my direction at random. The surrounding terrain afforded little in the way of concealment for Draconeans; even with their spring-grey scales helping them to blend in, the odds of them being spotted from above were too great. But there was a little hollow where one could crouch, and Ruzt was there. If matters here went badly, she would break cover and relay a warning to the rest of her people. I laid my flagpole down near her, exerting all my will not to look at the hollow, and waited.

The landing of the caeliger was a lengthy enough process that I had time to thank any deity who might be listening that we had developed synthetic dragonbone. Had my people landed in something obviously assembled from pieces of dead dragons . . . it did not bear thinking about. Someday we would explain that entire matter to the Draconeans, but not *that* day.

Shouts were coming from the caeliger, but at this close proximity the noise of the engine was too loud for me to make out any words. Men swarmed in the gondola—more men than our vessels had carried from Vidwatha to Tser-nga—carrying out the work necessary to bring it firmly to earth. I knew enough of such operations to be sure they were not quite done when one of the crew flung himself over the edge of the gondola, staggered on the thin spring grass, and set off toward me at a run. *"Isabella!"*

It was my brother Andrew, whom I had left behind in Vidwatha nearly a year before. We collided in the middle of the meadow, Andrew enveloping me in a hug so tremendous, I thought he might re-injure the ribs I had cracked crossing the Cheja Glacier. He was laughing hysterically, as well he might: it was clear that Tom and Lieutenant Chendley had made it back to the lowlands and the army there, and so Andrew had believed me dead.

Our collision swung me around so that I could not see what was going on at the caeliger. As soon as I could, I wriggled free of my brother's embrace so I could turn to look. Under ordinary circumstances I would have been delighted to stay where I was, for each reunion did more to strengthen me than any medicine . . . but I could not forget the burden of expectation that lay upon me.

Behind me, the caeliger was being staked to the ground. The number of men aboard made me certain their point of most recent departure was a good deal closer than Vidwatha. Hlamtse Rong, perhaps, or some locale even more remote, where the Tser-zhag were unlikely to notice them. Close enough that all they need do was get the caeliger up and over the col, whereupon they could seek a landing on the far side.

A man in winter uniform was standing not far away, looking as though he knew he ought to order Andrew to release me at once and behave as befitted a soldier, but was reluctant to disrupt our moment of happiness. When he lifted his goggles, I recognized him as Colonel Dorson, the fellow who commanded the caeliger base in Vidwatha. "Dear God, Lady Trent," he said when I faced him. "How can you possibly be alive?"

"Did the locals rescue you?" Andrew said. He still held my arm—as if, were he to release me, I might vanish in a puff of smoke.

I gave him a sharp glance. "What do you know about them?"

"The locals? Nothing, really."

Dorson intervened, clearly trying to regain some kind of command over the situation. "The original scouting flight saw houses. They aren't Tser-zhag, are they? All our reports say this is beyond the edge of the territory controlled by Tser-nga."

"It is well beyond their control," I said firmly. "In fact, the people here have been cut off from outside contact for a very long time. They—"

Andrew crowed in delight, throwing his arm around my shoulder. "You found a hidden mountain kingdom! Is it like the ones in the legends? Is there a palace of gold around here somewhere?"

He turned as if to look for a palace of gold, which made me very worried that he might see Ruzt instead. Fortunately for me, Dorson snapped out a sharp reprimand: "Captain Hendemore!"

My brother whipped back to face his commanding officer, startled almost to the point of saluting. "Sorry, sir. It's just—my God. She's alive!"

"I can see that," Dorson said.

A sudden thought came to me, strong enough that it diverted

me from my own course. I clutched at Andrew's hand. "Tom. Where is he?"

Andrew looked about as if expecting Tom to materialize at his elbow. "That's odd. Why hasn't he—"

Dorson coughed. "I'm afraid Sir Thomas is still asleep."

"*Asleep?*" I echoed, staring. Then I remembered our own flight from Vidwatha. "Dear God. The laudanum."

"We had to dose him pretty strongly," Andrew said, looking embarrassed. "But he insisted. Said your husband and that Yelangese fellow were out here looking for your body, and that on his own he'd have a better chance of scaling the pass from this side. He was awake for the flight yesterday, but two days in a row seems to have done him in."

Sure enough, Tom was curled up beneath several blankets in one end of the gondola. He was not, as Dorson had claimed, asleep; he was merely thoroughly fuddled. "Tom," I said, crouching in front of him. "Tom, wake up."

Andrew leaned over the edge of the gondola. "Look who we found, Wilker! No need to search for her body; she's been kind enough to bring it to you, alive and well."

I knew my brother's lighthearted tone was a mask for his feelings. Tom's response was to shake his head. His words more than a little slurred, he said, "I may need opium to ride in this infernal thing, but I refuse to become the sort of opium-eater who converses with his delusions."

"I am not a delusion," I said. It did not come out quite as tartly as I wished, for the rejoinder stuck a little in my throat. I could see a gleam at the corner of Tom's eye, threatening to fall. "A delusion would not tell you that she has solved the puzzle of that plaster cast—you know the one I mean. And if you get up, you will soon have a chance to see the solution with your own eyes."

This roused Tom enough for him to lift his head. "Actually, she might say that. But—" His mouth wavered. "But she would not look like ragged hell when she said it. Isabella—"

"It *is* me," I assured him. Then he came surging up out of his blankets to throw his arms around me; and I did not care how many soldiers were looking on, or whether this might renew any rumours about the two of us. I was coming to realize that after a winter isolated among Draconeans, it would take a *very* long time before I was tired of being embraced by those I loved.

Before we separated, though, I whispered quietly in his ear. "Gather your wits as fast as you can. Suhail and Thu are here, but their safety depends on our keeping the peace."

He stared at me as I drew back, but I dared not say any more. Colonel Dorson was waiting with thinly concealed impatience as I climbed out of the gondola once more, leaving Tom to pull himself together. "I imagine you have a hell of a story to tell, Lady Trent."

"I do indeed, Colonel. But before I do, I must ask: what are your intentions here?"

Clearly this was not the direction Dorson had expected our conversation to take. "That is a military matter, Lady Trent. I am very glad to see you alive, but I must remind you that your status as a scientist, or even as a peer of the realm, does not give you the authority to inquire after such things."

My mouth was very dry. "Ah, but I am not asking as a peer of Scirland, nor even as a scientist. I am asking as the appointed emissary of—of a foreign nation."

Andrew's arm dropped from my shoulder. He and Dorson

were not the only ones staring at me; by now the caeliger was fully secured, and the men from it were watching this exchange with interest. To my surprise, a number of them were Yelangese. Khiam Siu? They must be; only our rebel allies would be here, walking free in the midst of a military expedition.

Their presence only furthered my suspicions. "Let me guess: you are looking for an aerial route by which to invade Yelang. No—something more than that. Our caeligers cannot traverse these mountains so easily that overleaping the whole mass in one step would be feasible, not by anything other than the most lightly manned craft." The Sanctuary stretched out before us, the peak of Anshakkar shining in its center. My mouth kept working, taking input but no caution from my brain. "You want to use this as a base. It lies beyond Tser-zhag authority, and is unknown to the outside world; if you could establish yourselves here, then you could mount patrols or military excursions at will. It would allow you to control this entire region."

"Well, yes," Andrew said, as if he saw no point in denial.

*"Captain Hendemore."* This time Andrew did salute, but Dorson was no longer paying attention to him. "I see the keenness of your intellect is not exaggerated, Lady Trent. But what in God's name do you mean, calling yourself the emissary of a foreign nation? Are you talking about whatever yak-herders live here? I hardly think they can call themselves a nation, and I fail to see why they would need to appoint anybody to speak on their behalf. Or are you working for the Tser-zhag king?"

I wondered how much he knew about my actions in Bayembe, when I had, not entirely on purpose, undermined our colony there. At the time it had been a great scandal (I was even accused of treason), but I had won enough acclaim in subsequent years that not everyone remembered that incident. I said, "This has nothing to do with Tser-nga, except insofar as they have a neighbour they are not aware of. My purpose here today is to prevent a conflict which would be detrimental in the extreme to both this land and our own. I have done more than survive, Colonel; I have made a discovery of such magnitude as to cast all my previous work into insignificance by comparison. Scirland has the opportunity to share that discovery with the world—to establish our pre-eminence in ways other than military, which can only be to our benefit."

My declaration aroused a great deal of curiosity, which was as I had hoped. Dorson, however, remained skeptical. "Do you mean that carcass Sir Thomas claimed to have found in the mountains? If it is as he described, then I suppose it is of interest to scientific types—a new sort of dragon, one we didn't think really existed. But I fail to see what relevance that has for our situation here."

A glance over my shoulder revealed that Tom was on his feet, though holding on to the edge of the gondola as if it might be necessary to his continued verticality. I should have liked for him to be more steady, but I did not think I could delay any further.

I made myself smile, as if I had no fear in the world, only excitement for the news I bore. "It is far more than that, Colonel. May I have your word that your men will hold their fire?" Each of them bore a rifle, and while they had not unslung them and readied them for use, I was certain they could do so with great speed.

Dorson tensed at my words. "Lady Trent, asking a military man to hold his fire only confirms for him that there may be a reason to shoot."

"The people of the Sanctuary have no weapons to match yours," I assured him. "I only wish to forestall any misunderstanding that might result in needless bloodshed. If you please?"

A tense silence ensued. I dared not look away from Dorson, though I knew Andrew was staring at me, and I was desperately curious whether Tom had guessed my meaning. Finally Dorson said, "Very well, Lady Trent. Men, hold your fire—for now."

It was the best I could hope for. Now I spared another glance at Tom, and my grin, though still nervous, was also sincere. "This," I promised my colleague, "is *also* not a delusion."

Then I addressed them all, in ringing tones. "What we found in the col was more than merely another kind of dragon. It was the sad remains of one of the people of this valley." Turning, I called out in Draconean, "Ruzt, please stand up."

# NINETEEN

*More introductions—Tom's imagination—Engine malfunction—A good omen for the Khiam Siu—Distractions—Giat Jip-hau and the elders*

Ruzt had volunteered herself for this duty because she was more comfortable around humans than any other Draconean save possibly Kahhe, and I had accepted her offer because I trusted her more than any other Draconean, Kahhe included. But we both knew that if anything went wrong in that first moment, she would be the one who took the brunt of it, and I could not breathe as she stood up.

Dorson's men did not fire. Andrew swore as imaginatively as any sailor, and the colonel did not reprimand him. Ruzt, to my undying astonishment, made her very best mimicry of the curtsey I had given to the elders when I departed from their council, which I had explained to her was a gesture of politeness. I do not think anyone else realized what her movement was supposed to be.

I said, "This Draconean and her sisters saved my life after the avalanche. It is on their behalf, and that of all the Draconeans in the Sanctuary of Wings, that I signaled for you to land here today. If you are willing, Colonel Dorson, I will take you, Sir Thomas, and a small number of your men to meet with representatives from their council of elders."

Enough time had passed without violence that I felt safe in tearing my eyes away from Ruzt and the soldiers and looking at Tom. Judging by his expression, it was entirely possible he had not taken a single breath since Ruzt stood up. I could not help smiling: despite the tension, it was a pure joy to share this discovery with the man who had been my friend and colleague for so many years. Once the last of the laudanum had left his body, we would have a tremendous amount to discuss.

Dorson was staring too, but with a good deal more shock than revelatory understanding. In a limp and wandering voice, he said, "How is this possible?"

At least my encounter with Suhail and Thu the previous day had given me some practice in explaining. I delivered the most concise version I could, blessing the fact that military discipline meant no one interrupted me with a single question. The biological origins of the Draconeans I glossed over with a brief reference to developmental lability; Tom would have guessed a fair bit of it on his own by now, and the phrase would mean nothing to Dorson, which meant I could elide anything that might require me to utter the ominous word "blood." But I told him of the Downfall—a brief rendition of what I could piece together between the Draconean version of that tale and our own—and how, over the millennia, the survivors had taken refuge here. "And now, Colonel, you see why I call them a nation, for they are certainly not Tser-zhag."

"I should bloody well think not," Dorson said faintly. Then he shook himself. "You're able to speak to these . . . things?"

"I am indebted to my husband's work in reconstructing elements of the Draconean language," I said. "Beyond that, a winter with no one else to talk to is a wonderful motivator for acquiring vocabulary. I shall serve as your interpreter, Colonel, if you are ready to meet the elders . . . ?"

This sparked quite a brangle, for Dorson wanted to bring a full complement of armed men, and I wanted nothing of the sort. "Colonel," I said at last, "you should be aware that my husband and Thu Phim-lat reached the Sanctuary yesterday, not long before you made your first attempt at the col. They are currently the guests of the Draconeans—"

"You mean hostages," Dorson said, his entire posture hardening. "Say the word, Lady Trent, and we will retrieve them from these beasts."

"Dear God," I said impatiently. "How clear must I make it that I wish no bloodshed here at all? All you have to do is speak civilly to the elders—who, may I remind you, are no more beasts than we are—without looking as if you are here to finish what the Downfall started, and all will be very well. That means no more than two men with you, plus Tom." All would be very well . . . unless Esdarr or someone of her mind chose to start trouble. But I had to trust the elders to keep order on their end, for I had enough to occupy me on my own.

It was all well and good to insist on only two other men, but who would accompany Dorson? I was astonished to see the changes the army had wrought in my brother; he argued less than I would have expected when Dorson ordered him to remain behind and guard the caeliger. But matters became more than a little tense when the colonel refused to allow any of the Khiam

Siu to join him. "If this comes to blows, I don't want to catch your lot up in it," he said to their leader, a familiar-looking fellow I thought I must have met at one of those diplomatic suppers in Scirland, what felt like a lifetime ago. That man looked very unconvinced, but ultimately ceded the point.

Tom, in the meanwhile, had approached Ruzt. They could not converse at all, and I could not spare any time to interpret or even to really watch them, but he told me later that he had, through much pointing and other elements of mime, made clear to her his gratitude for my preservation. When I was finally able to rejoin him, he shook his head in disbelief.

"I had a whole winter in Vidwatha to think about this," he said. His restless gaze roamed the mountainside, never settling on any one thing. "You and I had wondered, after all, whether there might not be living specimens out here. I thought, what if there are? And what if—" His jaw worked silently for a moment before he could voice the rest of it. "What if they somehow saved you?"

I put one hand on his arm. He turned his head aside, so that I could not see his expression, and could barely hear his voice. "I wanted to believe anything that meant you weren't dead. No matter how impossible."

He pressed the back of his hand to his mouth. When he finally lowered it again, straightening his shoulders, I said lightly, "That goes to show just how astute you are, Tom. Now come: I think you will be fascinated to see what the ruff of a male Draconean looks like."

To my inexpressible relief, the meeting with the elders went off without violence.

Tom contributed substantially to that, for after a winter in Vidwatha, he knew Dorson far better than I did. The colonel had enough of an ego to enjoy the thought of being remembered as the man who established the first treaty with the Draconeans—and of course he thought of it in those terms, that *he* would be the one who achieved that triumph. (I, after all, was just the interpreter.) I let Tom exploit that angle for the time being, knowing that it gave Dorson a greater feeling of control, which in turn made violence less likely.

Suhail and Thu were both present, looking passably like guests instead of hostages. My husband's nod reassured me that they had not been mistreated; Kahhe and Zam were watching over them, much to my relief. But after that I could spare very little attention for them, as my efforts were entirely taken up by the role of interpreter, which I was sadly ill suited to.

I will not attempt to replicate all the points of conversation that day and the following ones. They would make for tedious reading, and would distract from the true turning points that sealed the fate of the Sanctuary and its Draconeans. The first of these involved Andrew, and the second involved Thu.

Dorson had every intention of sending the caeliger back across the mountains as soon as that first meeting concluded. He and the bulk of his men would remain in the Sanctuary, but there were others outside—as I suspected, they had established a temporary base nearby in Tser-nga—and he wished to notify them immediately of what he had discovered. When he returned to the landing meadow, however, Andrew informed him with a doleful expression that the caeliger's engine was malfunctioning. "I think fighting the headwind yesterday strained it something awful, sir," he said. "We're working to repair it, but the ship isn't going anywhere yet."

I prudently waited until Dorson was done castigating everyone for their failures, then snatched a brief moment of conversation with Andrew where no one else could hear. "A malfunctioning engine?"

Andrew shrugged. "It was pretty clear you wanted to keep this under wraps for now. But if I get caught and court-martialled, you should know that I expect you to come riding in on a dragon to save me."

(He was not court-martialled. I did, however, later take the precaution of securing him a pardon.)

My brother's act of benevolent sabotage bought me vital breathing space. At the time I thought it would only give me more opportunity to work on Dorson, persuading him to see the Draconeans as people instead of beasts, and perhaps even convincing him that Scirland must work to protect the Sanctuary from being overrun. Unfortunately, I suspected I would need a good deal more time than Andrew could give me. Dorson seemed willing enough not to kill the Draconeans . . . but I had very little faith that the Sanctuary would not wind up a possession of the Scirling Crown, its inhabitants treated as little more than exotic animals—possibly even put into a menagerie. And I could not see how to prevent that from happening.

"If I'd had a chance to prepare the ground outside," I said to Tom in frustration. I had explained to him the plan the elders and I had formulated—a plan that was now shredded beyond all recognition. "But without public sentiment prepared, what is there to stop the army and the Crown from doing exactly as they please?"

Tom shook his head. "I don't know. Dorson . . . he isn't a bad sort in his own way, but he'll put this whole place under military control, and be convinced he's doing what's best for everyone involved."

"Which will only persuade Urrte and Esdarr and their ilk that the humans must be fought," I said. "God help us all."

"You need leverage," Tom said. "But damned if I can see any."

My one comfort was that I was permitted to go freely between the caeliger camp and Imsali. The remainder of the council would not be there for days yet, and nothing could be decided until they arrived; in the meanwhile, I could see my husband and Thu.

Though both men were still considered hostages, they were not being kept in close straits. Suhail spent every waking moment studying the Draconean language, pausing only for his five daily prayers—an activity he pursued with more diligence than usual, on account of his tremendous gratitude for my survival. Thu was at somewhat looser ends, and frustrated that he could not speak directly with his Khiam Siu brethren. Two days after the landing, I had a question for him.

"Your countrymen seem very eager to meet the Draconeans," I said. The three of us were in the house of Ruzt, Kahhe, and Zam, which no longer seemed half so stifling to me, now that Suhail was there. "It could be simple curiosity, of course—but it doesn't seem to be. I don't suppose you have any idea why?"

He'd had no opportunity to speak with them yet, but it was clear he had been thinking about the matter. "If they are like me, they are thinking this is a very good . . ." He paused and looked at Suhail, who supplied him with the word he had forgotten. "Omen, yes. A good omen for the Khiam cause."

My knowledge of Dajin dragons was still woefully patchy, and I knew even less of how the Yelangese interacted with the creatures, owing to my premature deportation from that country a decade before. I did recall one point, though, which might be salient. "Because dragons are an imperial symbol?" Then I made several connections, quite rapidly. "Good Lord. Dragons are an imperial symbol . . . and the Taisên have been slaughtering theirs for their bones."

Thu nodded. "We say the first emperor of Yelang was able to unify the country because he had the blessing of the dragons. This is why they have always kept dragons, and given them so much respect. For the Taisên to kill them is very shocking."

"And for the Khiam Siu to encounter them en route to planning an invasion is fortuitous. Half dragons, anyway."

At my addendum, Thu's eyes widened. "You have thought of something," I said. "Is it useful?"

He did not answer me directly. Instead, choosing each word very carefully, he said, "In some versions of the tale, it is said that the dragons could take human form."

We all fell silent. It was the type of silence that seems almost clairvoyant, where no one speaks because it is apparent that everyone else is already following the same path of thought, and a mere cock of the head or lift of the hand is enough to communicate the next point. Finally Thu said, "If Giat Jip-hau—"

"We'd have to get him here, first," I said morosely. "And that would take months."

Thu looked startled. "Is he not with the soldiers? I would not expect him to sit back and let others lead the way."

"He—" I stopped, blinking. I had met Giat Jip-hau in Scirland, during those interminable diplomatic events, though I had not spoken to him above twice. He looked very different in the rough garb of a Mrtyahaiman expedition, with his facial hair grown to a thin scruff.

The would-be emperor of Yelang was in the caeliger camp that very moment.

And now I had a very good idea of why Dorson was so reluctant to allow any of the Khiam Siu to speak with the Draconeans. Suhail said, "Do you think you could arrange a meeting?"

"From the Draconean side, yes," I said. "I'm sure Kuvrey and Sejeat and Habarz would be willing. But from the Scirling side? Dorson will see it as an attempt to usurp his role." Which, in all fairness, it would be.

"Then don't tell him," Suhail said.


Even after a winter among the Draconeans, I could not always read their expressions and body language reliably. The three sisters, yes; their mannerisms were deeply familiar to me. The elders, however, were another matter. I therefore did not realize, until I suggested the meeting with Giat Jip-hau, that Kuvrey, Sejeat, and Habarz had taken a strong dislike to Colonel Dorson.

"We would like to speak to someone else," Kuvrey said, when she heard my proposal. I did not think it was my imagination that I read her words as understatement. All of Dorson's words went through me, and I did what I could to polish them, but by now the Draconeans had enough sense of human body language that they might well be able to detect his perpetual air of condescension. Even while negotiating a treaty, Dorson seemed as if he were speaking to a group of particularly clever animals, which could not possibly go over well.

Back I went to the caeliger landing meadow, for a hushed conversation with Tom and Andrew. "I think I can resolve this situation in a way that will work out to everyone's benefit—but it requires me to get at least Giat Jip-hau out of the camp without Dorson noticing. Better if it is him *and* some of his countrymen, but him at a minimum."

Andrew chewed on his lower lip. "I could make some kind of diversion—light something on fire, perhaps—"

"No!" I reared back in alarm, then made myself relax. If anyone saw us, we must not look like we were plotting conspiracy. (Even if we were. Especially *because* we were.) "You've already put your neck out far enough, Andrew. I don't want to see you in front of a firing squad."

"Dorson wouldn't do that," my brother scoffed, but all the confidence in the world would not have persuaded me to risk him in that fashion.

Tom said, "What about the Draconeans? If some of them wanted to meet with Dorson—"

"I would be needed as their interpreter. Which means I would not then be there to interpret for the Khiam Siu." Given time we did not have, Suhail might have been able to share that duty with me—but there were limits even to my husband's capacity for learning.

Tom had seen the flaw as quickly as I had. He nodded. "Nighttime, then. When most of the camp is asleep." He hesitated, then said, "We could make certain they sleep. All of them, except the Khiam Siu. I still have quite a lot of laudanum."

The prospect made me blanch. "That is nearly as bad as

Andrew's suggestion. They would know it was you, Tom—or they would blame the Khiam Siu for drugging them. No, we simply need the sentries to look the other way for a brief time."

"Then we're back to a diversion," Andrew said. "But one quiet enough that it won't wake up the whole camp. I'm on watch tonight, if you can arrange the meeting for the right hour, but there will be another fellow with me. And I don't think it will work for me to simply point behind him and say, 'What in the world can that be?'"

For the Khiam Siu to sneak out of camp, they would need a longer distraction than that. The three of us sat in silence for a time, broken only by the occasional aborted suggestion: "What if—no, never mind" and the like.

Finally a thought came to me, and a grin spread across my face. "I think I have the answer. But I will need something from Imsali first."

It was a mad rush, arranging everything in time. Tom spoke to Giat Jip-hau, as he could do so without attracting as much attention as I would; but I had to settle the place and time of meeting with the elders, and then I had to talk to Ruzt. She doubted my ability to carry out the plan on my own—rightly, I suspect—and so when night fell at last, I crept out of Imsali and toward the caeliger meadow with Zam at my side, and two squirming bundles under my coat.

When we were still far enough from the meadow not to risk being overheard, she muttered, "One group of humans; another group of humans. How much difference will it really make?"

All the difference in the world, I hoped. But what I said was, "How much difference would it have made had I been found by

Esdarr and her sisters, instead of you three?"

Zam spat something I expect was very uncomplimentary, and we left it at that.

At the edge of camp, beyond the light of their lamps and fire, we crouched down behind the same cover that had previously sheltered Ruzt. Zam released her own bundles first, with a quiet whistle to command them. My coat began squirming even more energetically; I opened it and let two more mews slip free. They lifted their heads and sampled the air; then one scurried away. They would have easy pickings in the camp's supplies: Dorson and his men had not learned from the Nying to set traps.

Andrew had been listening for the whistle, but he waited several minutes to give the scouting mew time to call in the rest of its flight. Once they had settled in for a thorough raid, he cursed softly, as if he had just noticed the invaders, and dragged his fellow watchman over to drive the mews away.

The trained kind are more difficult to scare off than their wild brethren, especially when Andrew was deliberately ineffective. The mews were still hissing and flapping about the watchman's head when I slipped away from camp, circling around to meet up with the aspiring emperor of Yelang and lead him to the Draconeans.

Once again I played interpreter, but this time for a very different sort of conversation.

Giat Jip-hau spoke very good Scirling, better than Thu's, but I wished my companion could have been there. It was, after all, his discovery of the first Draconean body that had put us all on this path; and without him, I would not have known to engineer this meeting. Unfortunately, the elders insisted Thu remain with Suhail, under guard in Imsali, as insurance against any deception. I had complete faith that the Khiam Siu intended nothing untoward; my sole concern was that we get the prospective emperor back to camp as soon as possible. Neither of us had much hope that he could return as discreetly as he had left, of course. But if we could keep negotiations from dragging on for so long that his absence was discovered, I believed all would be well.

When we arrived at the copse of dwarfish trees where the elders and their guards waited, he showed respect to the elders as I had advised him, crossing his arms over his body in imitation of wings. Then he bowed in his own manner—a tiny inclination of the body; as much as could be expected from a man of his station—and held out a small object. "Lady Trent, if you would give this to them. It is my gift, in gratitude for their hospitality."

A few torches lit the area, enough for me to see what he held. It was an intricate carving of a dragon, not very large, but all the more impressive for being executed so small—especially as it appeared to be made of jade, which is quite a hard stone. My naturalist's instinct made me want to study it more closely, to see if I could identify the breed, but I carried it to one of the guards, who passed it to Habarz.

With that to pave the way, I told the story of the first emperor of Yelang, as Thu had told it to me: how the dragons had taken human form and blessed the man, and how this blessing was believed to legitimate each subsequent dynasty in turn. And I told how the Taisên had slaughtered dragons for their bones—but honesty would not allow me to leave the matter there. "My own people have done the same," I said, "although now we have a way of creating the substance of dragonbone from other materials, as one creates butter from milk." I bowed my head. "Indeed . . . I myself have been party to the killing of dragons. It is necessary for my study of them. But I confess that after coming here, to the Sanctuary, my feelings on the matter are rather different from what they were before."

How could they not be? We still do not know which draconic species first gave rise to the Draconeans themselves; it may be a breed long since gone extinct. But I could not look at dragons any longer without seeing them as the cousins of the Draconean people. I believe this would have been true even had Ruzt not told me their myth, the one in which humans were born from the fronts of the four sisters, and dragons from their backs. I do not credit that story as factually accurate, but that does not prevent it from carrying a more symbolic truth. There are times when the death of dragons is unavoidable—they are, after all, still large predators who occasionally take it into their heads to threaten the lives of others—but ever since my time in the Sanctuary, it has been my habit to avoid killing whenever I can.

My revelation occasioned some muttering among the Draconeans, and a conference between Kuvrey, Sejeat, and Habarz, for which I stood well back and forced myself not to eavesdrop. At last Kuvrey turned back and said, "That is not the matter for which you brought us here tonight."

"No, it is not." I took a deep breath and brushed my hair from my face. The elders were correct; my own past behaviour was not the most important issue at hand. We were concerned now with nations, not individuals. "The alliance Giat Jip-hau proposes to you is this: if the council bestows its blessings upon his reign—

publicly, with one or more Draconeans accompanying him into Yelang for the purpose—then when he claims the throne, Yelang will in turn acknowledge and protect the sovereignty of this place." Figuring out a way to say "sovereignty" had occupied far too much of my time and Ruzt's. If the Draconeans ever had such a word, it had been lost during the ages in which they hid from all foreign relations.

Before the elders could respond, I added, "This also protects you against my own people. Scirland will gain more from a friendly dynasty in Yelang than it will from taking over the Sanctuary of Wings. If they fail to respect your borders, they will lose their alliance with the Khiam Siu. If the Khiam Siu fail to honour their agreement with you, then you can withdraw your blessing of them, which will endanger their standing in Yelang. Because both groups benefit from your continued independence, they will be your shield against anyone else who thinks to threaten it."

I knew full well that what I proposed was a house of cards. Others have built such things before, and seen them collapse, sometimes in catastrophic ways. It was, however, the only solution any of us could see: myself or any of my companions, human or Draconean. But the entire proposal hinged on one question: would the Draconeans bestow their support on a group of humans? It would cost them very little, and they stood to gain much . . . but part of the cost would be the willingness to look past the disputed history of the Downfall, their ancient fear of our species, and extend the hand of friendship in view of all the world.

Kuvrey looked at Giat Jip-hau. He did not cast his eyes downward, but met and held her gaze. According to the customs of the Draconeans—and in some ways, the customs of humans—his boldness constituted a challenge. I understood, however, his unwillingness to appear meek in front of potential allies. This man aspired to be the emperor of one of the most powerful nations in the world. He could not begin by showing submission to anyone. Even his bow at the beginning had been a noteworthy concession.

Finally Kuvrey said, "He will have no answer tonight. No decisions at all will happen until the remainder of the council arrives. But we will consider this proposal, Zabel, and weigh it against what the other human has said."

Dorson's offer was not nearly so attractive as this one, and the elders disliked him besides. I could not imagine them accepting his overtures, in preference to those of the Khiam Siu.

But those were not the only two options on the table. The Draconeans might decide to follow some third course entirely— one I could not begin to predict.

Sejeat asked, "Our people you wish to send with him. Would they be safe?"

I translated her question for Giat Jip-hau. He said, "I would do everything in my power to protect them. But I cannot guarantee their safety—any more than I can guarantee my own."

It was a fair answer. I gave it to the elders, who simply nodded; and then the meeting was at an end.

# TWENTY

*Sharing credit—The alliance is formed—Insufficient interpreters—A grand entrance—On the plains—Taking Tiongau—Giat Jip-hau's plan*

To say that Dorson was displeased by what we had wrought in the night is a profound understatement, but a more accurate description would entail words I prefer not to use in print.

He was displeased when Giat Jip-hau returned to camp— Andrew having dutifully woken him up when the other sentry spotted the prospective emperor returning. He was displeased when he heard that the leader of the Khiam Siu had met with the Draconeans, and I had engineered it. He was displeased when he realized that he could not punish me by shutting me out of his own negotiations, for without me, there could be no negotiations at all; he even went so far as to question my probity in translating their exchanges, and only desisted when Tom threatened to duel him then and there.

I thought of placating the colonel by offering a different kind of glory: allowing him to claim the credit for engineering the three-way alliance between the Sanctuary, Scirland, and the future Yelangese dynasty. But when I opened my mouth to speak the words, they would not come out. I had finished with such concessions. When others have contributed to my achievements, I am more than willing to give them credit. I would not have come to the Mrtyahaima had Thu not first located the dead Draconean's remains and identified them as something unusual; I would not have been driven into the Sanctuary, and the hands of Ruzt and her sisters, had Tom not spotted the second body in the col; I would not have been able to communicate half so well with the Draconeans had my husband not unlocked the first doors of their language. There are countless others to whom I owe thanks, ranging from my father to my first husband Jacob to Lord Hilford, from Yeyuama in the Green Hell to Shuwa in Hlamtse Rong. I even owe a debt to that unknown desert drake who laid her eggs atop the buried entrance to the Watchers' Heart.

Dorson had provided me with transportation into the Mrtyahaima, and had played a catalyzing role in sparking our negotiations that spring, not least of all because he brought Giat Jip-hau with him. But he had no part in the alliance, except to obstruct it—and I would not hand him those laurels simply to win his goodwill. As I said to Tom, "He can either join in and do his bit, for which I will thank him . . . or he can get out of the way."

The way in question was, of course, alliance. It did not happen overnight: the remainder of the council arrived on the same day that Dorson finally sent the caeliger back across the Sanctuary wall to inform the rest of his expedition of what he had found, and after that things got very, very complicated. But in the end, the council voted to proceed as we had discussed, blessing the reign of the first Khiam emperor.

Some delusionally optimistic part of me had thought that once this was arranged, I would be able to go home. I have rarely been prone to homesickness, but by then my longing for Scirland was so powerful I could taste it. Although I had been reunited with Suhail and Tom, my son still believed me to be dead, along with Natalie and all my family save Andrew, and all the good friends and colleagues I had acquired along the way. It would sadden me to leave behind Ruzt and Kahhe and yes, even Zam, but the Sanctuary was not and could never be my home.

My rationality soon reasserted itself, though. Suhail was devoting himself to the task of learning Draconean with a single-mindedness that astounded even me, and a rate of success that put me utterly to shame. Giat Jip-hau and several others were also bending their efforts to this task, albeit more slowly; and in turn we were teaching small amounts of some human languages to the Draconeans. Scirling and one or more of the Yelangese tongues were the most useful diplomatically, but the Draconeans made the greatest strides with Akhian, because of its relationship to their own language. As strenuously as we all worked, however, I remained the only person who could converse with both species in anything like a fluent manner (and even then, my limitations remained great). No one else, after all, had endured months in which there was nothing to do but herd yaks and acquire vocabulary.

This meant that any alliance expedition must necessarily have me along—and so it was that, ten years after my deportation from Yelang, I returned to that land in a convoy of Scirlings, Khiam Siu, and Draconeans.

*   *   *

Counting both those who came into the Sanctuary on that initial flight and those who had remained outside, the Khiam Siu accompanying Dorson's forces numbered just under a score, plus Thu Phim-lat. A pair of these remained behind in the Sanctuary, but the rest formed the core of our laughably small invasion force.

To these we added a round dozen Scirlings, including myself, Tom, and Colonel Dorson, and four Draconeans. The elders had decided upon a suitable punishment for the transgressions of Ruzt, Kahhe, and Zam: they would be the ones to accompany our group, risking themselves in a world full of humans. But in the end they numbered four, not three, because their clutch-brother Atlim insisted on accompanying them.

This occasioned yet another argument—I thought they would never end. To the Draconeans, four is an auspicious number, echoing the four sisters from whom their species is said to descend. But to the Yelangese, four is decidedly inauspicious; in most Yelangese languages, that word is a homophone for "death." But Atlim would not remain behind. In the end we resorted to numerical sleight-of-hand; there were not four Draconeans, but three plus one. Only the sisters would publicly bless the new emperor, with Atlim standing aloof.

So altogether we numbered thirty-three. This was, of course, not nearly enough to mount a revolution off our own bat. Should it come to that, however, we were already lost; for it would mean the bulk of the Khiam Siu movement, those revolutionaries who had remained in Yelang, had failed to rise to Giat Jip-hau's banner. Without them, we had no hope of success; more soldiers in our party would not change that.

And waiting for more soldiers would only put us at risk of

losing the element of surprise. Dorson's message to the outside world had of course been sent with strict orders for military security—but none of us (including Dorson, once his bluster faded) believed that would last for long. And once the Taisên learned about the Sanctuary, their own soldiers would be here as fast as their caeligers could fly. To avoid a pitched battle in this hidden valley, and to preserve the impact of the Draconeans' first appearance in Yelang, we had to move as soon as we could.

The remainder of the Scirling contingent, and a pair of Khiam men, stayed behind in the Sanctuary. Andrew argued vociferously to come with us to Yelang, but I took him aside and pled with him to accept command of the Sanctuary forces. "You are the only one among Dorson's men I trust to safeguard the alliance we have made," I said.

"Suhail will be here," he said, his jaw set in its most stubborn line.

It was not an argument calibrated to sway me. Leaving my husband behind was one of the most wrenching decisions I have ever had to make; after our winter-long separation, neither of us was yet ready to be parted once more. But it was the only feasible choice: with me gone from the Sanctuary, Suhail was the closest thing to an interpreter anyone there would have. His command of Draconean was still weak, but he would be competent with it long before anyone else could hope to be.

"Suhail's authority does not apply to the military," I said. "I need you both here. And—" My throat closed up unexpectedly. "I need you to watch over him. Whatever the council has voted, there are Draconeans who do not like this alliance at all. If something were to happen to him while I am gone—"

Andrew gripped my shoulders. "Say no more. I'll keep him safe."

I have never asked who it was that arranged for Suhail and I to be alone on my final night in the Sanctuary, with Ruzt, Kahhe, Zam, and Thu all quartering elsewhere. I think it must have been my husband; but it may have been one of the sisters. Not Zam, as she had little understanding of human notions of privacy and pair-bonding, but Ruzt or Kahhe might have done it. Regardless of the cause, we had one night in which we need not attend to anyone else's troubles but our own.

Suhail had made no secret of his reluctance to let me go, but he understood the need, and he was smiling as we cleaned out the bowls that had held our supper. I should not have had any appetite, but after a long winter of limited rations, my body had little concern for the distress of my mind. (In particular, the tins of lime juice from Dorson's supplies were exceedingly welcome. I had nearly forgotten what it felt like to have my teeth sit secure instead of loose.)

"How can you be so cheerful?" I demanded of him. Despite my words, a little smile of my own kept tugging at the corners of my mouth.

"I am just thinking," he said, "that most people will not have heard yet that you are alive. What a grand entrance you will make!"

This was so at odds with my own mood that could only stare at him. Then he came and enfolded me in his arms; and to my surprise, I found myself laughing. "Indeed," I said at last. If the shoulder of his shirt was damp by the time I drew back, neither of us commented on it.

And that is all I shall say of that night.

* * *

So it was that in early Gelis, just days before my fortieth birthday, we crossed the wall of the Sanctuary—the far wall, on the western side. The mountains there were even more deserted than the western edge of Tser-nga, but soon shrank into foothills, which gave out onto the high plains of Khavtlai. The people there had been subject to Yelang for over a century, but the Taisên presence was minimal: the imperial soldiers were content to hunker down in forts, leaving the trackless grasslands to the nomadic herdsmen of the region.

We could avoid the Taisên, but not the Khavtlek, who are as adept as Akhian nomads at knowing who passes through the vast empty spaces of their home. Fortunately for us, they had no particular fondness for their overlords, and could be persuaded to turn a blind eye to our passage. We had only to keep our Draconean companions hidden—for as much as we wanted their presence to make a stir, we did not want it to do so *yet*.

I should have foreseen our first difficulty. But after so many months cooped up in the frigid heights of the Mrtyahaima, the prospect of leaving them was, to me, an unmitigated joy. It did not occur to me, until our first night in Khavtlek territory, that not everyone in our party would view it the same way.

That the Draconeans had been silent during that day's travels, I attributed to the necessity of bundling them under cloaks for concealment. But they dove into their tent with such alacrity, I knew something was amiss. "May I come in?" I called from outside the flap, and entered when I heard Kahhe's reply.

They sat in a ring, facing inward with their wings partly spread to cup one another's backs. For them it is a comforting gesture, akin to an arm around a human's shoulders. "Is everything all right?" I asked. Then I waved the question away as foolish. "Is there anything I can do to help?"

"Make the sky smaller," Zam muttered, hunching her back.

What felt to me like gloriously open terrain was, to them, a daunting void. With each day we travelled, their beloved mountains receded farther into the distance, replaced by arid grassland and empty sky, as alien to them as a subterranean city would be to me. At home they were accustomed to gliding down the valleys from higher precipices; here they could scarcely fly at all, even if we dared risk such a display. The cloaks were both a blessing and a curse, helping them close out the sight of so much open space, but causing them to feel even more penned in than I had felt in their house.

It pained me that there was nothing I could do for them. The only solution would be to send them home again—and that was no solution at all. We needed them with us, and their elders had decreed this was their punishment. The council had chosen well indeed. Only Atlim could return before this affair was done; and he refused, as he had refused to stay behind in the first place. The sisters had no choice but to endure.

Matters would become both better and worse once we reached a more settled area. Our destination was the city of Tiongau, in the lower-lying hills that marked the far boundary of the Khavtlai plain. This was a hotbed of Khiam Siu, though they had been left quite leaderless since the failed insurrection at Diéziò; and it was here, Giat Jip-hau said, that he intended to proclaim himself the first Khiam emperor.

I did not participate in the initial infiltration of the city. Not only had I no desire to do so, I would have been worse than useless: a Scirling woman in the middle of a Yelangese city would have been *extremely* noticeable. Along with my fellow countrymen and the Draconeans, I lay in wait outside the city—which you need not think meant we were all huddling under bushes. One of the local magnates with an estate in the nearby countryside was a secret Khiam sympathizer, and he gave us shelter while Giat Jip-hau and his chosen companions went disguised into Tiongau, in search of the rest of their coterie.

As little as I wished to participate in another battle, waiting there was excruciating. Dorson spent the entire time pacing; he greatly disliked sitting idle while the Yelangese went about their work. But of course the presence of Scirling soldiers in Tiongau, even out of uniform, would only increase the chance of discovery. I did not pace, but I fretted all the same, spinning a hundred different scenarios in which we had to flee east on sudden notice, back to the shelter of the Sanctuary.

But disaster did not come. As is so often the case with such things, the waiting was lengthy, but the event itself brief. I shall not attempt to relate what I was not there to see; I will only say that once the fighting began, it lasted for scarcely two days. Pockets of resistance remained, but the Khiam Siu had overthrown the governor and taken possession of key locations around the city. Once those were secure, Thu reappeared with a bandage around one arm, and announced that Giat Jip-hau required our presence in the city.

I was not at my best when Tom and I arrived at the governor's palace. Although the arrival of the caeliger and the subsequent juggling of forces in the Sanctuary had done a little to acclimate me to human company once more, I was wildly unprepared for a city full of my own species. The last time I had faced them in such quantities was in Kotranagar a year before, on my way through Vidwatha to Tser-nga. I wondered how the Draconeans would fare, surrounded by humans. I was very glad that, for reasons of security, they would not enter Tiongau until they could do so under cover of darkness.

The prospective emperor had laid claim to the governor's own chambers. Austere for reasons of both personal inclination and political image, Giat Jip-hau had ordered the rooms stripped of much of their finery; what remained, however, was still more than elegant, with laquered screens and windows framing views of the gardens outside. I felt terribly out of place, even after my first proper bath in more than a year.

He wasted no time in making it clear why he had summoned us. "The governor of this place, like many of his rank, kept a menagerie, and in it there are dragons. I know the Draconeans trained those creatures in the Sanctuary for their own use—the mews. I want them to train the dragons here."

Tom and I exchanged glances. His minute shrug said he deferred to my knowledge on the matter. I almost wished he hadn't; none of my instinctive responses were at all polite. I managed to replace them with a question: "Train them to what end?"

"You rode a sea-serpent into battle in the Keongan islands," Giat Jip-hau said. "The dragons here are large enough to bear a rider."

I fear I gaped like a landed fish. Too many words wanted to come out of my mouth at once; they clogged my mind instead, leaving me with nothing. Tom stepped into the breach. "My lord, that is more like riding a wild mustang than a war-horse. The Keongans use the serpents in part because they have neither the firearms nor the artillery of a modern army; you do not suffer any such lack. Dragons would not be of much use to you as a weapon."

Giat Jip-hau dismissed this with a small cut of his hand. "Their use as weapons is secondary at best. But if my enemies see my generals riding into battle upon dragons, the effect on their morale will be enormous."

Insofar as it went, he was probably correct. That did not make the idea a good one, though. I found my tongue, and used it. "My lord, the Draconeans have spent centuries breeding the mews for their use, in much the same way that humans bred wolves into dogs. The fact that we can command hounds for our own benefit does not mean we can do the same with tigers; and I think it is fair to assume that the gap between mews and whatever dragons you have here is at least that large. If you had a decade to spend on this endeavour, it might be possible; but I presume your schedule is rather swifter than that."

I should have stopped there. My mouth went on, though, without leave from my brain. "And even if it could be done, I think it should not."

He fixed me with a steady gaze. "Explain."

I thought of the rock-wyrms that had attacked the boyar's men in the Vystrani Mountains, the fangfish that had savaged the Ikwunde, little Ascelin killing the Taisên agent in Qurrat and the sea-serpents thrashing in the waters around Keonga. But Giat Jip-hau would not be swayed by my qualms over my own past actions, nor by my newfound reluctance to see dragons killed for any reason other than sheer necessity. His care was for the future of his nation, not the well-being of a few beasts.

Instead I gave him a practical answer. "Battles are perilous things, my lord; you know that as well as I do. What omen would it be for your reign if these dragons were shot down in the field?"

"It would be the Taisên who shot them, and the Taisên upon whom the blame would fall."

"Perhaps. But they have not used dragons in battle; their own ministers would argue that you are the one who brought them to that fate. Some would agree with you, and others with the Taisên. It is a great deal of effort for dubious benefit—especially when you might more profitably attempt to train them for another purpose."

I spoke that last as if I had some plan in mind, held in reserve until that moment. In truth, it only took shape as I spoke; and even then, I hesitated to dignify it with the name of "plan." But Giat Jip-hau listened with interest as I shared the beginnings of it, and he and Tom contributed elaborations and improvements, and before long, I was committed.

To my part, at least. "I must consult with the Draconeans before I can say anything for certain," I reminded him.

"Then act swiftly," he said. "One way or another, we do not have much time."

# TWENTY-ONE

*Azure dragons—A blessing—The Khiam Siu rise up—The end of the rebellion—A letter—Returning home*

The entire plan depended on the assistance of the Draconeans. They entered Tiongau in the small hours of the night, when only Khiam Siu patrolled the streets, and were smuggled into the palace through a servant entrance.

Even traversing the city at night was a shock to them. "I owe you an apology, Zabel," Ruzt said when Tom and I met them, shortly after dawn. "You told us there were many humans in the world, but I never believed they could exist in such numbers. How many places like this are there?"

"More than I can count," I said. "And some are far larger than this. But you need not concern yourselves with that just now; I have something to show you."

The governor's menagerie was no miserable zoo, with animals kept in iron cages. Instead it was a series of beautiful gardens, with their bars, where necessary, concealed behind trees and flowering bushes. The most splendid of these gardens housed a pair of *ci lêng,* a species known in Scirling as the azure or eastern dragon; the latter name derives from their natural range, which lies in the eastern part of Yelang, and the former derives from their lovely blue scales.

Our Draconean companions reacted to these with astonished delight. Just as I had told them of the vast number of humans in the world, I had told them of other dragon breeds; and just as my words had failed to convey the true reality of humankind, so too had it fallen short of describing dragonkind. Despite my cautions, the sisters hurried through the gate and into the garden, where they sat utterly still until the *ci lěng* lost their wariness and came to investigate. There is no sight quite like a trio of previously mythical Draconeans sitting in a Yelangese garden with two azure dragons wending between them like curious cats; and in that moment, I felt as if all my suffering the previous winter had been more than worth it.

But of course we had a great deal to do, and not much time in which to do it. Nor, for that matter, did we have many resources to work with. The governor's dragon-men were of course no help, as they were all loyal to the Taisên; and Tom and I knew perishingly little about the breeds of western Dajin, on account of having been thrown out of Yelang before we could study more than a few. But the dragon-men had kept books detailing their arrangements, which Thu translated for us, and from this we were able to learn the means by which they fed, cared for, and worked with their charges. Kahhe, who was the best of the sisters at training mews, shook her head over the latter parts. "Is that how humans do it? No wonder you can't manage much."

I grinned impudently at her, buoyed by my excitement. "Very well—let us see you do better."

They set to it with a will, despite certain obstacles. True to Tom's predictions regarding the mews, our friends from the Sanctuary were too well adapted to high elevations and cold temperatures; the warmth of eastern Yelang in Gelis was as punishing to them as the Akhian desert in Caloris was to me. Fortunately the governor, being a wealthy man, had storehouses of ice brought down from the mountains. The four Draconeans took refuge there during the hottest parts of the day, working with the azure dragons in the morning and evening.

But they pushed themselves to their limits, for Giat Jip-hau insisted on swift action, and with good cause. The Khiam Siu rebellion needed momentum; their victory in Tiongau could not be allowed to grow stale, or the Taisên to gather themselves to resist. The moment of truth was upon us before we knew it.

It came on a brilliantly sunny day. The last of the resistance within Tiongau had been defeated; in celebration, the Khiam Siu and the people of the city were staging a great festival. Despite the destruction wrought by fighting, the burned houses and the grieving survivors, a raucous procession wound its way to the plaza in front of the governor's palace. There were drums and fireworks, dancers and priests, and an enormous puppet of a *hong lêng,* the dragon associated with the Yelangese emperor himself. This was carried by a whole crowd of puppeteers, and when I saw the puppet later, it reminded me a great deal of the *legambwa bomu* the Moulish had used to chasten me into shedding the burden of witchcraft, so many years before—albeit much larger and more brilliantly decorated.

I did not see the puppet until later because I was not standing with the soldiers on the steps of the palace, awaiting the emergence of Giat Jip-hau. I was with Tom, very gingerly leading a pair of leashed azure dragons through the corridors like enormous greyhounds, and hoping very sincerely that they would not decide to turn against us without warning. The *ci lêng* were relatively tame, as dragons went, but just as a cat or a horse may snap at its owner, so too may such creatures—with very injurious consequences.

The corridors, though grand, had not been sized for dragons. From behind us came a delicate crash. Tom and I both stopped, wincing. I cast a glance behind me, and saw that the tail of Tom's dragon had brushed against a vase in an alcove, knocking it to the floor.

"Do I even want to know what that was?" Tom asked.

"As there is nothing we can do for it now," I said, "perhaps it is best if we just continue on."

We made it to the great entry hall without further incident, and stood to one side, where we could not be glimpsed through the towering double doors. We had not been there long when I heard the footsteps of a great many people approaching, and then someone saying something in Yelangese. I turned just in time to see a Khiam Siu captain wipe the floor with a silk drapery, clearing away a souvenir left behind by one of the dragons before his emperor could step in it.

"Oh dear," I said involuntarily. "I, ah—my apologies."

If the incident troubled Giat Jip-hau, he did not show it. Perhaps his mind was so occupied by the impending ceremony that it simply could not accommodate any new sources of agitation; certainly mine would have been. He merely said, "Will it work?"

"I believe so," I said. Then, because that was clearly insufficient: "Yes." I prayed it was true.

He answered with a brief nod, and his entourage swept past us to the doors.

The roar from outside was tremendous when Giat Jip-hau appeared. I peered around a pillar long enough to see him raise his hands for silence, and obtain the closest approximation to it one can hope for from such a large crowd. But even had I been able to understand more than a dozen words of any Yelangese tongue, I would not have been able to listen to his oration; my leashed dragon was very determined to chew upon the gilded carvings of another pillar, and it was all I could do to keep her from swallowing a mouthful of wood and gold.

In a way, I was grateful for her mischief. It kept me from dwelling overmuch on what came next.

Thu seemed to appear out of nowhere, almost vibrating with excitement. "It is time."

Tom and I emerged from the great entry hall into dazzling sunlight and the renewed roar of the crowd. It seemed all of Tiongau was arrayed in the plaza below us, and every last one of them was shouting at the sight of the two *ci lêng*—for I have no illusions that a pair of Scirling strangers occasioned any notice, when there were azure dragons to see. The common people of Tiongau would never have seen the beasts except in paintings, and their presence next to the self-proclaimed emperor of Yelang was as wondrous to them as the sight of a Draconean had been to me.

But we had only begun to astonish them.

Three shadows passed overhead, and the crowd fell to dead silence.

Ruzt, Kahhe, and Zam had leapt from the roof above. Wings spread to their fullest extent, the sisters glided over the assembled dignitaries and down the palace stairs to a point equidistant between the emperor and the crowd. They stood there long enough for people to see them clearly, and to know that these were no humans dressed in masks and silk wings; they were draconic humanoids, creatures out of legend. Then they turned, wings and ruffs spread a little in display, and ascended the stairs once more to where Giat Jip-hau waited.

In this manner did the Draconeans make their public entrance to the world of humans.

All our pains to keep them secret came to fruition in that instant, and it was worth every ounce of effort. What might have been a moment of terror transmuted to wonder instead, as the Draconeans raised their hands to the sun and spoke a blessing in the local tongue that invoked an admixture of beliefs: a ceremony of Atlim's design, one part Draconean, one part Yelangese, and one part pure invention. Giat Jip-hau stepped forward, and Thu laid a golden robe over his shoulders; and in a powerful voice that carried to the far side of the plaza, he proclaimed himself the first Khiam emperor.

And the azure dragons danced.

Tom and I had unclipped their leashes while the sisters spoke their blessing. Following Kahhe's whistled signals, the two *ci lêng* flowed forward, executing a circle around Giat Jip-hau, down the steps a short distance, and back up again to where Tom and I waited.

For the dragons to be present at his proclamation would have been a boost to the new emperor's legitimacy—but they were only *ci lêng,* the dragons permitted to high officials, not the *hong lèng* that symbolized the emperor himself. But for the Draconeans to appear, as if conjured from nowhere, and for the *ci lèng* to dance at their command . . . could there be any clearer proof of his blessed state?

The Khiam Revolution did not achieve victory that day, of course. Although a great many people rose to their banner after Tiongau, quite a few did not; and the Taisên fought tooth and nail to retain their power, including many pitched battles that I was glad to sit out. By the time I left Yelang, almost a year later, the success of the Khiam Dynasty was a foregone conclusion, but the fighting still continued; by then we had repeated the grand display half a dozen times, to prove that the events in Tiongau were not simply a tall tale. Not all breeds were amenable to even that minor degree of training, but it did not matter: the story spread, and influenced public opinion wherever it went. Whatever the Taisên thought, the war was won on the day that a *hong lèng* circled Giat Jip-hau in front of the captured Imperial Palace.

The challenges for my Draconean friends were tremendous. They remained miserable in the heat, especially when we visited lowland regions; and Zam even expressed grudging sympathy to me at one point, saying, "Now I think I understand how you felt when we were chasing the yaks." Taisên agents made eight separate attempts to assassinate them, none successful. Thu told me it was a sign of desperation, that they would risk being blamed for such an act; but this of course is small comfort when one cannot sleep with both eyes closed. (They also tried to assassinate me, I think out of spite. I was far less of a threat to them than either the Draconeans or the new emperor.) It was a relief when I could finally install myself in a room in the Imperial Palace, safe behind a cordon of both Scirling and Khiam Siu guards.

By then my thoughts and Tom's were increasingly bending toward Scirland, despite the grand events occuring around us. "Will you come with us back to the Sanctuary?" Ruzt asked one day. Their exile had ended; the elders, well pleased with what they had done, were permitting them to go home.

A part of me wanted to say yes. We had been through so much together; it was strange to imagine being parted from my Draconean friends. But not only was the Sanctuary not my home, I had little desire to return there—at least, not so soon. I wanted the company of my own countrymen, the ease of speaking my native tongue, the comforts of my home in Falchester. I could not have any of these yet; but I could have my husband.

"Suhail is in Tser-nga now," I said. "Your elders will be negotiating with the Tser-zhag king soon, and I should like to be there for that. It will be a good deal faster if I sail to the other side of Dajin, instead of tramping through the mountains—and a good deal safer, too."

Ruzt's wings fluttered. "And you do not want to go back."

Before I could frame a response to that, she waved it away. "I understand, Zabel. Isabella. For you, it is a difficult place. But you will always be welcome in our house."

"And you in mine," I said reflexively. Then I laughed. "Though I will understand entirely if you decline to sail to the far side of the world to visit me." The sea had been even more daunting a sight than the plains of Khavtlai; it would be a very long time before any Draconean ventured out upon it.

Thu accompanied Tom and myself to the port of Va Nurang, where a Scirling naval ship was bringing a set of proper

*Blessing the Emperor*

ambassadors to establish relations with the new emperor. That same ship brought a letter, addressed to me. I went boneless with relief when I saw it was from my son—for he would not write to me unless word had reached him that I was alive.

Its contents, however, were most startling.

Dear Mother,

I am very glad to hear that you are not dead.

You may have noticed that this letter was not sent from Scirland. I fear you shall be very cross with what I have to tell you, but please understand that I did not mean it to happen this way. I had every intention of waiting until you came back from the Mrtyahaima before I made any decisions, so that I could talk to you first. (Like the good and obedient son I generally fail to be.) But then word came that you had died in the mountains, which put paid to any notion of talking to you—unless the spiritualists are to be believed, which I doubt. And it put me in the mood to do something rash besides, so I went ahead and did it. Now I've learnt that you aren't dead after all, but it's too late to take back my decision. Even if I wanted to, which I'm quite sure I don't.

All of that is by way of preface to telling you that I am no longer at Merritford, nor do I expect to ever go back. You see, my school chum Millpole has an uncle who sails with the Four Seas Company, not as a merchant, but as a scientist, studying the oceans. Right after you left for the mountains he gave a lecture at Merritford, and he and I fell to talking afterward. Well, the long and short of it is that he offered to take me on as his assistant—I think he meant after I graduated, but I ran away from school and joined him. So I'm writing you this letter from the deck of the *Osprey,* in port at Wooragine. Who knows how it will get to you, or even where you are now. Somewhere in Yelang, if that revolution is going well? I doubt we'll put in at any Yelangese ports—but, well, stranger things have happened, and quite recently, too.

I hope you aren't *too* angry at me. It isn't that I disliked university, I swear. But I don't see that there's anything I could learn about the ocean while sitting in a lecture hall hundreds of miles from the nearest salt water that I couldn't learn much faster at sea. Millpole senior is a splendid fellow, really quite brilliant—reminds me of you, honestly, except with fewer wings and more water. And male, of course. I'm sure you'll meet him eventually, whenever both of us contrive to be in the same place at once. I'd say in Sennsmouth the next time we call there, but for all I know you'll be out in the plains of Otholé or at the North Pole or something. But I promise I will write. If nothing else, I *have* to meet a Draconean in person. (I can't believe you truly found them! Or is that just wild rumour? Logic says it's rumour, but I know what my mother is capable of.)

Please do not die again, even if it turns out not to be true.

Your loving though wayward son,
Jake

I stared at this some time before dissolving into laughter and showing it to Tom. How could I be angry with my son? It was the sort of thing I might have done, had I been born a boy. And certainly I have done many more foolish things in my life, so I was hardly in a position to throw stones.

We sailed from Va Nurang on the same ship that brought the ambassadors. Thu saw us off: a very different farewell than the one we received when we were deported from Va Hing. "Thank you," I said to him. The phrase was wholly inadequate, but I had no better alternative; there were no words to express the true depth of my gratitude. "Had you not discovered those remains—had you not chosen to dangle them before me as very excellent bait—"

Thu bowed, in the manner of someone who knew the gesture was wholly inadequate, but had no better alternative. "It has been an honour and a pleasure, Lady Trent."

Tom went back to Scirland; I disembarked in Vidwatha, proceeding back to Tser-nga by less covert means than we had used the first time. There Suhail and I served as interpreters for negotiations between the council of Draconean elders and the Tser-zhag king. Letters between the two of us had been infrequent, owing to the difficulty of conveying them; when we were not carrying out our official duties, we talked ourselves hoarse telling stories of the things that had happened while we were apart. I told him of the dancing dragons; he told me about how he won over Esdarr and her sisters, which I thought was by far the more impressive achievement. He also showed me the modern Draconean syllabary, which he had learned from Habarz.

"So," I said, "we will finally be able to read all the inscriptions?"

Suhail laughed. "We will be able to pronounce them, at least.

And we can certainly make a much better guess at their meaning. I intend to ship a set of the most recent edition of the inscriptions to the Sanctuary; Habarz has shown a great interest in reading them." His smile lit up the room like a sun. "I thought it was impossible for you to find me a second Cataract Stone. Instead, you found me something far superior."

We left Tser-nga as soon as the negotiations were done, despite pressures to stay. Neither of us could endure the thought of living through another Mrtyahaiman winter, and by then there were others who could communicate to an acceptable degree—humans and Draconeans both. Moreover, my desire to be home had passed "overpowering" and reached a level for which no adjective could suffice.

Besides, I had business to attend to there. With the bright tone of one looking forward to a moment of perfect, undiluted triumph, I reminded Suhail, "I have something to report to the Philosophers' Colloquium."

# AFTERWORD

I would say that the rest is history, but as the entirety of my memoirs have been concerned with matters historical, it seems a bit redundant.

I returned home to honours and accolades, a thousand requests for public lectures and nearly as many dinner invitations. At a time when I wanted nothing more than to ensconce myself in my study once more, the world demanded my presence, and I fear I ran myself ragged trying to satisfy their insatiable hunger.

But one invitation I would have accepted were I on my deathbed from overwork.

On a beautiful Athemer evening in early Graminis, at a ceremony in their premises off Heron Court, I was inducted as the first woman Fellow of the Philosophers' Colloquium.

Compared with my elevation to the peerage, the ceremony was not particularly elaborate. The induction of new Fellows takes place in the Great Hall, around a little table with a book. This volume is the Charter Book of the Colloquium; its opening pages contain the royal charter that first created the institution, and the rest of it holds the signatures of the Fellows, inscribed in columns on each page beneath the Obligation that binds all members. That Obligation reads as follows:

*We who have hereunto subscribed, do hereby vow, that we will endeavour to promote the good of the Colloquium of Philosophers, and to pursue the end for which the same was founded, which is the Increase of Knowledge; that we will carry out, so far as we are able, those actions requested of us in the name of the Council; and that we will observe the Statutes and Standing Orders of the said Colloquium. Provided that, whensoever any of us shall signify to the President under our hands, that we desire to withdraw from the Colloquium, we shall be free thereafter from this Obligation.*

The room that day was filled to the walls with the current Fellows of the Colloquium; the street outside was filled with journalists, well-wishers, and hecklers. I did not like to keep all those people waiting, and so it was not until a later occasion that I had the opportunity to turn the thick vellum pages and peruse the signatures of the luminaries who had gone before me: Philippe Dénis, who proposed our taxonomic classification of organisms; Yevgeny Ivanov, the great astronomer and discoverer of planetary moons; Randolph Cremley, who created the periodic table we use to organize the elements; Albert Wedgwood, the theorist who gave us the concept of evolution; Sir Richard Edgeworth, whose book had been such a formative influence on my youth and my field.

Perhaps it is just as well that I did not have the time to survey the ranks of those I was joining. My hand might otherwise have shaken quite badly as I added my name to their company. But I did take a moment to look back a smaller distance, to the page that bore the name of Maxwell Oscott. He was not the Earl of Hilford when he signed; but he was, of course, the man whose patronage had launched me on my career, without whom I would not have been in the Great Hall that day.

I could not look for long. It would not have done my reputation any good for me to sniffle, or for a tear to fall upon the pages of that precious book. But I looked up and sought out Tom Wilker's eye, for he had benefited as much as I had from that patronage. We shared a smile; then I bent and signed my name to the book. If you have a chance to see it there, know that the slight gap in the column is intentional, for I felt it was only proper to place my signature to the right of Tom's.

After that there was a banquet, in which the President of the Colloquium stood up and said a great many flattering things about me, and many toasts were drunk in my honour. Much was made of the fact that the vote to award me a Fellowship was unanimous. Tom had told me in private that the President had taken a few recalcitrant gentlemen aside and informed them that if they did not vote in favour, they would not be welcome on the premises thereafter; for it would be to the eternal shame of the Colloquium if they failed to recognize the achievements of the woman who had found the last surviving population of the Draconean species. Those gentlemen had attended the signing, but absented themselves from the banquet, and I did not miss them. I did not need their dour faces marring that day. I said earlier in this volume that if the Colloquium had not admitted me to their company, I would have washed my hands of them without further ado; but it was much finer to achieve my girlhood dream at last.

For although the Colloquium is often a hidebound place, it is still a fine institution, and one that fosters scientific understanding in countless fields. My son Jacob is now a Fellow himself, having earned recognition through his work as an oceanographer—a field for which we did not even have a name when I was born. Natalie Oscott and her friends turned their attentions from the sky for a time in order to build him superior devices for exploring the world beneath the waves, and he has put these to excellent use. Suhail served as President of the Society of Linguists for a number of years, though he retired from that position a while ago; in his words, "If I never have to sit through another meeting again, it will be as good as attaining Paradise." (A part of me is relieved that no one has yet been able to stomach the notion of a female Colloquium President. I have no doubt that it will happen someday, and I will applaud the lady who takes that laurel—but I had rather it not be me.)

At this point I find myself wanting to make some comparison between the world as I knew it when I preserved my first sparkling and the world I live in today. But the latter is so familiar to my readers that any extensive description of it would be tiresome, and as for the former, if I have not conveyed the general sense of it with the previous volumes of my memoirs, I could not hope to do so now. The changes are pervasive: everything from the pragmatic facts of daily life (travel by caeliger, and the widespread use of dragonbone machines for countless tasks), to the fabric of Scirling society (vastly increased educational opportunities for my sex, and the right of women to vote), to the state of all scientific fields, my own not excepted. Those with a far greater understanding of anatomy and chemistry have begun to establish the various mechanisms by which extraordinary breath is produced: a thing I could not have hoped to puzzle out for myself, as my own education was so informal. And, of course, we know *far* more about developmental lability, and how it produced the Draconean species in the ancient past.

I will not pretend this knowledge is an unmitigated good. As one might expect, it has unavoidably led to a great deal of unethical experimentation, with disreputable types who hardly deserve the name of "scientist" attempting to create their own breeds for a variety of purposes. Some of them have even tried to make new Draconeans—or rather, new hybrids of dragon and human. Their efforts have succeeded in establishing that the theory I formulated while living in the Sanctuary (dragon eggs anointed with human blood) is likely correct; but the rate of viability for the resulting organisms is low enough that it must have taken ages of primitive dragon worship among humans before a breeding population was established. I personally suspect that the Draconean species arose from a single pair, the happy accident of two successes in close enough temporal and geographic proximity that they were able to produce offspring. From there, developmental lability ensured enough variation to avoid inbreeding.

We will likely never know for certain, though. These days we can read the ancient Draconean language quite well, but even the scribes of that civilization did not have records of how their species began, apart from myth. Records of the Downfall are also few and far between, as the event itself so disrupted the fabric of their society that it produced a great silence, a gap between that age and the rise of great human kings afterward. But translations and archaeology together produce a clear enough image, of a civilization fallen into decadence and cruelty, and of a great and merciless slaughter when some nameless human created a potion that could kill unborn Draconeans in the egg.

Of course someone immediately set forth to rediscover that, too. The value of firestone has fallen tremendously from what it was in my youth, as both its greater availability and the moral repellence of its origin have caused many wealthy individuals to cease wearing it.

But against these ills I may set the position of Draconean society today, which is unquestionably improved from the time during which they hid in the Sanctuary of Wings, with nowhere left to run. I will not pretend their re-emergence in the outside world has been without its difficulties; many humans are indeed hostile to them, and a counter-movement among the Draconeans has continually agitated for renewed isolation. But the more outward-looking members of their society have taken advantage of their new freedom, with the result that their population has nearly doubled since the creation of the Sanctuary Alliance. Many of these new generation were nurtured and hatched in less harsh conditions, which in turn makes it easier for them to travel outside the Mrtyahaima. In time they hope to re-establish a settlement in Akhia, where their civilization began—though opposition to them among certain Segulist and Amaneen factions is strong. For reasons both biological and political, I do not expect to see that happen in my lifetime.

One change, however, may happen quite soon. The final terms of the Sanctuary Alliance included the construction of a Scirling caeliger base there, for the protection of Draconean sovereignty. Although the garrison proved useful once or twice in the early years, it has not faced any significant threat in quite some time. The duration set for the base's operation will expire next year, and I am certain the Synedrion would not even think of failing to honour the promises they made then, that they would dismantle the base and return the Sanctuary fully to Draconean control.

I still correspond with Ruzt, who now sits on the council of elders in the Sanctuary. It is a wonder brought about by the use of caeligers; when we first met, to send a letter from Scirland to the depths of the Mrtyahaima would have taken half a year, and the other half for the reply to come back. These days I may converse regularly with friends all over the earth, from the Sanctuary to Yelang to Bayembe, and read the findings of scientific colleagues from countless other lands. As my enthusiasm for strenuous field expeditions wanes with age, I find this is a great convenience.

If there is any conclusion to my tale (apart from my death, which I hope is yet a good way off), it is that the heart of it will never truly end. Although my memoirs are of course the story of my life and career, they are also a story of discovery: of curiosity, and investigation, and learning, not only regarding dragons but many other topics. I take comfort in knowing that others will carry this tale forward, continually unfolding new secrets of the world in which we live, and hopefully using that understanding more often for good than for ill.

And so I leave it in your hands, gentle reader. Mind you carry it well.


Isabella, Lady Trent
F.P.C

ISABELLA

LADY TRENT

LOCKWOOD

*The memoirist, past and present*

# ABOUT THE AUTHOR

American fantasy writer Marie Brennan habitually pillages her background in anthropology, archaeology and folklore for fictional purposes. She is the author of the *Onyx Court* series, the Doppelganger duology of *Warrior* and *Witch*, and the urban fantasy *Lies and Prophecy*, as well as more than forty short stories. The first memoir of Lady Trent, *A Natural History of Dragons*, was critically praised and received a starred review in *Publishers Weekly*, who hailed it as being "[s]aturated with the joy and urgency of discovery and scientific curiosity." The second volume, *The Tropic of Serpents*, received a starred review in *Kirkus*, describing it as "admirable, formidable and captivating."

Visit Marie Brennan at www.swantower.com
or on Twitter @swan_tower.